THE TWISTED VINE

ALYCE CASWELL

First time in print: 2020

ISBN: 978 0 6481626 0 5 (EPUB)
ISBN: 978 0 6485444 1 8 (Print)

Cover design by Hampton Lamoureux, TS95 Studios © 2018, 2019

THE TWISTED VINE

CHAPTER ONE

When the laboratory collapsed, spewing equipment and the remnants of the machinery that had kept the platform floating over the soggy ground, Kuja knew who was responsible.

He sloughed through the mud barefoot, bending down to salvage broken bits and pieces before handing what he found to someone tasked with either writing the item off completely or cleaning and repurposing it. He was just turning around to search for more debris when he was jostled by a woman on a mission — she had swooped over to rescue a techpad before his toes landed on it.

'Creator God help me, that's six months of work flushed out the airlock!' Kuja's companion said, scowling down at a fresh splatter of mud on her form-fitting vinyl pants. Now cradling the damaged techpad against her chest, she rounded on Kuja. 'What have you people got against TerraCorp, Kuja? The starking lab wasn't hurting your precious topsoil — it was hovering a whole seven metres above it! You're lucky Bagaran, your otherwise primitive planet, has a law against murder or we'd have plugged all you sub-level god worshippers with lasbolts by now.'

Kuja backed away from her, holding up his hands. Though she was a head shorter than him and her flat brown hair was less confronting than his own wiry coppery mess, she still managed to intimidate him. He swallowed. 'Dr Hackett — Lorena. You cannot blame all of us for the actions of one unhappy person, though he really shouldn't have done this and I told him —'

'You told *him*, did you.'

Lorena's blue eyes might have been considered beautiful by some of Kuja's companions in the village, but like the more senior men and women who actually had a speck of common sense, he thought those eyes were more akin to chasmic ice: deep and dangerously deceptive. Even if he *was* tempted to find out what Lorena's lips would feel like against his, he'd seen what his oldest brother had gone through a few years earlier in the name of love and Kuja had no wish to invite that kind of pain and despair into his life.

Lorena would probably bite him if he ever tried to kiss her anyway.

'Who did this?' she asked, her voice simmering.

Kuja grimaced. Due to the mind-reading abilities he had inherited from his father, he knew practically everything that went on inside his rainforests. What he lacked, and badly needed, was the ability to keep his feelings from showing on his face or in his sea-green eyes.

He linked his hands together to keep them from fidgeting with his khaki shirt and pants ensemble, threadbare not from wear but from his fingers worrying over them. 'I'm not telling you. You'll just tell TerraCorp who'll then get GLEA to turn up with their lasguns.'

'Destruction of someone else's property is illegal on Bagaran *and* it's something the Creator God frowns on!' Lorena said, crossing her arms. The techpad, ruined though it was, remained clenched in her hand. 'It's kinder if I turn the perpetrator over to GLEA than deal with them myself, mark my words. But I suppose if GLEA hides them away in some dingy cell then they can feel the same frustration I am right now!'

Kuja tore apart the inside of his cheek with his teeth. The Galactic Law Enforcement Agency, if they could spare enough agents, would turn up on lucky — or unlucky, depending on how you felt about the Agency — planets to help enforce the local laws, to assist in capturing criminals and to encourage people to worship their god in return for their services.

GLEA's agents had chips in their temples that gave them special powers granted by the Creator God; this was why so many people referred to them as 'Chippers'. They could use forcefields to generate shields and move objects in a much more basic and laughable form of the telekinesis that some of the sub-level gods enjoyed. While Kuja's siblings could shrug off the threat GLEA posed, the Chippers were more difficult for him to deal with since he lacked that particular ability. He supposed being the youngest of his brothers and sisters had something to do with that. At least he was able to sense lifesigns at a greater distance than the Chippers could so he always knew when he needed to move further away from them. Their energy had a recognisable taint to it.

'Yes, well, go invite GLEA to Bagaran if you wish,' Kuja finally said. 'But I warn you. You'll lose more than a lab if they show up.'

'That a threat, Kuja?' Lorena demanded.

Overhead, a branch snapped. It crashed to the ground beside Lorena and she sprang away, dropping the techpad as she did so, her hand instead finding purchase on her heaving chest.

Kuja drew a deep breath, calming his temper. 'A rainforest can be a dangerous place, no matter what cool tech you have at your disposal. Do not forget that Bagaran was renamed in honour of our god, Bagara, and he does not tolerate those who insult or upset his people.'

'I'll bring GLEA down on you, god or not, you starking —'

Lorena's tirade was cut short when her colleague, a bulky alien woman with several chins and a large triangle-shaped smile, dropped a heavy tentacle onto Lorena's shoulder and gave her a healthy shove over to where the rest of the TerraCorp scientists were busily scavenging the wreck. Her lipless mouth shrinking into a terse pinprick, the newcomer reminded Lorena that she wasn't being paid to get into fights with the locals. Lorena didn't argue, but she banged a fist against her hip as she stormed away, clearly wanting to ram her knuckles into something else.

'Now me, I said to myself when I came here,' the newcomer began, 'I said, "Gerns, these people with their weird rainforest god and his mumbo jumbo, they're gonna cause you problems" and I was right.' Gerns paused to shake her grey, gelatinous head. She was a Jezlo, a native to the swampy world of Spetnusbani, and unsurprisingly enjoyed the humidity in Bagaran's rainforests. 'Still, 'least their god doesn't build temples all over the galaxy and insist everyone worship him.'

Kuja grinned. 'No, Bagara just sits around gnashing his teeth and waiting for his enemies to come all the way to Bagaran to single him out for attention.'

Gerns made a clucking sound that indicated her amusement. She slung one of her six tentacles over Kuja's shoulders and curled another around his waist as she guided him away to a less boggy patch of ground. They seated themselves on a fallen mossy log where Gerns bathed in the shade for several contented moments. Finally, she said, 'Kuja. You lot are harmless, mostly.

Nothing like the gangs on Yalsa 5 or the water god-worshipping nutjobs on New Sydney who keep blowing up GLEA's starships, but this is pretty serious. Even if no one got hurt, it'll set TerraCorp back a fair bit of money.'

'You should bring this up with the village headman,' Kuja protested. 'I have no sway here. I'm a stranger, like you.'

'Yeah, but they respect you,' Gerns said, the suction cups on her tentacles slowly peeling off him. Kuja had never found her touch unpleasant; he knew it was important to Jezlos to communicate their friendship through skin-to-skin contact. 'And you worship their weird rainforest god, you know what he's about. So I gotta know. Is this Bagara fellow to blame for the sabotage?'

Kuja's eyes widened. 'Oh, no. Never.'

'Huh, you sound so sure.'

'Well, not sure, just — I've thought about it, see.' Kuja found swallowing difficult so coughed instead to dislodge the lump in his throat. 'TerraCorp is here to study plant life to use when they next terraform a world. I think Bagara would be pleased with a company that creates more rainforests. If he lets them continue their work, he'll have even more planets under his control.'

'But the rest of his people don't agree with your thinking, I take it,' Gerns said, her massive head wobbling in the direction of the villagers who had come down to watch the TerraCorp employees clean up the mess that had once been a laboratory. The scientists looked filthy and out of place in their once-white garb whereas the villagers, in their array of brown and beige cotton, seemed more at ease with the setting.

'I won't deny it.' Kuja sighed. 'Some see it as stealing. Or insulting Bagara. Or even invasion. We don't have a temple or any worshippers of the Creator God here and many of your scientists come from worlds that do. I would understand if my companions are worried that TerraCorp means to bring GLEA here.'

'So it *is* a religious thing.' Gerns' tentacles straightened and shook, a sure sign of the Jezlo's irritation. 'Now me, I think that just because the Creator God and Bagara don't play in the same sandbox it doesn't mean their kids can't.'

'Why would you assume that the gods don't, ah, play together?'

Gerns bent one tentacle towards the destruction. 'Kuja, if they *were playing together*, wouldn't this Bagara fellow jump out and tell his folks not to mess with followers of the Creator God?'

'Free will is a common theme among the galaxy's religions, though — no god, sub-level *or* Creator, can make us do anything, and that includes being nice to each other,' Kuja argued, shrinking on the log and hoping the streaks of mud on his face were enough to hide his embarrassment at having to defend himself, no matter how abstractly. 'So...so Bagara can't *make* people do things.'

'Free will costs time and money and it might even cost me my job.' Gerns stood, her trembling tentacles now aimed at the gathered villagers. 'Kuja. Get this fixed. I don't like GLEA's agents any more than you do, always sticking their supposedly not-for-profit noses into places they're not invited, but if I have to call them, I will.'

As she plodded away, Kuja rested his chin in his hand, brooding. He glanced down when a vine reached up to tap his arm, asking if it could spend the day coiled around his waist since he clearly needed some comfort. Kuja shook his head. 'No, my friend. I will be fine.'

He rose from the log, leaving the dejected vine behind, and headed up the path towards Bagath, the village where he lived as a mortal. Once he was inside the palisade walls, he spent some time checking the generators responsible for powering the shield that protected the village against predators at night. It took him a while to realise that what he could smell wasn't decaying food matter in the compost heap (it was on the opposite side of Bagath, after all), but himself. Kuja winced. He really could use a wash. And he didn't want to give the visiting TerraCorp scientists the impression that he and the villagers were backwards or primitive.

He envied his beloved rainforests. They didn't need to worry about how they looked and nor did they need to remember which name they were supposed to be wearing at any given time. It was exhausting. He was called Kuja by those closest to him, designated as the Rforine in the Galactic Pantheon and referred to as Bagara by the complete strangers who worshipped him.

Sometimes he wondered if lying to the villagers in Bagath and pretending to be one of them was forgivable, but he always reminded himself that it helped him to understand them better. Other times he was afraid that living like a mortal would invite the wrath of his godly brothers and sisters. So far it seemed his life here hadn't upset the grand design because they hadn't yet come after him.

But he was always looking over his shoulder.

***

The new communal showers were a chrome eyesore beside Bagath, but they were so useful that no one complained that TerraCorp hadn't found a more aesthetically pleasing shape to drop outside the village gate. It also helped that the Bagathians had been told they could use the showers free of charge. It was a placating gesture, one meant to engender goodwill. How much longer TerraCorp would allow the showers to remain open after the lab's destruction was anyone's guess.

The frosted glass door whooshed open for Kuja as he approached it, allowing him to make his way through the misty air to the locker he always used. He shed his soiled pants as he went and binned them. The shirt he could probably keep — the hole wasn't *that* big and he could always patch it up later. He never wore boots, so there was no need to squeeze a pair of them into the small locker along with his clothes.

Kuja leaned his head against the door of the locker, enjoying the caress of cool metal against his skin, but it did nothing to dispel his dark mood.

What is the point of living forever, he thought, *when you must do it alone?*

The towel dangling from his hand dragged on the floor as Kuja shuffled over to the shower area, where someone else had already switched on one of the thundering water jets. He threw his towel onto a nearby rack, beside the fluffy blue one hanging there, and stepped beneath his own jet. It burst into life within moments, shooting hot water over him. He winced and adjusted the temperature. His lips went numb in under a minute but the icy spray seemed to be helping him clear his mind of the unwelcome desires that had flooded into it earlier.

'You can't wash away the guilt, you know.' Lorena's voice cracked through the room. 'You might as well just tell me who did it.'

Kuja's head snapped up in surprise. Flinging her hair out of her face, Lorena gave him a long, lingering look filled with so much heat it could have stripped the skin from his bones. Kuja glanced down at himself, then back at her similarly nude form.

'Erm,' he said and started side-walking to his towel.

'What in the Creator God's...' She trailed off, then burst out laughing. 'Kuja, are you *embarrassed?* I thought you rainforest folk showered together all the time.'

Tightly binding the towel around his midsection, Kuja glowered at her. 'We do. But my fellow Bagathians don't keep interrogating me about things I had no part in. And they don't look at me as you just did.'

Lorena planted her hands on her hips and arched her back. Her glistening breasts rose for his inspection. 'Maybe I haven't been very clear. I like the look of you, Kuja. At first I thought you were being coy, then I realised you didn't even notice I was playing with you.'

Kuja stumbled backwards, nearly tripping on the tiled steps leading up and out the shower area. His feet slipped around for several more agonising seconds until they found purchase on the rubber matting that was designed to keep such accidents from occurring. Lorena remained right where she was, watching him.

Kuja cleared his throat. 'Well, no, I don't...I don't tend to notice the women around me.'

'Why not?' she asked, holding her hand beneath a soap dispenser. It spat suds into her palm which she then began lathering down her chest. 'Would you prefer a man?'

Kuja actually had to think about that one. He shrugged. 'I, erm, don't know.'

The soap slid between her breasts, gliding further south. Kuja averted his eyes.

'So what's your glitch, Kuja?' Lorena asked.

'Apart from you threatening to bring GLEA down on us barely an Old Earth hour ago?' he demanded. His gaze had somehow found its way back to her.

'I might forget about doing that, if someone wanted to give me the right *incentive*,' Lorena said, her hands now roving liberally over her form.

Kuja sighed heavily. 'Lorena, I don't have...well, I *do* have the time for this, I just don't want to do it. In my experience, getting involved with mort — with women has never done my family any good.'

Lorena rolled her eyes. 'What, your brother have a nasty ex or something? Relationships are always messy. Deal with it. And it's not like we need to get involved, Kuja. We can just fuck.'

Kuja felt the rainforest outside Bagath immediately respond to his inner turmoil. Vines knotted, branches swayed, soil writhed and rocks began to unearth themselves, quaking, restless, desperate to carve their way into new territory.

'You wouldn't understand,' Kuja said and strode back to his locker.

When he made it outside, fully dressed and back in the pants he'd rescued from the bin, his breaths were short and sharp. He struggled to reassure the rainforests on several different planets that he was alright, that he didn't need their assistance. They were sceptical, but they dutifully quietened.

Not wanting to encounter any Bagathians returning from the lab site, Kuja fled to the hut that the village headman had allocated to him and sat in the corner, chin resting on his raised knees. He had fought so hard to shield Sandsa, the desert god, and his wife, Callista, from discovery when the other gods in the Galactic

Pantheon had demanded that Sandsa abandon his family and return to the deserts. Kuja's siblings had decided that there *must* be a deity roaming the sands; their father's perfect grand design could not be tampered with or ignored. It had taken everything from Kuja to keep his brother's family hidden. And he had failed.

Kuja caught the sob in his hand. Emanating concern for him, a vine crept in through a hole in the wall and wrapped around his legs — not like chains, but an anchor that grounded him and kept him from losing the human form he was currently wearing.

Now none of the gods dared to dabble in love, afraid they would be punished for straying just far enough from their duties that it threatened the grand design. The water god, Fayay, had also warned his brothers and sisters that since he was in charge of them now (Sandsa was the eldest but had been branded an outcast), he would take this responsibility very seriously and kill anyone who distracted his siblings.

There was no way Kuja would ever endanger a mortal's life by allowing himself to fall in love. But he couldn't help wanting it, wanting someone by his side for eternity, someone who filled his heart with joy and laughter once more.

'I am so weak,' Kuja said to the vine.

You will be strong again, it promised.

All of us know this, spoke billions of other plants across the galaxy.

Kuja could not bring himself to believe them.

CHAPTER TWO

'Don't you have anything better to do than call your mother and complain about your temple?' asked the communicator resting in Feiscina Neron's palm.

Fei plonked the device down on her desk and then let her forehead smack into the space beside it. Her long purple hair, kept soft and manageable by a strict routine involving several bottles of chemicals, puddled around her face. She snorted some strands out of her nostrils.

'Fei!' her mother scolded. 'I heard that! Don't hit your head — you need those brain cells!'

'I don't need brain cells, my code's compiling,' Fei muttered.

'Your what? Oh, honey, you need to run a medical app for that.'

Her mother hadn't yet told Fei to run some app to fix her 'twenty-seven and still single' status, but it was only a matter of time. Unfortunately.

Fei levered herself off the desk and stared down at its shiny surface. Her eyes were hollow — probably because she had set her electronic irises to a deathly white that morning — and her bronze skin was being washed out by the glow of the vidscreens. This gave her the appearance of a zombie, which was no laughing matter because a scientist had managed to cause an outbreak among the worker population of Londinium one Old Earth year ago. Fei's boss wouldn't be pleased if he saw her looking like this, but he rarely came to visit her down in the basement. She was safe. For now.

'My code's compiling,' Fei repeated. 'Which means I have nothing to do at the moment. So I thought, erroneously perhaps, that my own mother would want to hear from me.'

'You know I don't speak your programmer lingo.'

Fei pursed her lips. She could explain to her mother that she had to wait for her code to be translated into a language her console actually understood before she could run any complicated terraforming simulations, but that would mean having to yet again defend her job. People always asked Fei why she couldn't just go to a planet and throw a few seeds around to see how certain plants grew in certain environments. No one seemed to realise this would not be effective, cost-wise or time-wise. Simulations, based on the climates requested by TerraCorp's clients, were supposed to give you a heads up of how likely the terraforming job was to succeed, without wasting any seeds or funds.

Berale Neron, as usual, managed to think of something to say before Fei did.

'Fei, honey, if you really don't like the temple you go to at the moment, you could always try another one,' Berale said, her high-pitched voice due either to Fei's outdated communicator or maternal desperation.

Fei cradled her head in her hands. 'Mum. It's not about the temple. It's about...everything.'

'But how are you supposed to find a husband if you're not worshipping on a regular basis?'

'What!' Fei burst out laughing. 'Seriously? I work with plenty of guys who worship the Creator God. They don't go to temples.

They're too busy. Like me. Well, I guess I'm not busy right now, because my code's compiling, but if I turned up at a temple in the middle of the day no one else would be there. Defeats the purpose, doesn't it.' The chuckles began anew and Fei had to clamp down on them.

'Just tell me what's really bothering you, honey.'

Fei managed to rein in the sigh; she knew it would cause too much static on her mother's end of the call. 'I'm finding it very hard to feel...connected to the Creator God right now. I know, it sounds bad, but I'm just having a minor crisis of faith. It's fine. I'll get over it.'

'Have you tried talking to our god?' Berale asked.

Fei clapped her hands together and raised them to the ceiling, mouthing profanities. When she trusted herself to be civil, she said, 'Yes, Mum. Of course I tried that. I've been trying for months.'

'Are you thinking about talking to those sub-level gods instead?' Concern sharply became reproof. 'You know they are inferior gods who do nothing for their followers.'

Fei had only become aware of the multitude of gods people worshipped in the galaxy when she had taken this post as a programmer on the wealth-drenched planet of Enoc. Each terraforming simulation she was tasked with creating had to factor in a local population's predilection for worship. If someone on a client's planet claimed to follow the desert god, also known as the Desine, then Fei would have to appease them as well. She didn't mind. It was both challenging and fun to find a way to sustain a slice of desert on a world that someone had paid to make entirely wet.

'No, Mum, I haven't been talking to any sub-level gods.' Fei drew a breath. 'Maybe my crisis of faith has something to do with the fact that everyone I care about ends up abandoning me to go join the Galactic Law Enforcement Agency. Like having fancy powers obtained through tech is so much better than my own company.' Fei slammed her head back onto the table. 'Ow. Actually, yeah, that does sound better than my own company.'

Sniffling emanated from the communicator.

'Oh, Mum, I didn't mean...' Fei flung her exasperated grimace up at ceiling, wishing she could toss it all the way past the fifteen misshapen moons orbiting Enoc. 'You're always there for me.'

Silence. A nose was blown. Then — 'Your father was called to the service of the Creator God. That's why he joined GLEA, honey.'

'Yeah, but GLEA offered to relocate our whole family and he just went off without us,' Fei grumbled.

'Oh, honey, he said it was because they didn't pay him very much,' Berale reminded her. 'He was worried about providing for us.'

Fei picked her head up in her hands and swung it towards the console her code was being displayed on. The green progress bar continued to creep its way over to the right-hand side of the vidscreen, but it wasn't even halfway across yet. Already a dozen error messages were streaming down and out of sight. She couldn't bring herself to move her hand to the screen to scroll through them. Not right now anyway. It would mean admitting that her boredom-fuelled laziness had resulted in messy syntax inside her code.

'Right, Dad decided he'd rather provide nothing at all,' Fei said, rolling her top lip towards her nose. 'You worked two jobs just to feed us both when he left, Mum. And let's not forget that five years later he hinted he'd like to get back with you, so you moved us all the way to Gerasnin, the GLEA homeworld — only for him to not even bother seeing us. Not for a single second!'

'He's very busy, Fei. Agents have to go all over the galaxy, you know. And they do good work, honey. They maintain law and order so that we are safe to worship the Creator God.'

'They also stole the man I was supposed to marry!' Fei hammered her fists onto her desk. The communicator leapt to freedom but she snatched it out of the air before it could hit the floor.

'Fei, it was the Creator God's will that Zareth felt called to become an agent like your father.' When her mother pitched her voice low, it was an attempt at sympathy, which Fei did appreciate even if it didn't make her feel better. 'You could have joined up with him, you know. GLEA makes *very* generous accommodations for married agents, or so I'm told. Your father rightly pointed out that it wasn't my calling so I never...'

'I think the problem is me,' Fei said, glaring at the twentieth error that had popped up on her vidscreen. 'I must be pretty awful if both my father *and* my fiancé decided that a lifetime of shit pay and following orders was the better option.'

'Well, they *do* get those powers,' her mother pointed out. 'But it's more than that. It's very tempting to join up and make the galaxy a better place.'

Fei pinched the communicator between two fingers and held it over the bin chute beside her desk. All it would take was a snap of her fingers and the conversation end, instantly crushed and recycled into something better.

Static screeched out of the device. Berale must have sighed. 'I'm sorry, honey. I wish I was one of those mothers who could easily lie and say it wasn't you and that you really are a wonderful person.'

'Oh, my code's stopped compiling,' Fei lied quickly, skimming a palm over the vagrant tear on her cheek. If Berale realised how upset she was, then the conversation would *never* end.

'Does that mean you're finally off the toilet and have to do some work?' her mother asked.

'Mum! No! That's not what it means!'

'Well, I heard you talking about piles...'

Fei's reluctant grin slipped when a horrifying groan came from the hoverlift shaft. 'Mum. I have to go. And I'll think about trying another temple. Okay? Bye. *Bye.*'

The communicator made a discreet click. Fei set it beside her glass of water and positioned her fingers over the multicoloured lines on the desk that made up her keyboard. She began sliding her fingertips over the keys, humming to herself. None of this helped; her chest continued to constrict.

It's alright, it'll just be Moz and he's shorter than you, remember, Fei consoled herself, then winced as the hoverlift clunked into place. While it was quiet when passing most levels, one of the hoverpads was clearly malfunctioning because every time the lift came down to the basement it literally hit the bottom of the shaft.

Fei pressed her trembling lips together. *Oh, stark it. I hate being like this. I mean, I can tell myself that it's okay and I can handle it but when the moment actually...oh fuck, just work, Fei!*

Her boss strutted out of the lift, dwarfed by a strange duo Fei had never seen before. The ugly protrusions on their temples and the bright purple jumpsuits they were wearing immediately gave away what they were, however. Fei froze in place, her eyes flicking unseeingly over the vidscreen in front of her. GLEA agents! Here! What for? Had she broken some Enocian law? Were they coming to arrest her?

'My code's compiling,' she blurted as her boss passed the last row of empty desks that crowded the basement.

'Ah, programmer humour,' Mozel Zan said aside to the agents and guffawed. They simply stared at him. 'Ms Feiscina Neron writes the code we feed into our simulation software. She's in charge of Yalsa 5's upcoming transformation.'

The agents, though not at all similar in height, girth or colouring, could have been twins in Fei's opinion. Their heads swivelled towards her in one movement.

She swallowed. *Oh God. I know they can read energy, so does that mean they can read thoughts too? Do they know I'm having a crisis of faith? Well, not that I think the Creator God isn't there, per se, I just don't know if his existence matters to me anymore. Oh my God. They can probably hear me. Shit. Stark.*

'Neron,' the man of the pair repeated. He had one golden stroke on the left shoulder of his uniform, a feature indicating that he was a sergeant.

Fei wilted. 'Um. Yes. My father is one of you.'

'You should be proud,' the sergeant said. He must have seen her flinch because his indifferent expression wavered, bordering on disapproval.

Moz fluttered over to Fei's side and leaned across her shoulder, taking in the error messages. She wished he knew a little less about her work. Though he had grown slack since being promoted to middle management, with a stable of programmers at his beck and call, he still retained enough knowledge to know when someone was playing him.

Moz nodded, his lips bunching to one side. 'A few syntax and semantic errors. Don't bother fixing them. We need to alter the parameters and run a different simulation.'

'But I...' Fei's eyes fell to the surface of the desk. Her blank white gaze was soulless and passive, a reminder of what she was supposed to be. 'As you say, Moz.'

'You are wondering why,' the female agent spoke up. Her purple uniform bore four golden strokes, two on each shoulder. She was a major and also her partner's superior.

Fei offered what she hoped was a sweet smile, though it hurt her cheeks. 'I don't get paid to wonder why. I just input stuff.'

'Listen, Feiscina, this is very important,' Moz said, joggling on his bent knees beside her. 'GLEA has asked us to terraform the entirety of the planet. No deserts whatsoever. They say we can add some tundra as well because, honestly, no one wants a whole planet of tropical rainforests. That's a little boring.'

Fei's head snapped back up. She couldn't help herself. 'But this job was commissioned by Governor Bock Atsason. He's the one paying us.'

'He's also a major gang leader,' the male agent said, scorn running rampant through his words. 'We will not allow a criminal element to make the decisions for an entire planet.'

'Well, that's...that's...' Fei's vision sparked and her skin boiled at the very thought of speaking up, but she had to say it. 'That's silly. I mean, yes, he's the leader of the gangs, but he's also the elected ruler of Yalsa 5. That means you have to follow *his* rules, because as far as I know GLEA doesn't create laws, they just enforce them...' She trailed off when Moz cleared his throat. 'Well, alright. If that's what I'm doing.'

'You cannot seriously be prioritising a criminal's wishes

ahead of those of the Galactic Law Enforcement Agency,' the sergeant said, his eyebrows forming an unbroken line across his forehead.

'Oh, she's not, she just knows all this useless trivia,' Moz said, lifting a hand from the vidscreen to pirouette it beside Fei's head. 'She'll do it. It's fine.'

Fei stared at her reflection. A zombie stared back.

The female GLEA agent reached across the table and patted Fei's hand in what was probably meant to be a reassuring way. Fei jolted upright and snatched her fingers out of reach. 'Um. Sorry, Major. It takes me a while to let someone touch me. I mean. Yeah.'

'Is there something else that's bothering you?' the major asked her.

Fei bowed her head. 'I don't...it's not my place. So I'll just...shut up and work.'

The other woman stowed her hands at her sides and her face softened, distinguishing her markedly from her partner who continued to glower. 'If you have something you want to say, please say it. We can't read minds, Ms Neron. We can sense people's energy and sometimes their emotions, but that's it.'

Fei peered up at Moz. He nodded tightly. She swivelled her gaze to the desk again so that she wouldn't have to see anyone's faces while she spoke. 'There's a large faction of people on Yalsa 5 who worship the desert deity and they're not going to be terribly happy if we take away their access to him.'

'Don't concern yourself with that this time,' Moz said. His hand was now on the hoverchair, forcing it closer to the vidscreen. The chair gave an undignified whine. Fei wondered when *that* hoverpad would conk out too.

'Ms Neron is allowed to express concern,' the major said,

glancing aside at her partner when he snorted. 'Mr Zan, you should always allow others to say what they think, so that you can better help them understand your aims. Now. Ms Neron.' Fei started. 'You worship the Creator God, do you not?'

Fei shifted in her chair. Her knees hit the side of the desk and she winced. 'Yes. Yes, of course I do. But I don't think that's reason enough to...' She trailed off, but the other woman nodded encouragingly. 'It's not a good enough reason to dismiss people who happen to have another god on the other end of their prayers.'

The major smiled. 'I agree. But gang leader Bock has specifically asked for half the planet to remain barren, despite our entreaties to him. We think unguarded deserts make it too easy for pirates and slavers to come and go.'

'You could ask him why he's so insistent.' Fei hesitated. 'I mean, well, you probably have.'

'Of course we did,' the sergeant said, staring down his nose at Fei. 'He would not answer us which has made us all the more suspicious. So we would prefer to deal directly with TerraCorp.'

'Yes, yes, we cooperate with the authorities, always,' Moz said.

Even if those 'authorities' are a not-for-profit organisation that only lends out its services when its agents feel generous? Fei wondered. She had read plenty of anonymous posts on the Web about how it was dangerous to accept protection from those who were beholden to their religion before all else.

'Alright,' Fei said. 'I'm going to have to compile more code, I guess. Haha.'

Moz laughed along with her, masking her more tired attempt, then led the GLEA agents back towards the hoverlift.

'What the fuck, Moz!' Fei snapped once the doors were closed and the lift was heading for the foyer.

It was tempting to grab the nearest vidscreen and hurl it halfway across the room. Fei settled for a loud growl of frustration, glad she had the basement to herself. She might have gone mad if she couldn't show how she really felt now and then.

Oh well. If she couldn't yell at Moz, she could at least take her time in obeying him. She snatched her techpad out of the top drawer and allowed it to start displaying images of her and Zareth. Beside her colourful hair and sunny expressions, he looked troubled, distant, his expression absorbing none of the sunlight. He seemed like a shadow instead of a man.

She couldn't think of anything she'd said to upset Zareth — she'd been so good at keeping her feelings tightly wound, buried in her chest, afraid that if she unleashed them she'd drive him away. She wasn't sure why she'd bothered. He'd left her anyway.

Fei wriggled her hands over the brightly lit keys on the desk, pretending she was writing code, but her fingertips never hit the surface.

And her eyes never left the techpad.

CHAPTER THREE

Kuja stomped through the curved columns that lined the entrance walkway. They were white, soft, eternally smooth — and completely unnecessary because they did not hold anything up. Even if there had been a ceiling, it would have hovered without the aid of any tech, kept there by the impossibilities that existed in this realm.

Kuja had called it the Everything Portal since he was very small, because it was here that every god brought their unique array of powers. His brothers and sisters considered his name for the realm childish, much to Kuja's annoyance. He might be the youngest in the Galactic Pantheon, but he was now seventy-five years old. A mortal might even call someone of that age wise.

Kuja stopped by one particular column and stared at the floor. Years ago, he had watched Sandsa fall from grace in that very spot, cast out from the Everything Portal because he'd wanted to leave the deserts to seek the woman who had been haunting his dreams. Callista Krendasta — a beautiful woman, Kuja recalled, and she would stay that way forever. Though she had left the Desine, she had not given up the immortality granted to her by her marriage.

Kuja abruptly threw himself the side. A torrent of water exploded against the column a moment later, showering him with tiny pebbles made of liquid. Rolling onto his stomach, Kuja slapped the ground in an attempt to get to his feet, but his older brother's telekinesis was keeping him pinned. This would have been an excellent time to manifest that particular ability, Kuja thought sourly.

He gritted his teeth. 'Fayay. Let me up.'

'Still unable to defend yourself,' the Watine said, tsking. His dank hair fell over one side of his face in a wet, greasy curtain that complemented the strands of rotting seaweed he wore as a cloak. 'Did Sandsa send you here to whine to the Ine about his banishment from this realm? Or is he still sobbing like a baby because that woman left him?'

Fayay swatted the vine that Kuja had sent creeping over his shoulder, but the sharp point evaded the water god's touch and managed to open up a gash on his cheek. Fayay tore the vine in half in retribution, distracted enough by his anger to lose control of his powers. Taking advantage of this, the Rforine leapt up from the ground unhindered. Kuja then threw out his hands, streams of brown-streaked greenery tearing from him, swirling into a howling vortex that encased his older brother. A great crash told Kuja that Fayay had fallen to his knees.

But then he felt the breath on the back of his neck. Kuja froze. His attack subsided, leaving only bare floor in its wake. Fayay had teleported into a position behind him.

The Watine brimmed with vast power, as frigid and endless as the depths of an ocean. His lack of mind-reading abilities had never impeded him in an open fight. Kuja knew that firsthand.

'You are even weaker than before,' Fayay noted, his voice raspy. 'I could destroy you.'

'I haven't come here because of Sandsa,' Kuja said and winced when he heard how plaintive he sounded.

'But you have seen our brother. Do not deny it, Kuja.'

Kuja jerked his head from side to side. 'No! Not for a while, anyway. I wouldn't wish Sandsa's pain on anyone. Except maybe you.'

'Oh, I wouldn't have let that woman lure me from my duties the way she did Sandsa,' Fayay said, grabbing Kuja's shoulder and jerking his younger brother around to face him. The Watine towered over Kuja, his shadow eclipsing the rainforest god. 'You should have stood aside instead of hindering our restoration of Father's grand design.'

Kuja lifted his chin. 'I couldn't stand aside. I had to defend him.'

'Even when you knew your attempt was doomed from the start?' Fayay hissed at him.

'Yes.' Kuja swallowed. His failure had been inevitable, but he didn't regret what he'd done for Sandsa. 'If you ever try to hurt him again, whether by insults or by powers, I will kill you.'

'You would die trying.'

'I'd die for my brother,' Kuja said, planting his hands on his hips. He didn't care if it made him look infantile. 'Because I love him. You don't understand love. You don't understand why Sandsa wanted to leave us for Callista and his son. And it *terrifies* you that you might want the same thing one day!'

Fayay lifted a hand, a sphere of water rolling above his palm, but his threat lost its impact when a broad line of fire shot past the ball, turning it into steam. The Watine turned away to frown at the newcomer. 'Finara. You have no place in this quarrel.'

'The stark I don't,' said the goddess of fire, striding over, dark hair trailing behind her.

The Firine's olive skin was glistening, barely covered by her scarlet two-piece outfit, and her eyes were filled with flames, their hazel irises completely hidden. Only decades younger than Fayay, she was powerful, but didn't seem to care about proving this to her siblings. Kuja had to admit that this failing tended to afflict more sons than daughters of the Ine, known to the mortals as the Creator God.

Finara looked aside at the Rforine. 'Are you going to let him beat you up again?'

'I can't exactly stop him,' Kuja said with a sigh.

'Kuja, bro, the only reason you lost against him last time was because you used up all your power hiding Sandsa and his family for months.' Finara whistled in appreciation. 'That was really impressive. But hey, none of us could beat Sandsa in the end. *No one* can beat him.'

Fayay made a sound in his throat. It was somewhere between ominous and indignant.

'Well, you can't,' Finara said, spitting her older brother with a glare. 'You're still afraid of the Desine, otherwise you'd be over in the deserts antagonising him instead of going after our poor little Rforine here.'

'I'm not that little,' Kuja protested, but a grin exploded across his face. He had missed Finara. She was usually a recluse, preferring to hide out in volcanoes or lurk around buildings destroyed by fire, helping people to fix up the ruins left behind. She also had a habit of rescuing small children.

Kuja hoped she didn't think of him as one of those. But he was grateful for everything she had done for him. The Firine had threatened to singe off his eyebrows if he ever let the other gods know that she had nursed him back to health after that disastrous encounter with Fayay. She didn't possess healing abilities, but she did have a good deal of compassion. It seemed to embarrass her.

'We will speak of this later,' Fayay said and vanished inside a swirl of water that smacked onto the ground once he was gone.

Finara's expression became pinched. 'You really need to stand up to him.'

'I *can't*,' Kuja said, wringing his hands. He grimaced when he realised what he was doing and shoved his fingers into the pockets of the cargo pants he was wearing. 'I don't have his telekinesis and I'm not brave like you. And he's right. I'm weak.'

'Well, bro, I can't change your mind. But I can ask you why the stark you're here. Please don't tell me you're going to see Father.'

Kuja looked at his feet.

'Oh, *Kuja*.' The flames in Finara's eyes flickered, a hint of hazel peeking through. 'You can't do anything for Sandsa, not now. Our brother was the one who decided to jump out the airlock of sanity and into that mortal's arms.'

'The Ine as good as pushed him,' Kuja said, shooting a nervous glance down the long ornate corridor, half expecting to see the Ine walking towards him. But it seemed his father was busy elsewhere. Even though the Creator God now had plenty of immortal children to look after the galaxy's growing number of lifeforms, he still had important work to do.

Finara raised an eyebrow. 'Do tell.'

Kuja leaned forward and lowered his voice, despite knowing it was pointless to mask his words since the Creator God was aware of everything that went on in both realms. 'You know how the Ine lets GLEA use his powers through those chips in their heads, so they can protect other mortals? Well, Father made Callista have those powers naturally. She was meant to attract Sandsa's attention so that he would fall in love with her.'

The Firine rested a hand on Kuja's shoulder, squeezing gently. 'Are you sure about that? Could be that Callista was meant to do something else and Sandsa just blundered into it.'

'No, Finara, it's true,' Kuja insisted, shrugging off her touch. 'I asked Father about it. And he did not deny it. I was so angry. He lured Sandsa away from his duties on purpose! Do you know what the Ine said? He said it was a *lesson*. Sandsa needed to learn how to love mortals enough to care for them, so Callista provided that lesson. If Sandsa chose not to come back as the Desine, then he and Callista were expected to provide a replacement — they'd have had to give up their son! And Father stood by and let Fayay go after Sandsa's family, to force our brother to make a decision, so of course I'm upset and I'm — '

Kuja fell silent, horrified. Most of his siblings detested it when he rambled.

But Finara was smirking. 'I get it. Little Kuja's horny and he's upset that he'll get punished for falling in love and doing the nasty.'

'I am *not* — ' Kuja cut himself off, thinking of Lorena. His cheeks burned. Finara had to have seen that memory when it flashed through his mind, however briefly. She could read thoughts just as well as he could.

The Firine tutted. 'Kuja. It's normal. It's part of us.'

'What are you talking about?' Kuja demanded, refusing to meet her eyes.

'Well, our mother was born a mortal, wasn't she? It makes sense for us to have human desires!' Finara said, chuckling. 'And the Ine doesn't seem to care if we have sex, because he hasn't sent Fayay after me or the mortals I've gone to bed with. It's the love thing we can't do.'

Kuja gaped at her. 'You've had...*sex*?'

'Absolutely. You're really missing out, bro.'

'So if I...if I had sex, would that stop me having trouble around women?' Kuja asked, lining up his feet so that they were exactly parallel to each other. 'You saw how awful it was in my memories. That woman shed her clothes in front of me and I could barely think. Will that happen to me around men as well?'

Finara shrugged. 'Could do. I like men and women both.' She grinned. 'So? Are you interested? I know this great place in the mortal realm. I can pay for you.'

'How do you have mortal coin-chips?' Kuja blinked. 'I don't even have those.'

'Kuja. You live in a hut and work for food and board.'

'You live in a volcano!' he exclaimed.

Finara waved her arms around and streams of fire circled her body, seemingly unaimed but never leaving their tight orbit. 'I also work as a fire dancer at some luxury resorts. The mortals love that stuff. And I get to see how many of them take the fire goddess seriously.'

Kuja stood very still, hoping she would leave him alone if he didn't say anything.

Finara rolled her eyes. 'Kuja. You can talk to the Ine and get angry with him again or you can do something about your little problem. C'mon. Give it a shot.'

I wonder if Sandsa ever considered just having sex with Callista to get her out of his mind, Kuja thought, but then he remembered how his brother had looked at his wife on their wedding day in Atsa City. Sandsa's blue eyes had been swimming with moisture and he had felt so *alive*, thrumming with something even greater than the powers he had rejected.

Kuja shuddered. *Lorena might try to corner me again. I don't know what I'll do if she does. And I'd rather not do that with her. I don't even like her!*

'We'd better get this over with, and fast,' Kuja said as he and Finara began walking. They could have teleported out of the realm with their powers in an instant, but they both favoured the traditional exit between the last two columns.

'Don't worry, your first time won't take long,' Finara assured him.

Kuja didn't dare ask her what she meant by that.

CHAPTER FOUR

Fei eventually gave up hoping that Moz would come back to rescind his orders so she dutifully rewrote the code for the Yalsa 5 simulation. While the compiling program ran, spitting out a new bevy of error messages, she grabbed her techpad and headed for the hoverlift. It had taken her almost the entire two Old Earth years she'd worked here on Enoc to realise that every other TerraCorp programmer spent their spare moments doing more exciting things than calling their mothers. They often stepped outside to take in some natural light or even to get a cup of coffein.

Fei had at first prided herself on working harder than the rest of them, especially those who were in charge of inferior tasks such as writing code for Web-based advertising apps, but then she'd discovered that sometimes she actually needed fresh air to clear her cluttered mind.

Stepping out into the lilac fog spewing from the sea, Fei lifted her techpad and ran her thumb over the corner, activating the Web. Thanks to her, only communicators were allowed to connect to the Web inside the building.

That's one thing Moz finally listened to me about, she thought, shaking her head. *It's not safe for consoles or techpads to have Web access, because anyone could hack their way in and steal our files. I wish Moz had banned communicators too, because people might listen in to our conversations...but then I wouldn't get to talk to Mum at my desk...*

Fei caught sight of one of the other programmers exiting the building. She ducked her head, afraid he'd try to talk to her, but when she chanced a peek she saw that he was frantically tapping on his techpad, brow furrowed. Not everyone had been keen about the changes to Web access — Fei assumed they'd been watching vids on the Web instead of working — but after TerraCorp had avoided the data theft that other corporations had recently suffered, Moz had been hailed as a genius for *his* idea.

Fei clenched a fist inside her pocket, mindful of the surveillance vidcam hovering outside the foyer doors. She'd love to let Moz know how angry it had made her when he'd stolen the credit for her idea, but whenever she saw him she felt like she'd been struck dumb.

Fei sighed and flicked a finger over the screen of the techpad, pulling up her preferred Webchat feed. Several of the names listed there were familiar to her. She fancied she knew more about these anonymous, faceless people than she did any of her colleagues. Working in the basement wasn't exactly conducive to networking and she avoided people outside of work because they tended to get that blank stare which meant she'd been talking too much again.

Anticipation shivered through Fei as she brought up on the on-screen keyboard. *Hey, CC here. Anyone know why GLEA isn't tolerant of desert god worshippers?*

CC was her Webname, an acronym of Code Compiler. She had found this funny as a teenager, but now it caused her to cringe every time she signed in. At least no one else on the Web had figured it out yet.

'Why is it I can talk really well on this starking thing but I can't do it in real life, when it actually counts...' Fei muttered. 'Oh. Here we go. I knew I could rely on BozzMed.'

BozzMed, a regular of this particular feed (devoted to people who were fed up with their bosses or the corporations they worked for), had pinged her back almost immediately. *I've spoken to a few Chippers and desert tribespeople in my time. They've never had much love for each other; for starters, the Desine is considered a lot more violent than the Creator God.*

But it really depends on who's calling the shots at GLEA. There have been entire decades where GLEA doesn't mention the desert folk at all. But then the Agency elects a new Head General who's been nursing a grudge against the Desine's followers for years and suddenly has the power to go after them.

You're talkative today, Fei replied, throwing a furtive look between the surveillance vidcam and her colleague. She curved a hand over the top of her techpad, shielding the screen.

And you're not, BozzMed noted. *Why do you want to know all this?*

Fei bit her lip. *Are the Desine's followers a threat to GLEA? Enough that the Agency would want to destroy any deserts they come across?*

BozzMed's response arrived a lot faster than she expected. *Well, if you look at it with safety and security in mind, those with desert powers can turn them on innocent people and use them like weapons. It's another way to hurt folk and that could be why the Agency is concerned.*

Fei closed her eyes briefly. 'Yeah, like GLEA's agents don't have their own ways of hurting us.' She belatedly remembered to seal her mouth back up when her colleague gave her an odd look.

Ideologically speaking, BozzMed went on, *it looks bad if the Creator God's 'chosen' protectors of the galaxy have to get their powers from tech while the desert worshippers are born with theirs naturally.*

GLEA might want to wipe out the tribespeople simply because their existence is damaging the Agency's galactic reputation.

I've heard the Desine actually speaks to his followers, Fei sent to BozzMed, then glanced up at the sky, frowning. She'd never heard anything from the god she was supposed to worship, but then again, her father and her ex-fiancé must have heard something that had made them want to stick chips into their temples.

By the time she was done fighting back tears, more lines of text had appeared on her techpad.

There's a few sub-level gods who talk to their followers, BozzMed told her. *Oceania, water god. Renaei, tundra goddess. I could go on. Dare I ask what has inspired this line of questioning?*

The surveillance vidcam abruptly trained its lens on her. Fei forced a brittle smile. She might be able to hide a less-than-innocent Webchat from a vidcam, but the Creator God had to be sensing her turmoil. Shouldn't he make it known through some miracle or intervention that she shouldn't run off to some other god who might actually listen to her?

Fei covered her mouth with her hand. She felt physically ill. When she was able, she tapped out a message that hopefully came across as casual. *Oh, I've just been watching Webcasts about the historical tension between the two groups. I thought GLEA didn't believe in the so-called 'Magic' that the tribespeople claim to have.*

Do you believe the tribespeople have powers? BozzMed asked.

Of course. There have been documented cases.

Another question, CC. BozzMed was evidently on a roll today. *Are you thinking of worshipping a new god? Because that's exactly the sort of thing GLEA is worried about. Do remember — they rely on money, no matter how religious they are. They need to rake in donations from their worshippers to pay their agents. The desert tribes don't monetise their faith or show up on planets that don't want them. And I think that's contributing to GLEA losing some of their support.*

Fei's fingers shivered as she held them over the techpad. Despite her best efforts, the whisper escaped her trembling lips. 'I can't be talking about this. I shouldn't even be *thinking* about this!'

She powered down her techpad and shoved it back into her pocket, but she couldn't disconnect her mind quite so easily. *GLEA needs money to protect us. That's how they serve the Creator God, by serving us. Everyone knows that.*

So who are they serving when they tell a terraforming company to go against a client's wishes?

Appalled at herself, Fei scurried back inside to check on the growing list of errors filling the vidscreen in the basement.

***

The Enocian Harem was one of the most opulent places Kuja had ever seen in his seven and a half decades of life. The world it was based on, Enoc, had a government that created and passed laws, but its citizens and businesses were beholden to a queen who had the first say on how to spend the planet's treasury. The Enocians were rich enough that they didn't mind this arrangement, especially when their taxes were used in such lavish ways as this.

The Harem was so full of silksein that for a moment Kuja thought he had walked onto one of those ancient sea-faring ships his mother used to tell him about when he was young. She had been very old for a human, granted immortality by her marriage to the Ine, but unlike the Desine's missing wife, she had chosen to become mortal again upon leaving her husband. The memory of his mother's death felt, even now, like a hot blade passing through Kuja's ribs, right into his heart.

Kuja sat on one of the many couches inside the Harem's atrium, using a cylindrical cushion to support his lower back. Finara had already chosen a woman for the evening and had thrown her brother a suggestive wink before being spirited out a side door. Kuja watched the scantily clad bodies pass him by, wondering if he should rise and introduce himself or simply sit there, enjoying the view. Happily, someone else made the decision for him.

A woman bent down in front of the couch, her cleavage peppered with perspiration. It was very hard to focus on her pleasant smile and Kuja felt guilty when he kept looking elsewhere. Thin strips of silver were stretched over her hips, covering her intimate parts, but they did nothing to curtail the sweet smell that seemed to be coming from her. He watched as her fingers crawled up her thigh and briefly vanished. When they withdrew she offered them to him, her skin slick with moisture.

'Don't be shy,' she said. 'The first taste is free.'

If Kuja hadn't been able to see into her mind, he would have assumed she was joking. Trembling, he took her hand and held it to his lips. A finger slid its way into his mouth and the taste clinging to it was salty and strange, but somehow compelling. Kuja dug into his pocket, which was heavy with Finara's coin-chips, and thrust a fistful of the currency at the Harem employee. She rewarded him by smiling and leading him through a slit in the silksein that he had not noticed before.

He found himself in a secluded space that could have been a tent or a room cunningly disguised as one. No couches here, just sumptuous rugs and a small stack of shelves for clothes and shoes.

The woman swiftly unwound the strips covering her and lay on one of the rugs, brushing her palms over her body, playing with the nipples rising out of her skin. Kuja unbelted his pants and carefully folded them on one of the shelves. By the time he got to his shirt, he was more impatient so he settled for throwing it aside as he dived onto the rug.

'First time?' the woman asked, her gaze wandering to the unsheathed organ between his legs.

Kuja nodded mutely.

'Don't worry, I won't bite — unless you want me to,' she added with a wink. 'Now lie back and relax.'

Kuja obeyed, propping himself up with his arms beneath him, his elbows framing his head. An antique style lamp was swinging from the ceiling, brass if its appearance was anything to go by. He was intrigued by the false candle embedded inside the lamp, but was distracted from further study when lips latched onto the hollow of his neck, drawing a startled hiss from him. Her hot, wet kisses then travelled down to one of his nipples, evoking shivers and other pleasant reactions. Kuja nodded approvingly when she moved onto the other nipple.

'Interesting,' he said.

She paused, her silver eyebrows jumping up to the widow's peak that reminded him of the stern village headman back in Bagath.

'The sensations, they're interesting,' Kuja clarified. 'They're like...electric tingles. Or just tingles, as there isn't any electricity involved. I think. No, I am sure it's just tingles.'

'I'll give you more than tingles,' his companion promised.

'Cool,' Kuja said.

Her mouth continued to caress his chest for a time and Kuja

found himself wondering when they would get to the good bit, then mentally rebuked himself. He knew that mortals liked to engage in foreplay, even though it delayed their coupling. It was part of the experience.

Just as he'd prepared himself to wait, she cupped his balls and at the same time darted her tongue down the underside of his lengthening shaft. This caused a bolt of pleasure to course through him and Kuja jerked upright, exclaiming something, though he wasn't sure what. He was well versed in multiple languages and some came naturally to him because of his powers, but this was a word he had never before uttered in his life.

'Oh, I really ought to have tried this myself,' Kuja remarked, peering down at her as she continued to fondle her way around his intimate regions, alternating between carefully massaging his balls and gliding her fingers all the way up to his moistened tip. 'It would have saved my sister some money.'

The woman ceased her ministrations and gave him a pointed look.

'Um, sorry,' said Kuja.

'If you want to touch yourself while I watch, we can do that,' she suggested.

'Oh, no, I wouldn't know what I was doing. Please go on. I won't say anything else. Well, I'll try not to...' Kuja silenced when her lips clamped over his. Her kiss was salty and her tongue wriggled around as if it was searching for something. He refrained from snapping his aching jaw shut — he had a feeling she would not appreciate that.

To his relief, she did eventually stop kissing him, but only so that she could completely engulf his shaft in her mouth. Kuja's vision blackened for a several long seconds. When he came to himself, he was gasping up at the ceiling, his neck bent at an awkward angle as he thrust his pelvis against her. Her hands found his hips and forced him down.

'More,' a husky voice begged. It must have been his own.

Kuja gripped the rug beneath his fingers, feeling the soft fabric give and tear the more he stabbed into it with his nails. Potent heat was swelling below his abdomen, building his anticipation to almost painful levels — and then her lips abruptly left him.

Kuja made an indignant sound.

'You can finish in my mouth if you'd like,' she told him. 'But you have paid for the full service. Seems a shame to waste your coin-chips.'

Kuja groaned as she spread her thighs, showing him the moisture that had gathered along her exposed folds. After allowing him to enjoy the sight for a moment, she sank down on him in one go and got to work.

Kuja found himself staring at the ceiling again.

The draperies up there were a coppery colour that complemented the lamp — or was it meant to be the other way around? The woman's bosom heaved in front of him, sometimes blocking his view. She was attractive. He really should be paying more attention to her, but he couldn't think of any compelling reason to do so.

She cupped his face. 'Hello? Are you in there?'

Kuja blinked. 'Of course I am. I'm inside you.'

'You've gone soft.'

She climbed off him and his member fell limply to the side. Kuja peered down at it. 'Oh. I thought that once you got going, it built and built and then — well — you know.'

'Not always,' his companion said, lying flush against his body.

Kuja sighed. 'Well, that's disappointing.'

'Don't worry. It happens.' She began to play with his hair, apparently unbothered. This wasn't an unusual turn of events, if her thoughts and memories were anything to go by.

Goosebumps were crowding over Kuja's skin now that his body was no longer running hot with desire. Shivering, he sagged against the rug. 'I'm sorry. I don't feel...interested. Do you suppose that means I like men instead?'

'Did you like being inside me?' she asked.

'Oh. Yes. It was wonderful.'

She pursed her lips until they became distinctly button-shaped. 'I think you found me attractive but got distracted. Any physical problems, I've got stims for that — but I can't do anything about your head. You got a girlfriend or something? Some guys have trouble if they're feeling guilty.'

Kuja shook his head sharply. 'No, no girlfriend. Never.'

'You could play with yourself, like I showed you,' she said, her lips touching his temple. 'That might work.'

Kuja skirted his eyes down her form. She was beautiful, she really was. He thought very hard at his extraneous organ, but it crumpled even further. 'Oh well. I guess I just don't want to do this.'

She sat up and reached for her clothes. They looked more like ribbons now, out of context as they were in her hands. Kuja laced his fingers across his face and groaned.

'You alright?' the woman asked.

Kuja peeked at her. She was still nude. 'I'm not sure how I'm going to explain this to my sister — she's the one who gave me the coin-chips I paid you with. I've only been in here for a handful of minutes and she...well, she'll make fun of me.'

His companion's lips curled into a smile. 'Lucky for you, I know a few ways to pass the time.'

'Oh?' Kuja clambered onto his knees. 'Do tell.'

'It's obvious you want to go all the way one day,' she told him. 'I can show you how to touch a woman and how to please her. It's more fun if you both get something out of it.'

Kuja tapped two fingers to the side of his face, frowning thoughtfully. 'You mean, women also like being kissed and touched all over their bodies? I suppose I shouldn't be surprised. Does everyone know this?'

She laughed. 'You'd be surprised how many men don't.'

'Teach me,' Kuja requested.

More than an hour later, he sauntered into the atrium and threw a careless grin at Finara, who had been waiting for him. She actually applauded, much to his embarrassment. He ducked his head and hurried outside, his sister catching up to him there.

She threw an arm over his shoulders as they descended the Harem's gold trimmed steps. 'See? We haven't been struck dead by Father and Fayay hasn't shown up to berate us for abandoning the grand design. So I'll see you back here in one Old Earth week?'

'Oh, I think I might try to find someone on Bagaran,' Kuja said, averting his eyes from hers and diligently scrubbing his thoughts so that she wouldn't see the truth in them. 'I can't afford to return. I do only get food and board, you know.'

Finara snorted. 'Suit yourself. Anyway, I've got to go tell some stupid mortals their scenic volcano is rumbling for a reason. See ya, bro.'

The weight on his shoulders vanished along with his sister.

Kuja sank down onto one of the steps, suddenly feeling very alone. Thanks to his time at the Harem, he knew how to please a woman, but the ache inside him was even more painful than before. It was frustrating, in more ways than one.

He got back onto his feet but did not immediately disappear, instead choosing to walk the streets of Enoc for hours, deep in thought.

CHAPTER FIVE

Fei would have walked straight past the temple on her way home from work had a knot of worshippers not suddenly left, their eyes striking her like lasbolts and making her insides twist with guilt. Unable to remember anyone's names, she smiled vaguely at the group and began climbing the shallow schist steps. There were countless temples scattered across the galaxy, mostly square-shaped since that was GLEA's preference for their buildings on Gerasnin. Fei was glad the Enocians had insisted on designing their own places of worship. She found the uneven lines of this temple somehow soothing. Well, she *usually* did.

The moment Fei stepped inside she was embraced by cool, hushed air that was occasionally punctuated by the distant blast of lasgun fire. She looked down at the floor, as though she could see right through it to the bowels of the temple, where the agents stationed on Enoc were honing their skills. Some of them were probably even using forcefields to deflect the lasbolts.

Not all temples doubled as GLEA outposts, but this was the largest and most visited one on the planet. While the subterranean levels were given over to training, the higher levels were filled with sleeping quarters, eating halls and conference rooms in which the agents could discuss the protection of Enoc and its laws.

Fei wasn't sure how much GLEA received in donations, but

they must be doing well to have funded a temple like this. The Enocian worshippers were certainly grateful for it.

Fei didn't feel very grateful tonight. Tears seared her eyes as she sank before the altar. 'I'm sorry. I just can't feel you.'

'Are you alright, fellow child of the Creator God?' a gentle voice asked behind her.

Fei froze in place, wishing she could turn to stone and blend into the speckled grey floor. She waited for her unwanted companion to leave. Unfortunately, they knelt onto the floor, clearly intent on staying.

Fei kept her face hidden behind her curtain of purple hair. 'No. I mean, yes. I am very okay and I'm here to give thanks to the Creator God because isn't that we're supposed to do? Even if we can't hear him?'

A soft hoot, then another. Was it laughter? Fei turned to get a better look at the woman beside her. The newcomer was blue-skinned and had four thickly muscled arms that could have snapped a steel girder like a twig. Her smile was also inhumanly broad.

'It's normal to have doubts, I have them myself — everyone does,' the Lentarian (Fei thought she had guessed the woman's species correctly) reassured her.

Fei wrinkled her nose. 'That doesn't help. It just makes me feel worse because I can't get past this the way other people can.'

'Oh, you'll come through it, we all do.'

What if I don't? Fei nearly asked. Mercifully, her thoughts remained buried inside her, where only the Creator God could see them.

'You can talk to me,' the Lentarian said, tilting her head down until her eyes were even with Fei's. 'The Creator God has sent me to you so that I may serve both him and your needs.'

'How do you know that he sent you?' Fei asked. 'Can you hear him?'

The Lentarian shrugged. 'No, but I can feel him.'

'I can't,' Fei whispered. 'And I'm starting to wonder if I should even bother trying. There are other gods who have a more immediate impact and I'm thinking...'

'Stop thinking right now!' her companion admonished.

Fei tried. She really did. But her failure must have shown on her face.

The Lentarian unleashed a tirade, but it was the same argument Fei had used on herself many times. Yes, it was common knowledge that the Creator God had always been shared by different species on worlds light years apart. Yes, she remembered her history lessons, she knew that when the galaxy's species had developed faster space travel in the days of Old Earth, they had met and realised they shared a god. Since they were brethren, created by the same hand, there had been no ideological wars over planets and planetoids, only peaceful integration. This was long before any sub-level gods had appeared.

Fei knew she should just accept her place in the universe, accept that she couldn't hear the Creator God and accept that she should trust anyone who said they did.

But if the Creator God told Zareth to leave me, then my own god doesn't even want me to be happy...

'Please shut up,' Fei hissed at the voice inside her head.

The Lentarian woman reared back, offended. Muttering about rude young humans, she took her leave. Fei pressed her forehead to the floor and moaned in despair. She would probably need to find a new temple now.

When she finally managed to get back onto her feet, she noticed a copper-haired man sitting in one of the rear pews of the temple.

'Don't bother, this god's not listening,' she tossed at him as she marched out.

She ran most of the way home, her tears streaking messily over her face.

***

Kuja frowned as he took in the interior of the temple dedicated to his father, trying not to feel the energy of the Chippers in the building around him. He would not usually have chosen to come to a place like this, but he'd felt an irresistible urge to climb the steps of the temple. After taking a seat, he had listened to the two women talking, clenching his knees harder and harder with each passing moment, until the beautiful one, decked out in deep shades of purple that would make her appear invisible against the night sky of Enoc, had fled, crying.

'Father, I won't pretend to know every facet of your grand design,' Kuja murmured. 'But I don't see why your followers need to feel this isolated.' He crushed his eyelids together. 'At least you never do to them what you do to us. They can love without fearing that it's part of some plan of yours, without fearing that they'll get someone killed just by *looking at them for too long*. I don't regret helping Sandsa, even though I knew it was impossible to hide him forever, but...it destroyed me...'

He slipped into his memories, to the day he had been broken.

***

His rainforests demanded so much care, so much attention. He wanted to bathe them in his uninterrupted presence, but Kuja had to concentrate on concealing the pocket of happiness that contained Sandsa, Callista and their son, Kieran. Kuja continued to protect the Desine and his family, even though he felt like he had been reduced to the consistency of plastic film, stretched so tight a blunt fingernail could have punctured him.

Though he was struggling, he had not yet reached his breaking point.

But then Fayay, the Watine, came to Kuja's worlds.

The waterfalls fell silent, countless wells ran dry and the humidity thinned until every plant and animal began to wither. Bagara's people cried out for their god and Kuja had no choice but to come and defend them.

Fayay was ready for him. The Watine stole Kuja away to an ocean world in a telekinetic grip so powerful it could forcibly move the insubstantial form of a god.

Even when the pain began, Kuja still believed he was doing the right thing, defying the other gods so that Sandsa might enjoy the life of a mortal and remain a husband and father, the duty he had chosen over the one he had been born with. Sandsa did not yet know he had never needed to abandon his powers or his deserts to be with his wife. He did not yet know he was allowed to experience love so long as he kept guiding his people. And he certainly didn't know that Callista had kept this knowledge from him because she could not bear to stay with a god when she had married a mere man.

But Kuja's belief that his cause was just would not save him. His very being was dashed onto the rocks on the edge of a shore until his soul bore bruises. If he'd been in his human form, he would have broken every bone in his body. And Fayay wasn't done. He continued to claw and shred the Rforine's energy until Kuja wished he had a mouth to vent his agony into screams. Unable to take it anymore, he escaped into the part of his presence he'd left with Sandsa and collapsed onto the floor of the family's quarters on a barren mining moon, exposing its location.

That Fayay had managed to convince so many of Sandsa's siblings to come was not surprising. They all felt so strongly that they should be alone, forever watching over the happiness of their subjects, never tasting any of it for themselves. They saw it as their duty to force the desert god back to his rightful path, no matter what. Sandsa's love had become a distraction, one that no other god should be tempted to chase. It could not go unpunished. Not now, not ever.

Kuja was a broken shell. His siblings could have destroyed him. But they ignored their youngest brother and instead threatened a man who had once been the most powerful god among them.

Sandsa became the Desine. He fought his siblings. And he won. But using his powers cost him his humanity. Within seconds, his presence was gone, snatched back by the deserts he had abandoned for so long. Callista sank to the floor, cradling her husband's limp, empty body.

'Don't,' Kuja told his sister-in-law, not entirely sure what he was pleading her not to do.

Callista's mind was shielded from him by her unusual powers. All she allowed the Rforine to sense from her was that she would no longer keep Sandsa from the deserts or his people. Kuja's heart soared. So finally she was accepting all sides of Sandsa — the man, the god and everything in between. Sandsa did not have to abandon any part of himself. No one need suffer his absence.

Barely a day later, Callista and her son vanished. Not even Sandsa could locate them.

'*Don't make him choose between you and the deserts when he can have both,*' *Kuja had meant to say to her that day.*

Now he would never be able tell her, or convince her.

***

Kuja thought he understood now, years after the fact. Sandsa's duties required a great deal of his time, meaning that Callista would not always have the man she loved to herself. Worse still, she would have had to contend with a pantheon of gods who might suddenly decide she remained a distraction and needed to be removed altogether. They'd only have to wait until Sandsa left her side.

It was easy to see why Callista had taken her son with her: she had wanted to shield Kieran from the fear and danger he would have had to endure. No mortal would willingly choose that life for themselves or for their child.

But why did Fayay, who had threatened to steal Callista's son and turn him into a weapon, suddenly back off? It wasn't like the Watine to relinquish a valuable tool that could have helped him defeat the Desine, the sibling he hated most.

'As long as Sandsa's son remains unaware of his powers, I will not go after him,' Fayay had promised, a gleam in those blue eyes which were so much paler and crueller than Sandsa's.

It had taken time for Kuja to regain his full powers and he'd only managed it with Finara's help. The Firine had felt badly about what had happened to him, because she'd agreed to confront Sandsa with Fayay. But she hadn't wanted Kuja to get hurt. Kuja had forgiven her, but he refused to do the same for the Ine or any of his other siblings.

Kuja dug his knuckles into his thighs. Healed he might be, he was still that scrap of plastic, punctured and ruptured.

He stood and left the temple celebrating the Creator God, a being who had stood by and done nothing to protect his youngest son.

***

A thin band of lilac did its best to linger on the horizon, but within moments the sunset gave way to night. The days on Enoc lasted about eighteen Old Earth hours, only a third of which was spent at work or at one of the galaxy-famed universities, but lately they had felt like individual eternities. Fei hooked her fingers over the silver railing on her balcony and willed the system's star to come back and wash away the dark violet filling the sky. It refused.

Her apartment belonged to a building popular with TerraCorp employees, as it was near the company's headquarters and right beside the ocean, on soft chalk-like pebbles. The view was beautiful. But she gained no pleasure from it.

When she had first moved to Enoc, she had been relieved to leave her mother behind, along with the endless chatter and the backhanded compliments that were well meaning but still designed to alter her behaviour. Now Fei wished her mother would swoop in from somewhere. Berale would be a welcome interruption, loud enough to mask the gentle shhh-shhh noises the sea was making. It reminded her too much of Zareth.

Fei backed away from the edge of the balcony. But the waves still came for her, demanding that she relax and cast her cares away. Except that she couldn't. The past clung to her too tightly.

Shhh-shhh, you did nothing wrong.

Shhh-shhh, Fei. It's not about you.

***

One Old Earth year ago, she was standing in the middle of her apartment, keypass braced between two fingers as she watched him leave the bedroom. The small bag distorting the shape of his shoulder couldn't possibly hold more than a sliver of the items he had filled her apartment with. Most of his things were still strewn over the furniture and floor, like remnants of an explosion.

'I can do long distance, I know I can,' she said. 'And Gerasnin isn't that far. It's only three days away by starship. I can take leave to visit.'

'It's not about the distance, Fei.'

Fei felt her chin wobble. 'Are you worried your salary from the Agency won't support us? Zar, I already make more coin-chips than you. We can do this together.'

But his ebony face was set, determined.

'Don't do this,' she pleaded. 'You know what my dad's leaving did to me.'

The keypass slipped from her fingers and stabbed into the plush carpeting that even the queen of this world had on the floor of her bedroom. Nothing was too fine for the employees of TerraCorp.

Three days later Fei would rip up the carpet, exposing the ugly metal plating underneath.

'Shhh-shhh. I know your dad left to join GLEA.' Zareth's dark brown eyes were full of sorrow. Perhaps he was also remembering that he had always told her not to worry, that she could trust him and tell him what she was really thinking. She was glad she'd never been that careless. 'But when you're called to the service of the Creator God, it's impossible to *ignore and...look, I can't say no to this. It's more than a career. It's my destiny. My future.'*

'A future I have no part in,' Fei said dully, feeling as though she had been mined hollow.

'Fei...I want to focus on my duty. I can't let myself be distracted.'

'I get it. Our god's will is more important than me.'

'No, it's not like that — I know you don't understand, but —'

'Of course I don't!' Fei threw herself across the space between them, grabbing his vest and yanking him down for a kiss that he veered away from. 'I've never heard the Creator God calling me to his service! I've never...I've never heard anything...' She began to sob.

'Shhh-shhh, it's okay. Shhh. Goodbye, Feiscina.'

***

Every day since then she had left an empty apartment to walk to work, shirking the complimentary hovershuttle that TerraCorp provided. Some mornings were frigid on Enoc, others more kind, but at least Fei understood the factors that dictated the daily temperatures on this side of the planet. People were much harder to understand.

Sighing, Fei retreated into her apartment, the transparent plexiglass door sliding shut behind her. The sounds of the ocean mercifully died.

She hadn't made the bed that morning. Fei didn't care. It wasn't like anyone else ever saw it. She shed her clothes into an untidy pile then lay back against the silksein sheets that were a favourite import among the Enocian elite. Fei could see why; the fabric felt wonderful on her bare skin. But it still didn't compare to what her fingers could do.

During the time she had been alone, she had discovered more things about herself — including and not limited to her love of walking, her dislike of the sea and the fact that her body could sing, if it was given a chance.

She began to knead her breasts, working them closer together. The contact of skin on skin sent shivers across her chest and around to each armpit, raising a rash of goosebumps. Not to be denied, her scalp tingled, begging for some attention, so she ran her fingers there, through her hair, then over her lips, over her neck and back down to her breasts.

Her fingers circled a nipple, teasing it, never quite claiming it, driving her mad. When she could finally stand it no more, she pinched her nipple and gasped, tossing her head from side to side. Her other hand flew down her body and delved into the wet well between her legs, lathing her folds with slick moisture.

Fei squirmed, a moan prying her lips apart. She forced herself to still, then slowly renewed her ministrations. Her touch played along the edge of her labia, to the stretched band of skin beneath her weeping entrance, and then slid back inside her, deeper than before.

At last she gave complete attention to her swollen clitoris.

'Ah!' she cried out.

The resulting throb caused her hips to fly off the bed. Fei buried her hands into the sheets either side of her and tried to calm her breathing. She allowed herself a few more strokes before she once more abandoned her warm core, mewling in disappointment. This process continued, off and on, until she was grinding her mons against the heel of her palm in desperation.

It was time to stop denying herself.

Two fingers burrowed into her clenching folds, curving

against that soft part inside her. She continued to rub her clitoris slowly, in a circular motion, and quelled her impatience, knowing that if she forced herself to finish now, she would only be rewarded with a small burst. She wanted more. So much more.

Her body was slick with sweat when it finally happened. The orgasm began low in her abdomen, a heavy, growing promise that then shot out and struck her feet and hands, forcing them to curl. Hot waves of pleasure rolled through her, again and again, until she was spent, her limbs slack on the bed.

'Mmm,' Fei said, lying there in the aftermath, welcoming the tickle of sleep on her eyelids.

A smile graced her lips.

It would not last through her dreams.

CHAPTER SIX

'Are you going to dob me in, Kuja? It's not like anyone got hurt.'

Kuja turned from watching TerraCorp's scientists scurry about in the clearing below and bowed his head in greeting at Inesh as the other man entered the open-air watchtower. Inesh's thoughts were hard, uncompromising. He clearly wasn't there to enjoy the view of the rainforest on the southern side of the village.

Over the past five Old Earth years, Kuja had become friends with Inesh and the other villagers and looked forward to spending time with them. He liked that there were no coin-chips inside these palisade walls, that everyone's needs were provided for and that everyone worked together for the good of the village. If someone was not physically capable of manual labour, then they were given a role no less respected, be it as a teacher or even as an artist whose work could be traded in return for food or other supplies.

Inesh was the age that Kuja appeared to be, somewhere in his twenties, and had tawny-coloured skin, a feature that was unique in Bagath — most of those living in the village were much paler, like Kuja was. Inesh had been born on the other side of Bagaran, in a village that was known for being heavily armed and antagonistic. But Inesh's loyalty to Bagath had never been questioned. So long as one contributed and never picked up a weapon, they were welcome.

'No, I don't think I could stand the sullen silence you would punish me with if I *did* dob you in,' Kuja finally answered and dropped onto one of the wide wooden planks forming the floor of the watchtower. The wall here was low enough that he could still keep an eye on the scientists, not that he needed to. The plants in the clearing would tell him if TerraCorp's employees did something they shouldn't.

Inesh arranged himself into a cross-legged position beside Kuja, a deep scowl carved into his face. 'It's TerraCorp's fault for not using better tech. All it took was for one of those loud hoverpads to conk out and the whole starking thing fell.'

'You still think our god doesn't want them here?' Kuja asked, lifting a hand to direct Inesh's gaze to the downed laboratory. The squat buildings that housed the scientists at night sat on a rise above the clearing and were thankfully unaffected. 'Wouldn't Bagara want more rainforests under his sway? Rainforests that TerraCorp can create?'

Inesh shook his head. 'If Bagara wanted that, he'd make more of them himself.'

'Bagara didn't make...' Kuja began.

'The Creator God only dropped a few careless seeds, Kuja!' Inesh interrupted him. 'Bagara is the one who looks after us. And I don't see him creating more rainforests and expanding his control. Clearly he cares about what he has, not what he doesn't.'

Kuja opened his mouth, then closed it again. He couldn't explain that willing a rainforest into being was a draining process and he would have to pour a ridiculous amount of his energy into simply keeping it alive, especially if the soil beneath his construct was unresponsive. Kuja knew Inesh would not believe him if he said that TerraCorp was a better, more permanent option for altering worlds. So all he said was, 'TerraCorp is pestering me because of your actions, Inesh.'

'Taking the brunt of it, are you?' Inesh asked with a snort. 'That's your problem. You're the one who insists on consorting with them all the time.'

Kuja patted his cheeks with the back of his hand, trying to cool them. He couldn't remember the heat of his domain ever affecting him like this before. 'Consorting! No, thank you. Did you know that Dr Lorena Hackett, one of the scientists, tried to seduce me in the showers?'

Inesh raised his eyebrows. 'Tried — or succeeded? Judging by that blush, I'd say she failed! But why not, Kuja? You never have any fun.'

Kuja reluctantly let his lips form a smile. 'If by "fun" you mean sabotaging a lab and having sex in the showers, which are very slippery by the way, then I think we differ in our definitions.'

'Sounds like she was very slippery too.'

'Inesh!' Kuja cried, giving the man's shoulder an indignant shove.

They laughed together for several minutes before lapsing into a companionable silence. The village was preparing for the midday meal, judging by the clatter of pots and the wafting scent of meat-seeded rice baking inside vine leaves. Kuja's stomach, which didn't actually *need* sustenance, gave a hopeful rumble.

'It is good to hear you laugh,' Inesh said after a while. 'You always have this great big shadow on your face.'

Kuja sighed. 'Family problems.'

'Bagath is isolated and hard to find — how can your family get at you here?'

Kuja shook his head sadly. Revealing himself to a mortal was something he could never do, even if it would give him someone to talk to about the mess that was the Galactic Pantheon. Many of his followers were very devout in their worship of him and used their faith as a moral compass. He could not compromise that by showing them how little confidence he had in himself.

'Inesh, why do you worship Bagara?' Kuja asked. He could already see Inesh's thoughts on the matter, but he wanted to hear them out loud. 'You didn't witness his arrival like the older generations did.'

Inesh stretched his arms out behind him, grunting in satisfaction when something cracked in his shoulders. 'Bagara's only been here for a few decades. Seems to me that if a god gets old enough, they get caught up in the machinations of the universe and stop listening to the little people. Bagara still wants to please us. We should take advantage of this while we can.'

'I don't think you want Bagara overhearing you just now,' Kuja remarked.

'Hah!' Inesh smirked. 'He could learn a thing or two from listening to me.'

Kuja bit down hard on his tongue to keep from snickering. 'Oh? Like what?'

'I'll let you know when I think of something.'

'Cool, so I'll be waiting a while then.' Kuja's felt his good humour bleed away. 'But, Inesh, if Bagara really wanted the laboratory gone, don't you think he would have used his powers to throw vines into that hoverpad instead of expecting you to go blow it up?'

Inesh's voice took on a gentle, patronising tone. 'Even he must respect the free will given to us by the Creator God. Bagara has got to let us do things for ourselves. And how are we supposed to know what he wants? He only speaks to us once a year at the festival and it's always something so starking vague that it might as well not apply to us at all.'

'So you think he should speak to each individual follower?' Kuja asked, his forehead creasing.

'Oh yeah,' Inesh answered, smacking a bug that came too close to his arm. 'He could've told me to take a shower while Dr Hackett was in there. Wasted opportunity, I tell you.'

Inesh was still chortling as he scurried down the wooden steps, lured away from their conversation by the promise of food.

Kuja rested his chin on his knees, soothed by the distant croaks of the five-legged shingbats. He had spent so long letting his followers do as they pleased when perhaps what they had really needed was guidance. It was true that he only spoke to them during the festival, but he had intervened in extreme circumstances to save their lives and the lives of those visiting his domain.

But what if his people wanted more from him? What if they wanted someone more hands on, like Sandsa, who actually spoke to his desert-based followers when they asked for his help? Talking to Inesh as a god might have accomplished more; Kuja, as a man, could hardly convince his friend to do anything.

Kuja rolled his lips into his mouth.

It bore thinking about.

But not now. Not when he had so much to do.

Kuja attended the midday meal for as little time as could be deemed polite, then headed for the gate, making sure he threw Inesh a look of warning. The man held up his hands and shook his head, as though promising he wasn't going to bother the scientists in Kuja's absence.

No one in Bagath seemed fazed by Kuja disappearing so often and nor did they ask what he did while he was gone, for which he was grateful. He loved their company, enjoyed maintaining the village with his bare hands alongside them, and tried very hard to attend most of the meetings held by the village headman. But he wasn't one of of the Bagathians, not really. And he never would be. He'd have to leave them in a handful of years, before they started to notice that he didn't age. Before they realised what he was.

Kuja walked down the path outside, twisting his hands in front of him, though he did manage to pry them apart so that he could wave at Gerns as he passed. He then had to quickly duck behind a tree when Lorena exited her living quarters — he didn't want to see her, let alone *speak* to her, right now.

Once he was safely out of sight, Kuja collapsed to the ground in a heap of leaf litter. If he'd had a mortal body during this process, he would have laughed and danced and sung until his lungs ran out of air. He loved becoming one with his domain.

In this form, Kuja could touch every plant and creature on every world that bowed to the whim of the rainforest god. If there were humans or other sentient species living among the trees, he was drawn to their energy, their hopes, their needs —

Someone was in danger. They were calling for Bagara.

Kuja raced to their side to save them from falling off a cliff, then immediately hurtled into another situation requiring his presence. Then another. And another.

But no matter how far across the galaxy he went, no matter how long he spent in his insubstantial form, his unwanted thoughts and desires chased him. He needed to quell the ache inside him somehow. But he had no idea how to achieve this, especially since his visit to the Enocian Harem had shown him that his fear of Fayay was not the only obstacle preventing him from finding release.

Kuja's mortal body, the thing that made him *want* such a thing in the first place, seemed set on tormenting him for eternity.

***

It was still dark when Fei opened her eyes. She swung her legs to the side of the bed and leaned her elbows on her knees, swallowing her yawn as she sifted through the images from her confusing tangle of dreams. There had been a dark, faceless figure searching the shadows for her and, instead of being afraid, she had called out to him, revealing herself. Within moments his lips had claimed hers, his arm winding around her waist like a vine —

'I don't need another man in my life,' Fei told herself sternly, curving her hands over her thighs. 'Not even for sex. I can handle that just *fine.*'

She frowned when she remembered the last dream, the one that had actually woken her. Purple jumpsuits, empty of the agents who wore them, had been piling up beside her desk at work. She had kept tripping over them every time she'd tried to leave.

Fei gnawed on her bottom lip for a moment. 'Vidscreen activate.'

The vidscreen glowed into life on the wall, casting sickly shadows over the room. A line of text appeared, asking her if she wanted to watch some light entertainment or send a message to her mother. Fei grimaced. She really needed to do more with her vidscreen if those were the only two options it assumed she'd pick.

'Open Web,' Fei told the device. She briefly considered seeing if BozzMed was online, but she had already asked too many suspicious questions of him lately. 'I need information. Are there any GLEA agents on Yalsa 5?'

The vidscreen displayed a single word: *Negative.*

'So they've never been there.'

A GLEA outpost was established in Atsa City on Yalsa 5 three Old Earth centuries ago in an attempt to curtail gang-related activity. The outpost was decommissioned five Old Earth years ago.

Fei drew a silksein sheet around her shoulders, covering her goosebumps. 'Why would the Agency leave? The gangs are still in charge of Yalsa 5. Did GLEA just give up?'

She winced when she realised a response was already filling the vidscreen.

There are two popular theories. One states that the city is now safe to live in, rendering GLEA's presence unnecessary. The other theory states that GLEA agents became involved with the gangs and the Agency withdrew to avoid further corruption occurring within its ranks.

'Seems a bit strange that they tried to interfere with the gangs anyway, because GLEA isn't supposed to mess with a planet's system of governance, no matter how unorthodox,' Fei mused. 'I guess they could be right about the deserts making it easier to stage criminal activities...but if Governor Bock Atsason *is* doing something in those deserts, then he's probably written a law to make it legal. So it's none of GLEA's business. Unless BozzMed is right and GLEA really is worried about the Desine worshippers making them look bad...'

The screen was bare of words this time.

Fei sighed. 'My fault for treating you like a sentient being.'

Would you like to call your mother? it asked. *Please insert your communicator chip.*

'Oh, shut up.'

Fei rose and began to pace, the soft silksein sheet twisting around her ankles and nearly tripping her. No Web search would find what she was looking for. Since TerraCorp no longer allowed larger tech devices to access the Web inside their headquarters (Fei was keenly aware that this was her fault), any secret files that might explain the situation were offline.

She'd just have to go in and find them herself.

The sheet billowed as it fell to the ground, carried several paces away by the gust of wind she caused as she streaked towards her clothes. She threw them back on and hurried over to the door, slapping the keypass against her thigh five times in quick succession. If she neglected to perform this part of her ritual on the way out, she was guaranteed to lose the keypass somewhere on the way to TerraCorp.

The journey usually took twenty Old Earth minutes. Tonight it took ten.

Fei burst into the gloomy foyer of TerraCorp's headquarters, panting. The light strips overhead only roused themselves into a welcoming blast once she'd stepped inside the hoverlift and selected the basement as her destination. She thought she had grown used to the bang as the lift hit the bottom of the shaft, but this time it shot through her like a lasbolt.

Fei dropped into her hoverchair and opened an innocuous-looking program that was supposed to be debugging software. It took up relatively little space and on the surface seemed to do what it was meant to, not that Moz had ever bothered to test it. Shaking her head, Fei watched as the program sliced its way through security protocols, ignoring any prompts for passwords or retina scans.

There wasn't a folder titled 'why GLEA is messing with TerraCorp'. But there were plenty of financial documents that bore the acronym of the religious organisation.

Fei pushed herself away from the desk, her hoverchair all but shrieking as it carried her backwards across the floor, allowing her to take in the spread of files filling four entire vidscreens.

GLEA never charged for their services and most people were willing to accept their protection without asking too many questions. Some worshippers of the Creator God donated what they could, out of the belief that it would please their god, but Fei had always wondered if those contributions were enough to cover the costs of running GLEA, not to mention the agents' salaries.

'We're bankrolling them,' she whispered.

The files went back a full century. But that didn't mean they stopped there. Older data was kept on different servers, only to be accessed if necessary.

Fei brought up a list of the past few planets that TerraCorp had transformed. On each world the number of agents stationed there had multiplied by up to five times in the weeks following the final phases of the terraforming process. Any existing outposts had benefited from extensive upgrades and if the planet had lacked a temple dedicated to the Creator God, then it had been lavishly provided for.

'But what are we getting out of it?' she muttered, frowning so hard that she ended up squinting, the room around her fading to muted greys. 'They get their operational costs covered. They get refurbished outposts and shiny new temples, potentially attracting more followers. They get to mess with our work. So what do we get?'

The vidscreens abruptly darkened. Fei blinked at them, confused.

Then a high-pitched alarm began wailing overhead.

She shot to her feet and ran for the hoverlift. It failed to slam its way down to her when she called it.

'Oh stark,' she said.

Fei clasped her hands together as she backed away from the hoverlift doors, murmuring, 'Creator God, I know I haven't been very faithful lately, but I could really use some help. Please. Please tell me what I should do.'

Of course he didn't answer.

CHAPTER SEVEN

'This isn't like you at all, Feiscina.'

It seemed that Mozel Zan, like many others in Terra Corp's middle management, preferred to use wooden furniture imported from a world that was specially designed to provide timber. Though she would have liked to touch Moz's desk, Fei kept her hands linked behind her back. No one had threatened to arrest or cuff her yet, but her shoulders, elbows and arms ached from the position.

'I'm sorry,' she said.

Moz watched her closely, his eyebrows merging into a thick, disapproving line. 'You're always so quiet, you don't bother anyone — I never expected any problems from you.'

He was draped comfortably in a padded hoverchair covered with silksein and decorated with wooden panels that matched the desk. Of course, *his* chair was whisper silent, even when he changed position. Moz had been sitting there from the moment he'd been called into TerraCorp an hour ago and had made sure that the agents GLEA had dispatched to deal with the security breach had been sent away.

'But I never *really* know what you're doing down there,' Moz went on, scratching behind one of his ears. 'I just let it lie, because your output always meets our expectations. You really should tell me more about what you're doing, you know, or suggest any ideas you might have for improving our systems. I'd be more inclined to promote you if you spoke up for yourself.'

'I'm sorry,' Fei repeated. She wasn't going to mention the idea he'd stolen from her, the one about cutting TerraCorp's servers and consoles off from the Web. Right now she was wishing she'd never mentioned it in the first place, because being forced to come in to look for the files had led to her current predicament.

'Feiscina, just tell me what the problem is,' Moz entreated. His hoverchair jumped up as he rose to his feet. 'Is it because of your family history? You know it is considered an honour to be called by the Creator God to join GLEA.'

Fei sucked her lips into her mouth to stop herself from saying something that would get her fired.

'TerraCorp was never separate from GLEA, you understand,' Moz continued, moving closer to her, a hand outstretched. When his fingers came too close to her shoulder, Fei flinched and took a giant step away from him. Frowning, Moz pinned his arm back to his side. 'We were created to fund them so that they can provide their services free of charge. People could not afford their protection otherwise. And if we happen to help GLEA set up a new outpost or temple, that's not a bad thing. People need to be aware that the Creator God is looking after them.'

Fei kept her voice to a murmur. 'I know how important GLEA is. I do.'

'Then why this poking around?' Moz asked. He looked almost fatherly with his hair so uniformly silver, but it was the fashion on Enoc and not an actual sign of his age.

'Moz...' Fei swallowed, trying to find the words. 'This was my sanctuary. All that religion stuff — I didn't have to think about it. Not here.'

Moz nodded slowly. 'So you are having a crisis of faith and you're worried it will affect your job performance now that you know we are part of GLEA.'

'I just don't want anything to do with them,' Fei muttered.

'Maybe all you need is some time to think about it,' Moz said soothingly, backing her towards a hoverchair that matched his one behind the desk.

Fei reluctantly sank into the cushioned seat. Her jaw ached from holding in a bitter retort.

'A holiday,' Moz continued, still standing far too close for her liking. 'It will allow you to get your thoughts in order. You see, your father's calling may have been to join GLEA, but your calling is to work here, at TerraCorp.'

'That sounds...' *Like bullshit.* '...I don't know, Moz. It might take me years to come to terms with things.'

But Moz was smiling and shaking his head, as though she was a child who had asked him a stupid question about how the galaxy worked. She wanted to punch him but instead dug her fingernails into the arms of her chair. The fragile material gave and tore beneath her grip.

'This is what you need, Feiscina,' he cajoled. 'A holiday. A respite. A bit of time off. I know just the place.'

Fei gave a non-committal shrug. She had no real preferences for a holiday destination; her mother lived on Gerasnin, the GLEA homeworld, and she had no desire to go there.

Moz raised his hands in a triumphant flourish. 'Bagaran!'

'The planet we're currently sourcing data and material from?' Fei clarified.

The last few samples that had come through from Bagaran had been especially interesting because the topsoil on that planet was unusually deep. It was actually causing problems in her simulations since most plants in a typical rainforest had very shallow roots, owing to a lack of fertile depths. Millennia ago, some humans had made the mistake of assuming they could knock down rainforests and seed crops that needed much deeper topsoil. It had been a painful lesson, one of many that had destroyed Old Earth.

'Yes, yes, they've had recent setbacks because of vandals but it is a very pleasant place by all accounts,' Moz said, nodding repeatedly.

Fei performed the appropriate grimace when he brought up the laboratory's destruction. It had been recommended that GLEA not be called in because TerraCorp did not want to anger the Bagara worshippers in the area and the company still had important work to do on on the rainforest god's primary world. A new lab was being constructed on a nearby planet and would be shipped over in the next month or so.

Moz bounced back into his hoverchair and began sliding his fingers over his desk, its keyboard lighting up beneath his touch. 'Apparently the locals will be holding some sort of annual festival for their sub-level god soon.'

Fei sat up straight. 'I've heard about that one. Bagara speaks directly to them during the festival.'

'They *claim* he does, yes,' Moz said. 'It's probably nothing but propaganda. Now. About that holiday...'

He narrowed his eyes at Fei, clearly expecting a response.

She sighed. 'Alright. I'll go. If that's what you think I should do.'

Evidently it was, because Moz took her keypass and ran it through the reader on his desk, rendering her access to the building null and void for two months. The amount of time seemed excessive, but Fei said nothing and allowed Moz to escort her out into the violet night and onto the footpath that led to their apartment building.

'What we do here is so much more important than people realise,' Moz told Fei as he kept pace with her. 'You're doing the Creator God's work, Feiscina. Just keep that in mind.'

'I'll try,' she said, wishing she meant it.

***

The moment she set foot on the ground outside the village, Fei felt as though she had been plunged into thick, steamy soup. The air was warmer than she had expected and her hair immediately started to rebel in the humidity. She glanced down at herself, regretting her attire. While much of Bagaran was covered in rainforests, its spaceport was located on one of the planet's grass-smeared continents and could experience considerable gusts of wind.

She had tried to cater for both climates by pairing lime denim pants with a short-sleeved shirt bearing the bronze logo of a lasball team on Enoc, not that she'd ever actually watched them play. The sandals, meant to keep her feet cool, became impractical as soon as she stepped off the ramp of the small vehicle that had carried her from the spaceport; a rock immediately dug into one of her toes, drawing blood.

There was a conspicuous gap in front of the symmetrical living quarters that belonged to the TerraCorp employees, marking where the laboratory should have been. The scientists wore miserable expressions as they sorted through carefully stacked piles of debris, tagging what items they could for recycling. The village, by comparison, looked far more accommodating with its chaotic sprawl of huts and the frenetic movement going on inside its palisade walls. Fei even caught the strains of distant music before it rose into a crescendo and petered out, replaced by applause.

Bagath was one of hundreds of villages on this world. They all had access to the Web, thanks to the relay station orbiting the planet, and they were connected to each other by 'hoppers', tiny planet-bound vehicles that bounced across the atmosphere. The bubble-shaped hopper that had deposited Fei had already vanished, heading back to the spaceport two hours away. TerraCorp had chosen to stage their research near Bagath because it was the smallest village on Bagaran and the area was less disturbed by people.

Fei found herself walking to the village, her bag slapping her back as her mother's words from the night before her departure echoed in her ears. 'Bagaran? Isn't that a little wild for you, honey? They don't even have cities. I just looked it up. It's populated by heathens! Savages!'

'No, Mum, "heathens" just means they worship a different god; they're not actually savages,' Fei had responded while standing in front of the mirror in her apartment, three or four different outfits clutched in her hands. The electronic irises in her eyes had been blood red at the time, though she had been considering switching them to safe, approachable blue. 'And Bagath has a working shield. They say that if someone does attack us, we can retreat behind their walls. Isn't that nice of them?'

'Nice?' The incredulity in her mother's voice had raised its pitch into the stratosphere. 'They have no respect for the Creator God! And they probably indulge in impure behaviour...'

'Then I guess I get to indulge in *impure behaviour* for a couple of months,' Fei had retorted.

Instead of being appalled, her mother had sounded relieved. 'Oh good, you really do need to relax and have a bit of fun. Just make sure your pregnancy implant is working. And for God's sake don't catch anything.'

Fei waved at the few villagers she passed. Their casual clothes and boots would not have looked out of place in the universities of Enoc. These 'heathens' seemed ordinary enough.

But when she passed through the gate, she saw one that was more than ordinary.

Shoving copper hair out of his eyes, he grinned as he helped the other villagers raise brightly painted branches onto the eaves of the village's huts. The freckles on his face were spread in just the right way to emphasise how handsome he was. And there was something oddly familiar about him, something that made her want to walk over and ask him if they'd met before.

'Who let you in?' a much closer man demanded.

Fei nearly swallowed her tongue in panic. The bulky villager beside her was brown-skinned and should have stood out as much as she did among this crowd of beige-toned, pale-eyed 'heathens', but he didn't. This was probably due to the comfortable earth-caked clothes he was wearing, something many of the nearby Bagathians had in common.

Fei tried not to look down at her bright outfit again. 'Hi. Um. I'm visiting.'

'Are you here for the festival?' he asked.

Fei managed a shrug. Her sea-green hair flopped over one

shoulder. 'Maybe? I'm...I'm a follower of the Creator God, actually, but I'm...'

Disgust filled his features. 'You one of those Chipper-lovers then?'

Fei backed away against a hut, dropping her bag in the process. No words came to her rescue. When he continued to advance, her hands flew to her sides and found purchase on the vine that was growing on the wall behind her. It wouldn't protect her from this man, but holding onto something made her feel braver. She clenched the thin, ropey plant, her nails cutting in and drawing ooze.

'Inesh, leave her alone,' the freckled man Fei had seen earlier said as he jogged over.

'But she's a Chipper-lover and I'll bet she's from TerraCorp,' Inesh argued.

'Doesn't matter. You're being very rude when you could be helping us prepare for the festival.' The newcomer flashed a smile at Fei. 'Are you from TerraCorp?'

'Yes,' Fei answered and rubbed her hands together, grimacing when she realised they were now smeared with the ruins of the vine. 'Oh. I'm so sorry. I didn't mean to hurt it. Um. Do vines get hurt?'

'Are you alright?' was his next question.

Fei nodded mutely. With both Inesh and her anxiety now banished, she found herself completely entranced by her rescuer. He was even better looking close up. The loose cargo pants did little to hide his well-formed backside and the smattering of mud on his skin somehow suited him. Humming cheerfully, he reached for the leaking vine and snapped a piece clean off. He then coiled it into a circle and tied the ends together before taking her wrist and slipping it on like a bracelet. Fei held out her arm long after he had let go of it.

'That way it's not wasted,' he said, chuckling at her open-mouthed expression. 'The vine doesn't mind, so I won't.'

'I thought you were all...' Fei hesitated.

One coppery eyebrow shot up into his hairline.

'...savages,' she finished in a rush. Mortified, she clapped a hand over her mouth to keep anything else from escaping her. But he didn't seem to be offended.

'Well, I don't own any shoes so I can understand how you got that impression.' He poked his chest with his thumb. 'I'm Kuja Rforine. Forget Inesh. He has trouble remembering that Bagara doesn't care if the people in his domain devote themselves to other gods.' Kuja's lips firmed. 'Bagara will even let them worship Oceania, the water god, though he'd rather they didn't. He just wants them to be happy and well.'

'What does Bagara offer that the Creator God doesn't?' Fei asked, looking over his shoulder at the villagers. They were now stringing up gossamer banners that shimmered as light played over them.

Kuja shrugged. 'Depends on what you want from him. Would you like to come to the festival and find out?'

Fei bit her lip. What could it hurt? She was used to the Creator God ignoring her. A sub-level god doing the same thing wasn't going to feel any worse, right? 'Sure. I can do that. But I need to put my things down first and, um, let TerraCorp know I'm here.'

'Relax, you've got a few days,' Kuja said, his grin causing something hot to swell low in her abdomen. 'But if you're looking for something to do, I can show you around the area tomorrow, once you've settled in.'

Fei felt her lips tweak into a small smile. He had offered his time so quickly and without question. She supposed she should have been suspicious of his intentions, but there was something dark and serious in his emerald gaze and she found that she trusted him. And if he *did* have certain intentions towards her, well, Fei decided she had no problem with that.

'Sounds good,' she said and meant it.

She picked up her bag and left the village.

CHAPTER EIGHT

'She's one of *them*,' Inesh snarled.

The villager had his arms crossed and his shoulders were pushed out as far as they could go, as though Inesh intended to fill the gap left by the open gate with his body alone. Inesh was large, true, but he wasn't as big as a hovercar, which was the size he needed to be if he wanted to block Kuja from leaving Bagath that morning.

'Why would you *want* to waste your time with that TerraCorp scum?' Inesh went on.

Kuja glanced back at the huts. Most of the villagers were still asleep and those that weren't wouldn't come to his rescue — Inesh was known to be prickly and troublesome. Kuja sighed and braced himself. 'Inesh, they're not scum, they're my friends. And not that it matters, but she felt...she's different from them.'

Kuja wished he could explain that the newcomer was like a beacon to him. She stood out among a sea of lifesigns, not only because of her unique energy, but because every thought that occurred to her seemed to spring forth from her lips. She held nothing back. It was refreshing. And there was something...something very familiar about her.

Inesh scowled. 'She's not *that* pretty.'

Kuja didn't bother to fight the flush filling his cheeks. He directed his gaze at Inesh's boots. 'She's beautiful. But that's not the point. She's interested in learning about our ways and our god. I should not pass up this opportunity to educate her. And Bagara would expect me to offer her friendship and show her around, regardless of her interest.'

'Doing it in the name of Bagara, ha!' Inesh said, shaking his head. 'But you know our god never makes a nuisance of himself by trying to convert people. And we don't either. So don't lie, Kuja. You just want that woman in your bed.'

Kuja thought of the aching emptiness he'd sensed inside the newcomer, the same emptiness he knew was mirrored inside himself. She needed company. And Kuja could provide it. Was it selfish to hope that she'd give him the same thing in return?

Sighing, Kuja brushed past Inesh. 'Bagara isn't the only one who can help people. And she does need help.'

'Yeah, alright, but you seem to be helping yourself too,' Inesh chortled.

Ignoring him, Kuja marched down towards the TerraCorp sleeping quarters, hands clenched inside his pockets.

***

'So they do exist!' Fei exclaimed in delight when she saw the rows and rows of plants growing in the back of Head Botanist Gerns' room.

Fei had spent the night in the flat four-walled shelter assigned to her and had been dismayed to discover that most of the other rooms were just as bare and clinical. Gerns, the only scientist who hadn't been offended to hear Fei's opinion of the sleeping quarters over the breakfast buffet, had been more than happy to show off her cluttered, more homey shelter. It had been impossible to refuse the Jezlo because she was large and loud and possessed six

80

tentacles that gyrated in a hypnotic fashion. Fei had found that she liked the botanist and had managed to say a few sentences without embarrassing herself. Until now, evidently.

Fei grimaced and turned back to Gerns. 'Well, I knew the plants existed because I had footage and data, but seeing them in person is completely different from...well. You know. Don't you?'

Gerns clucked repeatedly, her entire body wobbling with mirth, then shuffled over and held out one of her tentacles, poking it towards a tray that was bare of plant life. 'Put your hand in there.' When Fei hesitated, Gerns added, 'Now me, I'd never hurt a colleague. I swear. Alright, maybe I would, but only if they gave me a good reason...'

Not entirely comforted, but also not wanting to offend a potential companion for the next two months, Fei gingerly slid her fingers into loamy soil that was studded with decaying leaves and insects. Her nose protested, crumpling against the smell, and she shot a betrayed look at Gerns.

'It's filthy!' she cried.

Gerns clucked again. 'What did you expect?'

'I know that dirt is *dirty*,' Fei defended. 'But where I work, there's none of this...this mess. I input data about soil and plants but I don't have to *touch* them.'

'Now me, I see that as just about the saddest thing — keep your hands there!' Gerns added, flicking her tiny eyes at a timepiece on the wall. 'You sit at your desk and throw code around without realising what you're actually doing. *This* is what you're doing, Fei. Creating whole environments! Actually creating something! Most people in the galaxy, now, they don't get to make anything, let alone life on another planet. Makes me feel sorry for them! Okay, remove your hands.'

Obeying, Fei looked longingly at a trough in the corner which held what appeared to be soapy water. But then Gerns made an excited ticking sound inside her throat, drawing Fei's attention back to her. The Jezlo gestured at the tray of soil which, at first glance, appeared to be as still as it had been during Fei's entire visit.

Then it began to writhe.

Tiny green shoots stabbed up through the soil and, like a rash, they spread throughout the tray, growing higher and higher. Small buds appeared on the ends of the shoots before exploding violently into life, the colourful blooms that escaped them stopping just shy of one of Gerns' chins. The abject joy on the Jezlo's face reminded Fei of how she felt when her code managed to compile without displaying a single error message.

'Amazing stuff, right,' Gerns said with a nod. 'Now me, I don't know why this is, but the acid on human skin seems to set this shrub off. I'm a little too alkaline, but stark it if it's not the most impressive thing we've found on Bagaran.'

'Have you run it through a splicer yet?' Fei breathed, wide-eyed. 'This shrub's genetics will be incredibly useful to study and replicate. We could speed up the terraforming process through more natural means! Our current method of accelerated growth puts stress on certain plants and weakens them and...' Fei cut herself off, embarrassed.

But Gerns seemed more interested in trailing her tentacles over the new shoots than in rebuking Fei. 'Not as much fun when it's just text on a vidscreen, right? Why d'you think someone like me, not so bad at coding and not so bad at tech, decided to become a botanist instead? It's not for the less-than-stellar pay. Now me, I like the joy my work gives me.'

Gerns then started talking quietly to her plants like they were beloved children, apparently forgetting she had human company, so Fei hurried over to the water trough and began scrubbing her hands. She'd been at it for a full minute when Kuja entered the hut.

He was wearing the same clothes from the previous day and wouldn't have looked any different, except that the grin he was sporting was now wider and much more excited. He also moved through the shelter with a bounce in his step, as though the gravity on Bagaran didn't lie so heavily on him as it did everyone else.

'Kuja, now me, I said to myself that I wouldn't let you anywhere near me until you sorted out that vandal of yours...' Gerns began, an undercurrent of warning in her tone.

'You like me far too much to enforce that restriction on yourself,' Kuja pointed out, then swung his shining eyes onto Fei. 'Feiscina Neron, right? Happy to take you out today, as promised. I have some time.'

'Time! You always have time.' Gerns shook her large head, clucking all the while. 'Running around barefoot, diving into waterfalls, swinging from branches. Makes a woman jealous!'

Kuja raised his eyebrows. 'I even spend some of my precious time with you, Gerns, though I'm not sure why.'

'I'm good company, that's why!' Gerns told him.

Fei opened her mouth, then quickly sealed it. She saw Kuja watching her, patiently waiting her out, his expression relaxed and unhurried. Encouraged, she tried again. 'Gerns *is* good company.'

'She's even better company if you buy her a drink,' Kuja said, winking at Gerns.

The Jezlo threw her tentacles up towards the ceiling, mimicking a frustrated human. 'Since when did you have any coin-chips to buy me drinks with? Be on your way, Kuja, and take Feiscina with you. I haven't got the time to be playing tour guide, even if I am *good company*.'

Once they were outside, leaving Gerns to her work, Kuja began talking about how much he liked the Jezlo compared to some of the other TerraCorp employees. Fei nodded along with this, entranced by the way he used his hands to emphasise what he was saying. She started when he suddenly asked her what she was thinking.

'I...I was thinking the weather's nice today,' Fei said haltingly.

'Really.' Kuja's cheek twitched. 'So you were biting your lip because the weather's nice today.'

Fei darted onto a rock, hoping it would keep her out of the mud. She wasn't wearing sandals this time, but she wanted to avoid ruining the only other pair of shoes she'd brought with her. Although, since they were canvas, she should just accept the inevitable, just like she should probably answer Kuja. Which she did. 'You'll think it's stupid and I'll regret having said it — and I'll sound so paranoid that you'll go back to that village of yours and never speak to me again.'

'If I don't speak to you for a while, it's only because I enjoy hearing your voice a lot more than my own,' Kuja promised.

'Um.' Fei cleared her throat nervously. 'I guess I'm worried that Gerns only talked to me because my boss put her up to it. It, uh, kind of seemed like Gerns was trying to make me find meaning in my work and that's something Moz — my boss — would want. I just hate that all these people have started talking to me lately and I can't figure out if they're doing it to be nice or because they want something.'

Kuja nodded solemnly. 'I see. And you're expecting me to leave because you just said a lot of words.'

'You wanted to know what I was thinking,' she reminded him, nibbling the tip of her tongue.

'So I did. And I'd like to hear more.'

'You're strange,' she said, eyeing him. 'I've never met anyone like you, human or otherwise. Should I be suspicious of you, Kuja?'

A shadow fell over his face and she regretted saying anything, but then his grin returned and brightened his features once more. 'Well, if you are, you can't help feeling it, so I don't mind. You're still getting a tour. And I'm not Gerns, but I do fancy myself good company.'

Fei gave him a wobbly smile. 'Whew. I need to be more careful about what I say. That could have gone badly.'

'It didn't and nor will it ever,' Kuja told her softly.

When he held out his hand, she forgot herself and took it without hesitation, allowing him to guide her away from the sleeping quarters. Once they'd made it across the flattened area where the lab had hovered, Kuja turned to her and said, 'I wish more people were open about what they were thinking. It'd make it easier to know if they really did care about you, or if they just want you to keep to the path they've created for you. I'm tired of being afraid that I'm straying and disappointing someone.'

He sounded bitter. Fei recognised that tone. She'd heard it inside her own head enough times.

'I think maybe we should find some happier things to talk about,' she said.

Kuja squeezed her hand. 'You're very right. Come on then, let me show you Bagaran. Despite what Gerns thinks, I don't have an endless amount of free time, though I am pretty good at multitasking.' He laughed to himself, seemingly amused at some private joke. 'But I'm happy to spend what time I can with you.'

'Why?' Fei asked, staring at him.

Kuja met and held her eyes. Fei found herself disappointed that he didn't give her a once-over. But what he said next more than made up for it. 'Because you need company.'

Fei blinked back tears. The humidity was sending rivulets of sweat streaming down from her temples and she really couldn't afford to lose any more moisture; the drink bottle she'd attached to her belt wasn't big enough to cover both a trek *and* a crying jag.

Her eyes still burning, Fei distracted herself by letting her gaze linger on the rear of Kuja's cargo pants as he marched down the dirt path in front of her. Her mother's suggestion for her to have a bit of fun didn't seem so silly all of a sudden.

I think I will enjoy him, Fei thought, allowing a wicked smile.

'Enjoy what?' Kuja asked, looking back over his shoulder.

Fei flinched. She couldn't remember saying anything, but knowing her mouth it had probably slipped out. 'Um. This walk. Your company. Everything.'

'Oh good, because there's a lot on offer,' Kuja said.

And then he smirked at her.

CHAPTER NINE

'Are you still there? Kuja? Hello?' Fei called up towards the canopy.

Kuja had left her side and clambered up a nearby tree about five minutes ago, gripping vines and latching onto branches in his rapid ascent. Fei had blinked once — only once! — and then he'd disappeared.

Her chest was starting to feel tight and her breaths came shorter and sharper with each moment he was gone. Fei had just convinced herself that he'd abandoned her when he slipped down another nearby trunk, clearly having switched trees somewhere above the canopy.

'Just had to take care of someone — something,' Kuja corrected himself. He wasn't wearing a communicator on his belt and nor did he have an earpiece, so Fei knew he couldn't have been talking to anyone. She had no idea what he'd been doing, but he *had* looked worried when he'd announced that he had to go up the tree. It must have been important to him and since he didn't seem to judge her for her strangeness, she decided she wouldn't judge him for his.

'It also looks like there's a storm coming,' Kuja added as he walked over to her.

'I don't suppose we can run back to the village before it hits,' Fei said, sighing, though she wasn't sure if being caught in a downpour would be any worse than swimming in her own sweat as she was currently doing. Her vivid magenta tank top was drenched and plastered to her skin. Fei was fairly certain the suede was permanently stained.

But her anxious thoughts disintegrated when Kuja took her hand.

'Come with me, Fei,' he said. And she did.

He led her into a surprisingly dry hollow that had been formed by a Bagaran Strangler; its roots spilled all around them, like a frozen waterfall of wood, and the sight was so beautiful that Fei couldn't stifle her amazed gasp. A few seconds later the rain began, white noise at first, but then it become a torrent that started driving into the roots at an angle. Fei drew closer to Kuja.

'You're going to ask me why I'm really here on Bagaran, aren't you,' she said. 'You know I'm not very good with words, Kuja.'

Kuja chuckled. 'You haven't run out of any good ones yet.'

'Oh alright, I'll tell you, but you really need to stop laying it on so thick,' she warned him, unable to kill her smile. 'I'm not sure I'll be able to concentrate if you keep complimenting me.'

Kuja ran a finger over his lips, as though sealing them shut. His silence emboldened her.

So she told him about her father, she told him about Zareth, she told him about her crisis of faith — she told him *everything*. Her voice croaked like one of the shingbats hidden in the foliage outside by the time she was done. At some point Kuja had wrapped his arms around her, which Fei couldn't remember him doing, but she didn't mind. He was warm. And gentle. And strangely patient.

'I'm not particularly fond of the Creator God myself,' Kuja admitted after a time.

'Why's that? Has he taken someone from you too?' she asked.

Kuja's eyes darkened and grew swampy. 'Let's just say I don't agree with his version of free will. If he really wanted us to find our own paths, he wouldn't rig it so we'd follow the ones he meant for us anyway.'

Fei blinked. 'You're — *angry* with him.'

'It's not unusual to be angry with an invisible deity, is it,' he mused. 'Especially when he stops being invisible and gives you an explanation for his actions instead of an apology.'

Fei pried herself away from his embrace, staring at him. 'You've heard the Creator God?'

Frowning, Kuja scratched the underside of his chin. 'Yes, I've heard him. Some might call it a privilege. I don't. I'd rather follow Bagara — he guides and protects his people but he doesn't insist they blindly accept everything he says or does.'

'What did the Creator God say to you?' Fei asked, wincing at how breathless she sounded.

She expected him to refuse to answer. She didn't expect to see the sorrow lining his face.

Kuja looked down at his bare feet. 'The Creator God only allowed my brother, Sandsa, to fall in love so that he could learn a *lesson*. Once that lesson was over, once the purpose of that love was fulfilled, the Creator God sent followers of his to tear apart my brother's marriage. It destroyed Sandsa. It's still destroying him. And now I can't even get Sandsa to sit still long enough for me to talk to him because he just...he just...' Kuja smeared a hand across his face, scattering his tears. 'I suppose you could say he's not...there's not a piece of humanity left in my brother anymore.'

Fei leapt to her feet and smashed her fists against the inside of the roots, again and again. When the wind outside roared at her, she roared right back at it, until her throat spasmed painfully.

'Thank you, thank you, *thank you*,' she said, turning to beam at Kuja.

'...for letting you hurt yourself?' he asked, looking bewildered. 'Fei, your hands.'

He drew nearer and encased her fingers in his, probably to keep her from taking another swing at the Strangler, not that she needed to. Not anymore.

Fei shook her head, her voice hoarse. 'No, Kuja. For making me feel normal. For letting me think and feel and *doubt* out loud. For trusting me with your thoughts and feelings in return. For being the only other sensible person out there. Well...maybe not sensible, because we're stuck here when we could have stayed in Bagath, kept dry and just now be sitting down to the midday meal...'

Kuja was smiling again, except this time it made her feel hot and cold all over.

Her heart stuttered for a moment.

Oh no, she thought. *This is just supposed to be a bit of holiday fun, Fei. And you don't even know if he finds you attractive...*

But it was difficult to worry about this when he was gazing at her like that.

Finally, Fei whispered, 'It's nice to know that I'm allowed to say these things, that I'm not going insane.'

'That or you have met someone equally insane,' Kuja countered, his face suddenly very close to hers.

Fei parted her lips, hardly daring to hope, waiting for a kiss that would set her ablaze — but then she was thinking of Zareth, of when he'd kissed her for the first time in that alcove, the rain pouring down around them. If she kissed Kuja now, she'd be doing it to wipe away an old memory instead of making a new one.

'Not here, not now, it wouldn't be fair to you, not that *it* was going to happen!' Fei took a giant step away from Kuja, towards the gap in the roots surrounding them. 'I think we should risk heading back. The rain should ease soon, right?'

'No, I suspect it will keep pouring for another hour or so.' He sounded so confident, stark him. But then he looked at her, really looked at her, and said, 'Thank you.'

'For what?' she asked, biting her lip.

'For being honest, for being *you*, for knowing we had to stop,' he said softly. Then he winked. 'I don't mind waiting. It will make it that much better when it does happen.'

Flummoxed, all Fei could do was stand there in silence as he darted outside. She heard a violent snap somewhere nearby and he returned moments later, carrying a giant green leaf that could have seated a small child — it even looked strong enough to manage it too. Kuja lowered the leaf for her inspection, showing her how the water droplets rolled right off it. He then held it up like an umbrella, an eyebrow raised, his meaning clear.

Giggling, Fei let him escort her from their sanctuary and into the rain.

CHAPTER TEN

When hundreds of balls of sand rose from the surface of the desert and began chasing him, Kuja had to admit that he probably should have listened when his brother growled at him to keep away.

Kuja ducked and rolled, but the missiles homed in on him and disintegrated upon impact, showering him with sun-blasted specks. He yelped and threw his arms over his head. But there was no escape. Though Sandsa lacked a corporeal body in this state, each grain of sand was an extra eye to find a target and an extra weapon to wield on the Rforine.

Leaf-studded vines grew down Kuja's arms, anchoring themselves to his skin and lengthening until he could whip them around. He slashed furiously with the fibrous cords, cutting down several of the balls as they came for him, but he wasn't fast enough to get them all. He cried out when one hit him square in the face.

'This isn't funny, Sandsa!' he shouted.

Go away! the Desine howled. *I don't want to talk about her!*

Kuja scowled. 'I'm not here to make you to talk about Callista, I just need you to *be my brother* — you haven't taken your human form in years!'

Because doing that worked out so well for me before? Sandsa said acidly.

A tornado bore down on Kuja, roaring and twisting, fed by

the endless sands on this desert world but never wholly satisfied. Now it craved a different food source.

Kuja opened his mouth to plead for mercy and instead swallowed a mouthful of grit.

Sandsa's voice cut through the shrieking winds. *I won't let myself become vulnerable again, Kuja, I won't! Living as a mortal cost me everything!*

'Are you going to keep attacking me?' Kuja gasped as his knees hit the ground.

What else will make you go away?

'Just talk to me, Sandsa!'

We are done talking!

Beneath Kuja the sand roiled, stirred by its master's anger, preparing to bury the Rforine. But Kuja was not giving up. Not yet. He sent roots scurrying through the sand, trying to temper the attack, trying to defend instead of antagonise, but within seconds the roots cried out as they blistered and burned.

'Fine,' Kuja muttered. 'Since violence is the only language you can speak...'

He transformed into a pile of leaves which then exploded upwards, escaping the grip of the sand. Once he was high enough off the ground, Kuja became a raging storm of branches, vines, leaves and even stones, beating back the tornado. Cowed, it retreated, unwilling to engage a god who could fill it with foreign, unwanted debris.

Then, just as Kuja had feared he would, the Desine abandoned his usual powers and reached for something else.

Sandsa crafted weapons from Kuja's domain, green fragments that screeched out apologies, powerless to fight a desert god who somehow commanded more than simple sand, who could wield fire and water and tundra and anything else should he choose to. Kuja sensed that Sandsa only used these powers when he was furious, when he wanted to make a point of his superiority, and was glad of this — if Sandsa practiced more often, he might be able to turn every rainforest in Kuja's domain against him out of spite.

The Rforine did not dare return to his human form, knowing that the thorny vines his brother was throwing at him would tear through his skin. Immortal he and his siblings might be, they could still die. But remaining incorporeal would only protect him so much.

Kuja's very being was soon stretched thin, like a piece of drenched cotton lashed between two poles that were constantly being pulled apart. He had felt like this once before.

When Fayay had come for him.

Kuja screamed inside his mind, wishing his brother would see, remember and know that he had done as much as he could.

Fayay broke me because I protected you! he cried.

It is your fault he found us! Sandsa roared back at him. *Your fault I had to use my powers! Your fault Callista left me!*

My fault? Kuja laughed darkly. His anger swelled and grew, bolstering his powers. *My fault you couldn't make Callista stay with you? It was her choice! She couldn't stay with a god! That's what she said in that letter she left you — so why can't you accept it? It wasn't my fault any more than it was yours!*

No, Kuja blamed the Ine for putting Callista into that position in the first place, a position no mortal could reasonably handle let alone *want*, and he blamed the Ine for ensuring Sandsa had fallen in love with only despair awaiting him. But the Ine wasn't the one who had left that letter. Kuja filled his mind with this truth, over and over, until the desert finally quietened around him.

The Rforine assumed his mortal form once more, dropping to the ground where he then balled himself up into a knot, sobs wracking his body. His mouth felt so parched he could have eaten the sand and found it moist on his tongue.

Right now he couldn't feel a single drop of sympathy for Sandsa.

Bare feet appeared beside him, slowly lengthening upwards into the body belonging to his brother. A few years ago, Sandsa would not have worn anything more exciting than beige fabric beneath his cloak. Since his foray into mortal life, he had chosen to clad himself in the black clothes favoured by the gangs on the planet Yalsa 5. He even wore a belt of scored and faded leather, though he no longer needed to hang a lasgun there, not as he had when his powers had been blunted by his desire to be nothing more than a man.

Kuja grabbed one ankle and pulled. Hard. Sandsa abruptly collapsed beside him, his blond mane falling across his stunned expression. He hadn't expected that form of attack. Chagrined, Sandsa tucked his hair behind his ears, revealing eyes so blue they were painful to look at for too long. The hands that could break Kuja disappeared back inside the folds of the cloak and the desert god's head sank to the side, pillowed by a rise of sand.

'Do you know what I've had to go through?' Kuja demanded. 'Knowing that I failed you? Facing Fayay when I know he can destroy me? Having to stop myself from caring too much about certain mortals in case he kills them?'

'And what of my pain, my agony?' Sandsa asked, shadows creeping over his face.

Kuja clenched his teeth. 'That doesn't give you the right to attack me.'

'Have you lost a wife and son, brother? *Have you?*'

Darkness submerged them, cold and deep, as clouds of sand rose to block out the sky. Kuja sat up, dusting himself off. He did not look down at the seething desert god, keeping his scowl aimed at the obscured horizon instead. 'No. But I lost my brother. Look at you, Sandsa. You're not used to your human form. How can you truly understand mortals if you refuse to acknowledge this part of you?'

'I am the Desine — my people need not see me to know I care for them,' Sandsa said flatly. The sand above their heads shimmered like the surface of an ocean, even forming dunes that crested and fell like waves.

'My name is Kuja,' the Rforine retorted. 'And you are Sandsa. Don't you remember how close we were?'

'You would do well to leave me now.'

Kuja curled his hands into fists, preparing for another battle. 'Why? Because you're afraid that love, even the love of your brother, will weaken you? That's stupid, Sandsa! I can't dampen your powers — only you can do that!'

Sandsa flinched. 'Do not speak of things you do not understand.'

'Maybe I don't understand some aspects of love,' conceded Kuja, thinking of Lorena and Fei and all the women he could never allow himself to develop feelings for. 'Still, our mother saw that we were happier when we spent time together. I was so much more *confident* in my powers when you were with me. Beside me. Shoring me up. And I gave you a reason to be *human* every now and then.'

Sandsa eased himself onto his elbows, the sand swarming up to support him until he could manage to sit unaided. He had to lift his legs into a cross-legged position with his own hands. It really had been too long since Sandsa had used his human form.

I should have come sooner... Kuja shook his head. *No. He would have killed me.*

I would never hurt you, Sandsa cut into his mind.

Kuja snorted. *You have already managed that.*

The desert god lobbed a paternal frown at Kuja. The expression would have fit well on the Ine's face. 'You feel older. And your mind is not as, well, bright as it was.'

'I am five years older, if you forgot,' Kuja reminded him with an impatient toss of his head.

'Then my son is five years old,' Sandsa said.

Something twanged in Kuja's heart. The anger that had been clenching the organ, forcing it into a rapid, erratic pace, suddenly dissipated. Kuja reached across and rested his hand on his brother's shoulder. 'Sandsa, if you can't sense your son, then Fayay can't either. Kieran is safe.'

'But I can't...I can't find him...' Sandsa whispered. A mournful wind howled on the bare sands. 'And I fear that Fayay will find him first and hurt him — or turn him into a weapon.'

'You can defeat Fayay, you have before,' Kuja said firmly.

'But if he twists my son's mind...' Grief clouded Sandsa's bright eyes. 'Kuja, you know how powerful my son is. He could very well kill me.'

Kuja squeezed his shoulder. 'Fayay won't bother your son so long as you rule the deserts and Kieran never discovers his powers. That was the deal, remember?'

Sandsa's chapped lips grated together. 'Yes. Strange that he would offer such a kindness to me.'

'I always wondered if Callista...' Kuja trailed off, then moistened his mouth, strengthening his voice. 'We don't know if she said anything to Fayay but...Sandsa, she would have done anything to keep your son safe. To give him a life free from the Ine's interference.'

'You are saying that *she* made that deal with Fayay...' Sandsa muttered, his forehead scrunching as he thought it over. Then his gaze snapped back onto his brother. 'Kuja, why are you really here? I sense more is troubling you than my current situation. And that is no business of yours.'

Kuja crossed his arms. 'It is my business. You're my favourite brother.'

'Who you clearly forced into human form not out of concern for me, but so that you could have someone to talk to. I can feel your worry and your guilt.'

'I *am* concerned about you!' Kuja exclaimed.

Sandsa raised an eyebrow. 'Have you fallen in love, Kuja?'

'What — no!' Kuja winced when he heard his own braying laugh. 'It's nothing serious, nothing that would invoke the wrath of Father or Fayay — I promise! She just...she deserves a bit of happiness, a bit of pleasure. And only Bagara can give it to her.'

Sandsa's sigh hissed over his lips. 'Kuja. If you want permission to pursue her, I can't give it. All I can tell you is that you should not abandon your rainforests the way I did the deserts. My people needed me. And I let them down.'

Kuja cast his eyes over the barren landscape, so different from the rainforests he loved, and said, 'Mortals don't need invisible deities to help them make their own decisions. I've seen religion make people wonder if there is something wrong with them simply because they have questions and doubts. The mortals might technically have free will but their fear of displeasing their Creator God, or any other god, is constricting them.'

'Guidance is not the same as outright interference,' Sandsa reminded him. 'Stop changing the subject. Who is this woman I see in your thoughts?'

'It's not like that. I just want to look after her, the way the Ine failed to.'

'So you are not trembling because you are afraid of feeling more for her,' Sandsa said dryly.

Kuja shot him an annoyed look. 'No, listen. She has been abandoned by both her father and her former lover because they decided that inserting chips into their temples and gaining a few fancy powers was more important than her.'

'Chippers,' Sandsa snarled. He'd never had much love for them, especially since they used tech to reach the Ine, someone Sandsa despised. The Desine had also tangled with some of GLEA's agents when he had been involved with the gangs on Yalsa 5.

'Yes, Chippers,' Kuja said, nodding. 'So of course Fei — Feiscina — has got the impression that she's not important, because her god has taken everyone from her and won't just speak to her and tell her she deserves happiness. She feels so guilty about her crisis of faith — she still thinks she owes the Ine her loyalty, even if it makes her miserable, and that's just awful!'

'Don't help this woman because you are angry about what was done to me,' Sandsa warned him. The carpet of sand above them was slowly parting, letting sunlight streak across their skin, and Kuja was glad, because it was a sign that his brother really was emerging from his dark thoughts. 'She isn't even one of your followers.'

'You told me once that the Ine's design has casualties,' Kuja said firmly. 'I want to help the casualties. I want to be the god that gives hope to those who have been spurned by the deities forced upon them by their families and their societies.'

'Just what has this woman been saying to you?' Sandsa asked, his thoughts even more incredulous than his voice.

'Enough to know that I have to change how I deal with mortals.' Kuja wet his lips. 'And anyway, I'm not in love with her. I'm just going to have sex with her.'

Sandsa stared at him. 'Sex? Is that all this Fei is worth to you?'

'All she wants is to have a bit of fun and Finara doesn't seem to have any trouble — '

'Hold on. I'll read it from your memories so we can avoid that blush of yours.'

'I do not...' Kuja winced, feeling his cheeks grow warm. 'Fine. So I blush. Easily. I think it's the hair that makes it so obvious. Do you know that Mother once told me of an Old Earth myth that says I have no soul because my hair is this colour? How backwards the mortals once were.'

'Hush, Kuja. You are distracting me.' Sandsa's expression cleared. 'Well, I don't see anything wrong with our sister's approach, given that there have been no repercussions. She has not abandoned her duties in her pursuit of...fun.'

'What was sex like for you?' Kuja asked.

Sandsa's lips twitched then reluctantly curled upwards. 'It was a uniting of souls, far beyond any physical sensations. Callista and I didn't have sex. We made love.'

Kuja captured his brother's smile in his mind, preserving it forever. He knew it wouldn't last — already night was stealing across the desert, erasing the twinkle that had briefly nestled in Sandsa's eyes.

'Sex was something that came after love for me, Kuja,' Sandsa said quietly. 'But I have seen into enough hearts and minds to know that is not always the case. Enjoy yourself, while you can.'

'While I can?' Kuja echoed.

Sandsa studied him closely. 'I can sense you standing at the edge of a cliff, brother. You will need to step away at some point or that woman will push you to your death.'

'The warning is thoughtful,' Kuja said, getting to his feet. His brother rose with him. 'But it is unnecessary. All Fei needs is a small spark of happiness and the knowledge that someone desires her, both of which I can give her, and then she will be out of my life. Father has not created her with the intention of teaching me some lesson. I'm sure of it.'

Kuja gasped, winded, when Sandsa abruptly gathered him into a crushing embrace. The Rforine blinked back tears, his heart threatening to outgrow his ribcage. His brother had not hugged him in years.

'Sandsa...' he whispered.

'I am here for you, Kuja, in whatever form you require,' Sandsa said, his words underscored with rust.

Kuja swallowed. 'Please assume human form when I'm not here. Just sometimes. Please.'

'I cannot promise this.'

'I know. But please try.'

Moments later, Kuja held nothing more a cascading lump of sand. Sandsa was gone. The Rforine stepped back from where his brother had stood, head bowed. He couldn't force Sandsa to maintain a form that had caused him so much pain. For someone who had lived as long as the Desine, the loss of his family might as well have happened yesterday.

Kuja vowed never to forget that.

CHAPTER ELEVEN

'It's so loud! Is it always so loud?' Fei shouted at him from beside the waterfall.

Kuja chuckled as he jumped over several water-slicked rocks to reach Fei's side. 'Yes! What did you expect?'

She scrunched up her face for a moment, then said, 'The ocean outside my apartment on Enoc makes annoying shhh-shhh sounds. I'm relieved this waterfall doesn't do that. But I didn't think sound was important enough to factor into my simulations, though I'm starting to reconsider this, because some plants get violent when they hear loud noises and I don't think our clients would be too happy if I put those species near waterfalls!'

Kuja smiled at her, enjoying the sound of her voice as it accurately translated her thoughts. The past few days had been wonderful — he had spent every spare hour with her, spreading his presence across several different worlds while staying physically by her side. He was finding it easier to split his focus, though it did give him a decidedly glazed look which Fei had occasionally made fun of. He didn't mind; he loved seeing her laugh so easily. Her memories of her former lover were now haunting her much less and her mind was full of images of Kuja instead. She was looking forward to taking him to bed, something she saw as the perfect addition to an already perfect holiday.

Kuja had worried for a while that he wouldn't be able to please her, because he was sure his body would fail to perform as it had in the Enocian Harem, but he had decided it didn't matter. He had learned how to pleasure a woman and it thrilled him to think of giving Fei his complete attention without asking for anything in return. She deserved that and more.

Fei leapt away from him, onto another rock, then shrieked as she slipped sideways. A vine swiftly whipped out from beneath her feet and wrapped around her hand. Fei's arm went taut and she jerked to a stop, suspended above the water. She hung there for several seconds, stunned, before reeling herself back in. She mused out loud that she must have snagged the vine on her way down, though she wasn't sure how.

Kuja shot a severe scowl at the vine responsible. *Stop that! She is not one of mine and might never be. And I do not want her noticing anything unusual. Do you understand me?*

We understand that you wanted to see her get wet, the vine responded in a coy voice that made Kuja's tongue feel as slimy as the seaweed that populated many of Fayay's worlds.

I did not, he snapped.

You enjoyed seeing the other one wet.

Kuja cleared his throat noisily and held out his hand to Fei. She accepted his touch, allowing him to lead her towards a less slippery side of the pool of water gathering beneath the falls. Kuja took a moment to admire his companion. Fei's hair was ruby red today and dusted with droplets of moisture. Her clothes were as bright and impractical as ever, but at least this time she was wearing sturdy closed-in shoes. She'd borrowed them from one of the TerraCorp scientists.

'I like it out here,' Fei said, seating herself on a soft blanket of moss that Kuja knew hadn't been there a handful of minutes ago. He barely refrained from berating this plant as well. 'There's no line of code that needs fixing, no temple or agent in sight, no one to hear me going on like this. Well, except you. But you don't seem to mind.'

Kuja sat beside her, tilting back with his hands braced behind him. 'I don't mind. At all. You can keep going if you like.'

She didn't need to be told twice. Kuja tried to focus on her words, but thanks to the scurrilous vine over by the waterfall he was now trying — and failing — not to envision what Fei might look like wet and without clothing.

We could have a look...and show you what we see... a withered, thin root offered as it crept over from Fei's left, intent on winding its way up into her shirt.

'Kuja, are you thinking about me naked?' Fei asked bluntly. 'Because I'm pretty sure that's what you're doing. I mean, I've started going on about how loud the waterfall is again and you can't be looking *that* interested about it.'

'Yes,' Kuja said, his gaze snapping back to hers. 'I am thinking about you naked. And wet.'

Fei blinked. 'Oh.'

He quirked an eyebrow at her. 'Is that a problem?'

'No.' Her lips began curling upwards. 'What about kissing me? Because I'd like that. So...are you? Thinking about kissing me, I mean.'

Kuja leaned over and stamped a hand over the root, setting it back into the ground. Now much closer to Fei and able to feel her warm breath on his face, he found he didn't want to relinquish this new position. 'Not right now.'

'Oh,' Fei said again, looking away from him.

His heart constricted. She sounded so defeated.

'Fei, your company is the best I could have asked for — you're talkative, alive and keen on sharing everything,' Kuja told her softly. 'My mouth on yours would only silence you and, besides which, I'm not a very good kisser.'

The gap between Fei's lips grew and shrank several times. 'But...what if I end up saying something you don't like? I feel like...like I'm always wrong. My boss talks over me and the other Creator God worshippers seem to think I shouldn't have any doubts — or at least keep those doubts to myself. I guess I should just find another religion,' she finished in a mutter.

'You don't strike me as someone who's able to accept something you can't question and look into,' Kuja noted, regretfully easing himself out of her personal space. 'No matter what belief system you end up adopting, you'll still investigate and find its secrets, just like you did with GLEA and TerraCorp. You can't help yourself, Fei.' He smirked. 'Bagara should be very afraid of you. But if he knows what's good for him, he'll answer every question you have. And if you find him wanting, he'd better find a way to appease you or he's not worth your time.'

Fei snorted, then slapped a hand over her nose. Some of her laughter still managed to leak out between her fingers. 'Oh my God, you're right, I have to find those secrets wherever I go. I can't *not* do it. Why are you so right — about everything?'

'I'm older and more experienced,' Kuja said with a wink.

'Then you should be a better kisser by now!' Fei told him.

She laughed even harder and fell backwards onto the moss, causing her loose teal shirt to ride up her navel. Kuja found himself staring, almost wishing the root would return to nudge the cotton fabric a little higher. As if somehow reading his mind, Fei curled her fingers around the edge of her shirt and gave him a grin that made something unfurl low inside his abdomen. She then boldly reefed up the shirt and shoved her rainbow-streaked bra band down, revealing breasts that would have out-sized his hands if he'd tried to hold them. A bead of moisture was sliding down from the peak of one dark nipple and Kuja imagined his mouth engulfing it — along with as much of her breast as possible.

The desire to taste her chased every reasonable thought from his head.

Fei snapped the bra band back into place and dropped her shirt. Her eyes danced and her lips began forming shapes that only served to distract him further. It took Kuja precious seconds to realise she was saying something.

'Still want to hear me talk?' she challenged.

Kuja cleared his throat. 'Oh yes. Especially when I lick my way up to one of your nipples. I imagine you'd say some pretty interesting things then.'

Fei started giggling, a hand pressed to her abdomen. 'I've thought about licking my way up something too.'

Kuja glanced at his shirt, then back up at her.

'Not what I meant,' she said, smirking.

He looked further down, to his pants, which were suddenly feeling a lot more constrictive. Kuja sighed inwardly. Much as he'd like Fei to touch him and sate his growing frustration, he was sure it wouldn't work. And this wasn't supposed to be about his pleasure — it was meant to be about hers.

Kuja shrugged casually. 'I do have some experience with that. It feels very nice. But I'd much rather lick you.'

'I'm definitely going to schedule some time for that later,' Fei said, then her eyes widened. 'I didn't mean to say that. You really shouldn't encourage me to blurt out whatever pops into my head.'

'Why not?' he asked.

Fei bit her lip, frowning slightly. 'You know what, I can't remember. So!' She sat up straight and clapped her hands together. 'Can we talk more about Bagara? You promised we would.'

'We've covered most of it already,' Kuja said after a brief hesitation.

'Well, it would give us something to talk about, not to mention something to distract you from those thoughts filling your head.' Fei waved a hand at him when he opened his mouth to object. 'They're written all over your face, Kuja! It's impossible to feel undesirable around you. I like that.'

Kuja's lips twitched. She grinned wickedly at him in response. Strangely, around her, he never felt undesirable either — and not just physically. Lorena had never been interested in seriously conversing with him, only in making him uncomfortable.

'Last time we spoke about this we agreed that Bagara could interfere a little more,' Kuja remarked. 'So instead of speaking to people en masse and restricting his speeches to a festival when only his followers are listening, he should also give his voice to those who are in their darkest, most vulnerable moments. It would help immensely for them to have someone to talk to, someone who offers no judgement, someone who simply...listens. No matter their religious preference. No matter what they can or cannot give in return.'

While he'd been speaking, he had rested his hand on Fei's thigh, rubbing his thumb along the line formed by the stitching on her soft cotton pants. Her hand now fell on top of his, stilling his fingers.

'Mm-hm,' Fei said, nodding. 'We did cover this. I think, yes, we definitely did. Wow, I find it really hard to think around you. But your plan — which is totally obvious, by the way — to distract me from discussing this topic isn't going to work. Just so you know.'

Kuja smiled. 'Maybe I should try harder then.'

They gazed at each other, unmoving for countless moments, then her hand left his, travelling to the hem of his shirt before dipping beneath the fabric and gliding over his stomach.

Her expression became incredulous. 'How are you not sweating? I feel like I've been swimming inside a swamp!'

'Acclimatised, I guess,' Kuja suggested. He silently asked the rainforest not to create a protective bubble in the weather patterns around him, not because he wanted to keep Fei from becoming suspicious, but because he rather enjoyed feeling like he had accomplished something and sweat helped with that.

Fei's palm skated along the trail of copper-coloured hair that led down from his belly button and towards the crux of his legs. 'Can I ask you a question?'

'You can ask several.'

'Why are you spending so much time with me?'

Kuja shivered pleasantly when her fingers slid beneath the edge of his pants and began rubbing gently, back and forth, back and forth, until he wanted to rip the item of clothing off entirely. He fought to keep his voice even. 'There's a couple of reasons. One, you seem to be interested in learning about our beliefs and, to be honest, I think that's something you need to do. I'm not saying you have to pursue Bagara, but you might find some peace in seeing that there is more than one way to worship.'

Fei's fingertips, belonging to the hand that was still roaming beneath his shirt, found a nipple and flicked it. Kuja gasped.

She blinked innocently at him. 'And what's the second reason?'

'I think you already know the answer to that.'

'Tell me anyway,' she said breathlessly.

'I'm hoping all this talking will lead to a lot less talking,' he told her in a low voice.

Fei wet her lips once, twice, seemingly incapable of forming a verbal response. There were no words in her mind either; only images. Her imagination certainly was vivid. But then her thoughts jolted back to their previous topic of conversation.

'I really shouldn't be thinking about Bagara just now,' Fei said.

'Bagara again?' Kuja chuckled. 'I wonder if I should be jealous.'

Fei made a face at him. 'I can't help it. You know that.'

'Don't even try to stop those thoughts, Fei. I want to hear them all.'

She fiddled with a tuft of moss beside her knee. 'Sometimes I feel like a fraud, because I don't feel connected and grateful like everyone else who worships my god. I keep turning up at the temple, pretending to be one of them, when all I really want to do is work on some code or go home and relax.'

'Bagara prefers his people to speak to him when it best suits them,' Kuja said, his eyes momentarily tracking a droplet of sweat that was slipping past her collarbone. 'And if they never acknowledge him, he doesn't mind. He will still care for them.'

'But don't they owe Bagara for looking after them? It's only fair.'

The growl rumbled low in Kuja's throat before he could stop it. 'Fair. There's nothing fair about making people feel they owe you something, just because you happen to reign over the environment in which they live. They had no choice in their creation. They owe him *nothing*.'

'But what does Bagara get in return?' Fei asked, looking confused.

Kuja blinked a few times, entranced by the amber eyes she'd chosen for today — this colour made her gaze as warm as liquid honey. 'He gets to watch the people he cares for enjoy their lives. If they want to worship him in return, then that is their choice. He just hopes they will care for others as much as he does.'

Fei pursed her lips. 'I see. That doesn't sound terrible. And you know what, I think I'd be more likely to do something nice for other people if my god wasn't demanding it of me.'

'It's easier to love someone when they actually let you exercise your free will,' Kuja agreed.

She stared at him.

'Just...an old grievance, with my father,' Kuja said by way of explanation. 'I can't talk about it. I'm sorry, Fei. I would tell you everything...but not that. Not now.'

'That's alright,' she said softly. 'I don't mind waiting.'

Kuja couldn't stand the melancholy now choking his thoughts and starting to infect hers, so he hooked his arms beneath Fei and hoisted her up from the ground. When she demanded to know if he was going to do what she thought he was planning on doing, Kuja gave her a wink and tossed her into the water, making sure she landed in the deepest section.

'It's cold!' Fei exclaimed, bobbing there with an indignant look on her face, her bright red hair puddling around her.

'Don't take that into account for your simulations either?' Kuja teased.

Fei poked her tongue out at him. 'Actually, I do. Because some plants don't like cold water and some don't even need water and some find water poisonous — so there!'

Kuja drank in the sight of Fei. He desperately wanted to watch her face slacken with pleasure as he moved his fingers around inside her, the way he had been taught to do on Enoc. She would be lost in the sensations he could give her, so far removed from the pain that had driven her to this world...

Kuja threw himself into the water, the cool blast of it against his skin a refreshing distraction. He swam over to Fei who splashed him when he got too close. Kuja arched an eyebrow at her, drew a breath, then dove out of sight and barrelled towards her. She darted aside at the last moment. When he resurfaced, their faces were a hand's width apart and Fei's amber eyes were glistening with mischief.

Oh Father, I so want to kiss her, Kuja thought. But he couldn't see if she was ready; her mind was in such disarray. He should ask her, an innocent offer that she could easily refuse —

Fei kissed him.

It was gentle, a peck, a knock at the door, and over far too soon. Kuja responded with a brief kiss of his own, though his landed lopsided, on her cheek. Laughing, Fei took his head between her hands and guided him back to her lips.

She tasted of salt and sweetness. He stored this away for future reference, relieved that kissing didn't do to him what it seemed to do to mortals. Some of them were struck by a sudden revelation of love or other such nonsense when they locked lips with someone, but it seemed he was immune.

Sandsa wasn't immune, a traitorous voice inside his head reminded him.

Kuja quickly back-pedalled and began swimming towards to the rocky shore. Fei crashed through the water after him, unusually silent, her thoughts blank and unable to provide any fuel for her voice. By the time they were walking towards the village, the sky was dark above them and Fei was smiling vacantly, her mind preoccupied with memories of what they had done together at the waterfall.

Kuja wondered when *he* would stop thinking about those kisses. Soon, he hoped.

CHAPTER TWELVE

Fei regretted leaving her communicator on such a high volume when her mother's voice blasted across the square in the centre of Bagath. Hunching down as several villagers glanced over at her, she clipped the offending device onto the collar of her yellow shirt so that she could keep her hands free. Today she was helping to wind dried vines into baskets. Her attempts, unfortunately, resembled stringy blobs beside the tightly-wound ones her companion, Lilliean, was making. The baskets were supposed to contain recently harvested produce, though Fei seriously doubted hers would even hold a single nectarino.

'Fei, honey, are you still alive?' Berale Neron demanded. 'Or have the savages cooked you into some awful and grotesque feast?'

Lilliean lifted her eyebrows.

Fei winced. 'Mum. These people are the furthest thing from savages. I'm fine. Really.'

'I'm surprised the call even connected!' Berale exclaimed. 'The savages must have a Web relay station in orbit.'

'I wish they didn't,' Fei muttered.

A small smile flitted along Lilliean's lips as she returned to her work. She was a patient teacher and didn't seem at all bothered whenever Fei interrupted her to ask for assistance. Kuja had vanished yet again and Fei had been desperate for something to do that didn't involve stewing about what he might be doing and who with. Not that it was any of her business. He was just a fling, a bit of fun to help her move on. He knew that. She'd mentioned it. Several times.

It was only thing she'd regretted saying to him.

'How am I supposed to know if you're alive if you won't call me?' Berale beseeched. 'You were a lot better at this when you were busy with work and that's saying something!'

Fei snorted. 'Well, it's not like I have any code to compile here so I don't have as much idle time on my hands.'

'You only call me when you're bored? Oh, that's lovely.'

Fei winced; she could practically see her mother grinding her teeth.

'But it doesn't matter,' Berale went on. 'I need to discuss something with you.'

Lilliean made a gentle tut-tutting sound.

Fei ripped her eyes away from empty space and mouthed at her companion, *I am paying attention to her, I swear!*

Lilliean gave Fei a pointed look, her fingers continuing to weave the basket in front of her. Fei realised that apart from the greeting the woman had given her earlier, Lilliean had not uttered a single word, choosing to instruct her student through demonstration alone.

They would have been working in complete silence if not for the nearby villagers discussing how best to display their stone statue of Bagara, recently removed from storage, so as to please the god when he arrived the next day. Inesh had already shouted himself hoarse over the position he deemed most suitable, but the village headman had insisted that Bagara was more interested in looking after his people than he was in where an image depicting him happened to be.

Fei found all this commotion a lot more comfortable than the tense energy of the tight-lipped scientists back at the shelters. Gerns, the only one of them Fei could stand, had been too busy with her plants to spare any time for chatting that morning and Dr Lorena Hackett had been particularly hostile towards Fei at breakfast, which made her wonder what she'd done to upset the woman.

'Are you even listening?' Berale demanded.

'No,' Fei blurted.

Static screeched out of the communicator; Berale had unleashed a long-suffering sigh. 'I thought so. Honey, if you're still this bad at focusing, you should get a doctor to give you those injections I told you about.'

'Look, Mum, you really need to stop believing everything that medical app tells you,' Fei said, managing to scrub some of the annoyance from her words. 'I've seen programmers lose their edge when they rely on the stuff in hyponeedles to concentrate. It can make them too rigid in their thinking, which I guess is handy depending on what they're doing, but I kind of need to be able to think my way out of corners. Anyway, I just drink some tea and I'm fine. I don't need anything stronger, okay?'

'Honey, I didn't call you to argue about this again.'

'Then why did you call me?'

No sound escaped the communicator for several long seconds. Fei was beginning to wonder if the connection had died by the time her mother's voice resurfaced. 'Your father requested a meeting.'

Lilliean's touch darted over, not to fix the vines Fei had just snapped, but to still the trembles racing along the ridges on the backs of Fei's hands. Fei sucked in a large gulp of air, but it compressed inside her chest, refusing to fill her lungs.

'Fei, please say something,' her mother said. 'Are still you there?'

'Yes,' Fei managed in a rasp. 'What did that fucker want?'

'Language!'

'I'll use what ever language I starking well want to, especially if it means people are more likely to listen…!' Fei cut off her ranting and forced a smile, hoping it would make her sound less confrontational. 'Mother. If you would be so kind, please furnish my knowledge on this matter.'

'There's no need for that kind of language either.'

'Mum!'

A ticking noise emanated from the communicator; sometimes her mother made sounds with her tongue when she was choosing her words. Fei wondered if she should do something similar so she wouldn't keep blurting out whatever was on her mind. *But Kuja doesn't care…*

She set aside the broken vines and took the new ones that Lilliean held out for her.

'Mum.' Fei softened her tone. 'Please tell me what happened.'

'Well, it seems he regrets leaving us all that time ago, which was lovely to hear.' Fei rolled her eyes, but didn't interrupt. 'Anyway, he was wondering if he could live in my townhouse for a bit. His superiors assigned him a new room in the temple but it's very small and very cold.'

Fei waggled her tongue between her teeth but it was nowhere near as satisfying as unleashing her thoughts, so she said, 'Oh, the poor man has to live in a tiny room! He could have combined his salary with yours years ago to get himself something nice outside the temple. But no. *He abandoned us.*'

'Does that mean we should abandon him in return?' Berale asked, her voice firming. 'The Creator God would expect us to assist one of his agents. And your father says that even if a better room becomes available he'll still stay with me...'

'Oh sure, sure he will! And in the meantime, I'll have to put up with him every time I visit you!' Another vine snapped in Fei's hands. Lilliean leaned over and rescued the mess from Fei's lap, deftly finishing the basket out of arm's reach.

'You don't visit at all now.' A sniffle escaped the communicator. 'What difference would it make?'

'Creator God, why are your followers so unlikeable?' Fei wondered out loud.

'Don't blame our god for this,' Berale chided her. 'He gives us free will so that we might live our own lives. We cannot blame him for the actions of those who abuse it.'

'So you admit my father abuses it.'

'Fei...'

'Mum, don't let him do this to you, not again,' Fei said, burying her eyes in her palms. 'The Creator God and his...his minions have done nothing but hurt us. Everyone tells me to just accept it, but I won't. I don't have to. There are plenty of other gods.'

'Fei!' her mother repeated, a good deal more sternly this time. 'You should come to Gerasnin immediately. It sounds like those temples on Enoc are not very good for you.'

'I'm on Bagaran, remember, there are no temples here and I love that,' Fei said, nodding at Lilliean who shrugged, apparently unfazed by the compliment Fei had paid her planet. 'Maybe there are some nice people at your local temple, Mum, but the Creator God worshippers I keep running into say it's my fault I can't trust a god who tells people to abandon me, a god who *ignores* me — and no one really knows what the Creator God wants because he barely speaks to any of us!'

'Honey, if you would just — '

Fei slammed her palm against the communicator, cutting the connection. She stewed for a time, passing the device between both her hands, then turned to Lilliean. 'Am I bad daughter?'

Lilliean shook her head. 'Seeking a path that diverges from what you were shown does not make you a bad daughter. But make sure you are not pursuing Bagara just because this path takes you the furthest from you mother's.'

'It's not about her,' Fei insisted. 'It's about what's best for me.'

Lilliean looked sceptical.

Fei scowled. 'I can make my own decisions!'

'Hurt makes us do things we regret,' Lilliean advised her, nodding at the broken vines littering the ground around Fei. 'No matter which god you choose, if you choose one at all, don't destroy what you have with your mother. She will need you when that rotten father of yours abandons her again.'

Fei threw up her hands in frustration. 'Okay, no more basket weaving for me. And sure, I'll be there for my mother when she needs me, since she's always been there for me. But I don't have to talk to her for a bit.'

Lilliean's lips twitched but she made no comment.

'Lilliean, why aren't you telling me off for being so strange and talkative?' Fei asked.

'You're not quite as *strange* as you think,' Lilliean replied. 'And Kuja's a good boy, so I'll not chase off the only one worthy of him. Don't worry; that Dr Hackett never caught his eye the way you have.' With a brief nod of farewell, Lilliean gathered up the intact baskets and left.

Fei's bottom lip bobbed up and down like a piece of flotsam bouncing on the purple waves of Enoc. Well, *that* explained why Dr Hackett was being so cold to her, though Fei wished she hadn't felt such a thrill at hearing Lilliean's words.

Fei stood up, grimacing when she felt the wet mud clinging to her backside. Brushing it off only made the gunk stick to her fingers which she then had to wipe on the front of her pants. There was no point in changing into fresh clothes since they wouldn't stay clean very long — a discovery Fei had made by her second day on Bagaran — so she did her best to ignore the mess and walked over to Inesh who was beaming, pleased that he had won the argument about the statue. When she drew nearer and used his name, he stiffened. His attitude towards her hadn't quite softened, but he seemed to be able to tolerate her presence now.

'Where does Kuja go when he's not in the village?' Fei asked him.

Inesh spat on the ground. 'Sometimes he helps your lot. I try to talk him out of it. Idiot thinks everyone's worth listening to.'

'His best and most baffling feature,' Fei said with a small smile. 'I actually came here today because Kuja didn't visit me at the shelters this morning and I...I wanted to see him.'

'He avoiding the TerraCorp scum for once? Good. They're as bad as Chippers.'

'There's a reason they're as bad as each other,' Fei said.

Inesh's eyes narrowed. 'What do you mean?'

Fei tried to keep her mouth shut. She really did. But it just spilled right out of her. 'You know I work for TerraCorp, right?

They're in bed with GLEA. They even bankroll them, can you believe that?'

Inesh snarled. 'I can believe it. Scum. Starking scum.'

'Tell me something I don't know,' Fei sighed. 'It just makes me so angry that TerraCorp will go around pretending they're an independent business when every time they're doing work for a client, they're actually finding ways to insert a temple and force their religion onto the local population. Other times they'll even let GLEA overrule a client's wishes!'

Fei broke off when she realised Inesh was staring at her. The anger that had twisted his features had dissolved into concern. 'This is personal, isn't it? What did they do to you?'

'Nothing, I guess,' Fei muttered. 'Except pay me. It doesn't matter if I refuse to do their bidding. It'll still get done by someone.' She refocused on Inesh, her heart thudding erratically inside her ribcage. 'Please don't tell anyone what I said. I might get fired and I'm not sure I want to lose my job just yet.'

Fei sucked in a few unsteady breaths and wavered on her feet, painfully aware that she had no idea if her plea would work on Inesh, someone who had no reason to like her much less help her. But then he was beside her, offering his arm if she needed to lean on it, which she did.

Inesh's voice lacked its usual snap when he spoke again. 'I won't tell anyone. It's your responsibility to say it, not mine. But now I think you need to lie down for a bit.'

'I want to wait for Kuja,' she protested as he began leading her away from the centre of the village.

'There's no telling when he'll get back,' Inesh said, then pushed her into Kuja's hut. 'I got no idea where he goes when he's not with the TerraCorp scum, but he's usually gone for hours so best to wait in here. He would not mind.'

Fei parted the netting strung around the single bed so that she could seat herself on it. When Inesh remained standing by the door, she asked him, 'Inesh, does it upset you that Bagara doesn't speak to any of you outside of the festival?'

'No. He doesn't need to.'

'Then how do you know he's there? That he cares?'

Inesh gestured at the window. 'He's always there. Even when we don't need him. Don't you feel it?'

'No,' Fei admitted. 'I don't even feel my own god.'

Inesh sat at the end of the bed, leaving several lengths between them. 'You may never meet a god or speak to one. But you can look, you can smell, you can taste and you can *listen* to the worlds Bagara tends and know that they are full of life because of him. He has given us places to connect with others and ourselves. What need have we for his constant attention when he has provided all this for us?'

She closed her eyes rather than tell him to leave.

'Just *listen*,' Inesh insisted.

So she did. She heard the whirr of the nashba bugs and the croaks of the shingbats, their combined chorus unending but never unwanted. She heard the constant hum of voices as the village prepared for the festival. And if she strained her ears, she could even hear the crash of the distant waterfall. It was so peaceful here. The ambient sounds of Bagaran quietened her mind in ways the oceans of Enoc never had.

Fei rose from the bed and walked to the window, resting her hands against the wooden sill. The wood grew wet beneath her fingers; a downpour had started, a comforting background noise that was in danger of pulling a yawn from her.

'I don't feel Bagara...' she began.

'But?' Inesh prompted.

Fei reached out, cupping her hands and then scissoring her fingers apart to let the rainwater trickle through. 'But I *feel*. I feel connected. To this world. To you. To everyone here. I don't need Bagara for that.' She glanced at Inesh, afraid that she'd offended him. 'Sorry. I'm not sure I can worship another god, even yours.'

'Kuja would say it doesn't matter, that it's enough that Bagara's domain has brought you peace,' Inesh commented, his gaze distant. 'Maybe he's not wrong.'

'He's not,' Fei said, believing it.

Her fingers began to catch tears instead of rain as her chest heaved, disgorging the weight of so much pain that had gathered over so many years. When she opened her eyes, Inesh had gone, but the rainforest remained, just outside the walls of Bagath.

Even in here she could feel it.

***

Kuja emerged from the thicket beside the TerraCorp shelters and waved at Gerns as she bowled over to greet him. Her tentacles were twitching, a physical echo of just how troubled she felt. Not for the first time, Kuja was tempted to suggest that the TerraCorp scientists take a day off to explore the rainforest surrounding them. They always viewed it as something to research and exploit, never considering that it might actually give them some peace.

'So this festival they're holding,' Gerns began, carefully navigating her way along the edge of the path and trying not to crush any plants. 'Do you think they'd mind us showing up? Now me, I haven't so much as *seen* a drop of alcohol in months, let alone absorbed it through my suction cups.'

'You should bring this up with the village headman,' Kuja said, the phrase an old, tired one between them, but he smiled as he delivered it.

Gerns flopped one tentacle through the air, a parody of a human's dismissive wave. 'You don't understand your role here, do you, Kuja? You're the go-between. My people can stand you. The villagers can stand you. Just about anyone can stand you! Now me, I'd say the Creator God placed you here to help us all get along.'

Kuja wrinkled his nose. 'I'm not here to do his bidding. Bagara is my chosen deity.'

'Must be nice, choosing from a pantheon of gods,' Gerns mused. 'My mothering circle was big on the Creator God and I'd feel guilty if I went against their wishes.' She aimed one of her tentacles at Kuja. 'Now me, I'll tell you this and it's true. I'd talk to the headman for you if our positions were reversed.'

'I'm beginning to think I let people walk all over me,' Kuja muttered.

Gerns clucked for several seconds. 'Oh no, Kuja. You're just obsessed with helping people and you can't say no to a Jezlo in need of a good drink, can you?'

Kuja sighed. He didn't say no.

When he entered the village a couple of minutes later, Fei jogged over to him, her gold hair slicked with rain and her eyes — green today, he noticed, almost the exact same shade as his own — shining with excitement.

'Kuja, I need to tell you something!' she said, then rattled off exactly what she'd been up to while he'd been on eight or nine different planets simultaneously.

Kuja gave her as much of his attention as he could, making soft sounds at all the right moments. He nearly lost the thread of her words a few times, as she seemed incapable of finishing one sentence before another occurred to her. Even having access to her thoughts didn't help; they were chaotic, as always.

'So it's okay if I never feel the rainforest god, because I don't need to,' Fei finished, beaming.

Kuja meant to rest his hand on her shoulder, but his touch began to inch its way towards her neck almost immediately. His fingers were soon stroking her exposed skin. 'You are so much more confident in yourself than you were a handful of days ago.'

'Is that a bad thing?' she asked with a tiny smile.

'No, it's actually quite sexy,' Kuja said honestly. His thumb reached her cheek and her lips emitted a soft sigh. 'Uh, not that you weren't already sexy to begin with. But it's a good look on you.' Fei's tendency to babble was apparently infectious, he noted.

Fortunately, her face exploded into a grin. 'Nice save.'

She accompanied him when he went to meet with the village headman, an older man with slightly bluish skin, indicating a Lentarian ancestor.

'If Bagara does not want the scientists here for the festival, then they won't be,' the headman said with a shrug. 'Invite them. Perhaps they may learn something about us. It pleases me to see that at least one of them already understands our ways, Feiscina, even if you are leaving us in a handful of weeks.'

The moment they left the headman's hut, Fei abruptly sagged, so Kuja went to her and delivered a hug which he meant to keep short and supportive, but she fell against him, trembling.

'I can't go back,' she whispered, her eyes distant. 'I can't do it. I can't terraform deserts just because GLEA doesn't like that the people in them worship a different god.'

'Why did you accept the job at TerraCorp in the first place?' Kuja asked her. 'I seriously doubt it was so you could live near the Enocian Harem.'

Just as he'd hoped, she burst out laughing. 'The Harem? God, no! I've never been in there. Tempted to, yes, but...no, I needed a high-paying job so Zareth and I could get our own place. I went to TerraCorp for him. He didn't make much off his paintings.'

'Then perhaps you need to find a job you actually want,' Kuja suggested.

Fei sprang out of his arms and spun to face him. 'But I like what I do. I like knowing there are planets out there with my mark on them. It makes me feel like I've accomplished something.' She deflated. 'Except I can't even visit the worlds I've helped shape, because it's considered costly and unnecessary.'

'I'm glad they let you visit this world,' Kuja said.

Smiling, Fei shuffled back towards him. 'Me too. Because I like kissing you. And I'm going to do it again, if you don't mind.'

Kuja's breathing quickened. 'I suppose I do need the practice.'

'Happy to help,' Fei replied, her straight face rapidly losing its integrity.

Kuja leaned in and kissed her. It was a gentle bumping of lips, just like their first kiss at the waterfall, but this time heat filled his face and flooded his very being. Kuja pried himself away, disturbed, and quickly erected a smile for Fei. 'I know you don't believe me, but I like hearing you ramble. It makes it incredibly hard not to kiss you when you go on as you do.'

'Um,' she said.

Kuja grinned. 'Nothing to say now?'

'You...' she attempted, blinking.

Then she dragged him behind the village headman's hut and exacted her revenge. Back planted against the wall, her body pressed up against his, Kuja found it hard to remember why he should be worried about the sensations she was causing inside him.

She drew back to lick her lips and must have seen his desire for more, because she renewed her attack. This time she pinned his wrists beneath her fingers and ground her hips against him, seeking so much more than a kiss, but Kuja wasn't sure what he could give her.

Fei pulled away again, gasping. 'That was fun.'

Her eyes travelled down to Kuja's obvious and emphatic agreement. He wondered if he should cover the affected area with his hands. But then Fei lunged in for another kiss and it seemed moot to feel awkward about her seeing his biological reaction when she was rubbing up against it.

He was, however, decidedly more embarrassed when the headman came out and caught them.

CHAPTER THIRTEEN

A lengthy Bagaran dusk had smeared the sky for three full hours when Fei came to stand in the doorway of Kuja's hut. She glanced down at herself, wondering if she looked ridiculous in the dress that Lilliean had lent her for the evening. Though they were a similar height, Fei's figure was much fuller and so the tan, suede item clung to her hips and every other curve she usually tried to obscure with looser clothes.

Fei's feet were bare tonight. She had been hesitant to shed her shoes at first, but now she enjoyed the mud squelching beneath her, massaging each individual toe. It was raining again, not too heavily, just enough to sprinkle droplets over her untamed hair like tiny pieces of glinting glass. She would have spent an extra hour smoothing out the strands with chemicals, so that her look would last the night, but she had felt the need to show Kuja who she was without all that effort — and what she'd look like in the morning if he woke beside her.

Kuja was in the same clothes he always wore, but at least he'd actually cleaned them for once. He'd also taken the time to slick his hair back with water, though Fei wasn't sure how long that would last. She had to admit that she hadn't been terribly specific when she'd asked him to dress up for her.

'That's what you're wearing?' she asked, her lips twitching.

Uncertainty crept into Kuja's expression. 'Should I be wearing anything else?'

The smile finally escaped. 'No. You look like you and I like that. Don't change.'

Taking his hand, she led him towards the square in the centre of the village. A wooden stage had been erected there, containing not only the statue that Bagara would be speaking through, but an array of buffet food ranging from fruit to smoked rice, freely available to the villagers and their god, should he choose to partake. Fei stifled a laugh when she saw that a couple of her misshapen baskets had made it into the display.

The space directly in front of the stage was filled with dancers moving to the beat of nearby drums. A pan flute provided a melody to go along with the rhythm, played by a man who was actually known galaxywide for the music he traded in return for any parts or supplies that Bagath needed. Fei eyed the patch of moist earth that served as the dance floor. She felt certain Kuja would oblige her, but she wasn't sure she wanted to make herself so obvious a target for everyone's eyes and attention.

Instead she chose to stay in Kuja's shadow as people came up to talk to him. When the villagers sensed her reluctance to be drawn into conversation, they would focus on him, allowing her to drift and enjoy the atmosphere.

'You look happy,' Kuja told her when they were alone at last.

Fei beamed at him. 'I am. I guess it's because I realised I don't have to force myself to be someone I'm not, just to impress some invisible deity. It's...it's *liberating*.'

'Bagara is pleased to hear this,' he said softly.

Fei blinked at him but didn't have time to muster a vocal response, because moments later the TerraCorp scientists arrived in one tightly-knit cluster. Fei supposed she should help ease their arrival and walked over, intending to greet them. She had made it halfway across the square before she realised what she was doing.

I must be getting better at this talking-to-people thing, she thought with delight as she grasped Gerns' proffered tentacle.

***

'Do you need company?' a feminine voice asked.

Kuja only turned away from speaking to Inesh when the other man made a low whistle. Half-lying against the stage to better accentuate the curves of her body, Lorena offered a smile while her scanty clothing offered a lot more. Kuja raised his eyebrows. He knew exactly what she looked like beneath the two-piece outfit, but his body gave no reaction to those memories or at the sight of her now. He glanced past her to the buffet tables, where Fei was talking to Gerns and animatedly gesturing at the baskets she'd made, and felt a persistent tug somewhere beneath his navel.

'I already have a companion for this evening,' Kuja told Lorena, lifting the drink in his hand and tipping it towards Fei.

But Lorena thought he meant Bagara's statue. Her top lip folded up towards her nostrils. 'You don't really believe he'll speak to you, do you? Even if this god does exist, he's not likely to bother with ordinary people. Not even my Creator God does that — and with good reason. We cannot distract the gods from their higher duties.'

Inesh chortled and said aside to Kuja, 'Listen to this woman! And you want me to let them trample all over Bagara's land?' Inesh jerked his chin at Lorena. 'You, Dr Hackett, do you realise that what your company struggles to make in years Bagara can do in one day? He can raise rainforests from the soil beneath any man's feet!'

'Then why doesn't he?' Lorena challenged.

While Inesh launched into one of his usual tirades, Kuja let his gaze wander back over to Fei. He wasn't sure where she'd managed to find the dress but it looked good on her and he liked that she'd chosen to do nothing with her hair. It showed how relaxed she was on Bagaran. Her bare ankles carried the proud marks of someone who had been trundling around the nearby paths in search of scenery, often with him, sometimes without. He joined her whenever he could — it wasn't as though the plants on his many worlds couldn't contact him if someone needed Bagara's immediate assistance.

But if I mean to expand my influence tonight, I will need to see less of her, he thought. Regardless, I will enjoy her remaining weeks here. And I will also enjoy giving her the pleasure she is so intent on finding in my bed when I am not there to see it...

The grin came unbidden but Kuja did nothing to banish it. The vines in his hut had been more than happy to share those arousing images of Fei. He had no problem with her passing the time in that way while she waited for him, even though it sorely tempted him to abandon his duties so that he could take human form and run his hands over her. She was a distraction, but not one he couldn't ignore if he had to...

Inesh's words were steadily growing more heated. Kuja dismissed them at first, but then Lorena's piercing retort coasted across the square, drawing all eyes and ears towards her. 'You think new rainforests just pop out of the ground, do you? Terraforming is hard work! And whatever your god creates, he can't do it without science. You can't make a tree grow if you don't give it the right soil — even a fool like you should see that!'

'Bagara knows all these things,' Inesh said stiffly. 'And if you were not so set in your own ways, Chipper-lover, then you would know that a tree flourishes best when it is loved by the hands that buried its seed.'

'You assume your god knows everything but he is only a handful of decades old,' Lorena pointed out, teeth peeking through the small, terse gap created by her lips. 'Tell me, has he learned the composition of all the different soils on all the rainforest worlds in the galaxy by now?'

No, I haven't, Kuja realised, then ducked his head to hide his blush. He would be lying if he said he'd never tried to grow a rainforest from nothing on an arid world, only to fail when his thoughts took him elsewhere.

Fei really must do something special with those simulations, he thought.

Kuja stepped forward, putting himself between his friend and the scientist. 'Bagara is younger than many other sub-level gods, it's true. He has time to learn, though. He is a god.'

'If he really was a god he'd know it all by now,' Lorena said with a biting laugh. 'The Creator God knows everything since he *made* everything. He's the one you should be worshipping!'

Inesh simmered. 'A god who never loves or tends to his people will lose them.'

'Lose them to what — your sad way of life?' Lorena gestured wildly at the nearby huts. Her hand froze into an awkward claw, fingers bent towards the sky, when she realised just how many people were closing in on her. Her voice took on a much sweeter quality. 'I suppose it's not for everyone, though it seems to work well for...some people.'

'Since when were you so devout, Lorena?' Gerns asked, her body swinging from side to side as she marched over, her tentacles wound around her midsection. 'Not you, no, I seen it myself. You can't expect our hosts to ditch their god just because *you* don't like him. It's pointless. And kind of rude, given that we're getting free booze — now me, I see that as a definite plus in this Bagara's favour.'

'If I'd known that alcohol would sway your opinion,' Inesh said seriously, 'then I'd've just got you all drunk instead of blowing up the hoverpad in that lab of yours.'

Kuja opened his mouth, but it was too late.

The uproar had begun.

CHAPTER FOURTEEN

Fei dashed over and hastily inserted herself between both human and Jezlo moments before it occurred to her that this was probably a bad idea. Gerns' tentacles were brandished now, the suction cups glistening with the poison that her species kept in reserve for those moments when they felt threatened. Inesh had barely moved, but his dark eyes were like bolts itching to be shot out of a lasgun.

Fei swung a helpless look at Kuja.

Please, please, be my voice, she pleaded silently.

Kuja stepped forward and laid a hand on her shoulder. 'I think Fei has objections to us turning this celebration into a fight.'

'This human has set us back weeks!' Gerns exclaimed.

'Bagara does not want you here!' Inesh hurled at her.

Kuja's voice was soft but it carried an echo that made Fei think of a snarling Bagaran Tiger, a rare but deadly predator. 'Inesh, we have talked about this. Bagara hasn't spoken directly on these matters, so we can't assume what he wants. Gerns, will you hear me out before you do anything?'

'I said to myself just then, I said, "Gerns, I respect Kuja".' Gerns aimed her tentacles at Inesh. 'Even if you didn't tell me it was your buddy here that destroyed the lab.'

'That's not what I asked.'

Gerns' tiny eyes fixed on Kuja. 'Then you better start talking before I wrap this man up in my embrace. Now me, I don't think he's gonna enjoy it.'

'Very well.' Kuja lifted his chin. 'Yes, I knew Inesh was responsible. He won't do it again. If he tries, or even so much as *thinks* about doing it, I will stop him. And believe me, I can.'

Overhead the sky rumbled, dissatisfied by the scene presented to it. Kuja was still speaking but his words, powerful though they were, hovered like a dead heat, never landing, never settling. They wouldn't be enough to convince his listeners.

Fei moved her hand to Kuja's waist and squeezed. He dutifully silenced.

Somewhere in the distance rain began to roar, the sheet of droplets drawing closer with each passing moment. Thunder growled, threatening anyone who dared to speak out of turn.

Everyone's eyes were now levelled at Fei.

She cleared her throat. 'Um. Hi. I work for TerraCorp, but I guess most of you know that already. So when I...alright, I'm going to talk about one of our most important rules. When I'm writing the code for simulations, the ones that get used to terraform worlds, I have to include the wishes of the local populations.'

'Fei, you need to pause and take a breath,' Kuja advised her in a murmur.

She gasped, glad that he'd interrupted, because she had been running out of air. When she was able, Fei went on, 'I have to appease both our clients and the rest of the people on the planet they want to change. If you have a follower of the Desine living there, you need to let them have some desert so they can still connect to their god. It's, you know, a compromise.'

'A compromise — our lab was destroyed!' Gerns' tentacles snapped into straight lines. 'And we're not trying to change or damage this planet, we just want to learn from it! The lab will be gone the moment we are, I promise you that.'

Fei nodded repeatedly. 'I know. I know. The lab's destruction affected me too, because now I won't have those new plants to include in my next simulation. Inesh, I like you,' Fei said, glancing at his stony expression. 'You gave me a chance. I don't think you regret it. So please try to do the same for my colleagues. And maybe tonight we can all drink together and, um, find some common ground. If we can. I don't mind if you get angry again tomorrow, but I'd rather not go through that right now, especially...' Fei offered a shy grin to Kuja whose emerald eyes sparkled in response. 'Especially since I'm here with a date and wouldn't mind scoring at some point.'

The square erupted into cheers, fed from both sides of the waning fight. The burdened clouds rumbled again, causing some people to tilt their faces skywards, their tongues extended in anticipation. But the worst of the downpour was elsewhere and only tiny pinpricks of rain were their reward.

Fei turned to Kuja just in time to catch his fervent kiss. When he broke away, he said, 'You should get a good spot near the statue. I have to go do something.'

'But...' Fei trailed off.

Kuja pressed his lips to her cheek. 'You don't need me, or my voice, just now. But if you call me, I will come to you. No matter what. Is that alright?'

'More than alright,' she said, watching as he walked away.

With nothing better to do, Fei moved towards the stage along with everyone else. She scrunched up her face in worry when she found herself standing between Gerns and Inesh, who were still shooting suspicious looks at each other. Fei forced a laugh when one of them made a joke, then quickly transferred an explanation to her other companion to make sure they knew it wasn't an insult. Within seconds all three of them were chortling and holding their bellies, even though the joke hadn't been that funny to begin with. But it was something. It was a start.

They silenced when the air inside the village grew charged and seemed to vibrate around them. An eerie yellow light fell from the sky, filtered through the heavy clouds, smearing over every exposed patch of skin. This must have been a cue of some kind because the Bagathians knelt, one by one, onto the muddy earth, looking expectantly at the statue.

Fei found herself holding her breath.

'Is the starking thing going to start walking?' Gerns asked.

'Walking? No.' Inesh snorted from his position on the ground. 'You better listen well because Bagara only blesses us with his voice once every year.'

'Once a year, huh — then he can't have told you to blow up any labs!' Gerns exclaimed.

Inesh bowed his head. 'True. That was my choice.'

'Now me, I think you need to make better choices. Or let your god make them instead.'

'I am sorry for my actions,' Inesh grumbled. 'But I won't be if you keep talking.'

Fei let her head drift to the side, reaching out with every sense she possessed, trying to feel the arrival of Bagara. There were some birds twittering nearby, but soon even they quietened. She wondered if the creatures were only following the lead of Bagara's worshippers or if they too understood that their god was coming.

Fei had to quickly lower her eyelids when the statue was struck with a blinding beam of light, as though the atmosphere had been rent apart, exposing everyone in the village square to the nearest star. Bagara's effigy thrummed with power and then grew in size, casting a shadow over them.

My people, I come to you now, said a low, measured voice, one that seemed oddly familiar to Fei, *just as I did over five decades ago. There are those that remember that time, but there are those that don't. Since then I have learned much about you and what you need from me.*

'Never heard anyone so eloquent,' Gerns remarked. 'Waste of words, if you ask me.'

Fei shot her a look of warning, then relaxed when Inesh said under his breath, 'Yeah. He's usually too busy to ramble on like this.'

The statue continued to conduct the voice of Bagara, heedless of this exchange. *I want to give myself to you, the way you have given yourselves to me. From now on, my voice will come directly to you when you need it, to guide you — and not just you, anyone who needs my help, anyone with questions. Even if they do not intend to worship me.*

'Even me?' Fei wondered out loud.

Even you, said the voice and she shivered, not sure if those words was directed at everyone or her in particular. *I freely offer myself, my guidance and my love. What you choose to do with that is your own concern.*

Spread my message. Tell others to ask for me. I am not a god who demands that temples of stone be built where they are not wanted. I understand that free will only works so long as you do not punish those who make use of it. And unlike the Creator God, I do not leave casualties.

I am Bagara. If you have questions, if you need help...you need only speak my name.

With a great sigh, the statue deflated, losing both height and importance. The sky had blackened at some point during Bagara's speech, but the clearing was now lit with twinkling solar lights that swayed in the gentle breeze. Those gathered before the stage seemed stunned, unable to move or speak. Then, slowly, the villagers raised their hands to the stars, murmuring their thanks and praises. Some of the scientists even bent down and joined the Bagathians on their knees. Others, like Dr Lorena Hackett, rolled their eyes and headed over to the buffet tables that groaned beneath the weight of assorted food and beverages.

Gerns was one of those who knelt. Fei quickly joined her.

'Now that, that is impressive,' Gerns said. 'This Bagara sounds like my kind of god.'

'I thought you were a staunch follower of the Creator God?' Fei asked, feeling dwarfed as the people around them began to stand, their knees covered in mud. She knew the dress she was wearing would also be dirty when she got off the ground, but since she knew it wouldn't bother Kuja, she decided it wasn't going to bother her.

Gerns' tentacles drifted, distracted and unaimed. 'Now me, I follow the Creator God, because I inherited him from my mothering circle — and because them at TerraCorp will only hire you if you worship the Creator God, you know that. But Bagara's right — there are casualties.'

Fei watched Gerns' skin darken, the alien woman's light grey colouring transforming into something more akin to coal. Fei wasn't sure what that meant for a Jezlo; Gerns might simply be sick or something much worse could happening to the botanist.

'Gerns?' Fei prompted, worried.

'Got a few things to say, I do, but not out here,' Gerns said in an undertone.

The Jezlo rose without another word and, ignoring the colleagues that offered to get her a drink, lumbered away, disappearing behind a nearby hut. Fei followed her.

Once they were far enough away from anyone who could overhear them, Gerns said, 'My Severs, I loved her and I told myself I'd never let her out of my sight, but she just had to go and join GLEA while I was at university. It's what she wanted, so I told her to do it, we'd call each other on the Web every night. But the agent she got paired with after she finished her training, now that lout made her think she was a terrible person for talking to me when she could have been using her free time to go to the temples. He said to her, he said, the Creator God wouldn't like that she put me first.'

Gerns broke off and made a low, globbing sound. Fei didn't know what she could do or say to comfort Gerns so she just stood there awkwardly. After a while, the Jezlo's skin took on its usual translucent hue and Gerns was able to lift her large head again.

'Severs took her own life rather than disappoint me or the Creator God,' Gerns continued, her voice flat and controlled. 'I told me, so I told me, "Gerns, TerraCorp will fire you if you stop worshipping the Creator God, but stark him if you ever get a better offer".'

Fei tried to keep her silence. But the drums from the festival were back, slowly and steadily finding their rhythm, forcing her blood to throb in her ears. She had to say it. She had to.

'Gerns, don't work for TerraCorp,' she said. 'You need to leave.'

Gerns' tiny black eyes darted around Fei's face. 'Why? You're still with the company. Now me, I wouldn't call taking a holiday funded by them at TerraCorp "leaving".'

Fei rubbed her forehead, trying to erase her growing headache. 'They wanted me to find a reason to keep working for them. And since you showed me all those plants and made me see how wonderful it is to create life, I thought...'

'You thought they put me up to to it?' Gerns shook out two tentacles in apparent agitation. 'Nah, just trying to focus on the good stuff in my life, since there's not much of it. So tell me, Fei. Why should I stop working for them? I don't need me much reason to leave as it is.'

'I don't have proof. It's not...it's not...' Suddenly Fei felt like she was back in the basement at TerraCorp with Moz advancing on her, his shadow encasing everything in its path. She let her gaze fall to the ground. 'Forget I said anything.'

'You got this far, you can't stop now,' Gerns told her.

Fei bit her lip. 'But you'll quit your job if I tell you. I can't...I can't be responsible for that.'

One of Gerns' tentacles fell onto her shoulder, but it wasn't heavy and neither did the Jezlo apply pressure. It was more of a comforting weight. 'Yes, you starking can. You know something. Now me, I'll be real unhappy if you don't tell me what it is.'

'TerraCorp was created to fund GLEA — Gerns, they're the same thing!' Fei blurted, then dragged in several long, laboured breaths.

Gerns' alien face darkened again. 'TerraCorp is GLEA. Now that's more than enough for me to wobble my way out of their clutches.'

'I don't even know if I should tell people,' Fei agonised. 'I don't have the files that can prove it. No one would believe me. And even if they did, do I want them to go to other terraforming companies? TerraCorp is the reason poorer planets have any protection from criminals, because they fund GLEA which lends out its services for free. I won't be responsible for endangering lives.'

'Now me, I think you *should* tell people.' Gerns removed her tentacle from Fei's shoulder and tapped one of her many chins. 'I'd rather have the truth so I can make a choice about whether or not I want to be mixing business with religion. But that's enough for tonight.' The tentacle dropped to Gerns' side. 'Go back to your date before Lorena gets her claws into him. Kuja's quite good-looking, or so our Dr Hackett tells me. I never can tell with you humans.'

'What will you be doing?' Fei asked, dreading the answer.

Gerns' triangular mouth shrank into a small circle. 'Tendering my resignation.'

'But Gerns —'

'Fei, sometimes you gotta say things because they need to be said,' Gerns told her. 'Some of us aren't meant to make waves. But you? You're gonna cause a tsunami on Enoc, on Gerasnin, maybe all across the galaxy. If I don't see it, now me, I'd be surprised.'

Fei held up her hand in farewell, but Gerns was already walking away, headed towards the gate. Worrying her lips together, Fei returned to the festival where she found enough smiles and laughter to wipe away the sadness and regret that had filled her stomach like bad wine. She was just thinking about looking for Kuja when he suddenly appeared at her side, as though he'd been there the entire time. He captured her hands in his and dusted kisses over her knuckles, gazing up at her in that way that made her heart jump.

'Kuja, it was wonderful, did you hear him?' Fei asked, squeezing his fingers to keep him from leaving again. 'It was as though Bagara listened to all of our conversations and wanted to address our concerns.'

There was a mysterious twist to Kuja's lips. 'Perhaps Bagara did listen to us. Now, Fei, we could talk about this or we could find other things to do with our evening.'

The shiver started at the nape of her neck before travelling lower, much lower. 'Do you mean dancing? Because I could maybe do that for a bit...'

'We can start with dancing, if you'd like,' Kuja murmured against her ear.

Fei leaned back, trembling. 'Kuja...I don't want to say this, but...but...'

'If all you want to do is dance, then that's fine,' Kuja assured her.

'It's...it's just that Zareth never asked me what I wanted in bed, he just assumed and did whatever made him happy and — I'm better off doing it alone,' Fei finished in a mumble.

Kuja's hand slid down her side then nestled against her hip. 'What if there was someone willing to take the time to learn from *you*, the master of your own body?'

'Then I would wonder why we're not dancing already,' Fei whispered.

His chuckle rumbled in his chest as he pulled her into his arms. Other dancers near them began partnering up as a slower song filled the square, the accompanying drums now as steady as a heartbeat. Kuja's lips found the hollow of Fei's throat and she lost any words that might have escaped her.

She never thought she would enjoy talking so much until she met him. And she never thought she would enjoy being silenced so much until he did it for her.

Eventually the song wound down and Kuja escorted her over to the drinks table. He chose to sip some carowaol juice, but Fei was after something a little stronger. She knocked back a fruity concoction in one go and immediately tripped sideways, giggling.

'That might be enough,' Kuja said, catching her in his arms.

She turned a grin up at him. 'I was trying to relax. I'm scared. I think. Or I was. Just so you know, the alcohol is going to make me feel very warm down there in a second or two and we're going to have to do something about it.'

Kuja hesitated.

'Kuja, don't pretend you're stalling because I've had a drink — it'd take more than one to lay me out, I promise.' Fei pressed a finger to his lips. 'It's not that. No. You're afraid this will mean more than it does.'

'Can you read minds?' he asked, frowning.

'No, no — I just...I just *know* you,' Fei said and moved her hand to his cheek. 'And we both know this can't be forever. But that doesn't mean we can't experience a little bit of happiness before we go our separate ways. I think we need this. And I also think that if we don't go through with it, we'll be too distracted for the rest of my trip to have any meaningful conversations about Bagara and I...'

'Come with me,' Kuja said, then led her away from the noise and the lights.

CHAPTER FIFTEEN

Kuja hooked an arm through Fei's as they walked towards his hut, pleased that a woman so amazing had agreed to share his bed. She reminded him of a quivering leaf that was shielding the vibrant soil beneath it, where secrets lay in wait, ready to surprise him and make him more in awe of her.

Fei stopped dead when he opened the door to his hut. 'Kuja. Are you sure you want to do this?'

Kuja nuzzled the side of her neck. 'Very sure. I intend on seeing you satisfied. I won't join in, since my limited experience has shown me that there's too much going on in my mind for me to find release. So this will be completely about you.'

She extracted herself from his embrace and danced towards his bed, green eyes gleaming. 'Well, what woman could refuse that offer?'

Kuja rushed to help her when she had trouble wrestling the tight dress over her head, but his efforts only caused her to overbalance. She laughed helplessly and fell back across the bed, him on top of her. Grinning, Kuja untangled her arms from the fabric so that he could roll the dress off her, then did away with the bra band. He stared down hungrily at her breasts as they fell to the sides, unhindered and beautiful.

'Could you...' Fei bit her lip. 'Could you...could you kiss them?'

Kuja brushed his palm over her cheek then moved down her

body. Each nipple sprang to life beneath his eager lips and she sighed with pleasure, stretching her arms over her head, a smile cascading over her face. Kuja drew as much of one breast as he could into his mouth, suckling gently, his tongue dancing over her slick skin. She made enthusiastic sounds, her hips rising off the bed, only to grunt in disappointment when he detached himself from her skin. But then he had her moaning and writhing again when his open-mouthed kisses found her other breast.

After a couple of minutes, Kuja sat up, grimacing.

'Something wrong?' Fei asked, an uncertain frown appearing.

He looked down at the tent his member was forming in his pants. 'I appear to be getting hard. Don't worry. It should go down. It always does.'

'Oh.' Fei blinked. 'You weren't kidding about this being completely about me.'

'No, I wasn't,' Kuja said softly.

'Don't let me stop you.'

He played with her magnificent breasts a little more before answering her unspoken request by skirting his fingers along her thighs, raising goosebumps as he went. Her underwear he slid off slowly, his lips following the fabric down one leg to her ankle. He threw the item of clothing haphazardly across the room, drawing another laugh from her, then spread her knees and exposed her to his gaze. When he began to tease the edges of her labia, she reached down to guide him, impatient, but he seized her wrist and pinned it at her side.

Using his other hand, Kuja pressed one finger to her clitoris and began a circling motion, light and teasing. When her breathing quickened, he swiftly dipped into her wet heat and then withdrew, lathering her folds with her own moisture.

'Oh, oh...' she moaned. 'How do you...how do you know what I like...'

Kuja firmed his touch and she bucked, her lips parting, her wrist wrenching around inside his grip and her thighs shaking beneath him. Fei's expression became transported and his name escaped her lips as the orgasm claimed her. He drew out her pleasure, continuing to wind his touch around her sensitive nub until finally she gasped, 'Stop!'

It took several minutes for Fei's eyes to lose their glazed look. When she refocused on him, she grinned. 'Kuja! You're blushing.'

'I can't help it,' he said defensively, lying down on the bed beside her. He saw Fei's gaze travel down to his pants, which felt like they were about to split apart.

She raised her eyebrows.

'I'm sure it will go down, it's supposed to go down,' Kuja fretted, patting his crotch.

Fei rested her hands on her abdomen, giggling at him. Unable to help the smile, Kuja abandoned his futile attempt to control his desire and instead chose to wait it out by embracing her. A strange heat smothered his heart as Fei snuggled into him.

'The Creator God doesn't deserve you,' he murmured.

'And Bagara does?' she asked.

Kuja hoped he didn't look as serious as he felt. 'Yes. Because he will only bring happiness to you.'

'I only want the happiness *you* can bring me, Kuja,' Fei whispered, closing her eyes.

When her face slackened and her breathing deepened, Kuja rose from the bed and went to the window. Across the galaxy, people were speaking Bagara's name, waiting for him to come to them, to guide them. Their demands on his time were stacking up into a great, seething pile that was swiftly growing more unsteady and threatening to topple. He couldn't let that happen. He had to leave. Now.

Casting a quick eye at Fei to make sure she was asleep, Kuja flattened himself into a puddle of leaves and soil which then vanished, leaving no trace of his human form. He divided his presence into countless fragments and sent them across the surface of multiple planets in under a microsecond. He could hear them all — old followers, needing reassurance that these changes would not alter their relationship with Bagara too greatly; new followers, wanting to know his measure; undecided souls with burning questions trapped beneath their ribs, fearful of the judgement of their peers.

And then there were the urgent prayers, from those who were in immediate danger. Kuja went to them, as he always did, but now instead of simply dealing with the problem and leaving without a word, he took his time. On one world, he kept a significant but still invisible part of himself beside a man while a rescue party was being assembled for him.

The man had begged him to stay. And so Kuja did, for one moment and then another. The man spoke of his life, his goals, his failures, and then asked that Bagara keep watching out for him, because a footographer's life was a lonely one, always wandering the stars in search of that perfect image, that perfect angle. The thought of having someone out there, someone who cared if he lived or died, would be a great comfort to him.

'This fall I took has really rattled my confidence,' the man admitted. 'Not that I had much to start with. Plenty of people say I'm mad for being a footographer. But I love it too much to quit.' He hesitated, his teeth gnawing into his lip, helping him deal with the pain. 'This...this feels weird, because I feel like I should have done something to deserve your help.'

Deserve? Kuja tempered his anger; it had no place here. *No. I gave you my protection because you pass through my worlds and I would keep all people in the galaxy safe if I could.*

'Isn't that going to take up all your time, looking after everyone?' the man asked.

If everyone turns out as pleasant as you, I don't mind.

'Oh, you're going to change your mind real fast, Bagara.'

It's a good thing I helped you before speaking to anyone else then, Kuja returned.

They shared a chuckle. Soon a ship was descending from the sky, coming to bear the man to safety. Kuja watched him go, then focused on the other parts of himself that were flying into dangerous situations or creeping in when more caution was needed.

Kuja felt wired, ready to take on the entire galaxy's problems if need be. And he might have to, he realised. He had opened his arms to everyone — and they were all flooding into his embrace. Many of them were victims of GLEA, an agency that had prioritised money and expansion over the physical and mental needs of vulnerable beings.

Father has a lot to answer for, Kuja thought. *And so do his Chippers.*

The next voice that called for him was surprisingly familiar. 'Bagara? You there? Don't want to waste my time if you're not actually listening.'

Kuja returned to Bagaran, filling the shelter belonging to Gerns with his presence and appreciating, not the first time, that the Jezlo had chosen to use bare earth as the floor of her home.

Standing beside one of her trays of plants, her entire body trembling, Gerns spoke again. 'I'd like you to be listening. I consider myself one of them casualties you were talking about and I'm a big fan of plants and things, so I figure I have a better than even chance of attracting your attention.'

I am listening, Kuja assured her. *And it would not matter to me, if you didn't like 'plants and things'.*

Gerns froze, her tentacles resembling the branches of a petrified tree. 'Well, just saying.'

What can I help you with, Gerns? he asked.

'I want to help you, actually,' Gerns said, swinging her gaze around the room, as though she could see him if she peered long and hard enough.

You do not owe me anything; even if you do not worship me, you will always be under my protection.

Gerns released a series of clucks. 'You don't get us mortals at all, do you?'

I have seen the sense of obligation destroy people.

'Nah, it's not obligation.' One of Gerns' tentacles danced over the glistening fronds beside her. 'It's called working together. Common goal and all that. You want to help people, I want to help people. You might think you can do everything, because you're a god, but you still need instruments. Any good scientist needs her tools.'

Kuja allowed amusement to infuse his words. *You would know this better than most. What can you do for me?*

'Not entirely sure yet,' Gerns answered. 'Now me, I got nothing but time and nothing to do with it now that I've quit my job. When you find something that fits, let me know.'

I will.

Kuja only left once Gerns had safely wobbled into her bed. There were countless worlds to visit and innumerous conversations to have — all before dawn swept into the village. He intended to be there when Fei woke up, to watch the smile spread over her features, to speak to her not as a god to a mortal, but as a man to a woman.

Bagara? another voice called.

Kuja immediately followed the thread back to its source, surprised to find himself within Bagath's wooden walls, tantalisingly close to where Fei was sleeping, her naked body free of the sheets. Kuja wasn't sure if he was annoyed or pleased that his plants had distracted him with this image, however briefly.

Inesh, he greeted, keeping his tone solemn.

'Bagara,' Inesh returned, seated cross-legged on the floor of his hut. His words were slurred from the alcohol he had consumed, but his mind felt clear and determined. 'You accepting that TerraCorp scum now, are you?'

I will not abandon the people I have promised to help just because you do not like it.

Inesh's face creased. 'Don't expect you to. Just saying...I can't accept it right now, but I want to. I do. So I guess...help me do that. If you can.'

Kuja gauged the truth in Inesh's words. The man would never apologise for what he had done, but here was a chance for Inesh to move past his old ways.

If I wish to create plants or animals or anything else in my domain, even I must obey the laws of science, Kuja told his follower.

'Look, I don't really care about all that,' Inesh said with a dismissive wave of his hand. 'You're telling me that those scientists and any other newcomers are just as worthy as me in your eyes. It's not fair.'

Kuja was tempted to retake human form just to display the grimace he was feeling. He still wasn't entirely sure how to deal with Inesh, but he had to come up with something to placate the man — and fast. As a god, Bagara was supposed to have all the answers. *Think of it this way. If I accept these newcomers, then that means there will be more people following me — and fewer people for you to fight and get annoyed at. You could channel your energy into something more worthwhile.*

Inesh deflated. 'I guess. I'll have to think about it.'

Please do.

Kuja scrubbed his presence from Bagaran after this, trying to resist the urge to watch a drop of sweat that was apparently wending its way down between Fei's breasts.

He really needed to have a stern word with the plants in his hut.

***

Fei jolted awake then fell back against the bed, groaning. She'd been gripped by an erotic dream in which Kuja had tied vines around her wrists, binding her to the bed so that he could walk his fingers all over her. The ensuing burst of pleasure beneath her abdomen had been wonderful — until she had woken up, alone and in need of attention. But that wasn't all she wanted from Kuja. She wanted more, so much more.

'You've had your fun,' she told herself. 'Just be happy with that and stop thinking about what you can't have.'

Shaking her head, Fei pulled on the mud-smeared dress she'd

worn the night before and glanced around. Kuja was nowhere in sight. She stood still for several seconds, trying to decide if she needed to cry or if she just wanted to.

'It's not fair!' she exclaimed and stomped her bare foot onto the earth-packed floor.

'What's not fair?' Kuja asked as he walked out of the tiny kitchen that was divided from his bedroom by a single board of wood. Balanced in his hands was a metal tray containing a small bunch of purple flowers, an array of fruit and a tiny metal teapot with two matching cups.

Fei smothered her face with her hands, equal parts delighted and mortified. 'You remembered that I like tea instead of coffein.'

Kuja set the tray on the bed and walked over to the window, where a vine was hanging over the sill. He gently nudged it outside then turned back to her. 'Fei, I don't, erm, usually do what I did last night.' His expression grew as dark as the storms that sometimes claimed the village. 'I've got good reasons not to.'

'Oh.' Fei looked down at the tray, then up at him again. 'I'm sorry?'

He grinned and swooped over to her, the shadows fleeing his eyes. Wrapping his arms around her and pulling her flush against his chest, he said, 'Don't be sorry. I had more fun last night than I've had in...well, years. Are you hungry?'

Fei licked her lips. 'Yes. For many things.'

Kuja raised one copper eyebrow, smirking, and threw her back onto the bed, alarmingly close to the tray. She shrieked with laughter as he bore her down, his lips whispering over her skin, then began to gasp and groan as his sure tongue and firm fingers played her to completion yet again. She was glad he hadn't bothered to make her a hot breakfast because they were able to enjoy it later, lying side by side while a breeze drifted in through the window.

The tea, however, needed rescuing.

CHAPTER SIXTEEN

Sipping a cup of tea that Kuja had left out for her, Fei read BozzMed's latest message on the Webchat feed for the third time in as many minutes. *I am currently researching this latest rainforest god resurgence. Anyone witness the speech Bagara gave to his people?*

Fei ran her finger over the text displayed on her techpad. It had been some days since she had bothered to check the Web and many more since she had thought about BozzMed and the answers he could give her. This time *she* was the one with the answers. There was a certain thrill that came with that.

She typed three small words: *I was there.*

CC, where have you been? BozzMed asked. *Hope those questions of yours didn't get you into any trouble.*

Fei's heart hammered across several ribs. She closed her eyes, shutting out the faint shimmer of pink hair in her peripheral vision, and tried to even out her breathing by thinking of Kuja and his frequent kisses. His mouth tasted like freshwater. She could only imagine what he tasted like elsewhere and she intended to find out — when he managed not to distract her with his confident touch. He seemed reluctant to see to his own needs.

Clearing her throat, Fei held her techpad up in front of her face, forcing herself to focus on the small screen of her device. *I did get in trouble, BozzMed. I nearly lost my job.*

I'm sorry to hear that, BozzMed replied. *You should have become a mediaist, like me. I get paid to ask questions.*

You're a mediaist? Fei asked, startled.

The profession was a lucrative one, given that mediaists with particularly large viewerships could charge outrageous fees if a company wanted a shout-out during a Webcast. And the best mediaists didn't just ask questions — they poked around until they found the answers they wanted. Having exclusive content was the best way to gather viewers and sponsors, after all. Mediaists might be motivated by coin-chips but Fei was more likely to trust them than GLEA, whose leaders were not so transparent about where their money came from.

Yes, BozzMed said. It was impossible to tell from that one word if he was proud of what he did. *So I'm sure you'll understand if I ask you what exactly went on at this event. The impression I got is that everyone's supposed to spread the word.*

The voices of the villagers outside grew in volume as some of them neared the hut. Fei reflexively ducked down and glanced over her shoulder, but the door remained closed. Kuja had left early that morning, but not before licking his way down her navel. His goodbye kiss on her intimate lips had lasted so long and felt so good that she hadn't been able to feel very sorry about grabbing his hair when she'd convulsed against him.

Fei squeezed her thighs together just thinking about it. She groaned in frustration. Not only did no one know where Kuja had gone, but they didn't seem to be able to contact him either — unlike the rest of the Bagathians, he had no communicator. Fei wondered if he saw little use for one, or if there was a reason he didn't want to be contactable.

CC? BozzMed prompted.

I'm here. The Web is slow out where I am. Fei grinned. It sounded better than 'I was just reliving some great sex from this morning'.

The text-based Webchat made it a lot easier to filter out embarrassing thoughts like that.

Tell me what happened, CC instructed. *And what everyone experienced. And why anyone would want to make this go viral on the Web.*

Fei began with the details of the actual festival itself, then ended with, *It's a very attractive offer. As someone who's well and truly over the Creator God and his followers, I like the idea that someone actually gives a shit about me and just wants me to be happy.*

I take it you're one of the people who made it go viral then, BozzMed said, his response flashing up almost immediately. *Can I interview you on vidcam?*

Fei darted another look at the door of Kuja's hut. She hadn't mentioned anything to Kuja yet, but she'd started making Bagara-related posts on certain Webchat feeds. And she wasn't alone. Thousands of beings across the galaxy were filling the feeds with discussion about the rainforest god. Many of them weren't even followers but they were interested in hearing more; others joined in just to make fun of those who were taking it seriously, or to point out that there were sub-level gods who were cruel and couldn't be trusted, such as the water god, Oceania.

Kuja didn't seem particularly keen about Oceania either. He hadn't said it in so many words but she'd felt it emanate off him, like a low-powered shield that swarmed a micrometre above his skin.

I don't think it's a good idea to appear in a Webcast, Fei finally typed. *I could get fired.*

BozzMed wasted no time in pursuing that lead. *I get the feeling your reluctance is due to GLEA interfering somewhere they shouldn't, maybe your workplace. Care to comment on that?*

Fei almost dropped her techpad in her haste to reply. *Forget I said anything. Unless your Webcast isn't all that popular and only two or three people watch it.*

My viewership is around ten billion.

Who are you, Ton Tinel? she demanded, naming the galaxy's most famous mediaist.

Yes. Again, a simple answer that revealed nothing about how he felt.

He was probably lying, Fei decided. Still, if he was Ton Tinel... *At least you're not one of those mediaists who gush on about GLEA. But even you don't ask them nearly enough questions.*

I think you know what happens when you upset or offend GLEA. His words might have been wry if he'd spoken them. *You strike me as someone who's figured that out from personal experience.*

Maybe, Fei said cautiously. *I've got to go.*

Can I use what you've written about the festival? BozzMed asked.

Sure. Just don't forget to say 'thank you for watching Ton Tinel'. If you are him, that is.

Fei signed off from the feed, deactivated her techpad and leaned back against the bed. Her attempt at relaxation was rudely interrupted when something sharp spasmed in her neck and starting aching. Sighing, she dug her fingers into the affected muscle and massaged it, straining to hear the soothing sounds of the rainforest that had faded into the natural soundtrack until Inesh had taught her to listen.

It was too quiet in here. She needed to submerge herself fully inside Bagara's domain.

Fei left the hut and put the village behind her. She took a moment to admire the new floating laboratory that the scientists were clustered underneath, then encased herself in trees, vines and thick heat. When she arrived at the waterfall, Fei knelt carefully onto the rocks, leaning over to coast her fingers through the pool's shimmering surface. She cupped some water in her hand and brought it to her mouth, the cool liquid kissing her lips before sliding down her throat.

With only one of her thirsts quenched, Fei sat back on her heels and said, 'I'm not sure if you'll hear me or if I'm even doing this right. But Gerns said it worked for her and...I guess what I want to know is...what can I do to help you? I mean, I get that we don't have to do anything in return but...I want to. Please speak to me.'

Her eyes burned but she kept them wide open, hoping the frustrated tears that threatened to fall would dry before they could. The boom of the waterfall seemed to grow in volume with each passing moment, causing her fear to multiply until her breaths became sharp and erratic.

And then Bagara came to her.

This wasn't like all those other times, when she was throwing out a hope, a wish, a prayer. She could actually *feel* him. One stubborn tear edged its way out, streaking down her cheek.

'You came,' she whispered. 'That's enough. You don't have to do anything else. You came.'

Her heart swelled.

***

Kuja had spent the day doing his best to answer the thousands of people calling for Bagara. Some of the mortals he visited lived in the domains belonging to his brothers and sisters, their curiosity drawing him to places far and wide across the galaxy. Word was spreading. People were already referring to Bagara as the god of lost causes and casualties. He was glad to be there for them, to answer their prayers.

And then she called for him.

Kuja filled the clearing near the waterfall with his presence, watching a delighted glow infuse Fei's cheeks in response. He wanted to tell her that this was all because of her, all *for* her, but if she knew what he was she would flee him just as Callista had fled Sandsa. Kuja didn't want to lose a single day of the weeks they had left, for any reason.

What would you like to do for me? he asked, making sure to mask his familiar voice with the sounds of leaves sighing and branches creaking.

'Bagara,' Fei whispered and fell to her knees. 'Oh. Um. I don't know. Whatever you want.'

You shouldn't make that offer, he advised her. *Make one that means something to you. All of this is pointless if you blindly follow me. I am not the Creator God.*

Fei nibbled her lip for a moment. 'Could I…keep spreading the word on the Web? I'm into tech so that's what I can do. I'd like to do that. That's my offer. I think.'

You're sure?

The smile on her face grew and grew, until it looked as though it would ring its way around to the back of her head. 'No. And yes. I'm just…so happy that you gave us a choice. And your people seem nice. And you'd tell me if I was doing something wrong, right? Right?'

He let her hear his laugh. *Of course.*

Fei chuckled along with him, though she might have only done so from nerves.

He bade her farewell, adding, *I hope you can always find answers here, Feiscina Neron, even if it isn't your permanent home.*

Fei's parting words followed him. 'I wish I could stay here forever.'

Kuja managed to address seven hundred and twenty-six other mortals by the time Fei's footfalls reached Bagath. He reformed his body behind the gate then jogged out to meet her. She stopped and turned her smile onto him, gushing about her experience and how she was going to share it with the villagers.

Deciding he'd rather her think about Kuja instead of Bagara, he encircled her with his arms and lifted her off her feet. Fei yipped in surprise, then coiled her legs around his waist as he carried her towards the showers. He nibbled his way along her collarbone and, briefly distracted, tripped on the uneven ground. Vines erupted from the soil to anchor him but Fei didn't notice; she was too busy throwing back her head and gasping. She had definitely liked him suckling on the tense muscle that ran down from her neck to the back of her shoulder.

'Kuja...' she managed weakly. 'How are you doing that...just to my neck?'

'Not sure but I'm enjoying your response,' he whispered against her skin.

Once the door of the showers slid shut behind them, he set her down, preparing to remove her clothes, but her fingers were quicker. Yanking his shirt up over his head and trapping his arms in the fabric, Fei bent over and captured a nipple in her mouth. Her eyes — royal blue today — peered up at him, curious at first, then downright mischievous as Kuja groaned and stumbled, his back slamming into the open frame of the locker behind him. Any pain he felt vanished when she began kissing his other nipple, her finger darting over the one she had already lathered, working the moisture around the pale brown bead that demanded more and more attention.

Just as he was starting to lose himself in the pleasant sensations she was giving him, Fei dropped into a crouch, pulling his pants down to his knees. Then her delicious mouth got to work, leaving a damp trail on the inside of his thigh. Kuja held his breath, waiting — and then she was on the other leg, driving him mad as she repeated the process.

'*Fei...*' he rasped.

'Something you want, Kuja?' she asked innocently.

His answer was lost in appreciative moans as her kisses travelled upwards again. Then, just as her mouth closed over one of his low-hanging sacks, two of her fingers grazed the fleshy part halfway between his interested member and his backside. Kuja jolted, banging his head against the locker. He attempted to say something, he wasn't sure what, but then she engulfed him, disrupting what precious little concentration he had left.

Anyone who needed Bagara right now would just have to wait.

Fei's tongue began to flick over a sensitive part of his shaft that was an inch or so from the tip. This sent hot sparks shooting down into his toes, forcing them to curl up against the tiles. When his knees weakened, his vines were quick to ask him if he needed their assistance to hold him up, or if he wanted them to hold *her* up so that he could slide himself inside her —

Fei jumped up and tore off towards the dormant jets in the shower area, throwing her clothes over her shoulder as she went. Kuja attempted to follow her but tripped over his pants and crashed onto the tiles. Muttering under his breath, he picked himself up and pulled impatiently at the fabric imprisoning him.

When he finally descended into the shower area, Fei stepped towards him, her concern bleeding onto her face. This took her away from the spray of water that had already claimed her; the wiry pink patch of hair between her legs was dusted with fine droplets.

Kuja stared at her, entranced by the beauty of the woman who stood before him, the woman who had inspired a god to do more than sit around and moan about how unfair the Ine was.

Fei glanced down at her body and self-consciously crossed her arms over her breasts. 'What is it? You're looking at me strangely and, well, it's flattering but also really weird. So, um, Kuja...would you just get over here before I start thinking there's something wrong with me?'

Kuja held his arms out wide, offering himself for her inspection as he advanced on her, his member lengthening with each step. The tightness of his balls and the excitement pounding inside his chest made it very hard not to lunge across the space between them and devour her. All of her. And all at once.

'You are wonderful, Fei,' he said softly. 'And no matter how long I live, this time we've had together will be the best few weeks of my life.'

There, there was the small, evil grin that reminded him of Finara when the fire goddess was up to something. Fei lifted her arms from her chest and arched her back, stretching towards the jet. Her breasts rose with the motion and her nipples jutted out even more, an irresistible lure.

'Better make some good memories now then,' Fei baited.

Kuja surged forward and kissed her, snagging her wrists in

the process and holding them against her abdomen. He backed her towards the tiled wall, one hand maintaining his grip on her while the other slid down between her legs. Though the jet overhead encased them in warmth and moisture, she felt so much hotter and wetter to his touch.

'That feels nice,' Fei breathed. 'And it'll probably feel *very* nice soon, but...'

'I know exactly what you want,' he murmured into her lips.

'Oh, do you? Prove it.'

Smirking, Kuja knelt before her, watching her teal eyes follow him down to the floor. He wasn't sure if he had ever seen her true eye colour — but that didn't matter right now, because her eyelids slammed shut the moment his tongue whisked along one side of her labia. Kuja kept to the edges of her sex, teasing out the impatient moans until she begged him for more.

His tongue pressed inside her, gently at first, but then he began to pump it in and out, seeking the saltiness that the water threatened to remove. Delight rained over her features but he was too busy to watch her take her pleasure; instead he drank it in, tasting it, swallowing the heat of her until she cried out his name.

Shuddering, Fei sank into his waiting arms. Kuja arranged them so that they were both half-sitting, half-lying against the wall.

After a minute or so, Fei's hand slid up his thigh. 'You're still hard, Kuja. I can deal with that.'

'I am sure it will subside any moment now,' Kuja said with a shrug. 'And I would much rather hold you. Then I will wash you. Very thoroughly.'

Fei released a sigh. Kuja would have mistaken it for one of

contentment, but she was stiff, unresponsive, and he could feel how upset she was.

'What's wrong?' he asked.

Fei turned an anguished look back at him. 'It's just...I haven't done what I'm supposed to do. If I did, it would help me feel like...like I hadn't disappointed you.'

'Fei,' he said, keeping inside his own mind and giving her some privacy; he never doubted that her true thoughts would make it onto her lips, 'what is it you want?'

'I want to make you feel the way I do right now,' she said, an uncertain scratch of a smile appearing.

'And how's that?' he whispered.

'Spent, sated, but still wanting more...'

Kuja held up a hand to silence her. The leafy fronds outside the showers were reporting that they had just been crushed beneath the boots of a certain Dr Lorena Hackett.

Kuja groaned. 'Someone's coming.'

'Someone already came,' Fei said playfully.

Kuja burst out laughing and only just managed to stand both of them up before Lorena entered the building. By the time the scientist descended the two short steps to join them, Kuja was soaping up his shoulders a respectable distance from Fei, who kept sneaking grins at him while wiping the same spot on her abdomen multiple times.

'I run into all sorts of people here,' Kuja said as he began edging his way back to the lockers.

Fei cast a quick look at Lorena, then said, 'I hope we run into each other again and again. And again.' She paused. 'And again?'

Grinning broadly, Kuja left the shower area and retrieved his clothes, Fei not far behind him. A jet was still running, but he knew Lorena hadn't come in here to get clean. The nearby ferns were quite insistent that she had been watching the building for several minutes before making her way over.

Without a single glance at each other, Kuja and Fei quickly dressed then passed through the exit with several paces between them. Kuja's crotch ached a little less now, though he wondered just how long he would have to put up with the lingering discomfort this time.

'Are you going somewhere again?' Fei asked quietly.

Kuja took her hand and squeezed it. 'Just down to the laboratory. It's Gerns' last official day of working for TerraCorp and I wanted to be there to welcome her to Bagath. The villagers just finished constructing her hut.'

'I'll come with you,' Fei said. 'Gerns needs all the company she can get. This has been really hard on her and I still feel like it's my fau — '

Master! The other one is following you! cried a shingbat swinging from a nearby branch.

Kuja bit the inside of his cheek and turned to see Lorena carving her way towards them, smashing aggrieved insects beneath her boots as she went. Kuja managed a cordial greeting when she planted herself barely two paces from him. Fei remained silent; she was wary from her past dealings with the scientist. Dr Hackett was noticeably brusque in Fei's memories.

'What's the deal, Kuja?' Lorena demanded. 'I practically threw myself at you and now you're hanging around with this programmer?'

'You do not want to have this conversation with me,' Kuja warned her.

Lorena swung her blazing scowl onto Fei. 'So what's she give you that I can't?'

'Maybe I actually listen to him, unlike you,' Fei retorted, then slapped a hand over her mouth, eyes wide with horror.

Barely a second later, Lorena launched herself at Fei, fists extended.

Anticipating this, Kuja did not move a single micrometre, instead asking an ancient, rotted tree on the side of the path to snag Lorena's foot with a root. It obeyed, immediately dumping the scientist onto the ground. Wheezing, Lorena pried her face out of the soil.

Kuja shook his head at her. 'Did you really think attacking Fei would make me dislike you any less?'

'But she doesn't put out, does she?' Lorena exclaimed. 'I'm right, aren't I? She hasn't spread her legs for you. I would!'

'What makes you think she's the problem?' he demanded while Lorena struggled her way out of the uncooperative undergrowth. Kuja turned back to Fei. 'Lorena should consider herself lucky that I didn't pursue her because I wouldn't give her what she wants.'

'Well, I don't care if we never have that type of sex,' Fei told him, then grinned. 'So long as you keep making me breakfast.'

'Oh, I don't actually...I...I have help.' Kuja blushed. He wasn't about to tell her that an intricate network of vines did most of the work for him, including selecting the fruit and arranging it. The tea was the one thing he did make, because he'd often prepared it for his mother when she'd still been alive.

'You shouldn't admit that,' Fei told him, smirking.

His hand still in hers, Kuja led her down the path towards the new lab, doing his best to ignore Lorena's parting words as they were shouted at his back. The scientist was particularly mean about Fei, which Kuja thought unfair because he had been the one to reject Lorena.

Can I, Master? Please? begged the old decrepit tree.

Oh alright, Kuja allowed.

He managed not to chuckle when Lorena tripped again.

Gerns, who had just exited the plastic tube that formed the laboratory's exit, was not so immune.

CHAPTER SEVENTEEN

Fei leaned over the edge of the bed, searching for her techpad which had dropped onto the ground at some point the night before — she'd happily been too busy to retrieve it then. She slowly exaggerated the curve of her backside as she reached for the device, acutely aware of Kuja watching her; he seemed to enjoy the view, judging by the low sound he made in his throat. Looking back over her shoulder, Fei saw the interested bulge in his pants and decided there was no point in retrieving the techpad. Its screen was dark anyway, which meant she had forgotten to place it near the charge emitter.

Fei swallowed, moistening her mouth, gathering her courage. 'You want to take those pants off, Kuja?'

'Fei...' he began.

'Before you say anything,' she charged on, 'I'm not doing this because I feel like I owe you — it's because I want to. Get it? I want to.'

'And does it matter what I want?' he asked, still lounging against the bed.

Fei glared at him as his grin continued to stretch, dimpling his cheeks. 'Of course it does, but I...I know you want to try, to see if it'll work with me. Don't ask me how, I just know. And I'm not above spanking you and I know you'd enjoy that. Probably. Maybe.'

'Definitely,' Kuja agreed in a husky voice.

'Or I could surrender to you again,' Fei mused. 'I'm feeling a bit greedy this morning and I doubt you'll mind indulging me...'

Kuja's hands, which had been lying flat on his stomach, began to creep lower, toward his belt. Tsking in disapproval, Fei rolled over and pincered his wrists, pinning them at his sides. She lowered her mouth to his, withholding the kiss his lips were already preparing for, and whispered, 'Now I will have to spank you.'

He opened his mouth to respond, then abruptly jerked upright, trying to wriggle out of her grasp. He only managed it just as Gerns' large bulk barrelled through the door. The Jezlo woman had wasted no time in shedding TerraCorp's sterile white uniform and had replaced it with a brightly coloured sarong woven from seaweed fibres harvested on her homeworld. It was a startling but flattering look for Gerns.

Fei glanced back at Kuja who was now sitting up, one knee raised above the other, skilfully hiding his desire.

How does he always know when there's someone around? she wondered.

Gerns looked grim as she held out a techpad. Hers wasn't dark; it glowed ominously, filling the hut with intrusive light. 'Your techpad and communicator both off, Fei? TerraCorp just contacted me in order to reach you.'

'But you resigned,' Fei said, leaving the bed to intercept the device from Gerns' tentacle.

'They know I'm still here. They also told me that I shouldn't even try to talk to my former colleagues — nice, aren't they?' Gerns' tentacles trembled with agitation. 'Now to me, that's no surprise, but what is surprising is that them down at the lab seem to be packing up. They can't be anywhere near done.'

'What does TerraCorp want from Fei?' Kuja asked. He moved forward to stand beside Fei, a warm hand wrapped around her waist.

The techpad, balanced in Fei's unsteady palm, began to wobble as she read through the text on the screen. Even though Moz's voice was not attached to the words, she could still hear him, still see him looming over her in the darkness of the basement.

Feiscina,

I realise I am cutting your holiday short, but an urgent matter has arisen. Our 'friends' have requested that we change the parameters in your most recent simulation and transform Yalsa 5 into an exclusively water-based world. As this must be done on short notice, we need you to return to work immediately. A starship will be waiting for you at the spaceport within a day.

Please note that TerraCorp will no longer be offering rainforest climes to our clients.

Mozel Zan

'Don't you have more than one programmer working at TerraCorp?' Gerns asked.

'Yes, yes, we do have more,' Fei murmured, re-reading Moz's message. 'But they're not as good as me. I think. Or maybe some of them actually have a way of saying no to Moz. I seem to be the only one incapable of turning down overtime.'

Kuja pressed his lips to Fei's temple. 'It's alright, Fei. You can say no. I will help you write a response.'

'Writing I don't have a problem with,' Fei said, lowering the techpad. It was shaking so badly she could no longer focus on the words. 'It's talking I can't do! And I can never stand up for myself when I really need to. Oh God, this isn't right — none of it's right!'

'Those *friends* would be them GLEA agents, yes?' Gerns clarified.

'Can't you send a message to the people on Yalsa 5 and warn them?' Kuja added.

Fei felt something hot hook her insides and twist. 'But would Yalsa 5's governor believe me? Some disembodied person throwing text at him? No, I'd have to...have to *talk* to him...oh God.' She shook her head frantically. 'But why a whole water world? Can't GLEA make up their mind about how they want to ruin Yalsa 5? The planet is a sandy wasteland, with nothing substantial between surface and bedrock — throwing an ocean on that would take away any topography, not to mention drown Atsa City because it's in a basin!'

'You told me that GLEA is concerned about the powers the Desine's followers wield and how they can make the Agency look bad,' Kuja reminded her. 'That explains their aversion to deserts. Could there be a similar reason for refusing to offer rainforests to their future clients?'

'Well, it's just something a mediaist said but he...' Fei trailed off. 'Oh. Bagara's message. It went viral. With my help. And oh my God, it's all my fault. GLEA now sees Bagara as a threat, because they know they could lose followers to him. The governor deserves to hear this from me. But how do I tell him? How!?'

Gerns trundled over and retrieved the techpad before it fell out of Fei's hands. Wrapping the object safely inside a tentacle, the Jezlo said, 'Open your mouth. Talk. The governor's got to listen, given it'll destroy his city, not to mention the whole starking planet.'

'I always sound so stupid when I try to say things,' Fei argued, her shoulders sagging. She felt like a plant that had been uprooted and thrown onto soil that could not possibly support it.

'Are you sure?' Kuja asked her. 'Or did your boss and other people in your life make you feel that way because they didn't listen when they should have?'

'That's not...' Fei said weakly.

Gerns slanted a look between the pair of them. 'Kuja, go with her. Fei's bound to end up out of a job the way she's going and that's no bad thing, but you seem to have a way of helping her out. Like you did at the festival.'

Fei bowed her head. 'Kuja. You're my voice. Please. Please come with me.'

She couldn't bear to look at his face, in case she saw something different to what she was so sure she was reading straight from his heart.

***

Watching both of them with his human eyes, Kuja sank his awareness into countless rainforests, checking in on those calling out for him and assisting them. He knew this must have given him that distant expression Fei liked to make fun of, but it had to be done; he could not abandon his duties. And while he would obviously love to spend more time in Fei's company...

If Fayay sees us together, he will get the wrong idea and assume there is a danger of her distracting me, Kuja agonised. I can't protect her against one sibling, let alone all of them.

But though Yalsa 5 was now much less dangerous than it had been before its current reigning gang had taken power, Kuja could not bear the thought of losing Fei the same way he had lost his mother — the same way he had nearly lost Sandsa when his brother had lived as a mortal in Atsa City.

There was no stopping Fei. She badly wanted to go; it was flowing off her in waves.

This made it easy, far too easy, to justify it to himself. *If Yalsa 5 really intends on gaining rainforests through terraforming, they will become one of my worlds. I can't wait for that to happen. They need my protection now. And Fei needs my help, especially if we have to convince a ship's captain to go somewhere other than Enoc.*

'It seems we will be taking a hopper out to the spaceport tomorrow,' Kuja said, but that was as far as he got before Fei seized him in a brief, searing kiss. When she drew back, he turned to Gerns. 'Fei won't always need me to help her find her voice. She has important work to do for Bagara and this is just the start of it.'

'A few days ago, now me, I would have disagreed with all of this,' Gerns remarked. 'But I said this to myself, I said, "Gerns, you can't call them crazy when you've also signed your sorry self up to help this Bagara". Now I just gotta wait and see how.'

Fei veered away from them and began throwing her things into the small bag she had brought with her to Bagaran. 'We need to do more than *react*, Gerns! Bagara said he'd be there for the casualties, but that's not preventative! If I do this, I can help people before they need saving.'

'Good luck shutting her up now,' Gerns advised Kuja and left the hut, clucking to herself.

Kuja felt a smile tweak his lips as he thought about all the ways he had managed to silence Fei so far.

Fei froze suddenly, looking stricken. 'Kuja, what if GLEA doesn't stop with Yalsa 5? What if they want to destroy all the deserts and rainforests in the galaxy because they feel threatened by the sub-level gods? What if they come here next?'

Kuja knew his expression must have darkened into something terrifying because she backed away a pace, staring at him.

'Bagara won't let that happen,' Kuja said roughly.

'Do you think Bagara can fight them, though?' Fei's lips trembled. 'The Creator God is behind GLEA! And he's so much older than Bagara.'

Kuja clenched his fists. 'Older or not, the Creator God lost his right to interfere with mortals' lives when he stopped caring for them. And now it's time someone did it in his place.'

CHAPTER EIGHTEEN

Fei paced inside the antechamber of the governor's office on Yalsa 5, wringing her hands in such a familiar way that Kuja glanced down at his own. He clenched his fingers in his lap, stilling them.

The walls were coated in yellows, creams and golds and filled with artworks, though Kuja wasn't sure if they were expensive or important — the imposing frames made of precious metals suggested that they were. This was a room belonging to a wealthy and powerful man, one who had been elected to two separate positions of leadership by the factions living inside his city. To the gangs who had once torn Atsa City apart, he was their Clan Leader. To everyone else, he had a more respectable title.

'What's the governor's name?' Kuja asked, belatedly realising he should have learned this earlier.

'Bock Atsason,' Fei answered, then launched into a breathy recitation of the greeting she had prepared for the governor.

Kuja's blood crystallised inside his veins, as though Fayay had flooded him with water only for Rasson, the Iceine, to freeze every drop of it. But it was too late to do anything, because the hut-sized door slid open, admitting a suit-clad secretary wearing more lasguns than Kuja could count in one glance.

'The governor will see you now,' the secretary said, more a command than a statement of fact.

Kuja remained seated. 'I'll wait for you here, Fei.'

She spun toward him, her chocolate brown eyes wide. 'Please. I can't. You're my voice.'

'And what do I know about terraforming?' Kuja demanded, a little more brusquely than he intended. He softened his features with a self-deprecatory smile.

'I need you,' Fei pleaded. 'I've only made it this far *because* of you.'

The secretary's lips thinned and her eyes flicked back to the door, showing her impatience.

Kuja rose to his feet and brushed his palm over the side of Fei's face. 'I will be right behind you. But you don't need me or Bagara to do this. I believe in you.'

The secretary made a disgusted noise in her throat and headed for the door. Kuja and Fei duly followed and allowed themselves to be deposited inside an office larger than some villages in Kuja's domain. The ceiling swooped up and out of sight, accentuated by an arching window that made Kuja feel as though he had just stepped into an endless expanse; the window's plexiglass was so clean that there was no apparent barrier between the room and the night.

Standing in front of the light-studded backdrop of Atsa City, hands linked over his abdomen, was Governor Bock Atsason. He wasn't the man who had ended the fighting and brought peace to this world — that had been all due to Sandsa, when Kuja's brother had lived here as a mortal. But, unlike the Desine, Bock had stayed behind to rule Yalsa 5 and look after its people.

Kuja sucked in a breath, hoping Bock wouldn't recognise him. He'd only met Bock once, at Sandsa and Callista's wedding, and the governor had been a teenager then. Bock's dark hair was now streaked with silver, even though he was barely halfway into his twenties, and the sleeves of his white suit were just short enough to reveal the tattoos swarming over his skin.

He wasn't alone. Lounging in the chair behind the centred desk was a woman — dark-skinned, bald and striking. One of her eyes was artificial, its red sensor aimed directly at the pair of intruders. Whereas she looked imminently dangerous, her cheekbones sharp enough to cut flesh, Bock exuded a subtler, quiet menace.

'I suppose you can tell me why TerraCorp's sittin' on their arses and playin' with my coin-chips,' Bock began, his voice an ominous rumble, 'instead of bringing their shiny machines over here to get the job done.'

When Fei didn't respond, Kuja moved forward and took her hand in his, slowly entwining their fingers. Fei drew a shuddering breath, then forced her chin up from her chest. 'I'm a programmer at TerraCorp. I'm not meant to be here. I should just do what they tell me to do. But I can't. It's wrong.'

'You'd go against the people payin' you?' Bock's companion queried, her mechanical eye zeroing in on Fei. 'Why?'

'Well, um, when I was working on a simulation, my boss...' Fei trailed off, biting her lip.

Kuja squeezed her hand. 'You can do this.'

Fei straightened and met the governor's fierce gaze with her own. 'GLEA is funded by TerraCorp. I found this out when two agents told me I was to ignore your instructions and make a simulation that would terraform your entire planet into one giant rainforest. And now my boss is telling me to turn Yalsa 5 into an ocean world, which would destroy Atsa City. I'm not sure they were even going to warn anyone.'

'Knew those douchenozzles were up to something,' Bock said,

seemingly unsurprised. Then his frown fell on Kuja. 'Have we met?'

'Um, I don't think so,' Fei said.

'I was talkin' to your man.'

There was no point in lying. Bock's mind was sharp; he had already figured it out.

Kuja grimaced. 'Yes. At my…at my brother's wedding.'

'Well, I'll just shoot meself,' the governor said, eyes narrowed. 'Or I could ask you to get the fuck out of here before I shoot you.'

'Bock?' the woman at the desk prompted. 'We need to do something about GLEA. We can't let them drown the whole starking city.'

'Ala, get this piece of shit out of my office!' Bock exploded. He marched forward, clearing the desk, and rounded on Fei, the long scar on the side of his face stretching with his scowl. 'Did you bring him here just to mess with us?'

Kuja grabbed Fei, whose lips who were flapping open and shut as the situation disintegrated, and placed her behind him, bodily shielding her from the wrath of a man who was not only in charge of an entire city, but its gangs as well. 'No! Fei has nothing to do with what happened. Your problem is with me. And not even me — my brother!'

'You know what Sandsa did to Callista? He destroyed her!' Bock jerked a hand at the woman in the chair — Ala was her name, Kuja recalled — then back at Kuja. 'Sandsa's brother!'

Bock was now holding a lasgun on his visitors, but the governor didn't need it. His eyes alone could have burned holes right through Kuja. The rainforest god curled his fingers towards his palms, tempted to unleash his powers, but he couldn't — not with Fei right there. She was saying something, trying to get his attention, but he blocked her out, unable to face the questions she must have for him.

'Enough!' said Ala, rising to her feet. 'You're wasting time fightin' about something that don't concern either of you.'

Bock opened his mouth.

Ala glowered at him. 'Sit down, husband. I'm not here just 'cause of this pretty face.'

The governor retreated to the chair Ala had vacated and suddenly looked like a small boy, engulfed as he was by the oversized leather furniture. Kuja released his grip on Fei and she swung around to face him, her confusion evident in her thoughts and features.

'I'm so sorry, Fei,' he said. It had been hard enough for her to divert TerraCorp's chartered starship to Yalsa 5 — and he had just made things worse by leading her into a feud when she was trying to save an entire planet. 'I didn't know how to say it.'

'Say what?' Ala stepped forward. The whole room seemed to tunnel around her as she took control of it. 'Nothing to be said. Not your fault, as far as I can tell. It's true Callista has had it rough. But she did what she could in a bad situation and even if I want to beat the shit out of the person responsible, you're not him.'

Kuja swallowed, not sure how to respond. He was grateful for Ala's words, grateful that Fei could still achieve her purpose here...and immensely grateful that he wasn't Sandsa.

Ala's red eye locked onto him for several long moments, then shifted to Fei. 'Fact is, the programmer's words are worryin' me more than anything you could say. Are GLEA and TerraCorp really comin' after us?'

Fei nodded continuously, her mind blank and her lips unmoving. When she began weaving on her feet, Kuja guided her into the lounge on their side of the desk and seated Fei beside him, a hand on her thigh. Her knee bounced a few times before stilling.

'He's gonna mess up your life, so I'd ditch him if I was you,' Bock said from his chair.

Ala slammed her fists onto the table. '*Enough.* You think you're so high and mighty, Governor, but you forget who got ya here.' She spun back around to face her audience, slinging one leg over the other as she hopped onto the edge the desk and perched there. 'Ms Neron. Can you refuse to create and run the simulation?'

'I'd...I'd lose my job,' Fei whispered.

'You knew that was gonna happen before you came all this way,' Ala said, crossing her arms. 'So why are you playin' with unemployment if you're so desperate to avoid it?'

Fei's expression warred between frightened and hopeful. 'I want...I want to do the right thing. I want to ruin GLEA's plans because of what they've done. The Creator God and those blindly following him shouldn't be allowed to get away with their crimes. Not anymore.'

Ala raised her one eyebrow at Kuja. 'Just what the stark are you doing with this girl? She's too good for you, ya douchenozzle.'

'I happen to agree with her,' Kuja replied. 'The gods have a lot to answer for, even the sub-level ones.'

Bock made a lewd comment about Kuja cavorting with sand lizards. Kuja frowned. He wished the governor had at least used an insult relating to his domain and not the Desine's.

Ala quietened her husband with a single glance, then said to Kuja, 'Callista's alright. If you wanted to know.'

'Is she here?' Kuja asked, glancing around even though he

knew Callista and her son would not appear simply because he bid them.

'No,' Ala said flatly. 'Callista travels a lot. To avoid that starkin' brother of yours, no doubt.'

'Is she happy?' was his next question.

Ala snorted. 'Happy? I doubt Ms Neron here'll be happy when she throws away her job just to impress ya. I want to make sure she's doin' it for the right reasons.'

Fei peered at Kuja, desperation hollowing her cheeks.

He shook his head, staying silent. *This is your moment, Fei. I can't always be there for you. Because...because if I do, they will see you as a threat to Father's grand design. They will come after you. And they will kill you.*

Not for the first time, Kuja was glad that Fei did not have the same mind-reading powers that Callista had. She would have read the truth from him within moments and — she would have hated him forever. He couldn't bear the thought of that.

Fei drew out her sigh. 'Fine. I guess it sounds better coming from me anyway. I'm doing this because I'm the only one who can. I'm doing this because it *has to be done*. I'm not doing it for Kuja; he's inspired me, that's all. Him and his god.'

Bock burst out laughing, then smothered his mouth with a hand when Ala shot him a look. Kuja shifted uncomfortably. Clearly they both knew exactly what he was; Callista must have told them.

Fei scowled. 'This isn't something you should be laughing about, Governor. Is risking my job going to come to nothing or do you actually care about saving lives?'

'He cares,' Ala said immediately. 'He just doesn't have all the brains. I'm the one who got him elected as both Clan Leader *and* governor, ha! Alright, what do we do? It's not like there are any galactic courts we can take them to. Good thing too; GLEA'd probably run the starkin' things.'

'We could just cancel the job, get a refund,' Bock piped up, fingers steepled beneath his chin.

'TerraCorp might just say that GLEA is their client and do it anyway,' Fei said, sighing.

Ala shook her head. 'Nah, they'll have problems with goin' that route. GLEA won't want to be seen throwing around that many coin-chips when they're supposed to only get donations.'

'But TerraCorp will claim client anonymity or some shit, to cover their arses,' Bock said with a snarl. 'We're in for a fight. Might even get physical.'

Fei worried her lips together for a moment. 'I think I can make it an even fight. We won't even need lasguns. We just need the Web.'

'Oh?' Bock looked curious, his previous anger deserting him.

'We're going to expose TerraCorp for what it is,' Fei went on, eyes shining. 'We're going to tell the galaxy. I can make it go viral. And then no one will want to deal with them *or* pay them.'

Bock nodded approvingly. 'I like it. Hit 'em where it hurts — their bank accounts.'

'People will still hire them anyway,' Ala pointed out. 'The galaxy's not gonna believe us just 'cause we said something on the Web.'

'But we have to try,' Fei insisted. 'At the very least, it will make their activities look suspicious. And maybe it'll discourage some people from donating to the Chippers.'

Bock trickled his fingers over the desk. 'So you're okay with losing your cushy job, huh?'

'Yes,' Fei said without hesitation.

'Might as well pay you then, since you're now workin' for us,' Bock mused.

Kuja enjoyed the smile that exploded over Fei's features.

'Good, that's settled.' Ala stood from the desk and made her way over to the door. 'I'm gonna go take our girlfriend out on a date. I'm late enough as it is.'

'I thought it was my turn with Ginsella,' Bock said.

Ala chortled. 'Check your schedule. It's not my starkin' job to keep track of your appointments. But, if you're good, maybe you'll find me in your bed later.'

Then she was gone.

Fei blinked. 'Governor, you and Ala...um...'

Kuja was also staring. He couldn't help it.

Bock shrugged, apparently unbothered by their reactions. 'This kind of marriage takes a lot of sharin' and a lot of talkin', two things I'm not actually terrible at. Now shut up for a moment. I have to check my schedule.'

CHAPTER NINETEEN

'Why didn't you tell me the governor would have a problem with you?' Fei asked as soon as she and Kuja were encased inside the silver hovercar that Bock had chartered to take them to a private apartment. 'I'd have let you stay in the antechamber, like you wanted.'

Outside the gleaming windows the city flashed by, full of blurred lights and flitting shadows — the hovercar was moving far too quickly for Fei to focus on anything. Their driver had explained, to Fei's interest, that no private vehicles were allowed on the streets after dark unless they belonged to the gang rostered on to look after the city for that night. Public transportation abounded instead, easily identifiable from specific markings on the doors.

Kuja slid his hand along Fei's thigh, his warm touch evoking a shudder of pleasure. 'I didn't realise the governor would recognise me until too late. And you still needed me.'

'It's a good thing Bock hates GLEA more than he does your brother,' Fei said.

'I'm glad Ala was there or he wouldn't have accepted our help,' Kuja murmured in response.

Nodding fervently, Fei leaned back against the seat. She could tell the fabric wasn't made of leather because it didn't stick to her hands when she planted them beneath her backside to keep them from roaming onto Kuja's body. She didn't want an audience for the things she planned to do to him tonight — and most hovercars had vidcams aimed at the back seat so drivers could keep an eye on their passengers.

'I suppose even planetary rulers need someone at their shoulder,' Fei mused. 'Someone to keep them from doing and saying stupid things. And to give them strength.'

'Does that make you feel better about needing me?'

'How did you know I was thinking that? How do you *always* know?' Fei wondered. 'Well. I can't expect you to stay with me for the rest of your life. Because this was just supposed to be a bit of fun, wasn't it.'

Kuja looked away from her, his lips firmly sealed. The driver coughed and announced that they would be arriving at the apartment building in about a minute, an unnecessary pronouncement but Fei felt grateful for it all the same. It had filled the awkward silence.

The moment the hovercar slowed, she slid over the seat and popped the door open before the driver could make it around to her side of the vehicle. She grinned when he muttered something about being about as useful as a lasgun drained of its charge, then ducked over to kiss his cheek. His mood immediately brightened and there was a bounce in his step as he escorted her to the foyer doors, Kuja trailing behind them.

Once the driver had returned to his vehicle, Kuja gained access to the building's foyer with a keypass Bock had given him, then guided Fei into the dark shadows beside the hoverlift, enveloping her in his embrace. His kisses began beneath her jaw before fluttering over to her earlobe, sending shivers racing through her. Then, when she parted her lips, he obeyed her unspoken command and claimed her mouth with heat and freshwater. She drank thirstily, wanting to drown in him.

But then his mouth darted away from hers. 'I can't see you again after you tonight. I'd like to...but I can't.'

Fei blinked back tears. She'd *known* this was coming, but hearing it spoken was even worse than she'd expected. 'I wish you could stay. And not just for, you know, sex stuff. It's...you being in the same room as me makes me feel like I can conquer the entire galaxy. And everyone listens to me. Everyone.'

Kuja's hands framed her face as he delivered a gentle kiss to her forehead. 'Just imagine me standing behind you, a little out of sight, and you will feel me.'

'That's not enough,' Fei muttered, leaning her cheek against his chest. 'It'll never be enough.'

Though Kuja's heartbeat was steady and unhurried beneath her ear, there was a sense of urgency to his voice. 'Please, Fei, this night is all I can give you. So take it.'

'If this is our last night together then I'd like to have you inside me,' she told him.

Kuja brushed her mauve hair out of her face. 'I'd like to try that. With you. Only you.'

Fei bit her lip as an impulsive thought occurred to her; she had to quickly bury it beneath her desire for him so that it wouldn't leak its way through her mind and then escape onto her tongue.

She was too weird to ever find another man and this perfect one was insistent on leaving her behind. If there was even a small chance that he might leave a part of himself with her, then she wanted it. All she had to do was duck into a bathroom and remove the implant she used for birth control. The lingering effects of the implant might stop anything from happening, but she was so full of hope she was sure her plan would work. It had to.

'Let's make it memorable,' Fei whispered. 'I might not remember all the things we did together, but I want to remember this night at least.'

But she would remember. She would remember everything.

Without another word, Kuja pulled her into the waiting hoverlift. Before the doors had even closed he was pressing her against the side, darkness shielding his hands as they slipped beneath her shirt, moulding against her breasts. He kneaded, he teased — and then he shoved the fabric aside to capture one of her nipples with a kiss. Fei gasped and tilted her head back against the plexiglass panelling that curved up and around, giving her an unobstructed view of the starry infinity stretching above her.

Her fingers found the trail of hair on his abdomen then skimmed further, past his belt, to cup him through his pants. His ensuing growl against her neck caused shock waves that began in her chest before plummeting down between her legs. Fei cried out and her hips jolted against him. Kuja had to hold her still as she laughed and laughed, slapping his shoulders.

'Kuja!' she said, grinning. 'You didn't even touch me there. And I still came.'

'Just getting started, Fei,' he promised.

The hoverlift drifted to a stop so Fei wrestled him away from her, trying to straighten her clothes, then wondered why she'd bothered when the doors opened directly into a penthouse apartment. Kuja hurled his shirt and pants onto the floor before advancing on her, his gaze hungry and impatient. He was slower and more romantic about divesting her of her own clothes; he kissed his way along each line of skin that appeared as he stripped away the barriers between them. Fei back-pedalled once he was done, mumbled an excuse and launched herself into the bathroom to deal with the implant.

When she emerged two minutes later, he carried her to a large, rounded bed smothered with silksein sheets. Kuja threw himself down beside her and she took a moment to admire his naked form, thrilled by the desire on his face as he returned the favour.

You are mine, she thought.

'Eternally yours,' he whispered.

Fei giggled, realising she must have spoken aloud, though she couldn't remember doing so. She leaned over and kissed his chin, then let her lips wander down to each of his nipples. He almost jerked upright when she claimed the first one, but she made sure to shove him back down onto the bed, covering his body with hers.

'I keep having this fantasy involving you,' Fei told him.

'Do...tell,' he gasped as she nibbled his shoulder.

'I imagine that we're out by that waterfall we both love.' She began teasing her tongue along his collarbone. 'I'm lying beside it, naked, the moisture licking its way over me.'

He groaned. The member hardening against her thigh shifted, its wet tip grazing her skin.

'Then the rainforest comes alive,' she continued, her lips now coasting up his neck. 'And the vines wrap around my wrists, trapping me there. I cannot move. I am completely at your mercy. And you definitely take advantage of that.'

Kuja's eyes rolled to the back of his head and his cock twitched. Fei glanced down at it, surprised. As she watched, it spasmed again.

'You are doing that on purpose!' she accused.

'I am...*not*,' he said, then fell against the pillows when it happened once more. 'Ah, ah. Fei, I'm yours. Do what you will with me. I think I'll go soft very shortly and I would rather you...rather you got what you wanted before then.'

Fei wrapped her hands around his shaft and squeezed gently. He leaked over her fingers, coating them with his desire. She wanted a lot more than her own pleasure. And she was determined to get it this time.

'Tonight I will give you what has been denied you for so long,' she vowed, gazing down at him. He looked magnificent like this, splayed out before her, the copper hair on his chest shivering with each ragged breath he drew. The power she had over him made her feel dizzy and she sagged to the side for a moment, resting her forehead in her hand.

'Fei?' he whispered.

I don't want him to know that I...I...

'I'm sorry,' he said, fingers trailing over her cheek. 'I'm sorry I can't be there for you. It's killing me. But please. Let me give you something that was denied *you*.'

'And what's that?' she asked softly.

'The freedom to enjoy yourself without fearing the consequences.'

Fei's heart constricted briefly. But then she allowed herself to release her thoughts and her fears, and forgot that Yalsa 5's star would rise to bathe her in light and reality. Tonight she had Kuja. Tonight he was hers.

Holding his gaze, she positioned his hard length between her hands, then wrapped her intimate lips around the head of him. When he pleaded for more, Fei indulged him and sank further down his shaft, engulfing as much as his member as she could. He was large and wide and felt *so starking good* inside her.

'Feiii...' Kuja groaned.

Fei bent over him, her hands clasped to his wrists. 'You will stay hard, or I will find a way to punish you.'

'Whatever...whatever you want,' he rasped, seemingly incapable of arguing.

Fei began to move, slowly at first, adjusting to the feel of him inside her. After she had given him several long, torturous strokes, Kuja's hands twisted beneath her own and he lunged forward, latching onto a nipple and making her cry out, 'Kuja! This'll be over way too soon if you keep doing that!'

He laughed and did it again. Fei sat back on him, forming a T-shape, hands on her hips. He offered her a guilty smile, though his green eyes were hopeful and bright.

Fei smacked the side of his rump, causing him to jolt up inside her.

'Behave,' she ordered.

Kuja went very still.

Fei rewarded him by moving faster; each small ensuing pulse of his hardness caused even more desire to swoop through her. Fei bit her lip as she bobbed up and down on him, trying to hold back, but it didn't take long — moans escaped her as she squeezed and tightened around him.

Desperate for more, Fei pumped him more vigorously, the room feeling as steamy as the air beneath the canopy of the rainforest on Bagaran. She began to gasp for breath as waves of intense pleasure continued to wash over her, weakening the knees that she had braced against his hips.

When she could finally see more than sparks, she stared

down at Kuja, wordless. She'd never had an orgasm last that long, never felt this way with Zareth, never felt this comfortable...

'I'm here. Not him.' Kuja's voice cut into her thoughts. 'And you are absolutely gorgeous when you're riding me.'

He offered her a smile, but it was a mask. Fei couldn't explain how she knew this; she just did. He was worried that she was upset, worried that she needed him, worried that he'd be unable to leave. Because he felt too much for her. She could feel it too, in her heart — the love swelling between them, far more potent than the pleasure she had taken from him.

He loves me. He loves me.

'I love you,' he echoed. 'Father help me, I love you.'

Fei laughed and wiped the tears from her eyes. 'I love you too, Kuja. Now shut up and let me show you what you're going to be missing out on for the rest of your life.'

When Fei licked his nipple, he begged her to do it again, the strain in his voice revealing just how close he was. He was growing inside her, so much so she was afraid he would hit her cervix. She squirmed on him, startled and anxious, but then she saw the adoration filling his half-lidded eyes.

He pulsed once more — and then exploded, releasing a hot burst that wrenched a startled groan from her. The sound that escaped his mouth was even more primitive and guttural. He shuddered for several seconds, eyes squeezed shut, his back arching off the bed. When at last he was limp beneath her, Fei reluctantly slid off him. He felt *amazing*.

And she felt wonderful and beautiful and loved and...

'You are all of these things,' Kuja said, stroking her back as she smiled giddily across the hair-dusted plane of his chest. 'You always will be.'

'I feel greedy for saying this, but I want more,' she admitted.

He obliged her immediately. Two fingers glided down to her dripping core, swirling around her clitoris while his thumb dipped inside her. She wriggled, her body almost too sensitive beneath his touch, but then suddenly discomfort faded into interest. Soon she was gasping, pleading, begging. And he kept at it, driving her mad. When she felt the first twinges, she opened her mouth to warn him — but before she could say a word, a wave of intense relief hit her abdomen and she spurted against his hand, a small puddle forming beneath her buttocks.

'Don't be sorry,' he said when she tried to apologise. 'I loved sharing that with you.'

Kuja's weight and warmth left the bed, causing her to subside into the soft sheets. Bereft, she made a soft, disgruntled sound — but within moments he was back, gently patting a towel over her thighs and across her still quivering mound, sending tiny shocks shooting through her. He lifted her hips and set the towel under her, then pulled her against his slick chest.

'I didn't think I would be able to finish,' Kuja mused. 'I wonder why it worked this time.'

'Probably because you love me,' Fei said with a smirk. 'You can't take that back. I've got it in my memories forever.'

Kuja combed his hand through her hair, winding some of the mauve strands around his fingers. 'And I will feel it forever.'

'I still don't know why you have to leave.' She didn't care that she whined when she said this. 'Is it something to do with why your brother couldn't stay with his wife?'

'You are exceptionally clever,' he murmured. 'And I should feel the appropriate amount of dismay that your guess is far too close for my liking.'

'But?'

He chuckled. 'It just makes me love you more.'

'If you love me then you'll tell me why I can't have amazing sex for the rest of my life,' Fei said, curving her palm over his chest. 'Please, Kuja?'

Kuja's face creased as he disappeared inside his thoughts. She knew the moment he relented; her heart sang before he even opened his mouth. 'I will try to say as much as I can without endangering you. There are people who...would not be pleased to know that I have found someone who could distract me from my duties.'

Fei blinked. 'Duties? Kuja, you live in a hut. And Lilliean and the other Bagathians don't seem to mind us being together.'

'I'm not talking about them,' he said, his frown deepening. 'I meant my family. The situation...I used to think it was because everyone obeyed my father in everything, but now I think they were jealous. My brother found love but the others couldn't stand it, couldn't stand that he was brave enough to seek what they wanted. They threatened the lives of his family to bring him back into line. Callista left him because she could not handle it.'

'And what if I decide I can handle it?' Fei demanded.

Kuja visibly gritted his teeth. 'Even if you could, I'm afraid that if I stay with you I won't be able to...to do my job.'

'That's stupid,' Fei argued. 'Plenty of people can work and have a family at the same time. Well, maybe not my father, but my mother managed it and she had two jobs! And I can do long distance; Bagaran isn't that far from here. Ugh, you know what — your family is seriously messed up and I'm going to have a word to them about it.'

'Fei...I can't protect you from them. They would tear you apart.'

'They're tearing us apart and I'm not sure that's any worse.'

'I agree,' Kuja muttered. His next words sounded like a warning. 'If I could stay, I'd ask nothing less than eternity from you.'

'And I'd give it,' Fei said. 'It'd make me extremely happy if I could die in your arms.'

'I am talking about eternity, which outlasts death.'

'Then I'd be just as happy to have you forever. So long as the sex remains this good.'

His laugh ended almost as soon as it began, his body shaking with the effort of suppressing sobs. Fei kissed his temple and made shhh-shhh sounds — until she remembered that she hated those and instead mumbled what she hoped were soothing phrases. Kuja eventually calmed down enough to speak. 'I'd like to stay beside you. Forever. Loving you, raising a family with you — that is *my* fantasy. I wish...' He sighed. 'I wish I could protect you. *But I can't.*'

Fei shivered. She believed him. But she didn't want to waste what time they had left by dwelling on what couldn't be. So she distracted them both from their dark thoughts by running her hands over his nude form. When he hardened again, both of them were surprised, but Fei was more than happy to take advantage of this. Before she could, however, Kuja took charge and rolled her beneath him, easing his way into her moist folds and claiming her, body and soul.

Later, when exhaustion weighed down on both of them, Fei entwined her limbs with his, trying to lock him into place. He didn't fight her, just gazed at her sorrowfully. It should have been impossible to follow him into his mind, but she knew exactly what he was thinking. He was worried and upset, remembering the loss of another woman.

Fei could picture this woman exactly, could even hear her voice. This was his mother, the one who had given him kindness and love and had taught him to embrace the emotions that made him so vulnerable.

I'm just dreaming, hallucinating even, Fei told herself, blinking away the images. But they were so real, so tangible, she couldn't have made them up.

Does love let you see into someone else's thoughts? she wondered. *Or is this something else?*

***

When Kuja roused from his doze he was startled, because as a god he didn't actually need to sleep. Gingerly, trying not to wake Fei, he used his powers to teleport out from beneath her steely grip and began looking for his clothes. He winced; there were spectacular aches running throughout his body, most notably in his arms which were unused to holding himself up over someone. His skin still tingled and he felt sticky but more sated than he had ever been in his entire life. He could not imagine why a god would want to stay in an insubstantial form when they could experience *that.*

He paused, his pants slack in his hand as he remembered that Fei had felt his mind as surely as he could feel hers. Strange — she didn't have any mind-reading abilities that he was aware of. How then had she known what he was thinking before and during the throes of ecstasy? If she did have powers of some sort, then that was another reason to avoid her, in case she was a trap cunningly designed by his father to teach him some sort of lesson.

Kuja held in the groan. He couldn't think these things now, not when she had given him so much pleasure and love. She deserved better than his suspicion.

He slipped into his clothes, painfully aware that he needed to leave, but that didn't mean he couldn't spend half an hour sitting in a chair beside the bed, watching the woman he loved slumber without him. Even though she was unconscious, Kuja could still sense her inside his mind, like the ever-present whirr of an insect hiding in a thicket. Some people might have found that sensation irritating. He enjoyed it.

Kuja stood. He couldn't pursue this connection between them, no matter how badly he wanted to. It would be safer for her if he left. So he did, walking from one world to the next, appearing on Bagaran in a vortex of greens and browns. Tormented, pursued by both her scent and her soul, Kuja ran to the top of their waterfall and stood there, arms held out either side of him.

When he could bear it no longer, he threw himself over the edge, wishing the rocks below would crush the fear and misery that were laying deposits in his bones, turning him into some brittle creature that would shatter the instant anyone dared to touch him.

He fell.

And then the vines that he cherished, the vines that loved him in return, soared across the space beneath him and caught his body. Lying there, stunned, furious, relieved, Kuja could only cry, his tears lost in the downpour that cascaded over him.

We are here for you always, the vines promised.

'But I'm not there for her,' he said.

You could be.

'My brothers and sisters would come after us both and I would lose!' Kuja cried, struggling to sit up in the rigid nest that the vines had formed for him. He lashed out, but they refused to give, instead absorbing his fury. 'I am nothing compared to Fayay! Nothing!'

But the water god has nothing to fight for, a nearby Bagaran Strangler told him, its tone rich in superiority. *You do.*

Kuja covered his face. 'That won't stop him destroying me. And I can't ask Sandsa for help. He might be able to defeat Fayay, but he'll probably say there's no point, that Fei will leave just like Callista did. And he'd be right! Even Mum left the Ine in the end. Who in their right mind stays with a god? What mortal would willingly *choose* eternity? I don't even want it!'

Did you give Feiscina that choice? the Strangler demanded.

'No! Because I'm afraid of what she'd say, you know that!'

You still should have let her choose.

Kuja closed his eyes and thought of Sandsa. After their mother had left, more than half a century ago, Sandsa had retreated to the deserts and let them absorb him, so that his pain would not become too overwhelming. It had been the Desine's only way to cope then and it was still his only solace now. He had lost almost everything he'd ever cared about, including his wife and son.

Kuja understood now. He wanted to disappear into the rainforests forever. He wanted to stop feeling, to forget entirely. Death would have brought that.

But his people needed him. And he could still be there for Fei, as Bagara.

Even if he'd much rather be there for her as the man who loved her.

CHAPTER TWENTY

The horizon was smudged with a sandstorm when Fei woke alone for the sixth Old Earth week in a row. Sitting in the bathroom with her blue hair cascading over her face, sucking her finger while a machine decided her happiness based on a single drop of blood, she allowed herself to feel hope. And then the pregnancy test read negative. Again.

Hope faded into disappointment, then melted into guilt. She'd been so desperate that night that she hadn't stopped to consider how selfish she was being. The implant...she should have asked him.

At least now he would never know what she had done. What she had tried to do.

Hugging herself, Fei went to the expansive window in the bedroom and took in the view. Down in the streets below, Atsa City was stirring into life. Artisan stalls, violently colourful and completely uncoordinated, were springing up as usual on Market Street. Those who were visiting them this early, before work and before the rush, looked like a handful of tiny nashba bugs. The hovercars slowly filling the streets weren't much bigger or any more impressive from this height.

Fei roved her eyes (emerald green, as they had been for weeks) around the hemisphere-shaped shield that kept the city safe from storms and weapons alike. It was hard to see during the day, but just at dawn the shield's faint orange hue was visible.

'Our shield can take an orbital bombardment,' Ala had said some days ago, creases running rampant over her face. 'Bock's not worried about GLEA showin' up and blockading us, but I sure as stark am. We need them starships to keep coming in if we want any food. Our hydroponics aren't that great so give it long enough and we'll starve. Can't fight the starkin' Chippers if we're dead.'

Unease gnawed low in Fei's stomach as she remembered those words.

'Bagara,' she whispered, her breath steaming the window. 'I'm scared. Is something going to happen today? I know there are no rainforests here yet, but maybe...maybe you can see...'

Fei drew a gasp of air, then rushed it back out, startled. She could now taste freshwater and the previously cool room was thick with humidity.

If something does happen, I will be here for you, Bagara promised in a voice that reminded her so much of Kuja that it caused her chest to ache.

'No offence but that doesn't help me,' Fei said, then bowed her head. 'I'm sorry. I know I should be better at this faith thing.'

I'd rather you have faith in your own abilities instead of mine.

'That's a lot harder and you know it,' she muttered.

The air became neutral and bland once more. Bagara was gone.

Fei strode over to the hoverlift, pausing only to grab a jacket. Despite Yalsa 5 being a desert world, the interiors of its buildings were often on the verge of freezing, thanks to the locals' insistence on overcompensating with their climate control systems. Fei wanted to avoid the arid heat just as much as anyone, but having seen the amount of power the city used on any given day, she had decided that she wasn't going to add to the strain on the grid until the ancient system was replaced.

On the way down in the hoverlift, Fei ran through the tasks that she needed to do. Bock had asked her to come up with the simulation he had originally paid for (TerraCorp had recently refunded his money, a move which Ala thought meant that hostilities were forthcoming), saying he'd buy some terraforming equipment and do the starking job himself. Fei had tried to explain that she would need to make a whole new program from scratch, but he still expected it to be finished in the same amount of time that Fei usually spent testing and finalising code on a single simulation.

Fei's colleague, Jalen, greeted her when she entered the techroom in Governor Bock Atsason's headquarters. Jalen was a Jezlo, like Gerns, and Fei couldn't help but feel comforted by the sight of the woman's six tentacles. Jalen was pale grey in colouring, which was typical of her species, and wore the seaweed sarong native to her world, but for whatever reason she also donned a bright pink cap that sealed over the top of her large head.

Fei bit a crevice into her bottom lip. 'I hope you had a good night's sleep. I definitely didn't. Has the shield been taken off the Web and put onto an isolated system like I requested?'

Jalen dropped the bowl she was eating out of — the metallic object clunked onto the desk, worryingly close to where the unlit keyboard was waiting — and slapped the side of her vidscreen with one of her tentacles, bringing it back to life. Jalen's head wobbled into a passable nod. 'Yep. No one's going to be able to hack the shield through the Web anymore. Good idea, that. Now Bock, Bock's not happy. He's been whinin' to Ala about how he has to go all the way to the shield generators to monitor them now that he can't do it on the Web.'

'But couldn't he just call someone stationed there and get them to check?'

'Nah, the governor said he don't trust anyone else to do it,' Jalen answered. 'Ala had a good go at him until he said he don't trust anyone else but *her*.'

A smile tweaked Fei's lips but she kept her tone professional. 'Alright, let's get started. It's not like we can't talk and work at the same time.'

'Might as well do something for the coin-chips we're gettin',' Jalen agreed. 'Another boring day of waiting for our code to compile then?'

'Once we get this simulation program completed, we won't ever have to wait again,' Fei said, seating herself at her desk. 'This one will have real-time interpreting. So as soon as we write a line of code, it's translated immediately into the console's language.'

It was a feature she'd always wanted to introduce to TerraCorp's systems but she hadn't wanted Moz to steal her idea or, worse, reject it completely. Bock and Ala had put Fei in charge of the techroom (and her only other colleague) and Fei still wasn't sure if she was ecstatic about this or absolutely terrified. Possibly both.

Jalen's body quaked violently; the Jezlo could have been shaking with mirth or shuddering. It was hard to tell. 'No more long hours of compiling? You mean, we'll never get to sit around and do nothing?'

'Well, it's not like we'll have much to do when the program *is* finally working.' Fei grimaced and rubbed her forehead. 'We can't run any simulations until we have actual data to put into them.

Bock and Ala will need to hire reputable scientists to start looking into plants and soils for us. And who knows how long *that* will take.'

Jalen noticeably cheered up after that.

They spent several hours running through the test suite the program needed to be subjected to. Jalen's skills weren't inconsiderable and she was quick to mention if she found an error in Fei's code — and just as quick to fix it. Fei found that she was making fewer mistakes now that someone was paying closer attention to her work. It was a welcome change.

During the third seemingly endless test, Jalen began passing judgement, once again, on Yalsa 5's lasball team. Some of the players were fine specimens, for humans that is, but they weren't very good and were likely to lose to Yalsa 3's team next week. Bored, and having no opinion to offer, Fei let her eyes slip shut. Her head, cradled by her hand, drooped, but never made it to the desk.

Because a screeching alarm chose right then to start drilling into her temples.

Yalsa 5 was under attack.

Fei jerked out of her hoverchair. Propelled by the sudden movement, the chair sailed backwards and collided with a desk on the other side of the techroom.

'What's happening?' Fei demanded.

Jalen wordlessly pointed a tentacle at the thin vidscreen that ran the width of one of the walls. Usually Jalen had the feed set to replays of old lasball tournaments, but the game had been interrupted by a Webcast that was showing a very familiar sphere of sand hanging suspended in space — Yalsa 5. Fei realised she recognised the mediaist on screen and might even talk to him sometimes, if BozzMed hadn't been lying to her about who he was.

'TerraCorp has refused to answer any questions about why they are doing this without the authorisation of its former client, Governor Bock Atsason, who my sources tell me recently received a refund due to non-delivery...' Ton Tinel paused, his gaze growing sorrowful, as though some great tragedy had occurred. 'It seems TerraCorp has decided to send its machines in. They claim this job was requested by a new *anonymous* client. So far neither TerraCorp or those on Yalsa 5 are willing to tell us what led to this conflict.'

Fei grabbed her techpad, flicking through various messages on the Webchat feed until she found him. *BozzMed, CC here. I'm on Yalsa 5. And I know who the anonymous client is. It's GLEA.*

She still had her doubts about his identity, even when she saw one of Ton Tinel's hands disappear from view as he continued to speak. Her techpad lit up with BozzMed's — and apparently the mediaist's — response. *I have long suspected that there is a connection between TerraCorp and GLEA. Can you tell me what you know about it? Don't feel you need to answer if your job remains at risk.*

Fei laughed as she typed her next message. *Don't worry. I quit my job. I have no proof but I saw the files — TerraCorp is part of GLEA. The Agency created the company centuries ago as a way to supplement the donations they receive. So TerraCorp will do whatever GLEA wants them to. And that includes eradicating deserts and rainforests because they're afraid of other gods.*

Tiny cracks began spidering over Ton Tinel's face as he glanced down at something out of sight — his techpad, Fei hoped. He was saved from having to explain his uncharacteristic silence to his audience when a member of his crew shouted something at him off-screen.

Tinel's grin snapped back into place. 'Ah. The general heading the flotilla of GLEA vessels that just dropped out of leapspace has informed me that TerraCorp is helping the Agency deal with some sort of criminal element in Atsa City. Could GLEA be the company's anonymous client? If so, this does make you wonder why GLEA has decided to deal with lawbreakers by terraforming an entire planet — *and* without consulting the planet's governing body.'

With one hand cupped to an ear in a futile attempt to block out the blaring alarm, Fei used the other to hammer out several more lines of text. *I can send you the message I got from Mozel Zan, a manager at TerraCorp. Basically it says that we're to turn the whole planet into an ocean. This will wipe out the city and anyone living in it.*

They have a shield down there, don't they? was BozzMed's response.

Jalen, who had also left her seat, leaned over Fei's shoulder, her beady eyes now fixed on the techpad. Fei was trying to think of an explanation for having this unauthorised contact with someone off-planet when her colleague said, 'Yeah, but the shield's pretty old. And it doesn't extend below the surface of the roads. So we'd still get flooded in from underneath even if we didn't get hit with waves. The buildings here are gonna topple over since their foundations aren't built for that.'

Fei provided BozzMed with this information in the Webchat. Moments later, the vidscreen on the wall was filled with the message Fei had received from Moz — along with additional notes that outlined what would happen to Atsa City. Ton Tinel was delightedly drawing conclusions about who this TerraCorp manager meant when he said 'our friends'. GLEA was Tinel's best guess.

'And while my sources cannot provide proof of this link between TerraCorp and GLEA,' Ton Tinel went on, waving a hand towards his ship's viewport which showed the TerraCorp vessel dropping small, compact machines towards the planet, 'it does make you want to ask more questions, doesn't it? Wiping out a city without even offering the so-called criminals a chance to surrender...? How curious. More updates to follow. Thank you for watching Ton Tinel.'

Fei released the breath that had started to ache inside her lungs. 'God, I'm glad I took the shield off the Web. GLEA might have hacked it by now and shut it off.'

'I ain't disagreeing there,' Jalen said. 'But I'll tell you what needs shuttin' off. That starking alarm. Gimme a sec.'

This done, Jalen dropped back into her chair and swore at the vidscreen. It gave them an uncomfortably good view of GLEA's ships using their weapons to shred the space-based defences that Bock kept in orbit. Several mediaists were now in the system and the Web was full of images of the destruction. Fei was wondering if she should call Bock or Ala when heavy boots stomped their way down into the techroom. She swung a wild look over to the door just in time to see Ala march in, her expression thunderous.

'Are their terraforming machines on the Web?' Ala asked. 'Hack 'em if they are. We need to shut those fuckers down.'

Fei's fingers flew across the keys on her desk as she opened her preferred hacking program. 'At least I never warned Moz to take those machines off the Web. I'd have grabbed our proof by now if I'd kept my mouth shut and let the servers at TerraCorp headquarters stay connected. Maybe that should be a requirement of every company; all your files must be hackable, just in case I need something to hand over to Ton Tinel.'

'Yeah, good luck getting Bock or Ala to agree to that,' Jalen said with a series of clucks.

Ala made no comment on that, her frown deepening with each charged second that passed them by. Finally, she said, 'Fei. If you stop these douchenozzles, I'll give you a raise on what we're already payin' ya.'

Fei didn't mind the incentive. But it wasn't going to help against the resistance her hacking program was encountering. The terraforming machines kept on coming.

'Oh my God, Moz's work isn't this good, it's never this good!' Fei cried, dismayed. 'The machines are protected by a firewall that I…I've never had to go up against something like this. My program is useless — I'm going to have to use a command-line interface to dig into their code!'

'But you *can* do it,' Ala said. It was not a question.

Fei flicked her a frantic look. 'I don't know!'

'You don't know that you can't, so try,' Ala instructed, placing her hands on Fei's shoulders and shunting the hoverchair forward so that the armrests hit the desk. 'Because if you don't, we're all dead.'

Fei's eyes danced frantically between lines of complex code, trying to find a weakness to exploit. She was tempted to call for Bagara but stifled the urge. Yalsa 5 might want to be part of his domain, but there were other planets who already worshipped him, planets that might need his help more far more urgently.

All she had to do was break through a firewall.

TerraCorp's machines were red-hot streaks in the atmosphere now. Their brakes were being applied, slowing them down so that they could hover above the surface of the planet without hitting it. Soon they would start to convert the planet's climate.

Bagara, I might have to use you as our Plan B, Fei thought, panic rising.

You won't need to, he said. *But I'm here. I'm here for you.*

That gave her the burst of confidence she needed. Fei funnelled all of her attention into her task and the techroom blurred into nothingness around her. Time became meaningless. Code became obstacles that she could hurdle or brittle shields that she could slash her way through. The growing ache in her fingers was irrelevant. She had more important things to worry about.

Fei jolted when Ala rained heavy slaps down on her shoulders. Jalen whooped enthusiastically. It took Fei a moment to realise she had managed to shut the machines down, causing them to drop gently onto the planet's sandy surface. She quickly began building up a firewall of her own — the machines were hers now and she wasn't going to make it easy for anyone trying to take them back.

'I wouldn't celebrate just yet.' Fei nibbled on the inside of her cheek. 'We're not out of danger. Even my firewalls aren't hackproof. And the machines are still functional and intact. Removing even just one in the chain would have rendered them all useless.'

'So, what, we take out one of the starkin' things and we're good?' Ala asked her.

'No Webattack can get around a physical problem like that!' Jalen exclaimed.

But Fei hesitated. 'It would mess up the current simulation

program they have, yes. But they could make a new program that works with one machine less. I was one of TerraCorp's best so I can do it, but my colleagues could also manage it, given enough time.'

'Alright,' Ala said with a sharp nod. She tapped the tiny earpiece that served as her communicator. 'Bock. You got Vom and his lot together? Yeah? Okay. Tell them to use that "Magic" of theirs to see if they can't take out one of the machines.'

Fei blinked. She knew there were followers of the Desine in Atsa City, but it hadn't occurred to her that they would be any use in a situation like this.

Bock's voice in Ala's earpiece was loud enough that even Fei could hear it, though the pitch sounded a good deal higher than usual. Fei saw Jalen hiding a triangular smile behind a tentacle. Ala's face, however, remained entirely blank as she waited out the governor's squawking. Then she said, 'I get that ya want to capture the machines so we can do the terraforming ourselves. Fei can make it work with one machine less. So quit arguin' and do it.'

The three women waited there in the techroom, so far removed from what was going on. The vidscreen didn't show anything useful — most Webcasts were focusing on GLEA's ships as they set up their blockade. The vessels were a lot easier to locate with vidcams than the compact terraforming machines.

Ala tapped her silver nails along the desk, causing a cascade of metallic chinking. Fei wasn't sure if the governor's wife was doing it to express nerves or impatience.

'It's done,' Bock announced.

Ala slapped her earpiece, cutting the connection. She held up two fingers and jabbed them in Fei and Jalen's direction. 'Make a simulation program that works with one machine less.'

Then she swept out of the room.

Fei slumped in her chair. 'Great. More work.'

'Stop moping — you stopped an attack on an entire planet!' Jalen said, bounding over to drop a mug of something that smelled far too strong in front of Fei. 'Time to celebrate, Defender of Worlds.'

Defender of Worlds? No, you're more than that, a voice mused inside Fei's head. She didn't think it belonged to Bagara, because it sounded a *lot* like Kuja this time. But he wasn't there. He couldn't be. Even if she could have sworn she felt him...

Shaking her head, Fei reached for the drink.

CHAPTER TWENTY-ONE

It spread like wildfire, stripping each and every nutrient from the soil, choking shallow-rooted plants and rotting trees from the inside out until they could no longer cry out for their god. Kuja crouched, a hand on the ground to brace himself as he sought out the source of the rainforest's pain. Its attacker had been born over a century ago and, if left unchecked, would take over every micrometre of Saren, a small but inhabited moon.

The virus was a natural, living thing and part of Kuja's domain. It even greeted him warmly, like an old friend. But within months it would invade the moon's only town, where buildings had only stood for two decades. The virus would not negotiate with something as temporary as a breeze fluttering its way through the leaves.

Kuja stood and walked over to the tree line to have another look at the town. It was nestled in a tiny valley, on fertile farming land that was not native to Saren. The settlers had barely been able to afford the small terraforming job that had granted them this sanctuary. If they'd had any coin-chips left, they could have charted a vessel to take them elsewhere or even rehired TerraCorp to eradicate the virus from the moon's surface. But they didn't. And couldn't.

While Kuja could halt the virus with his powers, a moment's

distraction on his part would allow it to grow again. The energy he'd need to devote to this fight might very well result in him being unable to save lives elsewhere, lives that might be in more immediate danger.

Kuja held out a hand, teleporting a communicator at random into his palm — he would have to return the device to its owner when he was done with it — and typed in Gerns' details. Though the Jezlo had spoken to Bagara once already, he knew she was far more comfortable with speaking to a human.

'Gerns,' he said. 'Bagara needs your help.'

'Now me, I just got rudely woken up, but I'll hear you out, Kuja,' the botanist grumbled on the other end and Kuja grimaced, remembering that it was night-time in Bagath. He had left the village weeks ago with an excuse about needing to see the galaxy. Truthfully, there were too many memories of Fei inside those palisade walls.

'Sorry,' Kuja said. 'But I was visiting Saren, a moon orbiting the gas planet in the Junim system, when Bagara came to me. He said you wanted to help and this is how.'

'What does he need me to do?' There was a crash; Gerns had knocked something over on her way out of bed.

'We have to find a way to stop a rainforest-based virus that will destroy the only piece of arable land on Saren.' Kuja paused for effect. 'And I think you're the only one both qualified and willing to do something about it.'

Gerns grunted, her tiredness causing her to think unsavoury things about him. 'Huh. How about that. Bagara using science. Gimme three days, tops. I'll meet you at the spaceport — or landing pad, whatever they've got. Saren...now me, I think

TerraCorp did a job there once. Doesn't GLEA have some sort of presence on the moon?'

'There's a small Chipper outpost. Saren was never deemed populated enough for a temple.'

'You should talk to the agents,' Gerns suggested. 'See if they'll evacuate the locals.'

Kuja ground his teeth together. 'They'd love to move people away from Bagara's domain, wouldn't they.'

'Now Kuja, I say this to you, you should ask the settlers what they want. It's their choice.'

I know that, Kuja wanted to snap. But then he thought of Fei — and the choice he never gave her. The choice he *couldn't* give her.

'Just get here as fast as you can,' Kuja told Gerns before he cut the connection.

***

'You could be lying about this catastrophic virus in an attempt to force GLEA off Saren,' Major Laura Minsra said, eyes narrowed. 'Why should I believe you? You're one of those Bagara degenerates.'

The GLEA outpost on Saren stood out amongst the cluster of silver shelters that made up most of the town. It was a stone building with a white exterior that needed to be scrubbed clean every morning — and it was also a lot larger than it needed to be to house the three Chippers stationed on the moon.

Kuja sized up the woman seated across the desk from him. Major Minsra wore a crisp purple jumpsuit with its long sleeves pulled down as far as possible; she clearly relied on the climate control system in her office to keep cool. The other buildings in the settlement had no such luxury, but Kuja could see in her mind that the major didn't know that. She rarely left her stone sanctuary to converse with the townspeople she was meant to be protecting.

He kept his voice calm and free of judgement. 'Unlike followers of the Creator God, we don't feel threatened by people of different faiths. And if my honesty really is a concern to you, I have an accredited botanist arriving in three days to inspect the virus.'

'Very well.' Minsra dusted her fingers over the golden strokes on both shoulders of her uniform. 'But what if this botanist of yours can't stop the virus entering the town?'

'I am painfully aware that the settlers cannot afford to put any more money into your coffers by paying for another terraforming job.' Kuja held up a hand to stop her denying it. 'I know where you get your funding.'

'Clearly not from this lot — they don't even donate,' Minsra said, blowing out a gusty sigh. 'And they're not the only ones. The whole galaxy's full of people like them. TerraCorp's profits are a lot more reliable than their sporadic donations.'

'I don't suppose you'd be willing to say that again and let me record it so the mediaists can use it against you,' Kuja said, fiddling with a thread that had escaped the hem of his shirt.

Minsra's expression soured. 'You will treat me with respect. I am a representative of the Creator God — the first god, the *only* god — and I'm much closer to him than you will ever be.'

Kuja swallowed the laugh and didn't correct her. 'Whatever god you or the Sarenites want to worship, that's not up to me. But Bagara doesn't want anyone to suffer.'

'Then he should stop the virus, shouldn't he,' Minsra remarked, smirking.

'Bagara won't just *stop* natural disasters.' Kuja shut his eyes briefly. 'Not in the way you're suggesting.'

'Even if it's to save his worshippers?'

'If the best thing for his people is to beg GLEA to evacuate them, then Bagara will tell them to do it,' Kuja told her.

'You want me to believe that Bagara will just...let them go?' Minsra leaned forward, holding his gaze. 'Would he do that, knowing they might worship in one of our temples instead?'

'Yes. Because he knows your duty is to protect all mortal children of the Creator God. His people will be cared for.' Kuja smiled grimly. 'Of course, if they happen to pledge themselves to your god because of what you've done for them, then that's a bonus.'

'A bonus,' Minsra echoed.

'They don't owe you anything.'

Minsra dropped back into her chair, chortling. 'They should at least make it worth our while.'

'Are all Chippers this mercenary or is it just you?'

'Look, Coo-coo, or whatever your name is — ' Minsra pointed at her temple, where her skin was stretched over the chip that was the source of her energy-based abilities ' — the Creator God gives us these powers and we pay him back by serving him. It's a transaction. That's how it works. If the people here want us to save them, they'll have to give us something in return.'

Kuja raised his eyebrows. 'So if they don't have the coin-chips then their faith will do.'

'We understand each other.'

'Many of them still worship the Creator God,' he pointed out.

Minsra shook her head. 'Not enough. We lost a whole pack of 'em six Old Earth weeks ago when that fancy statue belonging to the Bagara degenerates started going on about casualties.'

'So.' Kuja clenched his fists in his lap. 'You will only relocate them if they're *all* worshippers of the Creator God. How charitable of you.'

Minsra said nothing.

'Come outside and tell them this,' Kuja said, standing.

'Why?' she asked, warily eyeing the door.

Despite the anxiety rolling off her, Kuja could not bring himself to feel sorry for the major. 'Well, if they hear it from me, they might not believe it. They might think I'm twisting your words. And I'd much rather you disappoint them in person.'

'What if they decide to convert to save themselves?' she demanded.

Kuja spread his hands to better display his shrug. 'Then they will be safe and that is all Bagara cares about.'

Minsra's mind was full of suspicion, but she still sent out the two agents under her command to announce that she had something to tell the Sarenites. When enough townspeople were gathered in front of the outpost, Major Minsra gave her speech, one full of jerky hand movements that often singled out the sky. She shot a triumphant grin at Kuja when she was done.

Keeping his hands locked behind him, Kuja raised his voice above hers. 'Bagara has spoken to me, the way he has spoken to many of you recently. He wants you to be safe and will not begrudge any of you for choosing to worship another god if it means ensuring your survival. He is sending a botanist here to work on the problem in the meantime.'

Kuja felt a surge of anger emanate from the Sarenites moments before their muttering swelled into an uproar. Minsra took a large step back, towards the outpost, her eyes wide. One of the closest townspeople, a woman, pointed at the major. 'You worship the Creator God, like me. Is this what he tells you to do to your fellow beings? I guess I wouldn't know — I haven't heard anything from him. But all my neighbours hear from Bagara and he never says anything like this!'

Major Laura Minsra fled.

Kuja watched her disappear into the outpost, then turned his eyes back to the crowd. 'You may have just given away your only chance of being rescued.'

'Pah,' said the woman from before, shaking her head. 'The Creator God isn't the only god out there who can help us. Sounds like Bagara's already trying to do something about this mess anyway. When does his botanist arrive?'

'Three days,' Kuja answered.

'Then we'd better get things ready for them.'

CHAPTER TWENTY-TWO

A summons from Governor Bock Atsason could hardly be ignored, even if all Fei wanted to do was go back to her penthouse apartment and bury her head underneath a pillow. It had been a long day already. Clamping down on a yawn, Fei followed Caprice, Bock's secretary, up to his office and tried to wait patiently in the antechamber. This worked for about a minute until an awful thought occurred to her, one that made her go rigid in her seat.

'Caprice?' she called, trying to to keep her voice even.

The secretary looked up from the paperwork on her desk. 'What.'

'Is there a law against theft on this world?'

'Of course there is,' Caprice answered with a roll of her eyes. 'But our Clan Leader is allowed to take something into his possession for a short time if it will assist in settling a dispute. As the governor is also the Clan Leader, he enjoys many benefits.'

'Oh.' Fei bit her lip. 'Can Bock — the Clan Leader — use the things he's taken?'

'No. He can only hold them.' Caprice glowered at Fei. 'Any other pressing *concerns* I can help you with?'

'Um, is there a bathroom nearby?'

***

Fei paced in front of the stalls, running a hand over her scalp and wincing when her fingers met resistance. She hadn't attacked her hair with any chemicals in hours so it was starting to lose its sleekness. She cursed each and every strand for betraying her. There was no one else in the bathroom which was a relief, because she probably looked insane.

'But we can't use the machines,' she said frantically when her feet once again took her to the end of room. 'It's illegal for Bock to do more than hold them. If we *do* use them, GLEA will say we're criminals because we broke this planet's laws and that would justify their blockade! Stark it, stark it. I should never have said anything to Ala. I'm starked. I'm so starked.'

She smacked the tiles on the wall in front of her, wincing when the bony part of her palm caught the brunt of her frustration. Fei shook her hand out, muttering, 'They trusted me. They put their faith in me. And I've messed things up so badly. I failed! I really starking failed!'

You haven't failed yet, her god said, his voice coming unbidden. He sounded exactly like Kuja now. She wasn't sure if Bagara was doing that on purpose or because it was what she wanted to hear.

'Maybe I shouldn't tell Bock and Ala just so I can spare myself the *looks* they'll give me!' Fei cried.

They will order you to use the machines sooner or later, Bagara pointed out. *And in doing so, they will make GLEA appear to be the ones in the right. No mediaist would side with Yalsa 5 against the Agency then.*

Fei let the sigh bleed from her lips. 'God, I miss Kuja. I need him. Not to speak for me or stand beside me — I'm doing okay with that stuff now — I just want to *talk* to him about this and…and…I guess there's no point in asking you to bring him to me?'

I think you're afraid that one mistake means you have to stop trusting yourself, Kuja — Bagara — commented instead of answering her.

'Doesn't matter if you're right. I can't stop being afraid.' Fei tugged at her unruly hair again but it refused to lie flat. Her shoulders sagged. 'You should go. I'll be fine. I have to be fine. A lot of people are counting on me.'

She felt Bagara hesitate.

'You can't be there for everyone's little problems, surely,' she said.

His familiar laugh filled her mind. *I would like to. But then I wouldn't have any time for you. Farewell, Fei.*

Then he was gone, his sudden absence like a cold patch in a lagoon that she had swum into without warning. Fei shivered. Once more she was alone, so hopelessly alone.

With only herself to rely on.

'Oh, I *am* starked,' she moaned.

***

'…and this is fucking great news, because they've practically handed us the starking things so we can do our own terraforming,' Bock went on, tossing his booted feet up onto his desk. The metal caps on his heels soundly thumped the wood.

He had been going on like this ever since she'd entered the room. Despite herself, Fei found her focus slipping and started thinking about TerraCorp and how she'd always done the bare

229

minimum while working for them. Now Fei actually *wanted* to do things. She wanted to help Jalen became a great programmer, one to rival herself. She wanted to help Yalsa 5. And she wanted to terraform more worlds, because though TerraCorp hadn't been great, she'd loved knowing her fingerprints were on the end product.

But if she wanted to keep this job, then she'd better speak up. Bock was convinced he was going to make a lot of money out of the machines in his grasp.

Fei cleared her throat.

Bock didn't seem to notice. Ala, however, did. She nodded at Fei. 'Say what you need to.'

'Governor,' Fei began, swallowing when her mouth ran dry. 'I have to say something, please, if that's alright. Yes. Yes, it definitely has to be said.'

Bock stopped mid-word, his hands thrown up in front of him. He guided them back down to the arms of his chair. 'Go on then. I don't have all night.'

'We can't use the machines,' Fei rushed out. 'I'm sorry. I didn't think this through. While, um, we can physically hold onto them, we can't use them.'

'Why the stark not?' Bock demanded.

Fei flinched, unable to continue at first. But then she saw the frown descend on Ala's face. The thought of yet again watching the other woman intercede on her behalf made Fei's stomach churn. So she stepped forward half a pace. 'Because it's not legal on this planet. Since you're the Clan Leader, you can seize something that doesn't belong to you, but you can't use it. Which means we can't use the machines. No one would bat an eye if

GLEA punished you or the city for the theft. That'd be them enforcing the law, just like they always do.'

Bock stroked his chin. 'Aw, shit. Can we change the law?'

'No!' Ala snapped. 'There's a reason we have peace and prosperity in this city, you douchenozzle. The gangs would stop respectin' the laws if they saw the governor changing them whenever it suited him.' Ala leaned back against the edge of Bock's desk, arms crossed. 'Any chance the mediaists could find a way to make us look innocent even if we did use the machines?'

'I don't think so,' Fei answered. 'They have to report the facts. And the fact is it's illegal for us to use the machines — they belong to TerraCorp.'

Bock's eyes hardened. 'So what's the point in payin' you if you can't *do* anything for me?'

'Bock, that's enough,' Ala barked.

Fei tore a vicious chunk out of the inside of her cheek. Coppery blood flooded her mouth. She couldn't stand there in silence and let someone walk all over her. Not anymore.

'Because,' she said, her voice rising, 'I *am* doing stuff. I saved your life when I hacked those machines, Governor. I stopped them, not you. And I might've even got some of the galaxy on our side when I sent a message to Ton Tinel, one of the mediaists in orbit. It won't hurt to have people sympathising with us.'

'Now hang on, you shouldn't be talkin' to people outside — ' Bock began.

'Bock, I told you about this,' Ala interrupted, her tone severe. 'You gotta listen to the people who know more than you do. And you really need to shut the fuck up sometimes.'

Bock reached across the desk, his hand seeking his wife's — and finding it, when Ala allowed him to. 'You could phrase it a little more nicely, my dear, my sweet, my love.' Ala's lips twitched. Bock smirked back at her. 'You got me that voice coach, didn't you? I have to sound good for the rich folk or they'll start thinking I'm some sort of low life and not vote me in as their governor next time.'

Ala raked her eyes over her husband. 'Hey now, I like the low life.'

Fei studied her feet intently. There was something very intimate passing between Ala and Bock just then and it wasn't that it embarrassed Fei — no, it filled with her a very painful longing.

'Keep workin' on your simulation program, Fei,' Ala ordered. 'No matter what machines we use, TerraCorp's or somethin' else we buy, we'll still need to run the starking things.'

Fei nodded and headed for the door, but stopped when she heard Bock clear his throat. She turned back around, startled to see the governor giving her a sheepish smile. It was a strange look on him and wiped years off his face, making him actually look his age. 'Fei, I'm not any good at being nice. I'm best at barking orders and makin' sure they get done. So I guess I'm saying I'm sorry if I come off a bit gruff.'

'You're under stress, like we all are,' Fei said.

Bock shook his head. 'Nah, not a good enough excuse. So take this apology because I won't remember to give it again. And don't let people being shitty to you become normal. You're worth more than that.'

'You don't need to tell me,' Fei said, slowly smiling. 'I know that now. And I won't let you — or anyone else — forget it.'

Bock laughed. 'Look at you. Just look at you.'

CHAPTER
TWENTY-THREE

When Kuja entered the steel-walled warehouse that doubled as Gerns' sleeping quarters and laboratory, he almost didn't recognise the botanist. Her skin was midnight black and her beady eyes had ballooned to four times their usual size. Kuja couldn't imagine it was a good thing for a Jezlo to look like this.

'Have you slept at all in the past week?' Kuja asked her.

Gerns set down the test tube she'd been peering into and looped her tentacles around herself in a full-bodied hug. 'Now me, if I was sensible, I might have done that. But I'm not. And this virus isn't going to stop on its own. I've been seeing how it responds to some of the local plants and bacteria, thought maybe one of them could fight it, but the starking thing kills them dead in no time. Guess the only good news is that I now have data on a whole bunch of plants I can send to Fei. She'll need that stuff if Governor Bock Atsason ever gets himself some terraforming machines.'

Kuja buried his hands inside his pockets so hard and deep he actually felt the lining tear. 'You've been in contact with Fei?'

'You haven't?' Gerns returned, unwinding her tentacles so that she could brandish their poisonous suction cups at him. 'Now me, I said to myself, I said "Gerns, this Kuja's a nice man, he must have a good reason to treat Fei the way he is and he must be stewing on it if you can distract him from your failure just by mentioning her".'

'Gerns, I can't...' Kuja forcibly stilled his fingers when they caused another audible rip. 'I can't explain. I wish it was simple. I wish I could be with her. But I can't.'

Gerns' tentacles drooped. 'Huh. Sounds like we both need a drink. Go get me something strong from that dive they call a bar, but make sure you get yourself something first.'

Kuja made a point of letting his eyes wander over the multiple tables inside the warehouse, all of them cluttered with plant material, techpads and soil-stained shovels. 'You're going to...drink and work at the same time?'

'Don't be giving me one of them looks,' Gerns said, aiming the tip of one tentacle at him like an accusing finger. 'How do you know that alcohol doesn't work like coffein to my species?'

'Gerns, I'm sorry, I didn't — '

Gerns' large body shook as she released a string of amused clucks. 'Just messing with you, Kuja. Now get me that drink.'

***

The man dropped his metal cup onto the counter and it bounced, splattering the aluminium surface with what few droplets remained inside the vessel. He muttered a quick apology which apparently mollified the bartender enough to drop a hose into the cup to refill it. The man drank lengthily, blood-red liquid sliding over his chin, then banged the cup back down.

Having watched the man from the door for a full minute, Kuja sidled into the chair beside him. He didn't know this dark-skinned man but Kuja could feel his need for companionship. It made him think of Fei. Kuja prepared to be sympathetic.

And then he saw the purple jumpsuit underneath the leather jacket.

The Chipper glanced down at his uniform and rolled his eyes. 'Yeah, I'm with GLEA. Gonna judge me for my job or give me a chance?'

Despite his confrontational attitude, there was a sadness lining the man's deep brown eyes, though nowhere near as potent as what he was feeling. Kuja decided he would blame this for his decision to stay. 'Alright. You get a chance, because I want to know why you're drowning your sorrows in here. Your companions are not bothered by the problems facing this town. Does this mean you are?'

The bartender dropped a drink in front of Kuja. He tried to say he didn't order it, but the woman jerked her head at the GLEA agent. 'He's buying. For everyone. He agreed to these terms otherwise I wouldn't have let him in here.'

'You might as well enjoy that since I'm the one paying for it,' the man told Kuja. He flicked an impatient look at the bartender who, clearly hoping to eavesdrop, suddenly had something else to do in a back room. Once she was gone, the man sighed and pushed himself away from the counter. 'Okay. First of all, I've got my orders. I can't exactly go against them.'

'You can,' Kuja countered. 'There would be consequences, but you are physically capable.'

'I don't want to get kicked out, okay. I like being part of GLEA. I like what we do for the galaxy.' The man lifted his chin. 'We serve the Creator God. There is no higher calling.'

'And how does running a terraforming company count as serving him?' Kuja asked, crossing his arms.

'I don't know that we do run the company — I hope not,' the man with a grimace. 'I know what Ton Tinel's been saying. But even if we are using TerraCorp...it's for the greater good. It has to be.'

Kuja pinned the man with his sternest, most godly gaze. 'Bagara has no such ties. His motives are not tainted by coin-chips or a desire for expansion.'

The man snorted and reached for his drink. 'Okay. No desire for expansion. Whatever you say. So what do you call that viral campaign of his? I won't argue that Bagara probably has little use for coin-chips, but he doesn't have the operational costs that we do. Look, GLEA was founded eight centuries ago and has a proven track record of looking after the galaxy. And yet everyone's being encouraged to call out to this god who's virtually untested, who doesn't give his people any powers so they have to rely on his interference — and he's probably still adjusting to godhood because he's only, what, five decades old?'

Kuja bit his lip to keep from correcting the man. He had emerged into the rainforests as Bagara when he'd been about twenty. The mortals didn't know he was older than his reign.

'You Chippers get your name from your use of the chips,' Kuja said instead. 'You only have your powers because of that tech — even if,' he went on when the agent opened his mouth, 'the Creator God allows it, he didn't give them to you. Your abilities are unnatural. Bagara doesn't bestow any powers on his people because he trusts that they can succeed with their own abilities. He sent Gerns and me here, because of her knowledge and because of my compassion, so that we could protect the Sarenites.'

The man lifted his now empty cup, as though toasting Kuja. 'Okay, great, Bagara is doing something to help these people. Good for him. But I'll tell you this. Sometimes...I can actually feel my god. And when I do, I know I'm living my life the way I'm meant to.'

Kuja picked up his own drink and licked around the metal rim, scouring the sugar crusted there. He wasn't sure he should brave consuming what was inside the cup. 'So you are *meant* to abandon the Sarenites to starvation because they cannot donate to your organisation, either directly or through TerraCorp.'

'My superiors usually know what they're doing.' The agent paused, his lips curling. 'Usually. Sometimes I wonder. Major Minsra banned us from drinking any coffein and she's been downright unpleasant in the morning ever since. It could be affecting her judgement, huh? Now that I think about it, I didn't have any coffein the day the Creator God called me to his service...'

Kuja clapped a hand over his mouth, but he was too late; the laugh had already escaped. He detached his fingers from his face and waved them up and down the man's torso, indicating his purple outfit. 'If you'd had that coffein, what would you be doing instead of this?'

The man fiddled with the zipper on his jumpsuit. 'Oh. Well. There was a woman I could have married. But we weren't right for each other. We'd've both been miserable. So I let her go. She deserved a chance at happiness.'

Kuja nodded slowly. 'I understand. Sometimes it is better for them if we leave. You know, I'm glad I gave you this chance. I'm Kuja Rforine.'

'Zareth Sins,' the man said, extending a hand.

But Kuja recoiled. 'Zareth Sins. You are the one who broke Feiscina Neron's heart.'

Zareth's hand dropped to his side. 'You know Fei.'

'Did you realise that abandoning her would cause her to lose faith in your god as well as herself, or was that something you cared little about?' Kuja didn't so much as set his drink down as slam it. The liquid sloshed over his fingers, staining them.

Zareth slid along the counter, away from him. 'I can't talk about this. I won't.'

'Why not?' Kuja demanded. 'Because you would have to admit that your joining GLEA hurt someone and created the kind of casualty that Bagara wants to be there for?'

The trees standing above the town shivered, begging to express Kuja's ire — but other plants resisted and even scolded him. Unused to this reaction from those that were meant to be under his control, Kuja blinked and refocused on Zareth, who seemed more interested in studying the bright red residue left inside his cup than in defending himself.

'Not sure what you want me to say,' Zareth said at last.

'I'm not the one you should be talking to. Fei is the one you hurt.'

Something shifted in the depths of Zareth's eyes. 'I know. And I'll have to live with that. But I won't undo what I did. I'd never have made her happy. She deserves better.'

'She does,' Kuja said, unable to keep the bite from his tone.

'Why did you have to go and make this about her anyway?' Zareth asked, frowning slightly.

'Because I love her — and I've seen not just you but an entire organisation of people like you do their best to destroy her,' Kuja rushed out in one breath.

'You love her?' Zareth's face exploded into a grin and he leaned over to slap Kuja's shoulder. 'That's great, man. That is. I wish I'd managed to.'

Kuja stared at him. 'You...did not love her? But you proposed marriage to her.'

'It felt like the thing to do,' Zareth said helplessly, shrugging his shoulders. 'She wanted it. I think she did, anyway. She had so much trouble telling me anything and I...I guess I didn't care enough about losing her so I never put in the effort to figure out what she wanted.'

'You never listened to her,' Kuja accused. 'You didn't even try.'

Zareth's expression hardened. 'Look, man, I knew it would suck for her, losing me the way she lost her dad, but it would have been worse for her if she'd found out I didn't love her. My way was kinder.'

Kuja's retort died on his lips when his mind was suddenly flooded with images of Fei. She was busily hammering away on the keys in front of her on Yalsa 5, muttering to herself in a language better understood by a console than a living being — and then she said the words that struck him like a physical blow to the gut.

'I miss you,' she murmured. 'God, I miss you. I still don't understand why you left.'

Kuja blinked away the tears before they fell. *I treated her no better.* 'I'm sorry, Zareth. Can we perhaps reattempt our conversation?'

Both men sat there at the counter for several more hours, drinking and trading words, but never mentioning Fei or GLEA. Those would be arguments for another time.

Kuja perhaps shouldn't have been as surprised as he was when he and Zareth became so boisterous that the bartender called Gerns to come and remove them. The Jezlo was a good deal louder when she remonstrated them than she needed to be.

Kuja made a mental to note to never again forget to supply her with a badly needed drink.

CHAPTER
TWENTY-FOUR

Fei had wanted to spend her day going over the error messages her new simulation program, designed to work with twenty-nine machines that Bock wasn't even allowed to *use*, had spat out during the latest test suite, but instead she had to devote herself to defending Yalsa 5 against GLEA's next form of attack — a smear campaign on the Web. The Agency was trying to erode any support Yalsa 5 had from the rest of the galaxy. Fei couldn't let this happen.

She braced her fingers against her temples as she watched yet another Webcast from yet another mediaist on her vidscreen. Fei sighed. 'So they're saying this entire planet is a hotbed of criminal activity and there are bodies strewn through the streets.'

'Doesn't help that GLEA has the footage from those old gang fights, hey,' said Jalen.

'Should we send up our own images? Of quiet streets and smiling children and things like that?' Fei asked, wincing at the devastation in the footage. It had happened years ago, but the people watching the Webcasts might not realise that.

Jalen clucked, two tentacles thumping the desk in front of her. 'That'd be hilarious, doncha reckon? Everyone will think "hey, crime looks really good, let's try it out".' The Jezlo sobered. 'But we have to do something quick or Atsa's gonna lose all its tourism, even after that blockade goes. That's a huge chunk of the governor's income.'

'And, by extension, our income too,' Fei noted. She smiled when Jalen's tentacles clapped over the Jezlo's oddly-shaped mouth, a sign of the other woman's horror. 'Okay, but simply throwing images up on the Web is nothing compared to what GLEA can do to us.'

'Let's worry about what we *can* do,' Jalen suggested.

Fei cradled her forehead between her thumb and forefinger. 'Tell Bock and Ala we need some promotional material. Footage. Something. Anything.'

Jalen scampered away. Since the woman could have just used a communicator, it seemed likely that Jalen had wanted to rest her eyes. Fei's were burning — it came from looking at vidscreens for hours. She dropped her head onto the desk, intent on leaving it there, but the keyboard built into the surface pinged unhappily at her. Muttering under her breath, she pried herself off it and tried to decide if she should risk checking over the results from the test suite. Her new simulation program *should* have been finished by now. But whenever she dared to think about working on it, there was always some other problem to deal with.

Like all twenty-nine of the terraforming machines suddenly booting up on their own.

Someone was remotely accessing them. GLEA was getting ready to destroy Atsa City.

Fei groaned. 'Of course whoever made that firewall of theirs could get through mine *and* figure out how to use only twenty-nine machines. That was stupid, Fei, stupid! I should have gone out to every single machine and taken them off the Web. Ugh!'

Jalen exploded back into the room. 'Gods, you should see it. It's bad.'

'Can't, busy,' Fei muttered as she re-hacked her way into the machines. She erected another firewall, but she wasn't sure how long it would last.

'The machines started up and — ' Jalen began.

'Yes, I know, I just shut them down again, but if I don't keep them that way everyone is going to die — and if they die *it's all my fault!*' Fei broke off, gasping. 'Sorry.'

'Just tell me what to do,' the Jezlo said, flying across the room on her own chair.

A loud screech of static greeted them from the window, which was sealed shut and supposedly soundproof. Whatever was causing the noise had to be seriously loud.

'Tell me Bock doesn't have those giant vidscreens he's got plastered all over the buildings hooked up to the Web,' Fei said out of the corner of her mouth.

Jalen's silence was answer enough.

Fei slapped a hand to her forehead. 'Okay. Get ready to listen to some propaganda. GLEA's hacked the screens.'

She tried not to be distracted by the exterior vidscreens as they conducted the booming voice of some Chipper who was insisting that sub-level gods didn't exist but, if they did, surely they could not offer anything better than the protection of the Creator God, conveniently meted out by the Galactic Law Enforcement Agency.

'Fei!' Ala stormed into the room. 'Bock's not gonna want to shoot down them screens. And don't forget about those starkin' machines! What're you doing about it?'

'Don't you trust me?' Fei gritted out. She allowed two blinks to moisten her eyes.

'I'm tryin' real hard to do that right now!' Ala said and let loose a string of curses.

Fei considered giving her boss an apology, then very visibly shook her head. It wasn't her fault. And there was no time to blabber on like it was.

Kuja, I need your help, she thought. *I just can't seem to throw off this other programmer and I'm afraid all these people will die because of me. Stark, I meant Bagara. Bagara help me!*

Fei had barely finished her plea when a raging khaki and hazel torrent engulfed her. She opened her mouth to scream but never got the chance to unleash it — because suddenly she was in a dingy basement, standing behind a boy hunched over a vidscreen. His ankles were encased in bulky lascuffs that looked completely out of place on someone half Fei's size.

'So you're the one causing me all my problems,' Fei said as he continued to smash the keys lit up on the desk in front of him.

'No, please, I'm doing what you want — ' The boy broke off when he finished spinning around. His eyes lost some of their panicked width. 'Oh. You're not a Chipper.'

Fei arranged her face into a smile, hoping it didn't look as strained as it felt. 'No, I'm...I'm the programmer on Yalsa 5.'

'Uh, no, you're not on Yalsa 5 because they're halfway across the galaxy!' the boy said, diving back into his work. 'Don't distract me. If you distract me, I can't break their new firewall and get the machines under my control again. I can't fail — the Chippers'll kill my mother and I can't let them! I *won't* let them!'

'GLEA threatened to kill your mother if you didn't terraform Yalsa 5?' Fei asked, horrified.

'Yes! You win the jackpot! Now shut up.'

'But you'll kill hundreds of thousands of innocent people!'

'My mum's more important,' the boy said. 'I don't give a shit about anyone else.'

Fei's eyes dampened. 'Bagara. I can't do this. I can't be responsible for his mother's death. Please, give me another way to do this.' She knew her god could hear her; it felt like he was standing *right behind her*.

The boy released a groan of frustration. 'You still haven't shut up yet! Who or what are you talking to?'

'The rainforest god,' Fei answered.

'Oh, I've heard about him,' the boy said, his face glued to his vidscreen. 'The Chippers don't like him, say he's bad news, which must mean he's real because they wouldn't be so worried if — stop distracting me!'

'Bagara,' Fei said, raising her voice. 'Look at what the Chippers have done to this boy! He is a casualty. He needs you just as much as Yalsa 5 does right now and I can't do anything, I can't convince him — but you can!'

What would you have me do? Bagara asked in Kuja's voice.

Fei closed her eyes and used her thoughts to respond to him. *You brought me here, to another planet entirely, which means you can teleport people.*

The god sounded reluctant. *Yes...*

So teleport this boy and his mother to safety, somewhere GLEA can't get at them!

She knew she didn't imagine his hesitance. She also knew, somehow, that she was the only mortal he'd allowed the privilege of moving between worlds.

You can't give me special treatment, she told him, furious. *It's not fair to everyone else who needs you. Who will* need *you.*

No, it's not fair, Bagara agreed. *You make an excellent point, Fei. I'll do it.*

I love you, Kuja's voice added, but those words couldn't possibly have come from him — or from the god.

Fei watched the boy disappear inside a vortex of swarming vines, finding this method of transportation no less alarming to watch from the outside. She hoped the boy's mother was safe. She'd just have to trust that even though she couldn't see it, Bagara was doing as she'd asked.

Funny how I never had that much faith in the Creator God, she thought wryly.

Within moments her own personal vortex came and carried her back to the techroom on Yalsa 5. Fei leaned against the nearest console, breathing heavily, tasting bile. The room was starting to spin a little less by the time Ala touched her shoulder, a soothing pressure that grounded Fei.

'I'm fine,' Fei managed in a wheeze. 'Is the firewall still holding?'

'Yep, looks like it — so what'd your god steal you away for anyway?' Ala asked, correctly guessing who was responsible for Fei's disappearance.

'The Chippers forced a boy to launch those Webattacks on us,' Fei answered, sinking into the hoverchair that Jalen had steered towards her. 'They held his mother hostage so he'd work for them — they probably picked a planet where kidnapping isn't illegal. But it's alright. Bagara agreed to help the boy and his mother even though they aren't from a rainforest world.'

'For real?' Jalen's tentacles weaved with excitement. 'That's cool. Do you think he'll take on an extra planet? I mean, we're not even terraformed yet but...'

Ala removed her hand from Fei's shoulder to grip one of her lasguns. 'Those fuckers, threatenin' a boy. And they call *us* the criminals.'

Fei thought she might have agreed out loud, but it was hard to tell when she was buried in her work. First she strengthened her firewall, then she wrote some code which convinced the machines that they weren't on the Web (it might slow down the next Webattack since it wasn't an expected method of defence). Fei couldn't be sure how long this all took, because everything in her peripheral vision had faded to black long ago. When she finally looked up, Jalen had gone home. Ala remained, however, her red artificial eye glowing in the gloom.

Seeing that she had Fei's attention, Ala jerked her head at a vidscreen off to the side. 'Message came through for ya. At least I think it's for you, 'cause it looks encrypted and you're probably the only one who can open it.'

Fei recognised the boy immediately once she had managed to get the vid he'd sent to play. He spent several minutes explaining what the Chippers had done to him in detail, then he looked straight at the vidcam and said, 'Use this against them, lady. Get 'em good. For my mum. I'm going underground. See ya.'

'I didn't ask him to do that,' Fei murmured. 'Do you think Bagara arranged it?'

Ala shrugged. 'Doesn't matter. We've got ourselves some ammunition against GLEA now.'

'It might convince a few people, but it — '

'Won't convince GLEA to stop coming after us, I get it,' Ala finished, sounding grim. 'But maybe we can get enough of

TerraCorp's clients to demand refunds and hurt them a little.' Ala eyed Fei for a moment. 'I'd tell you to get some sleep, but you'n me both know this vid needs to go viral.'

'It'll be a lot easier to do that if I give the vid to the mediaist I know,' Fei told her.

Ala pursed her lips. 'Do it. Anythin' else you want to suggest? We're flyin' blind here, Bock and I, so any little bit helps.'

Fei leaned back in her chair, giving it serious thought, appreciating that Ala seemed willing to wait her out. Finally, Fei decided, 'We need to get our side of the story out there.'

'And this mediaist friend of yours won't make us look like right douchenozzles?'

'I don't know,' Fei said honestly. 'But we should give our fight a face, someone the galaxy can *see* and sympathise with. Because right now we're nobody. Everyone knows GLEA but they don't know us. Ton Tinel can help us change that.'

'I'll talk to Bock,' was all Ala said in farewell before she turned and left.

Fei grabbed her techpad and started searching the Webchat feed for BozzMed, aka Ton Tinel.

CHAPTER
TWENTY-FIVE

Once the boy and his mother had been dropped off on another world, one that had strict laws against kidnapping, Kuja returned to Saren and cast out his presence, seeking Zareth Sins. A plant inside the Chipper outpost informed him that the agent was alone for the moment. So, ignoring the closed door to Minsra's study, Kuja marched into the outpost's sleeping quarters and thrust a techpad he'd borrowed at Zareth. 'Watch this. It's everywhere on the Web.'

Zareth accepted the techpad, nodded and started watching the vid queued up on it.

'GLEA might've chips stuck in their heads, but that doesn't make them any better than you or me,' the boy Kuja had helped said, filling the small screen on the device. 'Anyway, it turns out they like abusing those cool powers of theirs. They kidnapped me and held my mum hostage, forcing me to run Webattacks against Yalsa 5. Why the stark did they do that? They're supposed to uphold the laws of a planet's governing body, even if said body is run by gangs who used to blow things up.'

The young hacker was briefly sidetracked, presumably by whatever was making that beeping sound off-screen, but then his face hardened again. 'Right. So. The reason GLEA chained me to a desk and made me attack Yalsa 5 is this — they don't like any planet that doesn't worship the Creator God. It really pisses them off 'cause they can't get donations out of these kinds of worlds. They're all about the coin-chips. They don't care about being nice people.'

The boy visibly shuddered. 'I'm probably going to have nightmares and they didn't even do much to me. But I haven't seen any sunlight in weeks and they threatened to kill my mother if I didn't do as they asked. That doesn't make them sound like the good guys in this fight, does it?'

Zareth waved a hand over the techpad, pausing the vid. He looked troubled. 'GLEA is not perfect. I never said it was.'

'Still think you should stay with them?' Kuja asked.

'Not this again,' Zareth said, flicking him an irritable look. 'Yes, I do. The galaxy needs us. Listen, I've been talking to a few of my friends and none of us like how the Agency is being run at the moment.'

'But you haven't left and nor have you done anything to curtail the Agency's greed,' Kuja said, pacing his way through the outpost's surprisingly large sleeping quarters. The room was lined with bunks, most of them looking as though they had never been slept in.

Zareth's lips reared back from his teeth. 'I won't disagree. Things need to change.'

'Do any of your friends have access to files on Gerasnin?' Kuja asked, turning to face him. 'Files that could show where most of GLEA's funding comes from?'

'Yeah. Maybe.' Zareth hesitated. 'But look, Kuja, even if it's true, GLEA provides a valuable service for people. We protect those who couldn't otherwise afford it.'

'Sounds like you need to spend more time convincing yourself than you do me,' Kuja noted.

Zareth threw the techpad onto his unmade bed. 'Also not going to disagree with that.' He cleared his throat, looking nervous. 'I have to make a call to someone on Gerasnin. Mind giving me some privacy?'

Kuja returned to Gerns' warehouse laboratory, hoping he would at least find some progress there.

***

CC, finally got some hard evidence for me? BozzMed asked the moment his real life counterpart signed off from his latest Webcast. *That kid's vid wasn't a bad start, but I need more than that.*

Lying in bed, the room dark but for the screen of her techpad as she held it above her, Fei swiped her finger over the device. *Unfortunately, no. But I have convinced someone to give you their side of the story. Exclusive access. But I need to know if you'll be able to come here, to Atsa City.*

Ton Tinel saw right through the words that Bock and Ala had allowed Fei to give the mediaist. *So whoever you're in touch with thinks my presence will make GLEA less likely to wipe out Yalsa 5. I'd hazard that we're talking about Governor Bock Atsason. Would I be right?*

Depends, Fei said. *Are you right about the planet being safe while you're down here?*

His response took a lot longer than Fei would have liked. *Yes. I'll make a special Webcast before I head down to the city. GLEA will be in for a lot of trouble if I am unable to keep updating my viewers. Can you really set me up with the governor?*

Fei let out an excited whoop, then hurriedly backspaced her initial comment to make it sound more measured and mature. *I will send you the details within one Old Earth hour. I hope I didn't just agree to something stupid.*

Only one way to find out, CC, he told her.

He left the Webchat feed, presumably to make arrangements. Fei sighed in relief — then cried out when the techpad dropped from her loosened grip and onto her face.

Rubbing her aching cheek, she mumbled, 'Kuja, this is your fault.'

My fault? his voice — definitely his and not Bagara's — mused, a smile tainting his words.

She didn't care that he wasn't really there. She wanted to pretend so badly.

'Yes!' she cried. 'If you'd stayed, you could have stopped me from doing all these stupid things!'

No, I think I'd still have let you do all these brilliant *things — that or do brilliant things to you,* he murmured before his presence faded yet again.

Grinning, Fei threw back the sheets, located her communicator and called Bock.

***

Ton Tinel's skin, in reality, was very visibly red, as though he had been left out in the sun for too long, and his bald head bore even deeper streaks of scarlet. He was clearly a Utalian and must have been applying a filter to his Webcasts to hide it. Fei suspected this was due to the fact that humans were the dominant species in the galaxy and many of them were disinclined to trust non-humans. Definitely not a disadvantage that any mediaist would want.

After perfunctory greetings, delivered in Ton Tinel's cool and cordial style, the mediaist and Bock sat at the same time in opposite chairs, their gazes connected, as though a plank of wood was resting beneath their chins.

Fei and Ala stood in the corner of Bock's office, both of them keeping well out of the way. Though Ala had proven herself unwilling to take the spotlight that Bock inhabited, she swung her weight from foot to foot, clearly wanting to take over from her husband. Bock had been speaking very well so far and had only managed to swear once. Ton Tinel was just as genteel and neither of them raised their voices, even when they reached the topic of the 'alleged' connection between GLEA and TerraCorp.

'Governor Atsason, if you had committed a crime affecting a subsidiary of the Agency, then surely GLEA would be well within their rights to hold you accountable, connected or not,' Tinel pointed out.

Bock's expression remained stony. 'First of all, I am this planet's ruler. GLEA is supposed to enforce *my* laws, which I haven't broken. And I should know — I created a fair few of them. Secondly, I have done nothing to TerraCorp that wasn't legal. We had a contract signed under Enocian law, one that I used to obtain a refund. GLEA should not be interfering, *connected or not.*'

Tinel ended the live Webcast with a slashing motion of his hand. While the vidsreens in the office filled with advertising from his sponsors, the mediaist held a palm to the side of his face and nodded, as though he was listening to someone speaking to him on a communicator inserted into his skin. Fei wouldn't be surprised if this was the case — the device's location would make it easy for him to hold conversations when he didn't want people to notice. Even an earpiece could be spotted at the right angle.

Dropping his hand, Tinel said, 'We'll be going live again shortly. Is there anything you want to ask me before we do?'

Fei stifled a grin when Bock's questions veered away from what Tinel had expected and became focused on whether or not there was a way for him to gain ownership of TerraCorp's twenty-nine functioning machines, given that the company had so thoughtfully dropped them onto his planet.

'Your laws forbid you from doing any more than holding onto them,' Ton Tinel said mildly.

Bock's grin showed teeth. 'Not what I asked.'

'You would have to convince TerraCorp to hand them over.'

'Not impossible, but.'

Tinel's expression, which had been so carefully controlled until now, cracked into a brief smile. 'No, I suppose not.'

The companionable moment was broken when the communicator in the mediaist's palm chirped. Ton Tinel turned his vidcam back on with another gesture (it had been dutifully hovering over his shoulder) and then held out his hand to Bock. 'GLEA extends to you the opportunity to discuss your differences in their main temple on Gerasnin. What do you say?'

'I'll only talk to them if they come down here and speak to me on my own terms,' Bock growled. 'It also wouldn't hurt if they offered me something. Say, an apology in the form of twenty-nine terraforming machines to use as I will...'

Ala groaned softly beside Fei. 'Idiot. Goin' off script and playing his hand too soon.'

Even Ton Tinel seemed taken aback by Bock's brazenness.

None of them, except maybe Bock, were very surprised when

GLEA refused to respond. And so the Agency's starships continued to orbit Yalsa 5, not attacking the planet, but not leaving it either.

***

Kuja was sitting on the ground outside Gerns' lab, exiled for 'talking too much and gettin' real irritating', when Zareth approached him and quietly explained that his friend in the Chipper headquarters on Gerasnin had found proof of the connection between TerraCorp and GLEA. Zareth didn't want to go to the mediaists with the files himself, which was understandable, though the agent did promise that he was working on changing the Agency from within. It would take time, but Zareth was sure it could be done. Kuja watched Zareth return to the outpost, overcome with a swell of respect he'd never expected to feel for any Chipper.

Kuja tried to tell himself that it was more secure to directly copy the files Zareth had given him onto Fei's techpad than it was to send them over the Web. But a few minutes later, when the Rforine looked over his shoulder at Fei's face, slackened by sleep and exhaustion, he admitted to the real reason he had come here. She was pushing herself too hard to save Yalsa 5, but he wouldn't have expected any less from the woman he lo...

No, don't finish that sentence, he warned himself. He knew he was being overly cautious, but if one of his mind-reading siblings happened to catch the stray thought and reported back to Fayay...

He left the techpad on the desk and sat beside Fei on the bed, leaning over to brush the sandy blonde hair from her face. He stopped himself just in time. He should have left then, but her mind reached out for his and he answered. She was having a very pleasant dream — they were both by the waterfall on Bagaran, both of them mysteriously missing clothes. She was lying beneath him, vines creeping around her wrists, pinning her there for him to ravish.

Kuja swallowed. He could blame the painful hardness in his pants for this lapse in judgement later. Bending down, he gently kissed her forehead and murmured, 'Fei.'

Her eyelids fluttered open. The darkness of the room made it impossible to tell what colour she had programmed her irises to mimic this time, but he didn't need to see them to feel her confusion — or her dazed desire.

'Kuja, are you really here?' she asked drowsily.

'Maybe, maybe not,' he answered, a hand gliding beneath the sheets and finding naked skin. He groaned in appreciation when his palm cupped her moist sex. 'But does it matter?'

Fei ripped the sheet off her body in response, then rapidly balled it up and tossed it aside. Grinning, Kuja kissed his way up her thigh, then let his lips roam further until they latched onto a breast. She had just enough time to moan his name before he rolled her over and nudged her onto all fours. Arching himself over her back and unbelting his pants with one hand, he used his powers to conjure the vines that tied her hands to the headboard. More vines ensnared her ankles before burrowing down the side of the bed.

Fei bucked impatiently when his fingers walked along the inside of her thigh. She had stopped asking questions. But he could still hear the wild thoughts tumbling through her mind. She wanted this. She didn't care if it was just a dream. She wanted him.

'And I want you *now*,' Fei added breathlessly.

So he gave himself to her, flicking a finger over her engorged nub to relax her and make his entrance easier for both of them. Her warm folds gave a hard clench when he seated himself inside her and she begged him to move his hand, because she might come too soon. Kuja obeyed, grunting when she pushed back against him, forcing him deeper.

Oh, Fei...

'Kuja,' she whispered.

He had planned to make love to her gently, but it had been weeks since they'd done this and his desperation made him drive into her. It was barely a minute before she spasmed to completion around him, causing Kuja to cry out against her shoulder blade. They collapsed into a tangle of limbs, both of them alternatively laughing or gasping for air. The vines, at Kuja's non-verbal command, had already fled the scene, vanishing before Fei could become too suspicious. Stretching luxuriously, Fei rolled onto her side and touched Kuja's face, tracing his contented smile.

'I don't want to wake up,' she said.

Kuja took her fingers and kissed all ten of them. 'You must. Because I have sent you the files you need. They link GLEA directly to TerraCorp and show who's funding whom. And I am certain that once you show them to Ton Tinel, GLEA will be very willing to come to Yalsa 5 to talk.'

Fei scrunched up her face. 'I'd rather have you than those files. It's just not fair. I'm going to spend the whole day thinking about this dream and how I'd really like to have sex — and I'll have no one to do it with!'

Kuja hesitated. 'You don't need to remain celibate for the rest of your life, Fei.'

But I want you to be the last person to touch me this way, she thought at him, her yawn smothering the words when she tried to speak them. *Kuja, I love you...*

She slumped against the bed, her cheek sinking into the pillow as she fell back asleep. Sighing softly, Kuja slid out of her grasp and vanished inside a vortex filled in with a confusion of greens and browns. Within moments he was perched on a branch on Saren, watching the town from his concealed position, wondering if Gerns would be able to put up with him again because he badly needed some company.

'You've got to stop doing things like that, Kuja,' someone said. 'Anyone could catch you mooning around after her.'

Kuja dropped from the tree and fell onto his knees, scuttling around his sister to make sure her arrival hadn't singed anything. Thankfully, it seemed the thicket had escaped any damage from the teleportation swirl fuelled by the fire goddess' abilities.

Kuja leaned back onto his haunches. 'I don't know what you're talking about.'

'Do you want to end up like Sandsa?' the Firine demanded, hands braced on her hips. 'And no, I wouldn't hurt your precious little plants. I don't get why you freak out about them so much. You can make new ones just by thinking them into existence.'

Kuja held out a hand, quietening the spiky ferns that quivered with anger on his behalf, then rose to his feet. 'Finara. What Fei and I have is merely physical. And Fayay doesn't even know she exists. She's safe.'

'Fayay *does* know,' the goddess countered. 'How many times did you fool around with the mortal near water, huh? You made it too easy for him to spy on you.'

'Why didn't you tell me earlier, Finara!?' he cried. His insides felt like they had been turned to molten rock. 'Has Fayay gone to Yalsa 5?'

Finara rolled her eyes. 'Look at you. You've only had her twice and you're this attached. It's weird, Kuja. Did you get this way about that woman in the Enocian Harem?'

Kuja clenched his fists, vines wrapping their way up his arms. 'Finara. Tell me.'

'I don't think Fayay has followed her there,' Finara assured him. 'But I wouldn't relax just yet. The moment he sees you hanging over her shoulder like a methane cloud...'

'I am her god,' Kuja said, relaxing his arms and ordering the vines to drop from them. He refused to unleash his powers on Finara; Fayay was the one he wanted to hurt. 'I am guiding her and listening to her prayers.'

'If that's what you call appearing in her room at night and making love to her.'

'How much did you see?' he demanded.

'Not much, bro, and I swear I won't snitch,' Finara said. 'I only looked in on you because I heard Fayay mention you'd had a bit of fun. He said it was lucky Sandsa hadn't rubbed off on you or he'd have to put an end to it.'

Something cold seemed to be pressing against the nape of Kuja's neck. 'I'd rather not know what Fayay meant by that.'

'Yeah, neither do I,' Finara agreed. 'But look, you need to be careful. Can you honestly tell me you'd leave that much of your presence with any other mortal?'

Kuja didn't bother to answer that. She wouldn't believe him anyway. He wasn't even sure he'd believe himself.

'Don't you dare give Fayay a reason to go after her,' he snarled instead. 'She's my follower so I am duty-bound to care for her. But

I guess you wouldn't know anything about that. You don't care about the mortals in your domain and none of them give a shit about you. No one worships or loves you, Finara. They just put up with you.'

Finara drew in a sharp breath, then exploded into a maelstrom of fire that soon became nothing more than a wisp of smoke.

Kuja winced and wished he could take back his words. Finara's hurt remained with him, like a heavy footprint left in drying mud.

'I'm sorry,' he whispered. 'I didn't mean that.'

Fuck off, you totally did, his sister sent before she severed the connection between them.

Shaking, hating himself even more, Kuja walked back down to the settlement.

CHAPTER TWENTY-SIX

When GLEA attempted to contact Bock directly — about five seconds after Ton Tinel told them he had files proving their connection to Terra Corp — the governor refused to speak to them and named Tinel as his chosen mediator. All communication was to go through the mediaist's shipboard systems and, as such, was at risk of appearing in a Webcast. So if GLEA dared to mention that the files were the reason they were proposing to hold negotiations down in Atsa City, they would incriminate themselves on a galactic scale.

Fei couldn't help but smile, even though the angry Chipper on the large vidscreen in Bock's office could definitely see her sitting next to Ton Tinel. Bock had insisted she be there for the call, since she was the one who'd netted them the files and 'deserved to take some of the blame'. But instead of being afraid, Fei found she quite enjoyed watching Head General Huw Hunslow squirm.

She still wasn't sure what to make of the previous night. She had woken up feeling as though she'd had sex and had even caught Kuja's scent on her pillow. Then, when she'd checked her techpad, she'd found the files he had promised her. Her confusion hadn't stopped her from using them — or from hoping that Kuja would revisit her dreams soon, especially if he was going to take her from behind again.

'Looking forward to seeing you at our *conference* in two Old

Earth weeks, Head General,' Bock said with a smirk. Clearly he thought the label GLEA had given their upcoming negotiations was laughable. 'All the security has been arranged. My best people will be there, packing lasguns. And trust me, they know how to use them.'

GLEA's highest-ranking agent flinched and swiped a hand in front of his face. The screen went dark.

Tinel leaned forward in his chair, a diagonal line of triumph slashed across his features. 'Of course you will now sign the agreement that states I have exclusive access to the conference.'

Bock chuckled. 'We'll see, we'll see.' He lobbed a grin at Fei. 'Did you ever think you could manage something on this scale?'

'No,' Fei answered honestly.

'Well, you have,' Bock said, then let his voice drop back into his usual accent. 'And don't ya forget it!'

Fei ducked her head, embarrassed by his praise.

Bock sighed and waved an impatient hand through the air. 'You have to get used to saying "thanks, I'm fucking awesome", because you're starking good at what ya do. And I intend to use you once them terraforming machines are mine. Gonna make TerraCorp hand them over to me in return for those files, that's the deal I'll be offering them. Even Ala likes that idea.'

Fei cleared her throat. 'Um. Thanks, I'm fucking...yes.'

'Now get back to work,' Bock ordered her.

***

A rumble filled the air, too steady and constant to have come from a storm. Kuja glanced up as a starship broke apart the clouds, splitting grey into blue. The egg-shaped vessel coasted down onto the cracked landing pad, its engines whirring endlessly instead of cutting out. The ship wasn't going to be there for long — all it needed to do was pick up three Chippers.

Major Laura Minsra hadn't announced the withdrawal until barely one Old Earth hour before the agents were due to leave. According to her, the Sarenites had lost their way and she could no longer help them find their path. While Kuja was sure this wasn't a surprise to the townspeople, they were still shocked and upset.

'They're leaving!' one woman cried, fingers clawing into her scalp. 'How could they leave?'

Other settlers used far stronger language. Some just sat in silence. Any children that were clutched to heaving chests cried out, not immune to the net of fear spun by their parents.

Gerns' beady eyes followed the Chippers as they took even strides away from the town. 'Was this our fault, for not encouraging the Sarenites to say they were followers of the Creator God?'

'No,' Kuja said. 'It was GLEA's actions that lost them both worshippers and potential funders of their galactic invasion.'

'Keep talking like that and this'll start sounding like a war,' Gerns warned him.

Kuja laughed darkly. 'Isn't it a war already? We might be the mop-up crew, Gerns, but something is causing these casualties.'

Gerns' made a soft huffing sound. 'Now me, I'm just wondering why we can't all get along.'

'Probably because the gods don't get along with each other,' Kuja muttered as he began marching up towards the landing pad. 'And they're supposed to be our role models.'

Major Minsra and one of her companions were facing the

starship, their expressions grim, as though they were being forced to retreat from a fight they could have won. Zareth stood apart from the pair, quiet grief streaking over his face as surely as tears. His fellow Chippers began to board the ship but he stayed right where he was, unmoving, unspeaking.

Kuja went to him, not bothering to keep his voice down. 'I know you're not like the others! You can't leave — you don't *want* to leave! These people badly need your protection.'

'I know.' Zareth's dark eyes blazed. 'Kuja, I'm staying. Minsra can run back to Gerasnin for all I care, but this is not how we're meant to do things. We're all children of the Creator God, doesn't matter if some of us worship someone else. I can't take anyone off this moon because I can't afford to chart a vessel on my salary, but I have a lasgun and decent enough aim. I'll protect Saren as best I can.'

'Private Sins, get over here now!' Minsra shouted from the boarding ramp.

Kuja held his breath; he'd sensed a flutter of fear inside Zareth.

But Zareth suppressed it and went for broke.

'I can't do that, Major,' he said. 'These people need me.'

Minsra's hand clapped down on her lasgun, but she didn't draw it. 'I'll have your chip ripped out for this, Private! Don't think I won't!'

'You better send someone else to do it then!' Zareth told her. 'Because you're too afraid to do it yourself, without any authorisation, aren't you?'

Minsra swore loudly, then turned her back on him. The ramp popped seamlessly into place behind her and moments later the vessel tore up into the atmosphere, one Chipper short.

'The Sarenites need to see me doing what's right,' Zareth muttered, his eyes travelling down the hill, towards the town.

'You don't represent all the Chippers in the galaxy,' Kuja pointed out.

'Neither does Minsra,' Zareth said.

'You're still just one man.'

Zareth spread his arms, as though to encompass the entire galaxy, and grinned carelessly. 'Yes. But it always starts with *just one man*, doesn't it. I want to make things right from the inside and convince the others to protect everyone as we should.'

Kuja exhaled in exasperation. 'That will take time — time Yalsa 5 doesn't have.'

'We'll just have to hope those files we gave Fei can stall my superiors,' Zareth said.

'You could go straight over there now and expose GLEA for what it is,' Kuja told him. 'It would make Fei think more kindly towards you. You're not a bad man, Zareth.'

'I can't.' Zareth ran a hand over his hair. It bounced back immediately once he'd removed his touch. 'I don't want her forgiveness. What I did was shitty, no matter which way you cut the cake.'

Kuja's bowels gave a savage twist when he thought about his own behaviour regarding Fei. He settled for a safer topic. 'So, if you do manage to get GLEA on track, I have to ask — what do you plan to do about the sub-level gods?'

Zareth looked pained. 'I'm not sure. But I won't be storming in and terraforming things against everyone's will. That looks bad enough even before the mediaists start doing their Webcasts.'

Kuja considered pressing his companion, asking more questions, but Zareth's mind was full of turbulence and disbelief

— mostly with himself, for doing something so foolish, something that had threatened his career. Zareth's fingers strayed to the bump on his temple, where his chip lay.

The agent didn't want anyone to take it from him. But he had risked losing it anyway.

Humbled, Kuja watched Zareth return to the townspeople. They crowded around the Chipper, all of them trying to lay their hands on him. Zareth looked distinctly uncomfortable with their praise; clearly the man wasn't used to receiving it. Reminded of Fei, Kuja walked into a nearby thicket then vanished, heading for that perpetually cool room where she spent her nights alone.

He stood over her for some time before rousing her. She said it was a dream. He did not deny it. Being with her was a dream that could never become reality. But he could be there for her in the shadows of night, making love to her and holding her close for as long as he dared.

He didn't regret the smile that painted her lips as she fell asleep in his arms.

***

When Kuja returned to Saren, the town was in the throes of a hot afternoon, having been deserted by the wind. Many of the settlers were uneasy and muttered amongst themselves, looking towards the tree line, where the virus lay in wait. Zareth was nowhere to be seen, but the potted plant inside the outpost told Kuja that the Chipper was hunched over on the floor of the antechamber, his head in his hands.

Kuja remained inside the dense grove, hidden from view as he knelt into the path of the virus. It rushed up to him like an enthusiastic child; the fronds beneath him died instantly, browning and falling apart before fluttering away like ash on a breeze. The virus danced around the Rforine, momentarily distracted from its destruction, and begged him for his approval.

This virus was created by the Ine, before I was even born, Kuja thought, his lip curling. *I suppose it's fitting that the Chippers abandoned the Sarenites to the destruction set into motion by their god.*

Master? the virus whispered.

Kuja sighed, wishing it didn't sound so in awe of him. 'I have something to ask of you.'

Anything, Master, it promised. *Anything.*

'Is there any way you can avoid the town in the valley?'

A pause. *If you wished it, your powers could bar me from anywhere you chose.*

'But the moment I lose concentration,' Kuja said, grimacing, 'you'll sweep into the valley and destroy the crops there.'

Confusion coloured the virus' words. *But, Master, you would never lose concentration.*

Kuja drew his thumb over a crease forming on his forehead. Several more attempts did nothing to erase it so he dropped his hand to caress the destroyed plant material beneath him. He was sad whenever anything died, but death always led to life and renewal inside the rainforests. It was a natural process, something he couldn't subvert without a great deal of will.

And Kuja knew he was capable of losing concentration. He doubted he had much mental capacity left when he was making love to Fei and that...that was something he'd decided he should be allowed to keep, even if he could never again see sunlight kiss her skin.

I have to think like Gerns and Fei, he decided.

It would take years for Gerns to find a plant that the virus couldn't eat, especially if it was not indigenous to the planet, and then there were the months needed to grow a protective circle around the town...

'Have you ever encountered a plant — or anything, really — that blocks you and hampers you from moving forward?' Kuja asked, watching the virus circle the fingers he'd left in the soil.

The virus delivered its answer after some consideration. *Not a plant. Myself.*

'What do you mean?'

If I come across plants I have previously killed, the virus explained, *then I cannot reinfect them or go past them. This is why I must always seek new ground.*

Kuja pursed his lips. Finara had once said something similar about the way fire reacted to material that had already been burned — flames could not easily cross an area they had destroyed. Some worlds, like savannah-clad Sundafar, actually torched their grasses in order to form firebreaks for when a more deadly inferno swept towards their settlements.

'Thank you!' Kuja said and sprinted back towards the town.

He slowed to a jog before entering Gerns' warehouse. The botanist, in lieu of any real progress, had continued to send data about the flora she encountered to Yalsa 5. Fei had mentioned it to her employers at some point, so Gerns was now on a salary given to her by Governor Bock Atsason. The Jezlo said this was a much better incentive than a rainforest god promising her goodwill and warm fuzzies.

When Gerns saw Kuja, she hopped off her seat. Kuja didn't even give her a chance to greet him; he immediately blurted out what he had deduced and finished with, '...so you'll need to work with the virus and get it to ring the town and somehow not let it get out of control.'

'Now me, I can infect the grasses around here, but I'm not sayin' I can control it,' Gerns said, waddling down one of the rows inside the lab.

Kuja frowned. 'But you will try.'

'What do you think I'm doing, Kuja?' Gerns stopped dead and slapped the tables either side of her with her tentacles. 'My brain's bigger than yours and it's already tickin' over. Now me, if I was you, I'd get out of here and find something useful to do. You'll only be in my way here.'

There was no point in trying to hold a conversation with her when she was like this, so Kuja simply nodded and left.

CHAPTER
TWENTY-SEVEN

Fei kept her eyes closed when she woke and stayed very still, maintaining her cocoon inside the sheets. The cold, sterile air supplied by the climate control system allowed her to maintain this position, which was dangerous because Fei was tempted to lie there in bed for too long, her anxiety mounting to unbearable levels.

Today GLEA would arrive en masse to attend their so-called 'conference'. And she would have to go meet them, sit with them, maybe even *say things* to them.

Fei lifted her knees, then bent over and rested her head between them, breathing deeply. 'Bock's doing most of the talking. You just have to provide data. And supporting arguments.'

But her stomach squirmed instead of settling. Fei groaned, pressing a hand to her abdomen. Ala had taken her out the previous night and plied her with alcohol which should have made Fei feel brave, but it had only made her feel nauseous. And her nerves definitely weren't helping right now.

Muttering some choice words, Fei dragged herself out of bed and into the shower. By the time she had scrubbed the phantom scent of Kuja from her skin and dealt with her hair, she was running extremely late so she had to sprint for the hoverlift, a piece of toast cratered against her teeth. Brushing crumbs off her lips as she stepped onto the ground floor, she caught sight of the heavily shielded hovercar waiting outside for her — and then she baulked. Dividing her from safety was a gauntlet made up of mediaists with vidcams and onlookers bristling with lasguns.

'Am I...supposed to go through that alone?' she demanded of the empty lobby.

Kuja didn't arrive to rescue her. But someone else did.

'No, that's what ya got me for,' Ala said, entering through the front door and supporting a bulky lasgun on one hip like a beloved child. 'They know not to fuck with the wife of the Clan Leader.'

'So he's the Clan Leader today, not a governor,' Fei noted.

'Same smell,' Ala replied with a smirk. 'But it'll make them Chippers uncomfortable if we remind them we've still got some real fight left in us.'

Fei knotted her hands together. 'Ala...I'm not sure I can do this.'

Ala watched Fei closely for a moment, then jerked her head back towards the crowd outside. 'Come on, Fei. The faster we get there, the faster it's over. And not that I'd ever let my personal life interfere with this shit, but it's my turn with Ginsella tonight and I really don't want this starking *conference* to run overtime.'

Fei reluctantly smiled and followed Ala out the door. The screaming crowd and the heat of densely packed bodies immediately pressed in on Fei, making her lungs seize up. She couldn't fault her protector, but while Ala's hands on her head and shoulder kept her beneath the worst of the tumult, they did little to comfort her.

Fei, you can do this, I know you can, Kuja told her.

She latched onto the voice of the man she loved, letting it guide her steps until she was safely inside the hovercar. Sliding into the front, Ala snapped her fingers at the driver and began barking orders at him, something about taking a more circuitous route in case the Chippers had installed snipers on the main road. Swallowing her panic, Fei closed her eyes and tilted her head back against the seat.

Oh, Kuja, Fei thought. *I need you with me.*

I'm always here with you, the voice of her lover promised.

Fei sighed. *If you say so. I've prayed to Bagara, asking for you. But has he really sent you? Or have I been dreaming these past two weeks?*

Kuja's ensuing chuckle was laced with desire and something else, something secret. *I know you want me instead of Bagara. Just...let him stand in for me.*

But I don't want to kiss him, Fei protested.

I don't want you to kiss anyone else either!

Fei laughed and opened her eyes to find Ala studying her closely.

'Do ya lose focus like that often?' Ala asked.

'Please don't tell me I need hyponeedles,' Fei grumbled. 'I get by without any enhancements, thank you. Why do you ask?'

'Because you had a look on that face of yours just then...' Ala frowned. 'Like you were talkin' to someone in your mind. I know that look. So were you? That Kuja dude?'

Fei wriggled her toes inside her shoes. They were flats, designed to mould to her feet, but now they felt too sweaty and too tight. 'I like imagining he's here with me. It relaxes me.'

'How do ya know you're not actually talking to him?' Ala asked, her one real eye blade-thin.

'It's just pretend.'

'Hmm,' was all Ala said to that.

Fei peered out the window as they approached their destination, a large hotel with silver cords that curled endlessly around the core of the building, reminding Fei of a twisted Bagaran Strangler. The hotel, shining so brightly it caused Fei to see its shape on the backs of her eyelids, seemed to be a newer addition to the cityscape, judging by the fact that it wasn't decaying and decrepit like some of the other buildings crowding Atsa.

Ala jumped out of the hovercar before it had fully stopped, clearing a path with threats and a wave of her lasgun. Fei dropped her feet onto the pavement — and then went very still. Hundreds of people were waiting for her, but one man in particular made hot fear curdle in her gut.

'You alright?' Ala shouted over the din.

Fresh briny air streamed over Fei's face, forcing her to blink repeatedly. The man kept watching her, his blue eyes so pale they were almost colourless. When Fei shivered, the man slowly grinned and turned away, disappearing into the crowd.

What is he doing here? Kuja's voice demanded.

Fei's jaw clenched and started aching. *Do...do you know him?*

You could say that. But it's alright. He's decided you aren't a threat. For now.

Fei realised a vidcam was aimed at her so she flashed a dazzling smile. *I wish I knew what it was you were actually protecting me from.*

'Ms Neron, Ms Neron!' someone shouted. 'If these rumours of a connection between TerraCorp and GLEA are true, why have you turned your back on a company sanctioned by the Creator God?'

Fei felt her cheeks tighten, enough to make the inside of them meet the edges of her teeth. Ala grabbed her arm, trying to pull her towards the hotel, but Fei dug in her heels and swung towards the offending mediaist. 'If the Creator God really does care about free will then he won't have an issue with it — and enough people accept me for me, so I don't care if one particular god doesn't like me. I'm done denying myself to please him.'

Fei lifted her chin, gave an imperious nod and then marched inside so quickly that Ala had to jog to keep up with her. The cool air awaiting them in the hotel lobby was a welcome change from the heat outside, but it made Fei immediately sneeze. She caught the spray on her sleeve, then belatedly realised that most of the conference attendees were staring at her. Ton Tinel was among them, the only mediaist allowed inside, his vidcam recording everything. Fei dropped her arm, mouth agape, and gave no resistance when Ala ushered her over to Bock's side.

The Chipper who was currently speaking to the governor had smooth dark skin and his hair lacked any silver which Fei thought unfair, given the amount he had caused to grow over her mother's scalp. Fei was glad she had tamed her own hair with a heavy dose of chemicals that morning, keeping it far flatter than his springy mop. The differences didn't end there — her strands were brilliant green today, matched by her eyes. His natural irises remained earthen brown.

'Colonel Lilon Neron,' Fei greeted when she was sure her voice would remain steady.

'Call me "Dad",' Lilon requested. 'You are well aware that I am living with your mother again. You might as well give me the same courtesy you do her.'

Fei felt a twinge of guilt. *You're the reason I haven't called Mum in a while.*

Bock glanced at her. 'This true? He's your dad? Could've asked him to help us out earlier.'

'Oh, he barely knows he has a daughter so there wasn't a point,' Fei said acidly. 'In my experience, Chippers don't care about anyone, much less their own families.'

Her father could have at least had the grace to look stricken, she thought.

'Fei — ' he began, his voice stern.

Head General Huw Hunslow, much more pasty and pinched in person, coasted over to insert himself into the conversation. His lips peeled back to display several layers of teeth, his face shimmering as it struggled to accommodate his predatory smile. Hunslow was poorly disguised by an illusion projected from the device on his belt, to make him pass for human in a predominantly human organisation. Fei thought her father was attempting to pass as a decent person but with less success.

'Let us be professional,' Hunslow said. 'This is not the time or place for personal issues — '

Fei opened her mouth, but Bock got in first. He laughed and patted the lasgun on his belt, a not-so-subtle warning. 'You lot didn't land yourself in this mess by being *professional*. Get in that room and into your designated seat before I decide this is all just a big waste of time and blast some extra holes in your worthless hides.'

As if waiting for this command, the gold floor-to-wall doors of the conference room swung outwards in an ancient style, revealing a brightly-lit interior. Ala followed the other conference attendees into the room but Bock calmly waited outside, letting everyone else pass ahead of him.

Fei cleared her throat. 'Thank you, Bock. But I think I can fight my own battles now.'

'I figured,' he said. 'But stark, I really like putting 'em in their place.'

Bock held his arm out to her.

Smiling, Fei took it and let him lead her to her fate.

***

That same potted plant inside the Chipper outpost on Saren warned Kuja when Zareth began packing. The Rforine swiftly formed a body and stomped down the hill, using the walk to query the nearby virus. It confirmed what Gerns had already told Bagara that morning — there was now a barrier in place around the town that it couldn't cross.

Kuja allowed a brief smile, impressed. *Gerns did it, she actually did it — I'll have to get her a drink for real this time, to celebrate.*

He made his way into the outpost's sleeping quarters and fixed his most potent glare on the moon's only remaining agent.

'So now that Gerns has saved these people,' Kuja said, shaking his head in disgust, 'you're going to leave and take the credit whenever a mediaist asks.'

Zareth stared at his visitor, a spare purple jumpsuit dangling from one hand. 'You can't seriously think that's what I'm up to. I'm going to Gerasnin — I gave it some thought and I realised I can't change things out here on Saren. I have to do what I can to save other worlds, the ones that don't have blackmail material to protect themselves.'

'I have a feeling that Bagara considers every moon, rock and planet under his protection, regardless of their climates,' Kuja said, his voice firm.

'No sub-level god can look after that many people,' Zareth said. 'The galaxy's too big for them. Us mortals have got to pitch in where we can.'

'Maybe mortals aren't meant to protect, just be protected.'

'Maybe,' Zareth echoed politely, his mind full of disagreement.

He resumed packing his things. It didn't take long; within ten minutes, he was bidding the townspeople farewell. Zareth told the Sarenites he would return one day with agents enough to protect the moon, either from pirates or opportunistic criminals. This didn't seem to be an immediate problem for Saren, but Zareth's promise made many of the townspeople emanate relief.

Kuja watched Zareth talk to each individual who asked for his time, thinking, *I wonder...I wonder if Zareth will manage to change GLEA. Is it possible that while mortals can corrupt the Agency's purpose, a mortal can also correct it?*

Kuja accompanied Zareth to the landing pad where both men waited as another egg-shaped ship descended from the sky, its hull covered in multiple solar panels that glinted in the sunshine.

'Will you go back to Fei?' Zareth asked. 'You don't talk about her much, but I get the feeling...'

Kuja shook his head.

Zareth turned to grip Kuja's forearms, his gaze deep and fervent. 'Kuja, you need to pursue what you want, even if it means risking everything.'

Kuja's chin hit his chest. 'I...I have failed before.'

'So you're giving up, just like that? You can't!' Zareth's hold on Kuja tightened. 'When you failed before, did you fail because you weren't good enough, or because you expected to fail?'

'There was no way to win,' Kuja said haltingly. 'I didn't want to give up but I...it was inevitable.'

'Was it?' Zareth challenged.

As the starship came closer to the ground, nearby branches whipped to and fro, performing a frenzied dance and slapping leaves onto the ground.

Zareth leaned further in, until their noses were almost touching. 'Fight, Kuja. Fight because it's the right thing to do. And who knows...you might even win.'

The ship finally settled onto the landing pad, throwing grit over their faces. Kuja kept his feelings churning low in his gut as he waved Zareth off, but when the ship rose into the sky, it sent a solid gust of air against his midsection, dislodging everything he'd tried so hard to hide.

Kuja clenched his fists and stamped his feet, a scream tearing out of him — raw, angry, defiant. Some plants begged him to calm down and others cheered him on, demanding retribution, but all of them carried the image of Fei, the woman who had inspired their god, the woman who was — *the Creator of Worlds?* Kuja paused, taken aback by the title the rainforests had given her.

Well, she does create worlds — and she needs me right now, he realised, feeling her distress.

He swiftly shed his body and sent a large portion of his presence over to Yalsa 5.

CHAPTER
TWENTY-EIGHT

The conference dragged on endlessly. Even after a short break for lunch it felt like an eternity had passed since Fei had left the warmth of her bed. She rested her chin on a bridge formed by the backs of her hands as she listened to various people repeat themselves over and over again. Her father was seated near her, much to her dismay, but between them were several bodyguards and even Ala, whose menacing mechanical eye frequently swiped in Lilon Neron's direction, keeping him in place.

Fei's stomach gave an unhappy twist. Ala's cup of coffein was throwing off the standard bitter scent, which usually wouldn't have bothered Fei, but today it burrowed into her nostrils and deposited greasy, acrid layers. She fought the urge to double over.

Ala looked at her. 'You alright?'

'It's just...just nerves,' Fei ground out, her forehead now low enough to graze the table.

Slowly, uncertainly, something unfurled inside her, a small, curious presence that reached for her the moment it noticed she was paying attention. Joy pricked the corners of Fei's eyes. She had to force herself to swallow the words she wanted to shout.

When she finally managed to lift her head, Ala's mouth was forming soundless shapes and the continuing murmurs around the table made even less sense than they had before.

I'm pregnant, Fei thought with such conviction that she almost laughed.

She heard a sharp intake of breath, as though Kuja was sitting beside her.

No, he protested. *No, that can't be.*

Fei hid her smile by pretending to cough into her hand and nodded along when Ala leaned in to enquire about her wellbeing. *So I wasn't dreaming all those times. I'm sorry — I am so, so sorry — but I took the implant out weeks ago. Before you left. It was stupid and selfish and wrong.*

Why didn't you tell me!? Kuja sounded upset. Fei had expected that, given what she'd done, but what she hadn't expected was the undercurrent of fear in his words.

Kuja, she said, not bothering to mask her annoyance, *I'm not the only one at fault here. Clearly you were visiting me and pretending it wasn't happening. If I'd known you were really there, I would have told you! Look, I know you're just part of my psyche, but it would be nice if you were at least a little bit happy about this...*

I am! Kuja cried. *And I would love to start a family with you — but he will come back!*

What are you talking about? Just tell me, Kuja!

An image of the strange man who had been in the crowd outside the hotel surfaced in Fei's mind. Her heart spasmed in fear and she grabbed the edge of the table to keep from falling off the chair that for whatever absurd reason didn't have a supportive back. Fei had to blink several times, stunned, because suddenly there were vines entwined around her arms, keeping her anchored to the table. It was as if they'd grown right out of the wooden surface.

A tiny blade shot out from the cuff of one of Ala's sleeves

and the other woman swiftly used it to saw through the vines. Ala then yanked Fei's hands off the table.

'Anything you want to share?' Ala demanded, her voice a harsh whisper as she swept the remains of the plant onto the floor.

'You saw that? It was *real?* Oh!' Fei's heart soared. 'Bagara! Bagara has given me powers so that we can fight the Chippers. This is great news, Ala — we need to tell Bock — '

Ala's nails dug into Fei's flesh. 'Tell no one. This is not what you think it is.'

'But the rainforest god — '

A low, strangled sound corded its way out of Ala's mouth. 'I don't doubt it's the rainforest god. But I don't think you should start splashin' this about.'

'But why else would he give — ' Fei began.

Ala hushed her, scowling. 'We'll talk about it later. Put that god out of your head for now and focus on the god that's actually causin' us this trouble.'

Fei quickly projected a mask of polite agreement, which she hoped fooled Ala. Fei was certain she'd had more than enough practice doing this; she'd spent two Old Earth years convincing Moz she was actually listening to him and not staring at his mouth, wondering when it would stop moving.

But then Bock turned towards her and she really did have to listen this time.

Fei nodded once, getting the gist of his words, then took in the wide, round table full of people waiting to hear what she had to say. She swallowed. 'Um. Hi. I used to work for TerraCorp but then I discovered they were bankrolling GLEA. We have proof of that now. But why not let the whole galaxy know that you are one and the same? Just be transparent. You wouldn't have to worry about us, um, releasing the files then. You could spin this any way you want to, make yourselves look good.'

Lilon rose from his chair, causing it to scrape over the marble floor. 'Feiscina, you refuse to listen to our god and so feel abandoned by those who do, those who know the path the Creator God has given them to follow. You are jealous of that faith and success. Admit that this is the true reason behind this farce. Admit that you are choosing this battleground for your personal vendetta.'

Fei raised her eyebrows at him, wondering if he expected her to shrink the way she'd always done before him. She'd suffered years of him talking over her and never bothering to understand her. Berale Neron was ten times the parent he would ever be.

I'm a grown woman and soon I'll have my own child, Fei thought, leaving her seat and gaining as much height against her father as possible. *I will not abandon my son. I will never let him think he isn't good enough. I had Berale. And he will have me.*

'Transparency.' Fei's voice was wispy at first and failed to rise above the mutters filling the room. So she lifted her chin and tried again. 'Transparency. You ask transparency of me yet won't give it yourselves. That is...disappointing.'

Fei caught Ton Tinel's approving nod and grinned at the mediaist. But her triumph faded when she saw her former boss, Mozel Zan, jump out of his chair.

Moz turned away from her, to the rest of the room, and said, 'Feiscina Neron was suffering a crisis of faith. She let her own personal doubts interfere with her work. And now she is letting those doubts create strife where there should be none. If you want transparency, there it is.'

'Sit down, Mr Zan,' Bock ordered. He worked his shoulders

against the air, apparently loosening them — or getting ready for a physical fight. But his words remained carefully chosen, his genuine accent buried. 'This isn't about Fei. This is about the fact that GLEA's bankrolling TerraCorp and not being entirely forthcoming to their clients or the people they're supposed to be looking after.'

Ala nodded sagely. 'Could be that GLEA's afraid the folk they've hurt will stop pumpin' coin-chips into TerraCorp once they find out the truth.'

Moz lobbed a pleading look down the table at the TerraCorp leaders whose vinyl suits shone beneath the piped lighting. Moz might be middle management, but even he was at the mercy of his superiors. They were using him in an attempt to rattle Fei.

She smirked. It wasn't working.

'Since you are now aware that TerraCorp belongs to GLEA...' Lilon Neron said, his voice booming across the table. Moz seated himself hastily. '...it's in your best interests to return the machines. Or there may be repercussions. Governor Atsason, just how many gangs do you have to fight a war for you? And would they? I was under the impression they are still separate factions despite being united by the man you ousted from power.'

'That is not how it happened,' Ala said icily.

Bock's forehead creased so much that his brow cast shadows over his eyes. 'Are you Chippers looking to start a war? You're insane. You're not in charge of any governments. And not everyone's going to let you walk all over them — some worlds even have armies larger than GLEA.'

'Makes you wonder why the Chippers are so keen to get an outpost on every planet,' Ala added. 'They'll end up taking over the whole starking galaxy at this rate. Is that what you're plannin' on doing, Head General?'

Huw Hunslow's pointed silence condemned the entire Agency.

'Oh, I see,' Fei said with a jagged shake of her head. 'Stark free will. We don't get to choose which god we worship.'

'Only one god has given his people the power to protect the galaxy!' Lilon roared.

His hands shot out in front of him, rising until they stood above his shoulders. The table, caught inside the forcefield his chip had generated, lifted at his command and began to hover a hand's width above the floor. Multiple conference attendees reacted in panic, pushing themselves away from the table, their chairs forming a concert of screeches.

Fei stayed right where she was, her fury outweighing her fear. 'And what about the desert tribes? Their god, the Desine, gives them powers — and they don't even need a chip to use those!'

'They are liars!' Hunslow shouted. 'There is only one true god!'

Fei laughed and laughed, incapable of holding the derision in. She felt Ala's fingers dig into her arm, trying to pull her back from the table, but she jerked away and raised her hands to the ceiling, just as her father had done. 'Bagara, god of the rainforests, hear me. I need you. The people of Yalsa 5 need you. They desire to have you, so come claim us!'

Vines exploded from her palms then twisted and wriggled their way across the table, seeking out those who hadn't yet moved far enough away. The table was her next victim; it shook beneath the weight of the plants growing on it before toppling to the floor, where gnarled roots cracked it apart.

Fei smiled, enjoying how everyone cowered before her, even the ones with ugly protrusions on their temples.

Well, nearly everyone was cowering.

Bock cleared his throat, hands pressed together as though he'd been applauding. 'Well now, I guess we were holdin' a conference with the wrong people, not to mention the wrong god.'

Ala shot him a look. 'Don't ya dare do this, Bock.'

'Can this Bagara of yours terraform my planet without any tech?' Bock asked Fei, apparently unbothered by the warning in his wife's tone.

'I...I don't know,' Fei answered.

'That Kuja dude will know,' Bock said. 'Can you get in contact with him?'

Fei trembled. She felt her control slip. Barely a heartbeat later, the vines tumbled away from her and vanished, as though vaporised by a lasgun. She staggered backwards into Ala.

'I can't,' Fei whispered, feeling her guts tighten. 'It's not safe.'

Bock sneered but Ala held up one hand to silence him, using the other to set Fei back on her feet. 'Shut up, Bock. She's right. And it seems to me that Kuja left so she'd have a chance at a normal life without all the shit that messed Callista up.' Ala drew a breath. 'You're pregnant, aren't ya, Fei?'

Fei nodded, confused. She was sure she hadn't given herself away.

'Then the best thing you can do right now is stay off everyone's radar,' Ala said flatly.

Fei threw a frown between her two employers. 'You're not telling me something. I'm scared enough as it is without being kept in the dark. Get back!' she roared when one of the Chippers tried to edge closer. They obeyed, meekly shuffling off.

But Lilon wasn't to be deterred so easily. He marched forward, back straight and shoulders jutting up towards the ceiling. 'Feiscina. You cannot do this.'

'What, shatter your faith in the Creator God?' Fei asked. She gripped her elbows with her hands to keep them from knocking against her sides. 'I don't mean to point fingers, *Lilon*, but you did it to me first.'

Behind Lilon, representatives from both GLEA and TerraCorp began retreating towards the door. Annoyed that they were trying to sneak away before she was done with them, Fei barrelled forward, swooping aside so that her shoulder would not collide with her father's, and made her way around the perimeter of the table. She stopped only when she'd managed to get out in front of the representatives. They paused, all of them watching her with wary eyes.

'You're not the first abnormality we've seen,' Head General Huw Hunslow finally said, the illusion of his human face flickering even more violently than before. 'We are aware of all threats to GLEA, including those desert magicians. You do not surprise us. Or frighten us.'

'So you *do* acknowledge that the Desine's worshippers have powers, fancy that,' Fei said, then looked at Moz. He was frowning. 'Are you surprised that I'm no longer the little doormat you kept walking over? I made it too easy for you.'

'Feiscina.' Moz stepped forward — but only after a frantic shove from one of his superiors. 'All of this unpleasantness could have been avoided. I was your boss. I was there for you. Why couldn't you just talk to me?'

'So you could brush me off or steal my ideas and take the credit?' Fei shook her head. 'No. TerraCorp and GLEA lost me. Bagara was the one who cared enough to listen.'

She sauntered towards the door, pleased that she was more than capable of standing up for herself, and ran into Ton Tinel who was practically radiating triumph, though his red skin might have contributed to that impression. He had a lot of footage that he could use as blackmail now — and GLEA was not going to like that. Not one bit.

Fei grinned.

***

Kuja ran over the dunes on some desert world, tears streaking down his face. He tripped and toppled over yet again, the sand caking the precious moisture that bathed his cheeks. He was so afraid that he already knew what his brother going to say, but he had to ask. He had to know.

Levering himself onto his knees, Kuja cried, 'Sandsa! Stark it, Sandsa, I need you!'

The Desine ignored him. But the sand and grit around Kuja shifted, interest piqued. Encouraged, Kuja cupped some of the nearby grains in his hand and spoke to them. 'Please, my friends. I don't know if you look after him the way the rainforests look after me, but you've seen his pain, you know how bitter it's made him. I don't want to be like that. I don't want to become him.'

The sand trickled away between his fingers.

And then a shadow fell over the Rforine.

Kuja looked up just in time to see his brother drop onto ground beside him.

'I'm impressed,' Sandsa said, eyeing Kuja. 'I would never have thought to use your rainforests against you in such a manner. I must be wary or soon you will wrest the deserts from me.'

'Only you seem to have the ability to command more than your own domain, Sandsa,' Kuja said, then bit down hard on his bottom lip. The ensuing sting told him he'd drawn blood. 'I...I...oh, Sandsa. See into my thoughts. Fei is in so much danger and Fayay will come for her once he finds out — and it's my fault!'

Sandsa's lips twitched. 'For gods, we are surprisingly irresponsible. We forget that more caution is required in certain situations.' When Kuja blinked at him, Sandsa clarified, 'Birth control. But it was a beautiful thing, to create life with Callista.'

Sandsa closed his eyes, his grief throwing lines over his immortal features.

Kuja distantly knew that he shouldn't try to make his case when Sandsa was like this, but he couldn't feel anything beyond his own fear. 'Sandsa! Please! I thought — I thought leaving Fei would keep her safe. I was so stupid, visiting her at night...please. Please help me. The way I helped you.'

'You *helped* me?' Sandsa laughed darkly. The dunes around them bent and swayed; some disintegrated while others grew to the size of skyscrapers. 'You were useless when Fayay came for my family. He forced me to become a god again...and you did nothing.'

Kuja winced. If he hadn't failed, if he hadn't let his brother down so badly, then Sandsa might still be with Callista...no. No, that had been Callista's decision, not Kuja's.

Kuja shook his head. 'This is not about you.' He sent vines streaking out beneath the surface of the sand in all directions, like dark green veins writhing beneath beige flesh. 'I still have a chance. If you stand by, if you do nothing, then I will lose my family. Please don't let that happen! I want to see if I can...if I can be happy, the way you were.'

'Happy! You think I'm happy, never sensing my wife or son, never knowing where they are...' Sandsa dropped his chin to his chest, looking like a broken man.

'Please, Sandsa, I love her!' Kuja cried.

'Love isn't enough,' Sandsa retorted. 'There is so much more to it than love.'

'What then?' Kuja demanded. 'Anything I need to do, I will do it!'

Sand began to choke the Rforine's vines, halting their growth and cutting them off at the source. Kuja breathed slowly, allowing the loss, willing himself not to rise against his brother. He needed Sandsa's help. Desperately.

But when the Desine spoke his voice was flat. 'Kuja. Even if you were strong enough to fight Fayay and Father, what happens when Fei finds out what you are? She will leave you, just as Callista left me.'

Kuja seated his fists in his lap. 'My son already has his powers and Fei is accessing them — they need my support. They need me to be there for them.'

'I cannot help you.' Sandsa stood and began trudging away. 'I cannot watch your heart break.'

The desert god's form dissolved into sand and the next gust of wind obliterated what remained of Kuja's brother.

Kuja sat there, unmoving, spine bowed, face drenched with sweat and tears. But instead of drowning in despair, he found himself thinking of Zareth Sins' parting words on Saren.

Fight, Kuja. Fight because it's the right thing to do. And who knows...you might even win.

'I might not win,' Kuja murmured. 'But I have to try. She deserves no less.'

When he rose from the sand, he was not just a god. He was a man fighting for everything he loved and held dear.

CHAPTER
TWENTY-NINE

'If you don't accept TerraCorp's generous offer, then I will continue to live with your mother,' Colonel Lilon Neron stated, his voice devoid of any emotion as he delivered his threat.

Fei's hands clenched and unclenched at her sides. She knew her mother wasn't entirely happy about sharing the townhouse with Lilon and she suspected he wasn't particularly pleased about it either — he had only moved in with Berale for the extra space, after all. But Fei wasn't going to let Lilon manipulate her, even if she had made the mistake of letting him into her apartment.

The conference had finished an hour before dusk, despite how badly things had gone earlier. Agreements had been drawn up, stating that Bock now owned the twenty-nine functioning terraforming machines in return for surrendering all copies of the files exposing the connection between the Agency and TerraCorp. But GLEA knew Fei was Bock's best hope for using the machines. So they'd sent her father along with a contract of employment. If she accepted it, Moz would be her boss again, but at least they'd offered her a pay rise.

'I see,' Fei said calmly. 'You are attempting to use my mother's happiness against me.'

'Don't be unreasonable about this, Feiscina,' Lilon said from his position at the window, where he was studying the streets below as they became steeped in shadows. Yalsa 5's nearest star was dropping below the horizon.

'Unreasonable?' Fei echoed. 'No. I'm not that girl you destroyed. And I don't think you cared that you did it. You certainly don't care about Mum — you're only in this for yourself. If you get me to sign this contract, your superiors will give you a better room and a promotion. That's it, isn't it?'

Lilon turned towards her, shaking his head, apparently disappointed. 'Very well. GLEA will report to the mediaists — but not that Ton Tinel fellow, even if he did promise he would never use the footage from the conference — that you are a disgruntled former employee motivated by jealousy and greed. Your colleagues had more impressive salaries, after all.'

'What!' Fei threw her eyes up at the ceiling. 'You mean I should have asked for more money before now? Is that it?'

'The other programmers at TerraCorp are not as good as you,' Lilon continued. 'You knew this, of course, and were angry about their work being rewarded when yours was so much more superior.'

Fei scowled. 'Moz. This is all on Mozel Zan. He wasn't paying me enough because he could get away with it — I bet the budget always looked good in his yearly reports! He took advantage of me not being able to stand up for myself. But he can't do that anymore, poor Moz...' Her laugh sounded harsh and inhuman, even to her own ears. 'You can smear my name. I don't care. Bock and Ala won't fire me over anything the mediaists say, so my position here is safe. Now that your stupid attempt has failed, what are you going to do?'

Lilon had the nerve to graze a knuckle against the corner of one eye, as though he was wiping away a tear. 'You don't care about your mother's wellbeing? How sad. She will have hoped for better from you when I tell her this. But I think she will still cook my food and sleep beside me, because she is desperate for any companionship.'

And then he smiled.

Fei's heart was flooded with hot fury that shot out through every vein before cycling back to stab into her chest. 'And you Chippers wonder why everyone's abandoning your god in droves. You're scum. The lot of you.'

'And you are an anxious little girl who is going to cause great pain to her mother *and* lose the only proper job she's ever had,' her father fired back.

'Oh, fuck off.' Fei glanced around, looking for Ala, but the words belonged to her. 'And I have a job. Here. Because you idiots handed over ownership of the terraforming machines. So go back to your temples and have a good sulk about it. I won't be your casualty anymore.'

'Fei...' Lilon tried.

She wondered how he could simulate remorse when he clearly didn't feel it. The corners of his lips were appropriately downturned and he even held out his arms to her, as though requesting one last conciliatory hug.

Fei shook her head. 'No. I'm sticking with the people who listen to me and apologise when they don't. You're nothing to me, Lilon.'

She raised her hand to better display the small vine curling its way through her fingers. She didn't need to ask him to leave. He got the hint and fled into the waiting hoverlift.

Fei's smile felt cold and brittle, but she kept it in place as she went to the window to watch GLEA's departing starships rise above Atsa City, blotting out the stars on their way to Gerasnin.

Ton Tinel might no longer have any proof of GLEA's collusion with TerraCorp, but the mediaist was good at making his audience wonder about it. Tinel had even told Fei that the footage containing the boy GLEA had held hostage had contributed to a thirty percent drop in temple attendance rates. The reduction in donations, as well as the recent loss of so many expensive TerraCorp machines, had to be hurting the Chippers.

Fei rested a hand over her stomach, soothing her son as he made his displeasure known. 'It will be alright. We won't have to deal with them ever again.'

Fei supposed she had better finish testing the simulation program that Bock wanted for Yalsa 5 — she no longer had any excuses. But her temples tightened and her skin went clammy at the very thought of sitting down to work again. There was no way she could get anything done feeling like this. And it wasn't like Jalen needed her help to run the test suite.

'I need another holiday, a real one,' she muttered, hoping — *pleading* — that this was the solution.

She picked up her communicator and contacted Bock, willing to bet he was still in a good enough mood from obtaining the machines that he'd allow it. She'd bet right. Bock was more than happy for Fei to 'sort your shit out' because he needed time to hire more scientists to gather data, seeds and genetic samples. The program wasn't going to do much without those anyway.

After Bock warned Fei that she'd have to interview potential new programmers when she got back, he asked her where she wanted to be dropped off.

Fei decided on Bagaran, because it was the only place she could remember finding any peace.

And she just might run into a certain someone there...someone who needed to be told that he was going to become a father. Because there was no way, no possible way, for him to know.

There was no way for him to be visiting you either, Fei thought, smiling.

She hoped she'd get to tell him off in person about that.

He'd probably have a thing or two to say about her removing the implant, but Fei was sure he would be happy to see her again. He had to be.

***

Fight. Fight. You might even win.

Despite his determination and Zareth Sins' words echoing in his ears, Kuja's heart still stuttered when he stomped his way between the white columns that heralded his arrival into the Everything Portal. He wasn't surprised to see Fayay waiting for him, the Watine's cruel smile parting as he prepared some biting remark.

Kuja didn't even give him a chance to speak.

He threw up a hand and thin, twisted branches whipped out from his palm like cords, binding the Watine to the nearest column. One particularly thorny twig snaked around Fayay's throat, tightening so that his attempted words became unintelligible croaks. Water began dashing down from the invisible ceiling but Kuja rose above the puddles growing on the floor, walking steadily across the ropey bridge that his vines created for him.

You can't do this — how are you doing this? growled the Watine, apparently remembering that he could revert to mind-speech. He gave a vicious tug against his bonds but the branches held.

Kuja wondered if his grin looked as maniacal as it felt. 'Because I can't fail. Not this time. I'm stronger now, so much stronger than when you destroyed me.'

What are you dithering about? Of course you can fail!

'Oh, shut up, Fayay,' Kuja said.

He took hold of the connection between them and hacked through it like a machete through dense foliage. Fayay's voice died completely. Kuja continued on his way, hands in the pockets of his cargo pants, trees and plants exploding into being around him. He had to dodge one particularly tall fern when his vines lowered him to the floor, the white surface now stained with roots and soil.

Kuja's triumphant smile slipped when he saw Finara and a handful of other gods standing in a line between the last two columns, barring him from the thousands of maze-like passageways beyond.

Finara bounced a ball of fire in and out of her palm. 'Kuja, what the stark are you doing? You can't seriously be thinking about challenging Father over that woman. Just go back to the Enocian Harem and sort yourself out.'

'Is that what you've been telling them?' Kuja jerked a hand at their siblings. One or two of them actually ducked, expecting him to unleash his powers, but Kuja had no intention of hurting anyone who didn't come after him first. 'That you can solve your ills by visiting a brothel?'

Several gods nodded mutely.

Finara's expression grew stony. 'Kuja, stop this right now. I don't want to hurt you, but I will. To protect you.'

'We *outnumber* Fayay,' Kuja said, moving his eyes along the line of gods, 'and you saw what just one of us can do to him. If you think ignoring what you want will make the desire for it go away, then you are all fools.'

'What does he know — he's just a boy,' Isabis, the goddess of savannah, said snidely. 'The youngest of us.'

Kuja levelled a finger at her. 'I'm young, sure, but unlike you I haven't forgotten who my mother was. We're half mortal. We *can* know love — Father even made sure that Sandsa experienced it so he would get better at caring for his people!' Kuja drew a breath. 'Sandsa would still have his wife if she hadn't left him. That wasn't the Ine's doing. It was *Callista's*.'

'Doesn't mean we're all allowed to jump out that airlock — and barging on in here with righteous fury won't help you against Father,' Finara warned. 'He doesn't want any of us messing with his grand design.'

Kuja slapped his thigh and Fayay dropped to the floor behind him, cursing. 'Did you see what I did to our brother? I can do that to any of you. So get out of my way.'

The gods parted to let him through. Fayay's heavy strides gave chase, but Kuja didn't bother to turn around. He knew his brothers and sisters would halt the water god with their own powers. Some of them called out encouragement, but most were silently watching, no doubt waiting to see if Kuja would be punished — or if they could benefit from his bravery.

Kuja heard the intake of breath when a ring of blazing white light swept from his crown to his feet. The colourless powers that bore him away belonged to the being who had created the universe, the being who had then created the sub-level gods so that all the galaxy's people, human or otherwise, could be cared for as they spread across a starry sea.

Kuja could not discern the limits of the room he found himself in; there were no walls, only a white horizon that spread out in every direction. He was alone at first, but then furniture arrived, clashing with the bare surrounds. Battered and brown, the chairs would have been considered prized Old Earth antiquities by the mortals. It was hard to know if they had been transported from that time or if they had been created in situ.

Kuja sank into one of the chairs and willed tiny roots to grow over his hands like wrinkles. He drew strength from his plants as they came to him, but they were silent, as though afraid to tempt the ire of the one who had given them life before they'd ever had the Rforine to watch over them.

A fire roared into being several paces away. Old blackened bricks rose to encase it. Kuja sat up straight, his chest constricting painfully when he saw what the flames were shedding their uneven light on.

The Ine's white hair and tidy beard did little to soften the frightful intensity of his blue eyes or the angular lines of his skeletal form. He lounged in the other chair as though he had been there for hours, nursing a mug of liquid that steamed and carried a floral scent. Tea, something the Ine's late wife had enjoyed. And it was also Fei's preferred drink.

Kuja swallowed. The tirade he'd been forming in his mind faded.

'Um, hi,' he said, then winced. This was no mortal to be swayed by friendly pleasantries. 'Father. I...I do not know how to say this, but surely you've seen my thoughts...'

The Ine set his mug down on vines that rose from the floor at his feet; the green cords curled around the item, keeping it clear of the ground. This display of Kuja's own powers was a deliberate reminder that the Ine could be bested by no one. He had no weaknesses.

Except his lack of compassion, Kuja thought, uncaring if his father heard it.

'Compassion is one of the gifts I gave to the mortals,' the Ine said in response to this. 'While it is not an attribute of mine I do possess an understanding of it, though I know you would disagree.'

Kuja gripped the arms of his chair. 'Do I need you fight you?'

'Why would we need to fight, my son?' the Ine asked, his voice grave.

'Because you'll have a plan for me that I won't like!' Kuja cried. 'And if I defy you, if I threaten your *grand design*, you'll stand by and let Fayay go after Fei — the way you let him go after Sandsa and Callista!'

The muscles in Kuja's legs screamed for him to leap up and defend himself, but he remained where he was, trying to calm his erratic breathing. He could admit that he was terrified at the prospect of dying. Did he and his siblings have the same options that the mortals did after death? Would he be given the choice between resting eternally or returning to make something better of himself in the next life?

Kuja wasn't so sure his father would allow him that second attempt.

'You do not need to risk your life,' the Ine said and waved a hand. His mug of tea slowly descended into the floor where it vanished, along with the vines he had created. 'I wish you and your brothers and sisters had come to me instead of letting your doubts affect your duties.'

'How are we supposed to come to you?' Kuja demanded. 'How? We saw what you did to Sandsa when he wanted to follow his heart! And worse, you made a lesson out of it — no wonder Callista ran! I can't blame her for wanting to take her son away from this mess. You know what? Stark you. Stark you for letting it get so far between me and Fei if all you were going to do was take her from me. I won't let you — I won't!'

He jumped out of the chair and kicked the furniture back a pace. His powers rose within him, conjuring soil that spun around his feet, birthing miniature versions of every plant he could control. Kuja felt the nearness of death with such clarity, such certainty, that he wondered why he'd ever been afraid of it.

'Kuja, sit down,' his father instructed.

'No!'

'You are not some mortal child — you are seventy-five years old.' The Ine gestured at Kuja's chair. No vines twisted there, no water dampened the cushions, no sand filled the dips in the fabric — the furniture remained innocuous and free of threat. 'Sit and I will tell you why you will not be fighting me.'

'Because I'm doomed if I do, right?' Kuja snarled.

'Do not assume that you know anything about my grand design,' the Ine said mildly. 'It is too complex for you.'

Kuja eyed his father, still wary. 'I won't be the last to challenge you and your grand design. The others will do it, sooner or later.'

The Ine's laugh was soft, as though riding a breeze. 'You are so much wiser than them, Kuja. They forget that they, just like my mortal children, are afflicted with fears and doubts and the guilt from decisions that cannot be unmade.'

'Am I about to make a mistake?' Kuja asked, lowering himself into his seat.

'Are you?' his father countered.

Kuja made a face. 'Just tell me what I'm not allowed to do so I know which points to argue with you.'

The Ine raised his symmetrical eyebrows; a gentle rebuke. 'Cease making assumptions. What do you know for certain?'

'Alright,' Kuja said. 'I love Feiscina Neron and I want to be with her and our son for eternity. I can't deny that because you'll see it in my head anyway.'

'And you believe that this desire is at odds with my plans for you.'

'It's not like you had any trouble punishing Sandsa for straying from the plans you had for *him*,' Kuja muttered.

The Ine released a heavy sigh. The effect it had on him was startling — it gave his face lines, shadows, even crow's feet. He suddenly had the appearance of a man who had long been wearied by the galaxy instead of the immortal being who had created it. 'In your pursuit of love, you have never once abandoned your duties or ignored your people. Sandsa, however, did. That was why I did not stop Fayay from forcing your oldest brother to return to the pantheon.'

Kuja gnawed on the tip of his tongue. He couldn't believe what he was hearing. It couldn't mean what he thought it meant. He couldn't be that lucky.

'It is not luck, Kuja,' the Ine told him.

'Not luck,' Kuja repeated. 'I suppose it's *not luck* that I found Fei and she's so perfect for me. It's *not luck* that she can read my thoughts the way I can hers. Me meeting her...was deliberate.'

The Ine bowed his head just slightly.

Kuja's laugh was wrenched from him like a piercing that was too new, too fresh. 'So she's been in your plan for me all along.'

'She inspired Bagara to reach out to those who needed him, but whether or not love followed was up to the two of you,' the Ine replied, his face smoothing out as he regained his usual mysterious countenance. 'If you mean to be with Fei, you must tell her the truth now or you risk losing her forever.'

'You want me to tell the truth, even though you've never done it yourself,' Kuja said, glaring at the fireplace, wishing he could hurl his father into it but knowing the desire was never going to eventuate into something real.

The Ine nodded gracefully. 'It is your decision, of course. I have no problem with you binding yourself to Feiscina Neron for eternity — and Fayay won't either, once he realises the opportunity has always been available to him. I will ensure that he feels my displeasure if he harms any of my children's chosen spouses.'

Kuja's lips trembled. 'Why didn't you explain this to the others earlier? You let them think that love was a distraction, a *threat* to the grand design. You let them think you'd send Fayay after them if they slipped up!'

'It was not the right time for my children to meet the mortals destined for them,' the Ine answered. As if that explained everything. As if it made up for years of fear and uncertainty.

'This isn't fair,' Kuja said through clenched teeth. 'It's downright cruel. And I'm glad you put us in charge of the galaxy because at least we inherited Mum's empathy. I'm afraid to know how you treated the mortals before you gave them to us.'

The Ine's blue eyes grew distant. 'Now you realise why I needed you and your siblings.'

'Did you forget the part where I said it was cruel?'

'You know your purpose now,' the Ine continued, relaxing against the chair, seemingly unbothered by Kuja's words. 'You have shown them, gods and mortals alike, that they are allowed to doubt. They should not blindly accept things the way they are. They need to ask questions.'

Kuja leapt to his feet. 'Father! Listen to me! I don't care — I don't care if my brothers and sisters can fall in love because it's the *right time*. I don't care if people like Zareth Sins can now challenge the status quo. You did all this in the worst and nastiest way possible — Mum would have *hated* you for it!'

The oldest being in the universe pressed two fingers to his lips, viewing his son with timeless patience, as though he was watching a glacier slowly melt. 'I will not explain my grand design to you. It would only incense you further and it is not your place to know.'

Kuja kicked his chair again. This time it flew out of sight. 'Fuck you!'

'Kuja, I suggest you go to Fei and be honest about who you are,' the Ine told him gently. 'You will be very happy with her.'

'Stop deflecting me!' Kuja cried. 'Are you going to tell your children they can know love or will I have to do it?'

'Would it not give you great pleasure to lord it over Fayay, that you succeeded where he never dared to try?'

Kuja backed away from the Ine, horrified. 'Cruel and petty. I think I understand where Fayay gets those attributes from. He didn't get them from our mother. I'm so glad she left you in the end. How did you not see that coming?'

The Ine's expression darkened, though it was hard to tell at first because he was fading away as he returned to oblivion.

'Your brother is right. There is so much more to it than love. Understanding, support and honesty...these things are paramount.'

Within moments Kuja was alone, invisible walls pressing in around him. Scowling, he turned and walked through one of them. This led him directly to the columned entrance where his siblings awaited his return. All of them were there now, not just the ones Finara had gathered to stop him. They stared at the Rforine, their faces filled with awe. Fayay kept to the rear of the pack — he would not attack Fei now, not when the Ine himself would punish him. But that was cold comfort to Kuja.

'It's allowed, so long as we don't neglect our duties,' Kuja said, clenching his fists, letting vines twist around his forearms. 'And Fayay has no right to come after our *chosen spouses*. We can balance relationships with our work, just like the mortals do. Happy now? Happy that you get to have what I fought for handed right to you? You better hope Father lets you fall in love without making some lesson out of it. He tends to choose who we're drawn to. As if we can't make our own decisions!'

He began storming towards the exit. He could have teleported away, but it felt good to stamp his feet into the ground, to make his knees ache and his calves burn. He deserved this discomfort. He was a liar. And he had no intention of telling Fei the truth.

He loved her, loved the unique connection they shared, but the mind-reading ability the Ine had bestowed upon her wasn't a gift. It was a curse. Because if Kuja was ever careless with his thoughts, even for a moment, she would realise what he was. And she would leave him.

'She'll never know,' Kuja vowed.

Even when she begins to show no signs of ageing? the Ine's distant voice asked. *The binding ceremony will confer your immortality onto her, my son. She deserves to know before you do this.*

Kuja ignored him.

CHAPTER THIRTY

Fei stood very still, a cup of tea tilting at a dangerous angle in her hand. She hadn't heard Kuja walk in and he hadn't knocked on the door, but this was his hut and he probably had no reason to expect to find her waiting inside for him. She was the one who didn't belong here, even though Inesh had insisted she did when she'd arrived a few hours ago, her rapid, anxious breaths practically choking her.

Inesh had approved of the strapless pink dress she was wearing and she suspected it wasn't just because he was trying to being nice. Fei had hoped to impress someone else with it and now he was here. Except she suddenly had no idea what to say to him.

'Kuja,' she whispered. 'I...um...'

'Yes,' he said, answering her question before she could even ask it. He swept to her, folding her into his embrace. 'I'm here forever. If both of you will have me.'

'How...'

'How do I know that you carry our son inside you?' He drew back to smile at her. 'I just do. We both made terrible decisions that led to this. But I don't care. I only care about being with you.'

Fei's eyes darted over to the door then back to him again. 'But you seemed pretty sure I'd be in danger if you stayed with me. I *saw* the fear in you. And I saw this strange man while I was in Atsa and he...he made chills run down my spine.'

Kuja cupped her face, his thumbs brushing her lips. 'We don't need to fear my family. I dealt with them. And that strange man? I fought him and won. No one can keep us apart anymore. *No one.*'

'You fought for me?' A wet lump formed in her throat.

'And I always will,' he vowed.

Her cup fell to the ground, tea spilling across the dirt as Kuja scooped her up in his arms and carried her outside. The nearby villagers stopped to watch, their broad grins nowhere near a match for Kuja's own. Fei laughed as he began to jog, his impatience getting the better of him.

'Shouldn't I be treated like fragile goods in this state?' she mock-sternly asked Kuja.

'Fei, you are the exact opposite of fragile and you know it!' he said, pressing a kiss to her temple. 'But don't worry. Nothing will trip me. Not here.'

She believed him. It wasn't just confidence she sensed from him; it was *certainty.*

'Kuja, do you ever wonder why we can see into each other's minds?' she asked as he effortlessly navigated the uneven path, passing the area where TerraCorp's two consecutive laboratories had floated. The company had left Bagaran weeks ago. 'It drives me mad, not knowing why...maybe it's a gift from Bagara for our loyalty to him...'

Kuja's dimples began to resemble jagged craters. 'I don't want to give it much thought. I'd just prefer to think of us as...lucky. That's it. Lucky.'

'It's a gift,' Fei said, smiling up at the light-laden canopy. 'So that we can always understand each other.'

Kuja's arms grew rigid around her, potent fear building layer upon layer inside his mind. Fei couldn't see what was causing it, but she didn't pursue the matter. She had a feeling he wasn't ready to explain — and she found herself oddly content to wait for him to do so. His thoughts warmed in response to her decision.

A gift, Fei repeated, brushing tears of joy from her eyes.

Kuja didn't agree, but he didn't correct her either.

By the time they reached the waterfall his smile was back in full force. Moisture sprayed gently over their faces as Kuja kissed her, again and again, until her knees grew too weak to support her. He pressed her onto the mossy ground and pillowed his hands behind her head, gazing down at her adoringly. Fei supposed her answering grin must have looked just as silly. But she didn't care, not when she could gasp his name as he slid inside her, not when they could become one again.

Fei leaned her head on his shoulder afterwards, her fingers swirling over his skin, drawing the streams of code that were flooding through her mind. She suddenly needed to be in Kuja's hut, where she'd left her techpad, so she could start making notes about all the other programs that the newly formed Yalsa Industries would need. There was so much to do before Bock's scientists gave her their data.

So all I needed to rid myself of my creative block was a bit of sex, Fei thought.

Kuja snorted. 'I seem to recall you being quite capable of handling sex on your own. I know what you were doing all those times in my hut while I was away.'

'Mmm,' Fei agreed, lifting her head to show him her dreamy smile. 'But there are some things that just work better with someone else.' When all she received in response was a burst of strangled thoughts, she leaned her elbows on his chest and hovered her face over his. 'Kuja? What's wrong?'

He gripped her hands, pinning them against him. 'Fei. I have no right to ask this, given that I abandoned you as so many others have before me...'

White sparks darted over Fei's vision. 'Kuja, just ask me. You know my answer. You've always known it.'

'Well, I...' Kuja floundered.

Fei laughed. 'Yes, Kuja. Yes. I will be your wife. I'm pretty sure we were meant to be together or we'd never have formed this...whatever it's called. There must be a word for it.'

'Bond?' Kuja suggested.

Fei beamed at him. 'Bond, I like that. I like being bound to you.'

Kuja's expression grew hooded and mysterious and his mind suddenly became closed off to her. She hadn't realised how much she'd relied on being able to touch his thoughts until the door had slammed shut between them. Fei drew back, hurt.

'I'm sorry,' he murmured.

'Say that enough times and it'll lose its meaning,' she warned. She winced when she felt panic cut through Kuja's mental shielding. 'But it's okay, Kuja. We have years, decades even, to figure this out. So just...take your time. I'm not going anywhere.'

He sat up slowly, carefully dislodging her, his eyes glinting like emeralds. 'Fei, do you want to get married right now?'

'Oh, we can ask the village headman to act as our witness — I think he has the authority to do that, doesn't he? — then upload the files onto the Galactic Database as soon as...' Fei trailed off, blinking. 'Or, um, did you mean something else? You *did* mean something else. But we haven't got any clothes on! Shouldn't I make myself look pretty first?'

'You are perfect as you are,' Kuja told her, smiling as he knelt before her.

Heart racing, Fei copied his posture until they were facing each other, his knees pressed against hers. Moisture beaded along his chest and Fei wanted to swoop over and lick it away, but he caught the mental images tempting her and chuckled, shaking his head. 'Focus, Fei.'

'Give me something to focus on then,' she challenged.

His breath escaped him in a tortured staccato. 'Alright. There is a custom in my family, a way to wed without involving legalities or the Database.'

'I like the sound of that. Legalities never stopped my father leaving.'

'Do you trust me?' Kuja asked, taking Fei's hands in his.

Goosebumps rose on her skin, spreading out from where he was touching her. Fei skirted the edges of his mind and found a giddiness inside him that matched her own.

'Yes,' she said softly.

'Close your eyes,' he instructed. 'And don't open them, no matter what happens. I warn you, this will hurt, but it will make our bond last for *eternity*.'

Fei shivered at how resolute he sounded, as if this really was for the rest of time and not just the rest of their lives. But she still closed her eyes, just as he'd told her to, and when his palms pressed urgently against hers, she threaded her fingers between the gaps in his. The boom of the waterfall, so loud and clear before now, dropped away until she felt like she was floating in a void. Her entire focus was tunnelled in on him.

'Kuja?' she prompted.

'Well, the wording doesn't really matter,' he muttered, 'but I wanted this to sound nice.'

'Take your time,' she said, repeating her earlier words.

Kuja's lips briefly touched her forehead. 'You have no idea what that means to me. Alright. I, Kuja Rforine, bind myself to you. I was always yours — you never lost me and you never will. My love for you will last forever.'

Fei smiled and tipped her head to the side, keeping her eyes sealed. 'That's really sweet. Um. Give me a moment and I'll be able to respond with something equally as...um...'

His chuckle warmed the air, but he neither said nor did anything to discourage her.

'God, I love you for that,' she told him. 'You were the first one who let me be me. And that's a big ask. Don't you dare say it's not because I know it is. You have the biggest heart in the galaxy, even bigger than Bagara's. So, um...I, Feiscina — Feiscina Rforine — take your name and bind myself to you. I'm...' She clenched his hands until the bones in her own ached. 'I'm not letting you slip through my fingers again.'

I love you, he said in response.

Fei bit her lip, also using her thoughts to communicate with him. *Are we done?*

Not just yet.

Even though he'd said it would hurt, she wasn't prepared to feel a red-hot blade being slashed across both her palms. She cried out. Kuja's mind buzzed with concern, but she gritted her teeth and said, 'I know, I know — I'm keeping my eyes shut — just get on with it!'

He grunted and then the pain abruptly faded, overwhelmed by the heat that ballooned inside her chest. It felt — it felt wonderful. She could feel so much of him, could even see where to find the secret he was keeping from her. He fled when she came too close.

Let me help you, she said and the spectre of him slowed, turning back to her. Though this wasn't happening on any physical plane, it still felt intensely real.

Fei conjured an ancient treasure chest in her mind, like the ones she saw in vids set on Old Earth, and erected a firewall that would keep it safe from even the most determined hack. Opening the chest for his inspection, she gestured down at the endless space inside it. *Put it in here — that deep dark secret that makes you so afraid and unhappy — and leave it until you're ready. But you will open this chest with me. Not today. Not tomorrow. But someday.*

Fei lowered the lid of the chest, then offered her husband a key that was shaped like a human heart. Pressing it to the lid, his eyes never leaving hers, Kuja locked the chest.

And then they were back at the waterfall, hands clasped once more.

'Wow,' Fei said, blinking against the sunshine, confused but exhilarated.

'I need to show you something,' Kuja said, rotating her wrists so that she could see her palms. On each of them there was a thin line of scar tissue running from the base of her thumb up towards her pinky finger. If Fei pressed her hands together the scars would match perfectly.

'Odd,' she said. She couldn't see a blade on him, but something must have pieced her skin.

'Is that it?' Kuja's voice was strained. 'Don't you want to ask me any questions?'

Fei shook her head. 'If I ask the wrong question, you won't answer me.'

Kuja offered her his own hands, also scarred. 'I'm not going to push you away. This is forever.'

'You say that now,' Fei said, Zareth's face coming to her mind unbidden. 'I'm sorry. I...he haunts me sometimes. Like an unwanted shadow.'

Kuja hesitated. She could feel that he wanted to say something, but then he nodded and different words escaped him. 'I know. I can see it.'

'I wish...'

'Do you wish I couldn't?' he asked.

Fei filled her smile to the brim, until her cheeks hurt, trying to reassure him. 'I love that you can. I just...have to get used to trusting. Loving. I can't...it's not easy to just...you know. No, maybe you don't know and I...I...oh.'

She refused to hang her head, especially when he was gazing at her like that, his thoughts promising another long, leisurely session of lovemaking, this time inside his hut. Keen to get started, Fei pulled on her clothes and took Kuja's hand, leading him back to the village.

'Alright, here's a safe question,' Fei said as they walked. 'Do you want to know how I dealt with GLEA on Yalsa 5 or do you already know?'

Kuja slid a hand around to her hip, cinching her to his side. 'I'd rather hear it from you.'

'You better not get that glazed look on your face when I carry on too much.'

'If I do, I'm sure you can think up an adequate punishment.'

Fei quirked an eyebrow at him. 'It's not a punishment if you want it.'

When they entered Bagath, they announced their union and immediately came under attack from knowing smirks and outright congratulations. The village headman offered to officially witness their marriage, but Kuja courteously refused him.

Fei inspected the scars on her hands. It didn't seem possible that they could look years old when she had only just received them. Was this some sort of ability, given to Kuja's family by Bagara?

Fei thought of the chest buried deep in the centre of Kuja's mind. In there lay the answers.

What are you so afraid of? she wondered. Kuja froze in the doorway of his hut, his eyes beseeching her. Fei shook her head. *I can't help thinking what I think. You don't need to answer me. Not yet.*

He pressed his smile against hers. *Then, by all means, keep thinking.*

I'd rather you stop me thinking for the rest of the afternoon, Fei said with a wink.

Kuja was most obliging.

CHAPTER THIRTY-ONE

Seated in the passenger section of a starship that looked about as bloated as she felt this close to the end of her pregnancy, Fei watched as a pair of children tore off their safety restraints and pressed their noses against the plexiglass at the front of the compartment. Harried parents arrived a moment later to carry them off, but that didn't stop them from staring at the viewport in awe.

Gerasnin was a startling sight the moment it ballooned from pinprick into planet. Large swathes of its hemispheres sparkled because of the world's expansive sapphire oceans and every limited patch of ground was covered in glinting white marble, even the streets. Gerasnin's quarry had yielded its last slab of stone centuries ago, but there were plenty of worlds the Chippers could source their favoured building material from — and Fei was willing to bet most of it was donated instead of bought.

I may have spent my teenage years on Gerasnin but I never belonged here, she thought, frowning.

As a student she'd talked too much and asked too many questions, so the local education system had granted her mother the use of a Websphere. Being encased in that ball for hours, connected to her classmates by vidcams alone, should have been a dismal, lonely experience. But Fei had loved it and had spent most of her lessons learning how to code instead. Ironically, that was the only skill she had used once she'd graduated.

Fei closed her eyes and recalled the worried expression that Kuja had worn when he'd bade her farewell at Bagaran's spaceport — it was more of a glorified field, though it was paved over and strewn with lights. Kuja had wanted to come with her to visit her parents but even Fei had felt the irresistible tug that stopped him from boarding the ship. He had been needed somewhere. Urgently. She no longer asked what mysterious duty he had to devote his whole being to, even though it was straining at the lock of the treasure chest buried inside his mind. His secret was hurting him. She wished he would let her help carry his burden.

Fei fiddled with the communicator attached to her belt. She'd bought Kuja a similar device and could call him anytime, he'd promised, but she didn't need the device to know he was alright — busy, but alright. Even across the galaxy she could feel him, like a warm hand beneath her shirt, resting over her heart. Fei opened her eyes, now able to face Gerasnin as it loomed before her, filling the viewport and blocking out the blackness of space.

Beside her, a man with a chip in his temple murmured, 'Ah, it's good to be home.'

Fei bit her lip until she could think of something pleasant to say to the Chipper. 'Yes, it's always good to return home.'

Except her home was a hut in the middle of a rainforest, surrounded by trees, waterfalls and people who had willingly shared their religion, not forced it on her. Fei also frequently called Yalsa 5 home, because there were times when Bock required her to be physically present.

On those occasions, Kuja insisted that Fei wear gloves, to cover the scars on her hands. Fei had agreed and found a fingerless variant that didn't restrict her work, but her curiosity had increased to painful levels, especially since her husband had asked her not to mention him or their binding to Bock and Ala. Fei got the feeling that Kuja was trying to stop her employers from exposing him somehow. It rankled that they clearly knew something about Kuja that she didn't, but she'd promised to wait him out. Even if it drove her half insane to do so.

Fei had managed to create her first simulation based on her own software just before taking maternity leave; the final test suite had yielded no errors, to her immense relief. But the actual terraforming would have to wait until Bock's growing cohort of scientists and engineers completed addressing the more physical issues, such as ensuring that the machines correctly duplicated their on-board seed and soil samples — and in enough quantities to cover the area Bock wanted to transform. Other scientists were rapidly growing animals that would be released into the future rainforest, making sure to equip them with essential genetic memory so that they could survive and reproduce without assistance.

But this was a problem for other people, not someone trying to distract themselves from the inevitable.

Gerasnin drew ever closer.

Fei tried not to hold her breath.

***

'Sandsa!' Kuja called.

Only an arid desert wind arrived to answer him. It wound around his ankles then left, clearly dismissing the rainforest god. Kuja slipped onto his knees, digging his hands into the sand and clenching it inside his tightening grip. The grains grew coarse and grated against his scarred palms, but he would not be cowed.

'I don't need an apology and nor should I have to keep giving you mine,' Kuja said, one lone tear eking its way out of his eye. It fell halfway down his cheek before it evaporated. 'What's done is done. I'm not asking for the protection you refused me, because I no longer need it — but I would be honoured if you stood with me at my son's birth. I want to share my joy with you.'

Sandsa's voice slammed into Kuja's skull with the force of a log flying down a fast-flowing river. *Joy? You call it joy? Lying to the woman you love so she will not leave you?*

Kuja winced and rightened himself, a hand on the communicator Fei had given him. Several simultaneous emergencies inside his domain had kept him from boarding the ship to Gerasnin with her. Even though he could now give her his full attention, he couldn't risk teleporting to her side when Bagara had made it clear to Fei that he would only move mortals between worlds in dire circumstances. A man who simply wanted to be with his wife didn't qualify.

'Stark you!' Kuja gritted his teeth, keeping any further curses trapped behind them. 'I won't deny it — it's *killing me*, lying to her. But it's just not...it's not the right time to tell her.'

She will not forgive you, Sandsa said. *Callista lied to me, you know, she made me think I had to choose between my duty and her. I will never forgive her. Not in a thousand years.*

'Fei will forgive me — she has to!'

Will she? A mocking laugh.

Kuja released a hiss of air. 'Maybe you could...help me? Help me keep it secret for as long as possible?'

You deserve to lose her, liar, Sandsa told him.

'You're just saying that because you want me to be as miserable as you!' Kuja bit back.

Sandsa gave him no answer but the dunes began to shake violently around the Rforine.

'*Please*,' Kuja whispered.

He waited, hoping, even as an immense wave of sand began to crest above him. The Desine was still there, still listening. But just as Kuja opened his mouth to plead once more, a tornado of fire roared up around his body and stole him away to another planet entirely.

Shaking himself out, Kuja threw an annoyed look at his sister. 'Finara, stark it — I was getting through to him.'

'Oh, bullshit,' Finara said.

Kuja glanced down and saw that they were standing on an impervious plexiglass platform that hovered a little too close to the planet's volatile surface. Around them, clad in bulky silver coats that insulated them against the intense heat, mortals made sounds of fright and awe as the shield volcano below them belched molten rock. Kuja had heard of this tourist world, but he couldn't fathom why anyone but the fire goddess would find it entertaining.

Finara held out one of the coats to Kuja. 'I'll protect you, but there's no point in making ourselves look conspicuous.'

Kuja accepted the reflective fabric and pulled it on. 'Finara, about what I said before...I'm sorry. It was cruel.'

'Not entirely wrong, though,' Finara said as she shrugged into a second coat. 'The mortals don't really care about me.'

'That doesn't excuse the way I said it.'

She looked at him for a long moment, then nodded. 'Apology accepted. Look, Kuja, Sandsa's like a toxic cloud of gas. He might love you, but he'll choke you if you hang around with him too long. You need to leave him be or he will end up lashing out and hurting you, no matter what he promises. There's no helping some people.' Her lips twitched. 'Or gods.'

Kuja hung his head. 'I know. I'll miss him. But I just...I just didn't want this to be the end of his story.'

'Well, it is,' the Firine said firmly. 'And what I'm feeling from you is that you're ready to move on and enjoy life. Sandsa's nowhere near that.'

'You've been there for me every time he wasn't,' Kuja realised. 'And I think I'd much rather have you with me in the coming weeks.'

One of the nearby tourists shouted as a jet of lava shot up and arced towards them. All Finara had to do was flick two fingers at it and the beast tumbled back down into its fiery origin.

'What do you need me for?' Finara asked once she'd turned back to her brother.

Kuja sighed and shrank further inside the coat. 'Right now Fei is over on Gerasnin, inviting her mother to visit us for the birth of our son. I imagine Berale, Fei's mother, will ask all sorts of questions that I am not prepared to answer.'

'You want someone else on your team, someone to even out the lasball court and help you field those questions,' Finara said, nodding. 'I'll do it.'

'You'll do it? Just like that?' Kuja was stunned. They might have been siblings but they'd never been particularly close, even after she had tended to him following his fight with Fayay. That had been more from guilt than anything else.

Shadows fell across Finara's face. 'I've been trying so hard to figure out how to deal with mortals, Kuja. Lava, firestorms, bushfires — those make sense to me. But the people who live in my domain are frustrating, you know? They ask me to stop volcanoes erupting but that's impossible to do for more than a few minutes. And they get so cranky when I don't force nature to go against itself.'

Kuja stared at her, thrown by the change of topic, but he didn't interrupt. He felt that this was important to her.

'I want the mortals to remember me when things *aren't* erupting or going bad for them,' Finara went on, waving a hand towards the nearest knot of tourists. 'I guess what I'm saying is — I need to learn from you. Yeah. That's why I'm helping you. To learn about mortals and how to make them listen to me. This is a trade, pure and simple.'

Kuja smiled. 'Of course it is.'

'One last thing.' Finara's flaming eyes narrowed. 'If Fei decides to punch you for lying to her, I'm pinning you down so she can have a decent crack at it.'

'I'd probably deserve that,' Kuja muttered.

'You sure would.'

***

When the door opened, Fei stayed as still as a statue, mirroring her mother's stance. Shorter and plumper than her, Berale Neron would normally have launched into an enthusiastic hug, but she simply stood there. Fei wondered if Lilon was making Berale so miserable that she had forgotten how to interact with people who didn't treat her terribly.

Berale's hazel eyes slowly crept to Fei's swollen stomach, a full eight months in the making.

Fei self-consciously rested a hand there. 'Maybe I should have mentioned something before now. Mum, I...I'm sorry I haven't

325

called you lately. I just couldn't stand the thought of Lilon being here and that...that was selfish of me.' Berale remained silent, so Fei set her bag down on the townhouse's white porch and pushed on, 'I'm married. And pregnant. Well, I guess that's obvious.'

'Are you done?' Lilon demanded, stepping into the doorway. 'You'll have us die of old age before you finish filling your mouth with nonsense.'

Fei clenched her fists in response and was pleased when her father stepped back a pace, apparently expecting an attack. She hadn't needed to use Bagara's powers since the conference, but she still felt them sometimes, as though she had vines tightening beneath her skin instead of veins.

Fei gave Lilon what she hoped was an infuriating smile. 'I'll talk as much as I starking well want to. You can't stop me, Chipper. And it's sad that you're only here to punish me, not because you love either of us. But I can probably *make* you leave, if Mum asks me to use my powers on you.'

'Fei,' Berale gasped.

'Yes. That's my name. Not something that could have changed overnight.' The laugh escaped Fei before she could clamp down on it. 'Well. Actually it did. I married Kuja Rforine and I'm much prouder to wear his name than the one I was born with. So...I'm Feiscina Rforine now.'

The three of them remained frozen for a time, like a static image thrown up on a vidscreen. Water slapped the stones nearby, disturbed by some swell further out at sea. Whereas the oceans back on Enoc spoke in gentle whispers, here there was nothing natural about the sound of the waves going to war with the marble in their way.

Fei picked up her bag and shouldered her way into the townhouse.

By the time she returned from putting her things away in her old room, Lilon was ensconced on the couch in the living area, dwarfed by a blaring vidscreen. Free of his gaze at last, Berale surged forward, arms outstretched, and delivered the hug that Fei had desperately wanted.

'You look happy,' Berale said, setting her at arm's length.

'You don't,' Fei returned.

Berale made a face. 'I was going to say that one day you might understand, but you've obviously found a far more superior husband than I did. Now tell me — is this Kuja a Bagara worshipper too?'

'Why do you ask?' Fei demanded, her eyebrows scrunching down low over her eyes.

Berale gently patted Fei's cheek. 'I don't want my future grandchild confused about which faith they're supposed to be adhering to now, do I?'

'I got plenty confused about my faith even with you and Lilon both following the Creator God.' Fei smirked when she saw her father's head jerk in her direction, though it didn't quite make it far enough around for him to show the glare he was no doubt sporting. 'And it doesn't matter. My son can choose whatever religion he wants. Kuja and I will always support his decisions.'

Lilon grunted.

Ignoring him, Berale embraced Fei again. 'Oh, Fei, your Kuja sounds so much better than Zareth. Running off to GLEA, never to be heard from again. Mind you, it's better when they do that...'

Fei's lips twitched when she saw her mother shoot an aggravated look over at Lilon.

'Should we go out for lunch?' Fei suggested. 'It's been a really long time since I was on Gerasnin.'

Berale brightened. 'I know just the place. They make the most fabulous coffein! And they do tea as well, don't pout. It's — '

'Don't say anything else,' Fei said, narrowing her eyes at the back of Lilon's head. She could tell he wasn't paying attention to the docovid he was watching about the low-tech life of people living on Alnia, a world some weeks from Gerasnin. 'I'd rather not find myself surrounded by Chippers when I'm trying to eat.'

'He wouldn't do that,' Berale said sternly. 'Would you, Lilon?'

He remained silent.

Scowling, Berale took Fei's hand and stormed out the door.

***

When Fei woke later that night, she knew immediately that the figure by the window was not some image of Kuja inserted into her room to set her at ease. She sat up and pointed at the empty doorway. 'Lilon. Get out.'

'These powers of yours are unnatural and must be dealt with,' Lilon told her. '*You* must be with dealt with.'

If she'd harboured any warm feelings for the man who had used her and her mother when it best suited him, those words would have caused them to disintegrate faster than magnesium held to a flame. Fei waved a hand over the sensor beside her bed, activating the room's light. The harsh beams it threw down from the ceiling revealed her father standing in his full GLEA regalia, the golden strokes on the shoulders of the purple jumpsuit carefully straightened. He even had his shielding device and lasgun clipped to his belt.

'The Creator God is silent so it is up to me to interpret his will and carry it out,' Lilon continued. There was a darkness in his eyes that not even the light could dispel. 'No abnormalities should be allowed to besmirch his grand design.'

'If I'm not in his grand design, then why did he make me in the first place?' Fei demanded. 'And why does he allow the sub-level gods to exist, to reign, to dole out *their* powers?'

'It should be me!' Lilon exploded.

Fei peeled back the covers and swung her feet to the side. The thin nightie she'd taken to wearing since becoming pregnant fell to her ankles but didn't offer much protection. She was going to need to use Bagara's powers.

She lifted her chin, smiling as vines began to creep down her arms. 'Of course it's about you, Lilon. You're jealous that I got powers naturally and you had to put a chip in your head. Makes you wonder who the Creator God actually wants looking after his people.'

Her feet slid into her boots. She considered calling out for her mother.

But even if Berale was conscious, she wouldn't have been able to do anything to help Fei against the pack of GLEA agents that suddenly swarmed into the tiny bedroom. Fei thrust out her hands, but she wasn't quick enough — the Chippers combined their powers into a large, potent forcefield that encased her and dragged her through the air, writhing and screaming.

She did manage to kick the side of Lilon's head, but this only caused the Chippers to shrink the forcefield until she couldn't so much as breathe. Again Fei tried reaching for the abilities given to her by Bagara, the abilities she so desperately needed, but they skittered away. She just couldn't concentrate when she had to focus on forcing air into her lungs.

Fei held back the whimper of despair.

Her father was now standing beside her, making shhh-shhh sounds as he grazed Fei's arm with a hyponeedle. Its tip punched in and out of her skin in less than a heartbeat.

Cold oblivion rushed up to meet her.

Kuja! was the last thought Fei could manage.

CHAPTER THIRTY-TWO

They took his wife into the largest temple in the galaxy, one staffed by no less than a thousand agents. He could sense all of their lifesigns, their energy, their power. It was overwhelming, even to a god.

Kuja remained invisible, hiding his presence behind a small potted plant that was resting on the table beside Fei's head. He could teleport her away within moments — she was no stranger to Bagara moving her around the galaxy in that manner. And, if he wanted, he could even attack the Chippers without physically appearing.

I need to show myself to them, Kuja thought grimly. *So they know who they're dealing with. So they know to never again come after my followers — or anyone else under my protection, for that matter.*

But if he took human form and attacked the Chippers, they would use his father's powers against him. Fayay had been just one enemy; here there were several. And since Kuja lacked telekinesis or the ability to manipulate energy the way the Chippers could, he would be at a disadvantage. But their fear and surprise might slow them down — he was willing to bet they'd never been attacked by a god before.

You'll reveal yourself to her if you do this, a voice piped up at the back of his head. *And she'll leave you.*

Not if I do it right.

She will find out eventually, his inner voice taunted.

I know that! I know that, stark it! Kuja snapped. *But if she wants to leave, to use her free will...* Agony lanced through his very being. *Then that is her right. I cannot refuse her that.*

A stray tendril reached for Kuja, distracting him from his thoughts, and he immediately traced it back to his wife.

I will never leave you, Kuja promised his son.

Emotions and wordless demands crashed against Kuja's mind. The boy was scared for his mother. The boy wanted the scary people to go away. Why wasn't his father doing anything?

Kuja was asking himself the same question.

***

The first thing Fei noticed when she woke up was that her bed was ringed by men and women garbed in purple, most of them with golden slashes on their shoulders, betraying them as high-ranking members of GLEA. Fei eased her way into a sitting position, using the wall behind her pillow for support. She still felt groggy from whatever sedative they'd used on her and her mouth was as dry and gritty as the surface of Yalsa 5.

'We can get some water for you if you'd like,' Head General Huw Hunslow offered. No slashes for him. He wore the stars of his rank.

Fei spitted a glare at Hunslow and didn't let up, not even when the illusion providing his human face flickered, revealing the scales beneath.

'Um, no,' she finally said. 'I wouldn't trust anything you'd bring me. Obviously you still see me as a threat given that there are fifteen of you in here and only one of me.'

'You are a threat to the Creator God's grand design,' Lilon Neron declared, standing far too close for comfort.

Fei snorted. 'No, I'm a threat to your self importance. I did nothing to any of you! Well, I mean, except for ensuring that you'll never set foot on Yalsa 5 again. But that doesn't justify kidnapping me. The mediaists will rip you to shreds for this. And I'm pregnant, if that wasn't obvious. This is just going to make you look even worse.'

'Your father informed us of your situation,' Huw Hunslow said, a hand outstretched and creeping towards Fei's stomach. 'Your child will be raised within this temple and taught to honour the Creator God.'

A vine shot out of Fei's palm and slapped Hunslow's hand back to his side. Fei breathed deeply as the vine disintegrated, fighting the heady rush that came from using Bagara's powers.

'Don't even *try* to touch me,' Fei warned, flinging her eyes around the room. Most of the agents looked at the floor rather than try to meet her gaze.

Her father's frown was unwavering, however. 'Surely you must realise that you and your child should remain here, so that we can use the both of you for the good of the galaxy and the glory of the Creator God.'

'Or,' said a very different voice, 'Fei has already done enough for the Creator God and she can return home whenever she wants to.'

'Kuja — how?' Fei whispered as he entered the room from the corridor outside.

His green eyes were soft when he glanced at her. *I can't explain. Don't ask me to. Just accept.*

Then he raised his hands. The Chippers began to respond

but he was quicker. Gnarled roots swept across the floor, tripping the agents in their way, then scrambled up the walls, cracking apart plaster and plexiglass as they went. Fei stared in wonder as Kuja stood on a bridge of vines above the chaos, letting the Chippers see how superior he was to them.

He was saying something to the agents, Fei realised, but he wasn't using his mouth. When she reached for his mind, to listen in, he withdrew from her, his fear as potent as the power he was wielding. Whatever he'd said to the Chippers, it was enough to send them running for the door. Not even Lilon or the Head General were willing to take Kuja on.

His face twisting beneath a grim smile, Kuja moved towards Fei and pulled her into his arms. When she pried her face away from his chest to ask him if he was alright, since he was still so *afraid*, she realised they were back in their hut in Bagath, surrounded by their things.

'So I'm not the only one Bagara has blessed,' Fei said, awed.

Kuja winced. 'I don't think you have powers, Fei. Not really.'

Fei held out her hand and a miniature tree grew out of her palm, no bigger than her tallest finger. She arched an eyebrow at her husband. 'See? I do have powers.'

'Those are our son's powers,' Kuja said, reaching over to brush her florid orange hair off her face. 'He inherited them from me and I believe you've been accessing them.'

'But Bagara...' she insisted, her heart skating to the edge of a cliff.

'Bagara is there for you, he is, but these powers are from me,' Kuja told her.

Her heart leapt and fell, crushed onto the rocks below by a raging waterfall that sought to bury her hopes and dreams.

Fei drew a shaky breath. 'But...but what does this mean? If he hasn't given me these powers and I only have them because...oh my God, this isn't fair! You're saying Bagara gave powers to my son and not me? Why?' The sob lodged in her throat until she spat it out. 'No! I don't believe you! I have powers and — and Bagara loves me!'

Kuja visibly deflated. 'I do love you.'

'I meant Bagar...' Fei trailed off. Her mind whirred. 'Tell me what's inside that chest in your mind, Kuja.'

He began to turn away so she grabbed his chin, forcing him to look at her.

'You already know what's in there,' Kuja said quietly.

'I want to hear you say it. Say it!'

His green eyes filled with tears. 'I am Bagara.'

'That's impossible,' Fei said, dropping his chin and taking a step back. 'You're human. I mean, your name doesn't show up in the Galactic Database...but that doesn't mean anything. Plenty of people don't have the names they were born with.'

'You looked me up?' His smile lasted for several seconds before it faded away.

Fei threw up her hands in exasperation. 'Of course I did. I'm not completely stupid. At least now I know why you made me wear those gloves. Ala and Bock know what the scars mean, don't they? You didn't want them outing you! So how come they knew and I didn't? Don't you think this is something you should tell a woman before you marry her?'

'Callista, my brother's wife, seems to have told Bock and Ala about Sandsa and myself.' Kuja looked pained. 'I wish she hadn't.'

'I bet you wish you hadn't needed to turn up and save me,' Fei said bitterly. 'Then you could go on pretending you were a man.'

Kuja surged forward, arms outstretched. 'Fei! I will always protect you! I should have said something, I know, but I was afraid that you would hate me and leave.'

'I might not hate you so much if you'd warned me not to start fawning over you as a god,' she snapped and darted aside, avoiding his embrace.

'It's...hard to explain.' Kuja wrung his hands. 'I'll open the chest in my mind. You'll see. You'll understand why.'

Fei backed further away from him, until she hit the door. 'It's not the same! I shouldn't have to read your mind to know who you are. I just want you to *tell* me. I tell you everything. *Everything*. And all you've ever done was lie to me.'

He pressed his lips together instead of defending himself. Fei could read from him that he'd told some truths, but not nearly enough. He knew that. And he was so very sorry, especially when she found that last awful secret in his mind.

Fei looked down at her hands, tracing the lines on her palms. 'The scars. They transferred your immortality to me. Just how permanent is this binding?'

'Fei, please...'

'Tell me!'

'The scars can be removed,' he said, his voice shaking. 'But I don't want you to do that.'

Fei nodded curtly. 'Thanks for not lying to me. This time. When were you going to tell me I'd signed up for immortality?'

'I love you.' He was whispering now.

'I can't even look at you for three seconds without feeling ill,' Fei bit out. 'I'm not sure I can handle an eternity in your presence.'

She marched out of the hut, ignoring the confused looks many of the villagers sent her way, refusing to stop when they called her name. They would only ask her awkward questions about how she was already back from Gerasnin and she had no idea how to answer them. Kuja was the one who'd lied; he could deal with the consequences of his actions.

She couldn't stifle the shivers. *No matter where I go on this planet, he'll find me. He'll fucking find me.*

I could, Bagara's — Kuja's — voice said softly as she picked up the hem of her nightie and began to run. *But I won't come after you. It's your choice to return or to...leave.*

Callista, his sister-in-law, had made a choice like that, her memories told her — no, those memories were his. The pain that came with them squeezed Fei's heart.

Her fingers curled reflexively over the scars her husband had given her.

But she didn't turn back.

CHAPTER
THIRTY-THREE

With night falling fast and the thicket now impossible to navigate, Fei perched on a rock beneath a large tree and watched the glowing nashba bugs parade through the branches sprawling above her. So long as she didn't move too quickly or annoy the insects, they wouldn't unleash their stingers on her — or would they unleash them at all? They wouldn't want to anger their god by attacking his wife, would they? Fei grimaced.

She had stumbled around for hours, losing her way after deliberately veering off the well-trodden path outside Bagath. The booming waterfall she had once enjoyed listening to had been too loud, too constant, so she'd ignored it and kept going, until only insects mocked her with their tinny voices.

And now she was here, wherever 'here' was. Fei's hand dropped to her hip, but her techpad was still in her bag on Gerasnin. This meant that she couldn't pass the time by jotting down notes about an idea she had for debugging software that could pick up any mistakes in the code the moment they were made. But what would be the point? Anything she accomplished in her life was useless compared to what Kuja could do as a god.

If the people in your life don't end up abandoning you, they'll make you wish they had, Fei thought and sealed her eyes against the precious moisture that threatened to escape them. She was already thirsty enough.

When she managed to open her eyes again, she immediately regretted it. In front of her was a sea of quivering leaves that definitely hadn't been there a few moments earlier. One particularly large leaf glided forward, heavy with water, and nudged her hand until she lifted it to her lips, draining it. The leaf darted off, its mission complete. Others crowded forward in its place.

'No, no,' Fei said, shrinking back against the tree behind her. 'No. Stop. You don't have to do this, you're only doing it because of him — or because of my son. I'm just human.'

She allowed herself to hope that they'd leave her alone. But then the vines wrapped around the tree struck — they coiled themselves into a crown and dropped over her head, squeezing hard once they found their mark. Fei gasped when something punctured her temples. Her fingers rose, desperate to wrench out the vines that must have looked like squirming tentacles beneath her skin, but the tree threw down thin branches to capture her wrists. Fei prepared to keep fighting, except suddenly she forgot why she'd wanted to.

Because now she didn't just hear or smell or see the rainforest. She *felt* it.

Old and endless; young and renewed. Those parts of it that were tired and worn dropped and died, replaced by fresh plants and animals in a constant cycle. The rainforests had served the Creator God since the beginning of time, never knowing another master — until Kuja came to them.

The plants showed Fei an image of a boy, small and wiry, with bright green eyes that didn't yet hold the shadows that belonged deep inside caves and plunge pools. He had been so young and so full of light then, unmarked by fear or despair.

He breathed new life into us, a voice told Fei. It was high and reedy, demanding her attention, and somehow suited the vines it belonged to. *The mortals in his domain were drawn to his positive spirit, like a flower turning towards a shining star.*

'That's not what attracted me to him — the god, I mean,' Fei said. 'He didn't demand. He just offered. And he understood mortals. At least, I thought he did...'

Another plant spoke, sounding so wizened and ancient that she had to strain to catch every word. This had to be the tree behind her. *He was made wise by his pain. He lost his mother because she removed her binding scars and shortened her lifespan, but he was glad for her. She was so much happier as a mortal.*

The scars on Fei's hands throbbed. 'And his brother?'

You speak of the Desine...

A younger voice, belonging to the glistening leaves in front of her, interceded as the older one faded. *The desert god's wife left because she wanted to pursue her own path. She wanted to know who she was beyond the wife of a god. The Desine did not understand. He did not listen.*

'She kept the immortality scars,' Fei murmured, knowing it to be true. 'She kept them. Why?'

Why do you keep yours? the vines asked.

Fei tilted her head back and looked up at the branches. The nashba bugs continued to dance worryingly close to her, but she felt safe beneath them. She could actually sense how much they cared for her. They would even bow to her wishes, should she have any.

Fei's vision swam. 'Do you only respect me because I am his wife?'

No! cried a thousand voices. *You are Feiscina! Creator of Worlds! Spreader of our seeds!*

'But it was just code, all I did was write code,' Fei said, wiping the back of her hand over her face, scraping the tears away. 'The engineers who look after the terraforming equipment do the heavy lifting. And the scientists — you remember them, don't you? Before they left Bagaran? They're the ones who go to other planets and collect seeds and cuttings. I don't create anything.'

We remember them. But they took. They did not create. Not like you.

Fei nearly sobbed in relief when the branches that had captured her wrists released them. She immediately gave a futile tug at the crown encircling her head. The wound the vines had inflicted in order to connect with her might not be hurting anymore, but she could still *feel* something pulling on her skin, forcing her to talk when she'd rather sit in sullen silence.

Fei glowered, not sure which plant to target with her fierce expression. 'Simulations! That's all I do, you know. Or maybe you don't. It's all done virtually, not in real life. Um, I'll try to explain it but...'

We understand, the plants chorused as one.

'I'm not so sure you do,' Fei muttered, then swallowed a wave of nausea. Her son had shifted inside her, roused by her disturbed feelings. She moulded her hands to the curve of her stomach. 'It's alright, honey. It's alright.' A new thought occurred to her. 'What about my son? Is he...is he allowed to live as a mortal? Does he have to help Kuja rule the rainforests? What?'

A spiky fern, which stood out amongst its gentler brethren who weren't so barbed, answered her. It sounded like a venerable old mediaist, honest at the cost of viewership. *That has yet to be determined. The Old One will not say. But why could your son not create worlds, like you do?*

'I don't create worlds! Don't you get it?' Fei blew out a breath, trying to keep her anger in check. She knew she had failed when her son's unhappiness rolled out of her stomach and up her throat, gathering bile until she felt the need to throw up. 'I'm not a god! I'm nothing!'

The nashba bugs tumbled, rocked by a giant gust of wind, and went shrieking for cover. Trees bowed away from Fei, turning their bark-covered backs on her, and the vines snapped out of her temples and withdrew, but not before radiating hurt.

'Um, look, I'm flattered that you think so well of me and I didn't mean to upset you,' Fei said, holding out her hands and smoothing them over the nearest leaves. They trembled beneath her touch. 'But I'm nothing special and you're only being nice to me so I won't leave him.'

A nearby branch snapped, plummeting to the ground. Fei threw a nervous look skywards when she heard more creaking overhead. The next branch came closer, causing her to stagger away from the trunk. But the tree wasn't the real threat, she realised. It had only been herding her.

She was now standing in front a whirling, human-sized vortex that seemed to be made of twigs and assorted greenery. Fei tried to step back towards the tree but the vines were faster. They ensnared her wrists and yanked her clear into the air. She didn't even have time to scream.

The vines were already tossing her into the vortex.

***

Kuja crouched in a tree on a world halfway across the galaxy from Bagaran, hands clenching and unclenching by his sides. He'd brought himself here in a desperate attempt to ignore the temptation to return to his wife's side. It was working. So far. But it took supreme effort not to eavesdrop on Fei's thoughts.

The communicator on his belt broke the silence, buzzing insistently and causing his shirt to shiver over his skin. Kuja glanced down, startled. There were only two people who knew he now had such a device and since Fei had expressed no desire to ever speak to him again, it had to be...

Kuja grabbed the communicator and held it up. 'Gerns, is something wrong?'

'Kuja, it's Zareth Sins.' The usual confidence that Kuja had come to expect from the Chipper's voice was eroded by tension. 'Gerns gave me your communicator details — look, I wouldn't have asked her for them, but something bad is happening. And I can't stop it in time.'

Kuja's heart shuddered, then pumped even faster to make up for the pause. 'Tell me.'

'Colonel Lilon Neron, Fei's father, claims that the rainforest god launched an unprovoked attack on Gerasnin,' Zareth replied. 'He says we need to respond in kind.'

Kuja frowned. 'Lilon kidnapped Fei and Bagara rescued her. My god was defending one of his followers, not making a declaration of war.'

'Yeah, well, the colonel doesn't see it that way. So he's...' Zareth paused. Static jumped from the communicator. 'I'm on a ship headed for Bagaran, your homeworld. Lilon convinced Head General Huw Hunslow to put the orders through — we're to strafe all the rainforests from orbit. And we're not stopping there. This is just the first planet on our hit list.'

'What!' Kuja felt as though someone had thrown a rope around his ribs and was tightening it, crushing the fragile bones. 'But we've done nothing.'

'Except refuse to worship the same god,' Zareth reminded him. 'It's not right. I know it's not. Look, I've spent months quietly talking to other agents about changing things. Some of them are on the ship with me, but they need an extra push before they even consider disobeying Lilon. They won't risk their careers just because I've raised some doubts. And I figure that by the time the mediaists hear about it and come to Bagaran, it'll be too late. I don't suppose you could get Bagara to help you out?'

Kuja gnawed on his lip for a moment. 'Zareth, Bagara could destroy your ships. But I don't want him to.'

Zareth laughed shortly. 'Don't hate me that much anymore, huh?'

'I'd rather you didn't die when you're the only chance GLEA has of becoming anything halfway decent,' Kuja said and blinked, realising he meant it.

'That's nice to hear, but we've just dropped out of leapspace near your planet, Kuja. You better do something fast.'

Kuja winced. He had to act soon, but he didn't want to make a decision on this scale without Fei. He'd seen what had happened to Sandsa and Callista when they had made choices independent of each other.

But Fei hadn't called for him yet. And he wouldn't go to her before she did.

'Give me some time if you can,' Kuja murmured.

He switched off the communicator and summoned a tornado

of vines and twigs that rose from his feet, preparing to take him back on Bagaran.

***

The vortex had sent her to a completely different planet. Fei was more resigned than surprised.

She skirted the edge of a temperate rainforest, fascinated by the savannah-based grasses that cut their way along the trees, forming a solid barrier between them and the rest of the planet. Fei remembered one world, ruled by a very wealthy caste, that had commissioned TerraCorp to make distinct square-shaped habitats with strict borders. They had wanted it set up this way, so that their world could be as ordered and rigid as their society.

Fei glanced at the sky, counting the moons just to be sure. 'This is Butisl, in the Ratanni system. I don't know what you were hoping to achieve by sending me here, but...'

A leafy sprout shot out from a nearby tree and affixed itself to her temple. Fei stopped dead. Her chest heaved, but once again the pain only lasted a moment before she was gifted with an awareness of the nearby plants. This small, fabricated rainforest wasted no time in also showing her an image of Kuja. But now Fei saw him holding his mother's hand as she ushered him towards his much older brother.

But what would the Desine know about teaching a god who would rule over plants and budding life, not arid and desolate worlds? It made no sense.

The partnership had not been for Kuja's benefit, Fei realised. It had been for Sandsa's. Their mother had wanted someone to

346

be there for the desert god, to keep him company throughout the endless aeons.

What about Kuja? she wondered. *Who's there for him? Me? I can't be. I'm nothing compared to him.*

Creator? a timid voice asked.

Fei shook her head roughly, clearing her vision, and found herself back at the tree that had imprisoned her inside those images of the past. 'Kuja is your god. He looks after you.'

But you gave birth to us in your code — our god only tended what you began, the tree said, sounding quiet and cowed, like a child who had been scolded. It was so easy to forget that this immense tree, with its expansive roots and its ancient genetic memory, was only one Old Earth year old.

Fei softened her voice. 'I...I had a really, really small part in making you *you*. The bits inside you came from the rainforests tended by your god. And he could have made you appear in seconds just by thinking about it. He doesn't have to spend months writing code.'

The tree paused, considering this, then rejoined brightly, *But he would not have known about the special grasses. The lundi grasses. Our friends.*

'Friends?' Fei glanced at the safari-style square that the Butislans had asked for. 'Oh. I chose the lundi grasses because they were known to communicate with other intelligent plants in their savannah climate on Alnia. I picked your species for a similar reason. The simulation I ran worked; it said the barrier wouldn't break down because you and the grasses would cooperate. I imagined you two having long conversations or even throwing wild parties.' Fei snorted, shaking her head at the memory.

Friends, the tree repeated happily. *Our god would not have thought of that. He would have forced his will upon us and kept us growing through might alone. It would have taken effort. And once his thoughts turned from us, we would have ceased to be.*

Fei's throat burned. She swallowed. 'So if Kuja got distracted you'd wither away or be overtaken by the surrounding environments.'

Yes, yes! You are so wise, Creator of Worlds.

'I'm not a god. Not like Kuja.'

God? The tree made a sound that seemed to simulate distorted laughter. *What use is he? He only looks after us. He doesn't create anything. Not like the Old One. Not like you.*

A chill ran the length of Fei's spine, as though someone was running an icicle over each and every bump. 'The Old One. The Creator God.'

Yes, yes! Creator! Feiscina!

'I am *nothing* like him!' Fei cried, backing away. The shoot that was attached to her temple strained and nearly snapped. 'I am not a creator! I'm not him!'

Confusion filled the tree's voice. *But we don't want you to be him. We want you to be you.*

Fei's stomach twisted uncomfortably. She glanced down at it. Her son wasn't even born yet, but already he was making himself heard. He saw his parents as celestial bodies rotating around him — the god *and* the creator. They were beautiful, both of them, shining like stars.

Fei closed her eyes, breathing heavily, but the dizziness swamping her did not abate. When she staggered, a hovercar-sized fern caught her — a plant she had selected and chosen to be there, because it would help ensure the rainforest's survival.

Beside her the lundi grasses whispered gently, their words

lost, buried in a language that only other plants could understand; they belonged to another god, so Fei couldn't hear them through the sprout in her temple. But the tree, a forever friend to the lundi grasses, translated for her.

Creator of Worlds, the grasses chanted, over and over again.

Fei crouched to run her hands over their soft blades, startled and pleased when they caressed her in return. 'But I might not be able to create as much as I did at TerraCorp. Yalsa Industries is very small and hasn't got any clients yet.'

None of us would ever bow to TerraCorp as we do to you, the tree vowed on behalf of so many plants from so many different environments. They knew who had given them the chance to live, they knew who had decided to include them on this planet — and they knew that their brethren on Bagaran were in imminent danger of falling prey to GLEA's weapons.

'Take me back!' Fei commanded. 'Now!'

Another vortex appeared beside her, whirling and spitting out tortured sounds. She was afraid to see Kuja again so soon, but she could not turn away from the rainforests who needed her just as much as they needed their god.

Holding her breath, she stepped into the vortex.

CHAPTER THIRTY-FOUR

Kuja felt his heart leap the moment Fei arrived back on Bagaran. His joy then swiftly became confusion. His son's powers were growing, but they were not yet strong enough to cause teleportation. When Kuja opened his mind to the foliage around him, to ask them about it, he heard smugness in the thousands of voices that answered. *We are older than you, young god, and much wiser. We only did what was needed. And now so must you. Go. Go to the Creator of Worlds.*

Kuja hesitated. 'I want to go to her but I...I'm afraid. I'm afraid she'll never stop hating me.'

Do not let your fear destroy your chance for happiness, a nearby vine cautioned him. It wriggled beneath his chin and forced his gaze up towards the sky, where GLEA's starships hovered, invisible beyond the atmosphere. *And do not let your fear cause us to perish. We have brought both god and creator here to save us. So save us.*

Kuja stepped inside a new vortex that took him directly to Fei. She didn't flinch at the sight of him, which was a start. He held his breath as she drew nearer.

'I can't believe GLEA's doing this,' she said, her cheeks hollow. 'They'll, oh my God, they'll destroy your rainforests and everyone in them. I won't let this happen!' Her eyes blazed.

Fittingly, she'd programmed the electronic irises to appear magma red at some point. 'I won't!'

'Good, because I'll need your help,' Kuja said, reaching out when he felt her need for his touch — and her reluctance to ask for it. 'I don't want to destroy the starships outright. I have a friend up there.'

She stayed still, accepting his caress on her cheek, then offered him a wobbly smile. 'I'm still mad at you. Really mad. You'll have to spend a lot of time making it up to me.'

'We have eternity for that,' Kuja said.

'Kuja, I'm scared.' The whisper barely escaped her lips. 'Eternity is a *long* time.'

Kuja wound his arms around her, savouring her warmth, grateful for her very presence in his life. He made sure she felt that. 'We'll be together and that's what counts, Creator of Worlds. Magnificent title. Wish I'd thought of it.'

'Yeah, way more impressive than "sub-level god",' Fei agreed, her smile growing. But then her eyes rose up towards the canopy. 'If those ships are using the same systems as TerraCorp, then I should be able to paralyse them without any trouble. No one needs to get hurt.' Her red eyes narrowed. 'Unless they try to hurt us first.'

'Ready to save Bagaran with me, my Creator of Worlds?' Kuja asked her.

Fei gave him her answer, then tensed as brown-streaked foliage swirled up around them. Kuja watched her, worried, but she drew a breath and nodded reassuringly at him just as the vortex tore them away from the surface of Bagaran and deposited them into the bowels of one of GLEA's egg-shaped starships.

Her mind flush with delight at what he could do, at what he

could share with her, Fei grabbed Kuja's shoulders and yanked him into a fierce kiss. The feel of her, and the taste of her, very nearly tempted him to stop what they were doing and make love to her right there.

Fei drew away from him when she saw this thought. 'Kuja! We have eternity for that, remember? The Chippers can sense energy, so there's a good chance they've noticed two extra lifesigns appear on board. We don't have much time.'

'I don't think their abilities are as sensitive as mine,' Kuja said dubiously.

'Well, that or the shipboard sensors will notice there's two blips where there shouldn't be any,' Fei told him, her eyebrows knitting together. 'Right. I need to gain access to their systems so I can hack them. And then we're going to need to have a chat with the Chippers upstairs. I suspect Bagaran is only the first of many worlds that they've decided to go after.'

'That's what I've been told,' Kuja agreed.

'Okay, that's enough standing around doing nothing,' Fei said. She spun on her heel and waddled as fast she could towards a console set into a bulkhead in the corridor.

Kuja followed, keeping his senses alert for any approaching lifesigns, and watched as she hunched over a keyboard that sprang out from the wall. The vidscreen in front of Fei appeared to be running script but she immediately dismissed it, muttering something about redundant processes, then began skimming her way through the systems.

Her mouth bunched to one side after several moments. She seemed to be chewing on the inside of her cheek. 'GLEA's hit list is pretty long. And most of these worlds are poor and don't have a fleet of ships to defend them. This…' Lines curled around her eyes. 'This is mass murder.'

'I wonder how they were going to explain it to the mediaists,' Kuja mused.

'Ton Tinel would have ripped them to shreds,' Fei said with a sharp nod, then went back to work.

Kuja leaned over to study the vidscreen. 'So…how are you going to paralyse the ships?'

The grin was obvious even from his position behind her; it coloured both her words and her chaotic thoughts. 'I'm creating a virus, a very simple one. If I corrupt certain executable files, I can kill engines, weapons, shields *and* communications. GLEA's ships are connected to each other via the Web so it's pretty easy to do them all in one go. Idiots. There's a reason I told Moz to keep TerraCorp off the Web. Basically, any criminal with moderate hacking abilities could take down every Chipper ship in the galaxy.'

'Fei…' Kuja lowered his voice to a murmur. 'Much as I love hearing your beautiful voice, I can sense people approaching our position. Are you done?'

'I will be if you quit distracting me!'

Leaving her to it, Kuja turned around and crossed his arms, trying to make himself look intimidating. The pair of Chippers that had been creeping up behind him stopped dead, panic flitting over their faces. Their hands touched their lasguns but the weapons stayed holstered. For now.

Neither side did anything for a very long moment.

'Colonel Lilon Neron told you to kill us, no questions asked,' Kuja finally said, rifling through their most recent thoughts. 'But you've been arguing about those orders all the way down here.

Because neither of you believe that destroying rainforests on innocent worlds is truly just or right.'

They both blanched.

'Can you read our minds?' one of them asked in a whisper.

Kuja grinned at their combined discomfort. 'Of course. I inherited this ability from the Creator God. I'm his son.'

'His son?' repeated the woman of the pair.

Fei's mind was still occupied with lines of code so Kuja decided to buy her some more time. 'Where did you think the sub-level gods came from? They're your god's children.'

'But you — you attacked our headquarters on Gerasnin!' the woman cried. She drew her weapon and aimed it at Kuja. 'There are vids of you! And Hunslow said you threatened everyone in their minds, told them you would kill anyone who angered Bagara. But you won't have surprise on your side this time, rainforest god. I bet I can squeeze off more lasbolts than you can block.'

'She probably can,' Fei said, now leaning back against the console, her work apparently done. She added silently, *You don't have telekinetic abilities, do you, Kuja?*

Kuja grumbled at her mentally and she threw a very audible laugh back at him. The Chipper's lasgun retrained on Fei, but then the woman realised Fei was pregnant and dropped it, babbling apologies.

'Private Clarin, put that away before you hurt someone,' the Chipper's companion said with an irritable shake of his head. Kuja used a glancing touch on the man's mind to learn that his name was Losson. 'Mr Bagara, many of us have problems with how GLEA is being run at the moment, not just our mutual friend. He told me you would come here and help stop this madness, but I...I didn't believe him. I thought you'd just kill us.'

'He might still do that if we let him!' Clarin exclaimed, eyeing Kuja.

'Anyway,' Losson went on, 'our mutual friend said GLEA should be working *with* you, helping you care for the galaxy — oh, and he also said you're the only god he's ever seen drunk.'

Kuja knew exactly who this mutual friend was, but he didn't dare think his name, in case Fei heard it. He wasn't entirely surprised that Zareth had figured out who he was — according to Losson's memories, GLEA had just finished circulating footage of Bagara attacking them so that their agents knew what he looked like. They had been ordered to shoot on sight.

Clarin scowled at Losson. 'We should at least cuff him before we take him anywhere, Lieutenant.'

Fei jerked a thumb at the vidscreen behind her. 'Oh, I doubt you'll cuff either of us. If you make us angry, or we die, then you'll never get this virus off your ships. You won't be going anywhere until I let you.'

Losson grinned, completely unfazed. 'I guess we better get this over and done with then. My husbands expect me home in a week.'

Kuja and Fei followed both Chippers up to the bridge. There was no time to admire the gently curving silver walls of the room or the twinkling starscape filling the expansive viewport. Several lasguns were trained on Kuja and his wife, though many more remained holstered.

'Don't get any ideas, Bagara,' Lilon Neron warned.

Kuja glanced at Fei, but her snarl was aimed at a different man. She had spotted Zareth. 'Of course you're a part of this. You want to hurt as many people as possible. What did they promise you, Zareth? A promotion? Or didn't you need any incentive to participate in mass murder?'

Zareth's eyes flicked between Fei and Kuja. 'Fei, if you would just let us...'

'No, I think I've had enough of being talked over.' Her hands coiled into knots at her sides. 'You don't get a say.'

Lilon rounded on Losson and Clarin. 'Why are they still alive?'

'Ask Lieutenant Losson,' Clarin grumbled.

'Ms Neron says she put a virus on the ships,' Losson said. He seemed to have no trouble answering Lilon, unlike his companion. 'Begging your pardon, sir, but these worlds have committed no crimes that we can punish. And it goes against GLEA's best interests to attack harmless worlds. The mediaists will not forget this and neither will the civilians who worship the Creator God — we're having enough trouble getting them to donate as it is!'

'Shut up!' Lilon barked at him. 'There is no virus. We have firewalls!'

Zareth cleared his throat and stepped forward. 'Fei probably *built* those firewalls. We share the same systems as TerraCorp because we're the same entity, even if Head General Huw Hunslow doesn't want to admit it.'

Zareth hooked his thumbs onto his belt. This was apparently some sort of signal, because every agent who hadn't yet drawn their weapons fell in behind him and copied the gesture. After several tense seconds, a good portion of the remaining Chippers holstered their lasguns and joined the growing crowd. Lilon frowned deeply at Zareth and his supporters.

'They also said...' Clarin hesitated, ducking her head to avoid Lilon's furious gaze when it fixed on her. 'They also said that the sub-level gods are the children of the Creator God. Is that true?'

'Of course it isn't!' Lilon snapped. He began ordering one of the tech-minded agents still loyal to him to trawl through the ship's systems. He explicitly told them to find nothing.

Almost immediately, his beleaguered inferior announced that they couldn't raise the other ships and nor could they move or fire any weapons. Beads of sweat broke out on Lilon's forehead.

'Interesting,' Zareth mused. 'The sub-level gods are the Creator God's children. This certainly explains why he's done nothing to curtail their powers.'

A glower started to creep across Fei's face so Kuja swiftly showed her what had happened between him and Zareth. But within moments her voice cut across the bridge, silencing the growing murmurs from the gathered Chippers. 'Zareth, you were a shit to me and suddenly I'm supposed to trust that you're on our side?'

Zareth sighed deeply. 'Fei, this has nothing to do with us. But look, Kuja listens to you in a way I never could. He loves you. You're much better off with him.'

Zareth nodded at Kuja and moved closer, holding out his arm. Kuja was momentarily confused, because the gesture the Chipper had in mind was not the one he was used to seeing among Sandsa's people in the deserts. But he allowed Zareth to squeeze his hand and give it a firm shake. Several agents gasped at the companionable display.

Zareth released Kuja's hand and said wryly, 'I'm impressed that you haven't speared every one of us with branches by now. I'd be tempted to in your position.'

'I don't think I like you two being friendly with each other,' Fei grumbled. 'And I think we should all be focusing on the immediate problem. GLEA is out to destroy rainforests and countless lives because they're afraid of Bagara and can't stand the thought that not every planet wants to be under their heel!'

Zareth turned to face the pack of Chippers behind him. 'Where does it stop? Do we attack every planet that has a grain of sand, or a single drop of water? Do we keep going until there's nothing left in the galaxy?'

Kuja could spot Zareth's most loyal supporters from their firm, confident nods. Others still looked uncertain.

'Remove this virus *now!*' Lilon roared, sweeping over and knocking Zareth out of his way.

'No,' Fei said, lifting her chin.

Snarling, her father gave the air in front of him a vicious shove with his hands; the ensuing forcefield slammed into Fei and sent her flying. Kuja reacted immediately, his vines causing metal to scream as they took root in the floor, providing as much of a cushion as they could for the Creator of Worlds.

But they were not needed.

Fei was floating in midair above the hard deck, arms flung out either side of her. A score of Chippers had their own hands extended as they projected the combined, much stronger forcefield that had halted her fall. As one, they lowered their arms back down to their sides. Fei coasted gently onto her feet.

Zareth marched up to Lilon. 'Colonel Neron, we serve and protect all children of the Creator God, mortal or otherwise. Stand down!'

'I will not take orders from some — ' Lilon began.

Zareth sliced a hand through the air, commanding silence.

'We just found out that Bagara is a son of the Creator God, just as I am. I won't hurt my brother. But it sure looks like you'd hurt your own daughter.'

'I will not allow any of my fellow agents to harm an innocent being,' Lieutenant Losson piped up.

'And neither will I,' echoed several other Chippers.

Kuja felt triumph boil off Zareth.

'Hunslow will rip out your chips!' Lilon hissed, lunging forward.

Zareth stepped aside and the older man overbalanced, hitting the deck. '*All* of our chips? I think it might just be easier for him to rip out yours. Think your wife will still let you room with her?'

'She better not,' Fei muttered.

'Can you get us in touch with the other ships?' Zareth asked, turning towards her. 'You don't need to let us go yet, but I do need to get my message out there. To let everyone know how things are going to be inside GLEA from now on.'

Kuja could see that a lot of the words popping into Fei's mind weren't particularly pleasant, but she understood what Zareth was trying to achieve. Even if she still disliked him. Intensely.

'Alright,' Fei said and seated herself at a console. While she restored the flotilla's communications, agents flooded over to hold Lilon down with both limbs and powers as Zareth clamped lascuffs onto his wrists.

'What's going on over there?' Head General Huw Hunslow's voice demanded through a speaker in the console.

Zareth looked at Kuja and Fei, a hand hovering over the sensor pad that would let him respond to his superior. 'So what *is* going on here? We're all getting out of this alive, right?'

'Angling for a better rank, Zareth?' Fei asked sourly. 'I

imagine this'll look good for you, being friends with a sub-level god. You'll have a whole bunch of people willing to support your promotion now.'

Kuja rested a hand on her arm. 'Fei, Zareth is nothing like your father. He's doing this for the good of the galaxy, not himself.'

'I don't care — he hurt me!' she cried.

'I had to leave you in order to achieve my true purpose,' Zareth said, then winced. 'That sounded bad.'

Kuja snorted. 'You think so, do you?'

Zareth's eyes skated towards the viewport, a much safer location to pin his gaze on than Fei's scowl. 'It was my fault. I couldn't...I couldn't give you what you needed. And then I realised...oh God, this sounds even worse. I realised I didn't love you. I'm sorry. But I found my calling and you've found yours. Let's move on, Fei. Please.' Zareth nodded at Kuja. 'This man loves you enough to share entire worlds with you. And I'm well on the way to changing GLEA for the better. Do you still think we should have stayed together? 'Cause I don't.'

Kuja rested a hand on Fei's shoulder, squeezing gently. She was ready to forgive Zareth, because he was right and she was so much happier without him, but she sure enjoyed watching him squirm. Fei flipped a quick smile at Kuja when he coughed, trying to mask his laughter.

'Husband,' she said conversationally, 'I'm not sure I'm comfortable with the fact that I like some of these Chippers now.'

'We just had a few bad eggs,' Lieutenant Losson said and poked Lilon with the toe of his boot. He darted back when Lilon brandished his teeth. 'Very, very bad eggs. I'm going to enjoy binning this one.'

Zareth cleared his throat and the bridge fell silent. 'Am I right in assuming that we'll get back control of our ships in return for GLEA promising to fix up its act?'

Fei's lips remained defiantly sealed until Kuja nudged her side. She sighed. 'Oh, alright. But if you dare mess up again, I'll rig all of your ships to explode.'

'Fair enough,' Zareth agreed.

CHAPTER THIRTY-FIVE

'I still don't like it,' Bock said, glowering at Fei from his chair.

'But it's good business to have the Chippers guarding your terraforming machines when you send them to other planets,' Fei said, linking her hands together over her bursting stomach. 'Knowing that GLEA is protecting your property will make your clients more confident about choosing you, right? And it's not like it will cost you anything. The Chippers don't charge for their services.'

It had taken weeks and another so-called 'conference' to create this arrangement between the governor and GLEA. Fei suspected that the negotiations had been mostly helped along by Zareth accepting Bock's challenge to survive an all-night drinking session.

Bock muttered under his breath, stewing.

Ala, casually draped across his desk, answered for him. 'He's just upset that GLEA didn't shut TerraCorp down because they're tough competition. And since those Chippers revealed that they own the company, all the devout clients are gonna stick with them.'

'Fucking Chippers!' Bock burst out. 'I don't care if they say they're cleaning up their act and ripping out the chips of all the bad ones. I still don't want them crawling around my machines!'

'You agreed to it,' Fei reminded him.

'I don't mind that ex-boyfriend of yours, but the rest of them might be up to somethin'!' Bock gripped the edge of his desk, his biceps bulging inside the sleeves of his suit. He looked like he wanted to snap the furniture in half. 'And why couldn't Kuja just wave his hands and transform half the planet for us? It'd be easier and cheaper, that's for starking sure.'

Ala flung an annoyed look at him. 'Shit, Bock, she explained this. I'd rather our brand new rainforest didn't disappear just 'cause Kuja lost concentration.'

Bock was still grumbling when he reached for the switch on his desk, the one that would signal his terraforming machines to start up. He stopped himself just in time, apparently reconsidering. He then waved an impatient hand at Fei. Honoured, Fei wasted no time in marching forward and flipping the switch for him.

It was silent inside Bock's office, but Fei knew that across the planet twenty-nine machines were rising into the air and turning her simulation into a reality. Fei released a hiss of relief. Her first terraforming job for Governor Bock Atsason was complete. Her next project, impatiently moving around inside her, was threatening to tumble out at any moment.

Ala nodded at Fei's stomach. 'Your kid got a name yet?'

'Micadei,' Fei replied. 'After my mother's father.'

Bock's lip curled. 'Make sure he picks a better gang name. Can't really use that one on the streets, can he?'

'I'm raising him on Bagaran,' Fei said firmly. 'He won't need a gang name there.'

'What the stark do they do all day on that planet if they don't have gangs?' Bock wondered.

Unable to hide her smile, Fei farewelled her employers and allowed a vortex to take her to Kuja, who was some way outside the city. The roar of the machines out here was deafening and the wind being kicked up by them was vicious — it buffeted her, threatening to knock her over, but Kuja kept her rooted.

The scrub that exploded into life around them was excited to explore this world it had been given. It said over and over again, *Thank you, Creator of Worlds! Thank you! It's wonderful!*

The trees were not so shrill in their assessment of the situation. They reminded Fei of cats, aloof and more sure of themselves. They were less impressed with Kuja than they were with her; they knew that the special soil that had allowed them to grow so well and so fast had been chosen by the Creator of Worlds, not Bagara.

Fei stepped back as one tree spurted up from the ground near her feet. It attempted to apologise. She laughed and assured the tree that she didn't mind, that she wouldn't dare suppress anyone climbing their way to their full potential.

Within hours half of Yalsa 5 was well on its way to hosting a rainforest, one that might even see out the eternity that Fei had ahead of her.

An eternity without locked treasure chests or the secrets inside them.

I hope I can continue to rebuild the trust between us, Kuja said, pressing a kiss to her temple.

Fei snuggled against him. *I know you will. I love you, Kuja.*

And I love you, Fei. Forever.

***

Two Old Earth days later, Kuja had to blink several times to make sure he wasn't dreaming.

Berale Neron, his wife's very mortal mother, was arguing with (and apparently winning against) the immortal goddess standing in her way as she continued to sweep inside the hut — an entirely moot exercise since the floor was comprised of bare earth. But the chore seemed to help Berale in the same way that blurting out every distracting thought helped Fei.

Finara held up her hands, aggravation flowing off her like waves. 'Really, Kuja? You wanted a wife who came with a mother-in-law? I'm glad I'm single.'

While the Bagathians thought that Kuja's family members, who had suddenly appeared out of nowhere, were odd, they had been far too polite to say so. This didn't stop them from shooting him amused looks whenever he escaped the arguments in his hut, however.

'I'd like the two of you to put aside your differences for now,' Kuja said, 'since Fei is currently giving birth.'

'Out there?' Finara asked, eyes skirting to the window, her horror evident.

Berale dropped her broom and marched over to grab Kuja's arm. 'Take me to my daughter, rainforest god, or I promise you I will spend the rest of my life making you miserable. And don't think I won't teach my grandson to handle the rest of eternity for me.'

Kuja led both women down the path towards the nearby waterfall, where Fei had been swimming with him before the labour pains had arrived. The rainforest had come to Fei's aid already, forming a bed of the softest moss, providing her with leaf-loads of water and ensuring that she had copious amounts of a particular plant that could dull the pain of childbirth. But none of this seemed to be helping her mood.

Kuja knelt beside his wife, kissing her sweaty forehead. 'Fei, my love, this doesn't need to happen out here. We can use the village infirmary.'

'I like it here, so deal with it,' Fei muttered. 'And since we're isolated it won't matter if Micadei accidentally uses his powers on his way out because no one will see it. And ow. These nefarg stems are supposed to be a mild analgesic but they're taking their starking time in working.'

Kuja thought that Fei looked adorably grumpy.

'I'm not adorably grumpy, I'm just grumpy!' Fei snapped.

Finara's fiery eyes were wide when Kuja looked back at her for help. 'Yikes! No way am I ever going through this. Good thing I can't impregnate anyone.'

All through the afternoon Fei kept up a stream of words that was almost impossible to interrupt. She began talking about how the parameters in the simulation for Yalsa Industries' first client needed to be reset — but only if Bock would get Jalen and the other programmers to do it, because Fei was clearly going to be too busy to dart over to Yalsa 5 for the next few weeks.

'Honey, I'll be looking after your son while you go to work, remember?' Berale told her, then winced when Fei grabbed her hand and crushed it. 'My God, I swear I didn't give Lilon this much trouble when I was giving birth to her.' She glanced at Kuja. 'Just how old are you? I suppose you might have been around for that.'

'He's old enough to be your father, mortal,' Finara said. 'And I'm even older. The shit I've seen over the centuries...'

'I don't care how old anyone is!' Fei exclaimed.

Later, as the sky had darkened, Fei pillowed her head in Kuja's lap, dozing and shoring up her strength for what was to come. Berale and Finara remained standing nearby, waiting in solidarity. Finara's presence meant a lot to Kuja. She had not been his first choice, but she had been the right one. With his help, she was becoming much more in touch with her mortal side and her domain was benefiting from it. Kuja asked nothing in return from sister, glad that he no longer needed her assistance.

Finara was there to witness the greatest moment of Kuja's life. And that was better than any other gift she could have given him.

***

Fei was so exhausted she could have fallen asleep there and rolled right into the water without waking up. The culprit was tucked into her arms, wrapped up inside a flexible frond that could be wound around him like cloth. Micadei's skin was amber in tone, not quite as dark as her colouring or as light as Kuja's, and his head lacked any hair. His tiny green eyes were familiar; his cry less so.

'You'll get used to it,' Berale said, a soothing hand resting on the back of Fei's neck. 'Soon you'll be able to tell the different cries apart.'

Around them the rainforest stilled. Trees and vines bent towards them, eager to see the son of both god and creator.

'Can I show him to them?' Kuja asked Fei.

She nodded, smiling.

Finara chortled. 'What, are we going to pretend that your precious plants have feelings? They're not people, Kuja. They're *things*.'

'Don't be rude!' Berale told her sternly. 'You might upset them.'

Surprisingly, Finara said nothing more, though she did roll her eyes.

Fei handed her son over to Kuja who then walked towards the tree line, vines dropping from the branches around him and curling towards the bundle in his arms. The nearest trunks shivered, disgorging all manner of creatures that must have been waiting for this moment. Those that could bowed; others chirped. Fei was stunned breathless by the scene, by the knowledge that she and her family would always be safe here, watched over by the rainforest that loved them.

Silence fell as Kuja began to speak to his domain. 'This is my son, Micadei. He has the blood of your god and the Creator of Worlds. You will treat him as you do us, but you will not bow to him until he decides which path he wants to walk.'

The nashba bugs, which had been lighting the clearing in front of the waterfall, danced with joy. Plants and animals alike continued to celebrate, even as they left the clearing or shrank back into place. Berale moved closer to Fei, muttering something about how it was all a bit much for her.

Fei raised her eyebrows. 'Just say the word, Mum, and I can have you back on Gerasnin in an instant.'

'Oh, really?' Berale pursed her lips. 'I might take you up on that, when Micadei is older. I do have a new career in mind and it's not exactly easy to pursue out here. Not the way you can do your — what is it called? — code compiling on that shiny new console the governor sent you. It's so nice of him to let you work remotely.'

Fei groaned and buried her head in her hands.

'I'll miss you too, honey, when the time comes,' Berale sniffed.

Kuja walked back over to them, smiling. '*I'll* even miss you, Berale.'

His mother-in-law gave him a very suspicious look.

When Kuja passed Finara, his sister reached over and waggled her fingers in front of Micadei. He blinked sleepily in response. The fire goddess' face lit up. 'I definitely have to get me one of these.'

'Finara!' Kuja exclaimed, sounding — and feeling — appalled.

'Well, Fei and I will certainly help you if that happens,' Berale promised. 'Won't we, honey?'

'I think Finara might rather my company,' Fei said.

Finara nodded vigorously. Berale sighed, but she didn't seem too put out.

'So what now, Creator of Worlds?' Kuja asked, kneeling onto the ground beside Fei.

Fei accepted her son back from Kuja, her hand lingering on his. 'I guess I'll have to figure out how to juggle my work for Yalsa Industries, my first forays into motherhood and that little side project of mine.'

She had begun to use her skills to expose other organisations that did not have the best interests of the galaxy at heart. So far GLEA had been behaving, even co-operating. They didn't seem too concerned that she darted into their files every now and then, to ensure they were on the right path. Transparency was now at the core of their philosophy.

'You've got eternity so I'd pace myself if I was you,' Finara advised Fei. 'And anyway, it's hard enough for us gods to balance family and duties without factoring in little side projects. You're still just a human, even if you are immortal.'

Berale reached down and stroked Fei's fuchsia hair back from her face. 'Honey, she's right. You're only human. You can't do it all.'

Just watch me, Fei thought, grinning. *I'm the Creator of Worlds.*

She caught the amusement on her husband's face when he heard this, but he didn't dare say a word. He believed in her. He believed she could do anything.

Funnily enough, Fei was starting to believe that herself.

ABOUT THE AUTHOR

Alyce Caswell lives in Sydney, Australia with zero cats and one husband. When she isn't drinking her way through a giant pot of tea, Alyce is a keen reader and writer of science fiction and fantasy.

You can contact her via e-mail (alycecaswell@outlook.com) or on Twitter (@alycecaswell).

ALSO BY ALYCE CASWELL

The Galactic Pantheon Series
The Tortured Wind
The Twisted Vine
*The Flickering Flame**
*The Shifting Ice**
*The Whispering Grass**
*The Creeping Moss**

**novella*